Welcome to Stanley Elkin's Magical Mystery Tour! You will never meet more memorable—or entertaining—children than the seven terminally ill kids who have been chosen to go to Disney World for a last hurrah; Disney World becomes for Elkin's children a kind of Lourdes. Bearing their painful afflictions amidst Disney's magical fantasy, they are funny, tough, and heroic in their comic-shock "stand against death."

Four other Stanley Elkin novels are available in Obelisk editions: *A Bad Man, The Dick Gibson Show, The Living End*, and *George Mills*.

belisk

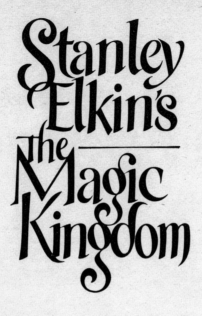

Stanley Elkin's
The Magic Kingdom

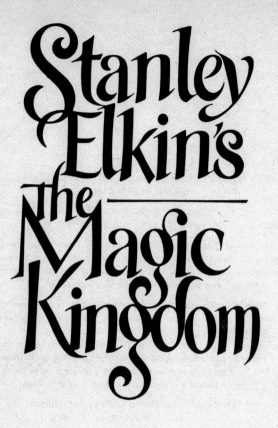

Stanley Elkin's The Magic Kingdom

A Dutton Obelisk Paperback

E. P. DUTTON / NEW YORK

This paperback edition of The Magic Kingdom *first published
in 1986 by E. P. Dutton.*

Published in the United States by E. P. Dutton,
a division of New American Library,
2 Park Avenue, New York, N.Y. 10016.

Library of Congress Catalog Number:
86-70433

ISBN: 0-525-48211-3

Published simultaneously in Canada
by Fitzhenry & Whiteside Limited, Toronto

COBE

Designed by Mark O'Connor

10 9 8 7 6 5 4 3 2 1

For Joan

I

1

Eddy Bale took his idea to the Empire Children's Fund, to Children's Relief, to the Youth Emergency Committee. He went to CARE and Oxfam and the Sunshine Foundation and, because he was famous by then, a famous griever, managed entrées to the boardrooms of Rothschild's and British Petroleum, ICI and Anglo-Dutch, Marks & Spencer and Barclay's, to Trusthouse Forte, to Guinness, to British Rail. He wrote to hospices; he wrote physicians on Harley Street and called at surgeries and hospitals. He spoke to high-ups in the National Health and dashed off letters to the national newspapers. He had an interview with Lord Lew Grade and worked up a proposal for Granada and the BBC. Because the idea was dramatic he ap-

3

proached the Directors of the National Theatre and the Royal Shakespeare Company. He had a sign made which could be put in taxis and minicabs.

What convinced him his idea made sense, he said, was the fact that none of these children was under the care of a pediatrician. Not one. (Charles Mudd-Gaddis, eight, was being seen by a gerontologist.) They'd been handed over to the specialists. Specialists diagnosed them and other specialists treated them, if you could call their courses of experimental drugs and dollops of nuclear medicine and being zapped by lasers treatment. They were tortured not into health, he said, but into, at best, brief periods of remission. They died in pain, language torn from their throats or, what little language they had left, turned into an almost gangster argot, uncivilized, barbaric as the skirls and screaks of bayed prey.

He spoke, he reminded them, from experience, and here his auditors looked away or cast down their eyes, for by this time there could hardly have been an adult in all the kingdom who hadn't heard of the ordeal of Eddy Bale's son: eleven operations in three years, the desperate flights to Johannesburg and Beijing; even, though the Bales weren't Catholic, to Lourdes; and even, though they weren't suckers by nature, to the gypsies—to anyone, finally, who promised to lift the curse. There had been a woman in Leek Street who read the toilet paper on which Liam wiped himself, and a witch in Land's End who fed him the eyes of rabid dogs and the testicles of great sea birds wrapped in toad's skin like a bleak hors d'oeuvre. Bale and Ginny together had all they could do just to hold him down long enough to get it past his jaws. When the stuff backed up he started to retch from his nose and the witch pinched his nostrils. "No," she said when Ginny protested she was smothering him, "it's supposed to mix with his puke. That's what seasons it."

"You know what practically his last words were?" Eddy Bale asked the great men with whom he'd had interviews. " 'May I die now? May I die now, please?' "

"Please, Mister Bale," a Lord counseled softly, "you oughtn't. . . ."

But Bale was crazy.

"Canisters!" he pleaded. "Just let me leave canisters with your publicans and newsagents. Let me put canisters in your tobacconists' and greengrocers'."

There were dozens of angles. Eddy wrote quiet businesslike letters to top rock stars suggesting they do a ballad about these children. He wrote Elton John and the musician replied, sending along with his letter a haunting and very beautiful song he'd written which he said Bale could have so long as the composer's name was never linked with it. Bale showed the song to the managers of half a dozen of Great Britain's most important artists with no success. All recognized the song's genius but refused to allow the people they represented to have anything to do with it. Eddy even got apologetic phone calls from two of the Beatles and a long overseas call from Yoko Ono. Once, near a recording studio in Hammersmith, he actually heard someone whistling the mournful, catchy melody in the street, but when he stopped the man to ask what the piece was and where he'd heard it, the fellow, a particularly vicious punk rocker Bale recognized from his photographs, became embarrassed and rushed off as if actually frightened.

It was a question of taste. No one would say so; no one wanted to hurt a man who'd been through so much, who'd put the nation through so much. Two or three of the country's biggest executives actually agreed that it was a wonderful idea for a promotion, worth probably hundreds of thousands to their firms, but when pressed declined to explain their reluctance to participate in his campaign. (Because even Ginny had abandoned him by now, having left just after burying Liam.)

Though no one had to tell him. Eddy Bale may have been mad but he was no fool. During the four years of his child's illness he had submitted to—and survived—many exquisite attacks of pained, assaulted taste and wronged form. He'd lived with camera crews, gone on the wireless, wept for photographers from the mass circulation dailies till he could have wept, participated in a hundred stunts and publicity tricks, become the U.K.'s most visible, most recognizable beggar. He'd gone door-to-door, his hat quite literally in his hand, to raise the close to one hundred thousand pounds that kept Liam alive. He sold exclusives to the press, each more humiliating than the last, drawing them forth from a reserve, a storehouse, a treasury of indignities, intimate detail—giving Liam's public honest measure, unstinting, honorable as a craftsman, an artisan of the unspeakable: BALES DISCLOSE DETAILS OF DYING LIAM'S GROWING SEX DRIVE!; HOW THEY BROKE THE NEWS: PARENTS TELL TWELVE-YEAR-OLD ALL HOPE DEAD! (It was all they would accept, finally, passing over his and his wife's suffering and the considerable heroics of the child's determined resistance, ignoring Liam's struggle, whatever value he might still have as an inspiration to others, defying human interest itself at last—once it was established he couldn't live—homing in on the macabre, the exotic, all the screwy, built-in ironies of premature death.) And he *was* humiliated. (And Liam, a terminal fame victim, as interested as the readership itself in the vicious aspects of his own story, taking a sort of cold comfort from its documentation, in a way grateful that others could be drawn in, driven to cliché, weeping as his father read these accounts to him of his own last months—for he was too weak to hold a newspaper now—sobbing condolence—"I've suffered so much, my death will be a blessing"—and offering his comments almost as if he'd survived himself.) And said to Ginny what Ginny could at any time have said to him (for they were in this together, collaborative as kidnappers, hijackers, ideological as terrorists), their hearts' mutual weights and measures, lashed by the same hope, doomsday'd by identical misgivings: "We're mugs, m'dear. Ants at the picnic. They hate us. They despise Liam. They wish we'd go 'way and eat our grief like men. 'Your father lost a father,/ That father lost, lost his,' et cetera et cetera."

And if they were on Claudius's side in this, why, so was he. So was Ginny. So, for his part, was Liam himself. Much as he was eager for others to know what he'd gone through, the child had despised his routines for television, for the press. "It's mush, Daddy. It's all cagmag and codswallop. And you know the part I hate most? The medical stuff. Pictures of my bone grafts, my deformed platelets, those awful blowups of my bombed-out retinas."

So because he could get nowhere with the country's great public firms and private men, nowhere with the public itself (despite Eddy's protestations that the money in this instance was trivial compared to what it had given him last time, twenty thousand pounds as opposed to a hundred thousand), he determined to take his case over their heads. He decided to seek an audience with the Queen.

On the strength of a condolence letter—"My husband and I were distressed to read in the *Times* of your son Liam's death. We have been following the course of your boy's tragic ordeal and his valiant struggle. Our hearts are with you in this gloomy hour"—he wrote Her Royal Highness's Appointments Secretary and was promised an audience just as soon as one could be worked into her busy schedule.

Which is why Eddy Bale finds himself on a fine spring day at Buckingham Palace.

He is dressed in a suit of black funeral clothes, the one he'd purchased for Liam's burial service. He wears his mourner's band, tight on his arm as a blood-pressure cuff. He is, he's surprised to learn, not in one of the public rooms at all but in a sort of royal rec room in the Queen's private apartments. To get here he has climbed the Grand Staircase and come down long elegant corridors behind a tall, slim young woman in custom jeans and a sort of country-and-Western shirt with the royal arms emblazoned on the back in an elaborate filigree. Her expensive Western boots seem to click on the carpet. "Bess normally sees subjects in the Appointments library, Mister Bale, but we're fitting you in."

The young woman, who has not bothered to introduce herself, leaves him in a very high and plush chair beside a card table on which a Scrabble game is still set up. Eddy means to ask about the protocols, but she is gone before he can even frame his question. Bale is able to read a few of the words the players have formed and abandoned—"peasant," "serf," "primogeniture"—but a child of perhaps seven or eight, either a page or one of the young royals, comes up beside him, and Eddy glances quickly away as if he has been caught poring over state secrets.

"What's your name?"

"Eddy Bale."

"You a commoner then?"

"I'm afraid so," Eddy tells the boy.

"That's all right," the kid says. "Oh," he says, "Bale. That was the name of that boy who died—Liam."

"I'm his father."

"Oh, I say," the boy says, "he was quite a brave chap, wasn't he? All those operations, all those heroic interventions and procedures. He won all us nobles, just walked off with our hearts. Many an aristocratic eye was moist when Liam succumbed. Did he *really* say, 'I'm proud to have been English'?"

"We never falsified an interview," Eddy says uneasily but can't recall the quote. He's a little startled by the child's T-shirt: *Buckingham Palace* in embossed Gothic above what would have been the breast pocket. It's less outlandish than the rampant lion filigreed in tiny pearls and gold leaf on the blouse of the young woman who conducted him here, but somehow he would have been less surprised if the child had appeared in a tiny bowler or carried a miniature furled umbrella, cute, like a kid in a sailor suit. Perhaps, among themselves, the royal family—he is in their private apartments, after all—enjoys a bit of high-camp informality now and again. Perhaps it's their idea of patriotism.

Bale is uncertain about the child. He could be anything from a duke to a baron, could command the income on great estates in Surrey or collect the rents in downtown Leeds. He seems a kind enough young fellow, and Bale, who for all his interviews with the kingdom's most powerful men, has never yet had audience with peerage, sketches his idea for the kid.

The child hears him out and concedes, "That's a *smashing* plot!"

"Thank you, sir."

"Blast, I wish *I'd* the lolly, but I don't come into my inheritance for just ages yet. Your troubles would be over if I did."

"You're very gracious, Your Grace."

"Not a bit of it, Mister Bale. We all admired young Liam."

"Thank you."

"Twenty thousand," he says, considering, stroking his chin, imagining ways it might yet be done.

"Yes?" Bale says.

"Well," he says, "it's just a thought, of course."

"Yes?"

"We could put on a horse show."

"A horse show."

"Or sell lemonade."

"Lemonade's a thought," Bale says.

"*I* know! We could hunt for buried treasure, raise the Spanish armada from Davy Jones's locker. There must be just thousands of doubloons lying about."

"Well . . ."

The Queen of England enters the family room carrying her purse. Bale rises and improvises a few courtesies. He completes his obeisances by pulling a chair out for his Queen on the other side of the Scrabble board. Queen Elizabeth II gestures for him to be seated, and Bale returns to his chair. The Queen is silent and Eddy clears his throat, is about to speak, when he sees that he does not have her complete attention. Covertly, she appears to be studying the rack of letters before her.

They play for money, Eddy thinks; they play for trips and dogs and horses. They play for cooks and butlers, for invitations and the use of castles. They play for gossip and regiments. He is a long way from his cause, and he thinks not of the children—in any case he hasn't come to save the children; now his old notions are tempered, toned, almost temperate— but of himself.

He is calmer than he has been in months. Eddy Bale and the Queen of all the Englands are in a strange conspiracy of mood, she because she is Queen, unaccountable, irreproachable, the kingdom's most private citizen as he is its most public beggar, and he because he has volunteered for scorn and is in the presence of one who has set all scorn aside, who has had it flushed from her system, an emotion not so much above her character—he doesn't know her character—as beyond her biology, who could not have lived so long with such power and such privilege and *not* have dispensed with it, scornless from birth, from lifelong pet and pamper, public croon and cherish. Perhaps even surprise itself would be vestigial in her, useless to her as her appendix, and Eddy realizes he could not have offended her with his makeshift bowings and scrapings, his quick and nervous touch-flesh salutes. A woman who's seen it all—though the empire is shrunken now—a queen shaped to tolerance and ceremony, who has sat in whatever place someone has told her to sit and observed all the strange dances of welcome, all the queer inverted struttings and high-souled arabesques and flashy, prescribed abasements and ceremonial mortifications, who has heard the odd music and seen the war paint—all the leaf mascaras, all the bark rouges and earth cosmetics, for whom the world and all behaviors are only a sort of anthropology and fierce loyalty, a kind of ethnic nationalism. She would never scorn him—for if he does not know *her* character she hasn't a clue to his—and for a few seconds Bess and Eddy have this mutual moment. It's as if—the child has left the room—they are married, in bed, side by side, reading . . .

Which puts Eddy into a sort of remission—gives himself back to himself, that is—and for the first time since Liam died and Ginny left him, for the first time since he's had his idea about the children or delivered his new pitch to his famous but secular patrons, he is suddenly quiet, not at rest but unobsessed. The refusals he's so patiently listened to—and understood, and even in his heart embraced—from men who've listened so patiently to him, have depleted him; just arranging all the appointments that have so conflicted other people's schedules has: living by deadline, his opportunities foreshortened—despite their patience—spliced into ten- and twenty- and thirty-minute intervals, and even his own eye on the clock, not, as you might think, because he has just so many minutes to make his point before he is politely dismissed but because he has buses to catch, underground trains, other appointments to make.

And sometimes he wished they weren't so matey, the chairmen and managers, wished they were as businesslike as himself, could forgo the cuppas and glasses of sherry, all the bright riffs of decorum, all the easy perks of the obligatory genteel. He apologized and declined whenever he was invited to lunch. A smoker, he refused even cigarettes when they were offered and, in his turn, and even when Liam was alive, withheld his own beggar's knee-jerk God-bless-you's, even when, as so often happened when Liam lived, he was successful. (Because Liam was appealing, even handsome, and lived—and died, by God—under the dreadful curse of his outside chances, his long-shot, high-roller, break-the-bank, one-in-a-million possibilities.) Because I *am* mad, he thought. Not so much grief-struck as driven. Ginny had seen it clearly and, though she'd been as tireless as himself while Liam was alive, wanted no part of this new business. Two hours after they returned from the cemetery, a taxi was waiting to take her away. (The taxi, like the food they'd lived on during their son's illness—Eddy had taken leave of absence from his job in order to be with his boy—like their clothes and rent, like their phone bills, airfare, hotels, and utilities, like the cost of the boy's burial itself, had been paid for from funds pledged to cure Liam, to keep him alive. Solicitors had put their two lives in trust, and just one of the peculiar results of their tragedy was that they'd come to live the managed financial lives of children of wealth, say, who'd not yet achieved their majority, or film stars on allowance, accepting doles and quarreling with accounts managers, dependent, special-pleading their special needs—though they were always merely Liam's honest brokers: rails for the bed in his room, a remote control for his telly, down pillows, colored prescription lenses cut from blanks identical to the material that went into stained-glass cathedral windows—and both of them developing a sort of privileged rich kid's cunning charm, turning them into nephews, nieces; a kind of undergraduate glamour, the exuberant flush of an overdraft youth upon them, the sense they could not help giving off—

though it was never true—of people with gaming debts, their tailors and dressmakers unpaid, heavily into their publicans, their grooms and servants; a raffish couple, committed to weekending, to leisurely country pleasures, imbued with some nostalgic, almost larky spirit of the throwback, all the more—and all the more oddly—"modern," for that the type had disappeared about the time they were born.)

It was, of course, an illusion. Inland Revenue was far too conscious of them. This was no fiddle. No fiddle was intended, no fiddle would have been allowed. Nevertheless, their lives in receivership, they *seemed* lifted from responsibility, what they did for their child, even those terrible "exclusives," a kind of sinecure, like a plummy-placed commissionaire, or the man who changed the guard outside this palace. And Ginny had absconded with the last of the taxi fare, throwing neither reproach nor their common loss at him so much as the diminished fact of herself, taking her weakened leave, so that the cabman had to help her down not only with her two or three bags but even with her umbrella, and she seemed, well, found out, undone, all in, cashiered, disgraced, ruined, sent down, as if she'd actually been the type she had—they had—merely seemed. "Where will you go?" he'd asked, the words, despite his sour mood, unaccountably sweet because of their melodrama. Because it was a time in his life when he had absolutely legitimate recourse to the great phrases of melodrama, when entire conversations were built around them, exhorting contributors, reproving medical science, comforting Liam, tongue-lashing God. By turns angry, enraged, or gently depleted as an actor, and, late at night, with Ginny, when they returned from hospital or while Liam still slept in the next room, all the heavy, distilled oom-pa-pa of crisis and crunch on him. When he'd outlined his scheme. And Ginny had called him Boots the Chemist. "Boots?" "You fill needs like prescriptions, Eddy."

The letter she'd left him unread. Not even opened. His wife. They'd lost a child together, a marriage, done chat shows, been to the necromancers. They'd always been intimate, but the very night they lost Liam, returning to their flat (reporters had been there, at the London Clinic, consigned to wait in the lobby until the Bales should appear, Ginny, who ought to have known better, surprised at their presence, even alarmed: "What are they doing here, Eddy?" "I sent for them." "You?" "Please, darling, don't go all upset on me. Stories properly have beginnings, middles, and ends." "Eddy, you dumbshit, you damned son of a bitch." "Thanks for coming, gentlemen," Bale had said. "I've terrible news. Our Liam's gone." Though when they'd pressed him he hadn't told them the little boy's last words, had told them little enough, really, content to allow the child's doctor to speak for him, for Ginny in shock, who could hardly have spoken for herself, the specialist reciting the facts of Liam's case, letting the press in on its dark pathology, then Eddy stepping forward, nodding at the doctor as though the man were merely some compere at an awards dinner, as though the doctor's dry recitation of their son's passing had been only a sort of introduction, thanking him—you could almost see microphones—and, smiling thinly but almost hearty, relieving him, making his statement—you could almost see text—thanking *all* of them, the doctors and nurses, the splendid staff, the press who had so kindly come out on this wet night, who'd been so cooperative throughout, who'd taken the message of their son's strange and terrible illness to the magnificent British people, whose response to the plight of one small, unfortunate, doomed little twelve-year-old boy, and whose consideration of that poor doomed boy's poor doomed parents—pressing her close now, practically holding her there, applying the invisible forces and vectors of some secret body language, as you'd guide a horse with a barely discernible pressure of your knees, and actually saying the words "On behalf of my wife and myself, on behalf of our son, Liam . . ."—had been the manifestation of the generous spirit of a generous people), they had fallen into each other as into actual furniture, actual chairs, actual beds, not undressing each other, pulling off clothes, so much as tearing at belts, shoulder straps, zippers, ties, tugging on sleeves, elastic, undoing one another like gifts, packages, grasping as children and, naked now, as though they had uncovered puzzling, unassembled toys, or a clutter of treasure, say, reaching randomly for pieces, parts, touching features, lifting and turning over limbs, scenting fingers, handling rashers of flesh, inspecting, examining, now squinny-eyed, now all gawking open rubberneck and abandon, no surveillance or vigil, no cool peep or snoop, neither peek nor pry but committed, bristled stare, some in-for-a-penny-in-for-a-pound plunder of the other, Ginny forcing the cheeks of his ass, her face close as a detective's and, shifted sudden as wrestlers, his eye at her cunt myopic as a man who's lost his glasses. Not even fucking finally but transport, some courtship of the head, their very wills consummated, a will seduction that ends in the giant swings and fluctuate spasms and shudders of orgasm, coming, coming, come, autonomous but reciprocal, too, as the shuttle of a rocking chair or a kid's seesaw, both feeling the private, internal seismics of self, percussive as a drum roll of glands—not even fucking—a convulsion of spirit, overwhelmed, rushed, jerked as boxers by jolts of lovepulse involuntary as seizure, some absurd, choreic twitch and flop-flounder fishthrill, the shaking of all the body's lymphs, jellies, and puddings, and last declining flickers, tremors, and almost gentle aftershock and ripple of nerves, a sort of jitters, the groggy, pleasant, irregular cramp raptures, subsultive, succussive. "Wow!" says the bereaved man. "Oh, Jesus!" groans the woman whose child will be buried the day after tomorrow and who will leave her husband two hours afterward. Then both look up, stricken, and recover their clothes. (They have been through so much—the chat shows, the necromancers, the marriage, the kid. They have been through so much—the so handsomely rewarded begging; their life on the handouts of chairmen of boards, great merchants and managers, significant tradesmen; their odd raffishness, their queer, soiled fame.) And both realize, as they'd realized their detached, mutual frenzy of moments before, that the death of Liam is not without its compensations, that they are without his intrusive presence, that they have, in ways they could not have contemplated earlier that day, been freed. (They have been through so much. He speaks for both of them.) "Well," Eddy says, "weren't that a corking way to have a bit?" (He speaks for both of them and slips into their old slangy banter, the dated style he does not even remember they have not used with each other since Liam's illness was diagnosed.) "Coo!" he says. "I daresay neiver of us has ever been brought off like that." "Fair fizzing dinkum, it were," his wife answers unexpectedly, but without energy. "I know *I* didn't feel the draught," Eddy tells her. "We was brung off just by looking, the both of us Harry starkers. We never even had it in." "Jack it, Eddy, it was flaming doolally," Ginny says. "You've got *your* rag out." "Eddy, jack it," she says listlessly. *"You're* a long streak of misery." "And you're in high feather." "Want to jig a jig then?" "You've got a hope!" "Come on, then." "Eddy, you neddy." "Pongy, were it?" "Were mine?" "Yours? No, la, yours was pukka. Yours was pure pukka quim, Ginny darlin'. Want to have it off?" "It's not on," she shouts. "Jolly good, luvverly," her husband says. "Wasn't we randy though?" she says more softly, and Eddy puts his arm about her shoulder. "If we're going to do it," he says, "I ought to Jimmy riddle first. It's up in me marbles." Ginny starts to cry. "We behave like this because he's dead, Eddy." "It's not as if it was off the cuff, old girl," Eddy says quietly. "Because he can't hear us. If the phone rings it won't be hospital." And now *she* is speaking for both, resuming ordinary English, setting aside their old language as earlier they had dispensed with the actual need for actual fucking. "Why were they there? Why did you bring them in? The reporters? What business was it of theirs?" (They miss their stress, he sees, the full-fathoms pressure of their deep-sea lives. Stress was what organized it, kept it under control, kept it civilized. It's at this point that Eddy knows Ginny will leave him. Like Eddy she can't accept the gift of grief, all loss's break-bank boons and benefits, the perks of tragedy. Oh, he thinks, what we could have done with each other! This evening's outrage only a taste, the tip of their new iceberg privacy!) "Liam was never the press's creature. He was never the hero of those accounts, that ordeal. We were," he tells her. "Liam was just the little boy who died, only the victim."

And now it is the Queen of England who does not have *his*

attention. She taps a Scrabble tile lightly against the game board.

"Oh," Bale startles. "Forgive me, Majesty." And begins (not without wondering whether it isn't being in a palace which has somehow caused his—their—lapse, the trance, the magic narcotics of his frozen animation: Has a century passed? Is Elizabeth still queen? Has the boy come into his inheritance by now? Enjoyed his tenure and relinquished it to a child itself no longer a child who for his part has handed over the depleted yet intact privilege of his title to the next in line in the orderly take-turn, marathon sequences of life and death? Is the kid ancestorized now, his portrait in uniform hung in a hall?) to tell his schemes.

"When I realized," he says, interrupting himself, overriding his improbable, inopportune parentheticals, "we had pretty well come to the limits of my son's medical options, I began to question whether he had been justly served. My wife, Ginny, and I had embarked on this search for a cure for what we'd been told at the outset was incurable. After the docs had conferred, after the second opinions, after the tests and operations and experiments, I began to see that Liam was really no better off than when his difficulties had been first confirmed in those initial interviews with the doctors in that first surgery of the National Health. Worse off, really. For by now the invasive procedures had been introduced. They beat my kid up, Your Royal Highness. With the best will in the world they worked him over. They took off his hair with their toxins and gave his liver third-degree burns. They softened his bones like modeling clay and grew little ulcers in his gut. They turned his blood into dishwater. They caused him such pain, Monarch. It's not as if they didn't warn us about the side effects. Every other word out of their faces was side effects: diarrhea, nausea, depression, and drowsiness"—and has some idea where his vagrant notion of a spell had come from just now—"weakness, fatigue. And everything with his parents' permission. All, all of it approved at the outset, Sovereign, the sacrifice added to his sickness like a cover charge, risk built into his bill like the V.A.T. We were dippy for risk, spellbound—enchanted, I mean. Desperation whips up courage. It clothes consequence and dresses the bogeyman in

high fashion. Oh, I think we were mad. Into science like as-
trology. Beside ourselves as gamblers doubling up on their bets.
You're ruler here, Ma'am. Tell me, is there a law of diminished
returns? Should you hope with your head? Wouldn't we have
been better off if we'd boarded the ship for the sunny isles?
Chosen the course of the stubborn old bastards, the ones who
stuff pleasure into their winding sheets like a sort of Egyptians—port and cigars and a pinch for the nurses that doesn't
just elevate blood pressure but positively launches it? Hey, the
only thing my kid never lost was his looks. Those he had on his
deathbed. You saw his pictures, you followed his case. Did he
go like a goner? Did he look like one? Teenage girls wanted his
autograph. He was dreamy as a rock star, they said. Wouldn't
we have been better off to have given him a cram course in de-
bauchery? Whatever it took? The rarest dishes and the richest
sauces? Ardor, toys, and all the final cigarettes and secret wishes
of his imagination?

"Well. You see what I mean. Where we went wrong. We
never rewarded him for his death. He should have lived like a
crown prince, Queen. We should have sent him off to hunt in
a red coat. We should have brought him to opera and sat him
in boxes. We should have hijacked the sweet shoppe and turned
him loose at the fair. We ought have sent him on picnics with
hampers of ice cream. We should have ground his teeth down
on scones and flan and ruined his eyes on the telly. We should
have sent him to sleep past his bedtime. We should have burned
him out on his life, Dynast. We should have bored him to death."

"Oh, I say," the Queen says, clutching her purse. Bale knows
that the woman—he recalls her odd patience with weather from
photographs, news clips, her jungle and rain-forest tranquillity,
her snowstorm serenity, her comfort in climate—has seen it all
but wonders how much she's heard. He senses her alarm, is
alarmed himself. This is not the way he presents himself to patrons. With financiers he is reserved, refined as their boardrooms, sedate as a bank. Only to his suzerain has he said these
things. Nor, till now, has he given much thought to his distinction, all that's been granted him: his private audience with his

Queen, his presence in the strange, off-limits room. He's never seen it in photographs and cannot now remember how he reached it, has only a vague memory of having climbed a staircase, come down a corridor, rather, he imagines, like the corridors in First Class on good steamships, a queer notion of being pulled along. *Yes*, he thinks, in the wake of the beautiful young woman, sluiced as wood, debris, sucked and maelstrom'd, shipwrecked, beached. Even the sight of his Queen's pocketbook strikes him as not only the most informal thing he has ever seen but the most intimate as well. I saw her cheat, he thinks, then wonders, My God, did *that* set me off? I *am* mad, I *am*. I'm lucky she don't call the coppers. Which, he sees now, is not quite the case. Footmen have appeared. They stand along the walls in their livery, their rococo chests puffed as the breasts of birds. Bale is certain they have been signaled, high-signed. Or perhaps the room is wired.

Sending his own signals, Eddy moves his shoulder slightly forward, shifting the arm with the mourning band, favoring it like a man with a game leg. He actually touches the black cloth. It is some private rigmarole, reflexive but loaded with a meaning he hopes will carry across the abandoned game board. He is not calling attention to his loss—tears form in his eyes, choke his throat, but this is because, like Ginny, whose taxi had been paid for with the last bit of Liam's cure money, his armband has been purchased with (what?) the last of the mourner money—but to his vulnerability, his madman's amiable harmlessness. He holds the black armband as if it were a white flag. And Elizabeth II understands. She smiles. Even the footmen seem to have uncovered his intentions. Invisibly, they seem to relax, expel air from their chests, breathe normally as other men.

"Yes?" she says, encouraging him.

"Over two hundred children can be expected to die of rare terminal diseases in Great Britain this year."

"Oh, my," says the Queen.

"You should understand that nothing further can be done for them," Bale says, and he is recovered now, as decorous as if he is addressing a tycoon, a newspaper magnate. "For many of them, additional treatment would make them even more uncomfortable than they already are and only hasten the day of reckoning. In several cases their therapies have already stopped or will shortly. This is at their parents' request or, in certain instances, at the request of the patients themselves. Their physicians have placed them on a sort of minimum maintenance: restricted diets, courses of high-potency vitamin injections, carefully monitored sleep regimens, even, when the discomfort becomes too great, narcotics on demand."

"*Les pauvres!*"

Bale pauses. A peculiar thing has happened. He discovers that, at the crunch, he is unable to bring his argument round, that the kingdom's foremost beggar, a man who has passed the hat among the nation's leading industrialists and press lords and brought his case to the public not only through those shameless exclusives he sold but who, in those early days of his son's illness, even climbed soapboxes in Hyde Park Corner and accepted Liam's weight from Ginny, handing the child up to him at the end of his spiel as if the boy were conclusive, telling evidence in a legal proceeding, and who on one occasion actually walked along beside the buskers working the crowds in London's theater district, Liam's sad legend printed carefully across a sandwich board—this man is suddenly and quite inexplicably mute in the presence of a woman who, to judge from her assenting clucks and royal coos, is already sympathetic, predisposed toward the children who are now his cause. Perhaps he feels himself an intruder, inhibited by the wealth she represents, the difference her sympathies could make. Perhaps he is having second thoughts—indecisive at the last moment as a child choosing which chocolate to take from a box. Perhaps that's it, that he's caught among need's swerving priorities, its competing demands on good men. Or that what he feels are the once-burned-twice-cautious misgivings of the wish-privileged in tales, and what he's searching for is precise language, seeking to clause request in legalese, to seal it in the metric measurements of ironclad engagement. (But Bale knows. He is frozen by the peculiar kicks of juxtaposition, the odd sense he has always had of misalliance, incongruence, all the thrilling, discrepant mysteries and asymmetries of disrupt geometry. Once, before Liam had become ill, he and Ginny had left the child with an aunt to go on holiday with friends to the French Riviera. In Nice, quite by accident, they had come upon one of the nude beaches. "When in France . . ." his friend's wife had said and removed the halter of her bathing suit. He had known the woman for years and, though she had always been attractive, he could not recall ever having thought about her sexually. Afterward, back in London, he could not look at her without remembering how she had appeared to him on that beach in Nice. Nor was he particularly aroused at the time. What he subsequently could not forget was that he had seen his friend's wife's breasts. He had never touched her, yet he could not get the incident out of his mind, and a part of him believed, and believes still, that he had somehow cuckolded the husband. What he felt, God help him, was a sort of pride. Another time, before he ever met Ginny, he had lived for a while with a girl named Ruth. They'd led a placid, almost deferential life together, each conveying to the other a wish to please. They never argued; were, for the six or seven months they'd been together, completely at ease, agreeable as twins. Only once, when a package they'd been expecting arrived at the flat, did they come anywhere close to quarreling. Ruth had gone to the door to accept the delivery. "Look, Eddy," she said coming into the lounge, "the bed lamp from Heal's, I think." Bale took the carefully wrapped package and began to tug at the cord which bound it. It was strong stuff and he was having difficulty. "I'd better get a knife," he said and got up from the couch on which he'd been sitting and started toward the kitchen. "Oh, don't bother, luv," Ruth said, "I'll manage." He turned to look. The tough cord snapped in her hands like a biscuit. "How'd you do that?" Bale asked. "Look," she said, "it's the lamp, all right, but the nits have sent us the wrong color. This one is green." "How'd you do that?" Bale repeated. "Do what?" "Break the cord like that." "Well, I don't know. I guess I just pulled extra hard." He took up the cord from where it lay on the floor and wrapped it around his hands. He couldn't break it. "You're trying to jerk it," Ruth said. "Just pull. Here, see?" The cord seemed to stretch like elastic. She broke it effortlessly. They'd never argued, never fought. Without thinking about what he was doing, Eddy reached out with his open palm and tried to slap her. Instinctively she caught his hand and forced it down. She's stronger than me, Bale thought. It's not even a goddamn contest. Afterward it was Ruth who was embarrassed. "I'll make us some tea," she said. When she returned with the tea he wouldn't drink it, and though neither ever alluded to the incident, Eddy was never again comfortable with her. It was the disparity, the misalliance, his nervous apprehension of her great physical strength, which he found at once threatening and compelling and with which he had become strangely obsessed, that made him move out. He was ashamed of himself, repelled by his new attraction for her.

(Now the cat has his tongue because this queen has once again kindled the disparities, stunned and bewildered him by the Mutt and Jeff arrangements of the world, the absolute unapartheid provisions and tableaux he so yearns for and dreads, the surreal displacements of his heart.)

"What I want," he begins carefully, "what is needed—"

"May I go with them, Ma'am?" It's the little boy. He's seated to Eddy's side and slightly behind him, one leg comfortably crossed over the other, swinging freely, at once as poised and at ease as an assistant brought back in an illusion. "With Mister Bale and the sick children? The little dying boys and girls? May I, Ma'am? May I? To Disney World? On their dream holiday? Oh, I hope so. I hope I may! There's nothing to *do* in the palace."

"Disney World? Dream holiday? What's Clarence saying, Mister Bale?" asks the Queen.

"Well, that's my idea, Your Majesty. What I was leading up to. They're terminal, you see. One little fellow is in the last stages of progeria. That's a sort of premature old age. Charles Mudd-Gaddis. He's only eight but he already wears bifocals and suffers terrible constipation. He's feeble, of course, but he has all his faculties. He's very alert. Really. He's sharp as a tack. We should all be in such shape at his age."

Queen Elizabeth stared at him.

"What I mean—" Bale breaks off helplessly to watch the Queen, who has opened her purse and begun to rummage through it as if looking for her compact, a handkerchief, her car keys.

"Continue, please, Mister Bale," Her Majesty says.

"Well," Eddy says, "there's this eleven-year-old girl in Liverpool who's already had a hysterectomy. They should have been tipped off by the hot flashes, but even so they wouldn't have caught it in time."

The Queen has found what she's been looking for. "Yes?" she says when Bale pauses.

"I know the names of almost all the terminal children in England, Ma'am," Eddy tells her, "and who would qualify for the dream holiday—who would benefit, I mean. Twenty thousand would do it."

She takes a checkbook and gold pen from her purse. The checks are imprinted with her image and look rather like pound notes. Bale notices that they've already been signed; only the amount and name of the payee remain to be filled in.

"Of course there are lots of arrangements to be made," Eddy says nervously. "I mean I've got to decide whether to remove my mourner's band in the presence of the children. There's plenty that remains to be worked out."

She is writing his name on a check. "You will be wondering why I am never without my handbag. Very well, Mister Bale, I will tell you. You having shared so much with us," she says slyly, barely glancing at him. "We clutch it this way because of the muggers," she says, and tears the check out of the book and hands it to him. It is for fifty pounds. "Don't cash it," she says. "Show it round. The money ought to come pouring in. When you have what you think you need you may send the check back. You needn't deliver it personally. Just put it in the post."

"It isn't for keeps, Your Majesty?"

"Nothing is for keeps, Mister Bale."

"You want it *back*? Fifty quid? You want it *back*?"

"Does the pope shit in the woods?" asked the Queen of England.

2

He put his staff together like a collection, like partisans, like a crew in a caper. And liked, even as he recruited them, to think of them that way, something faintly illicit about what he could not really think of as trained specialists so much as a band or gang, some troupe of adventurers, a rash ring of the madcap, spunky-emboldened, stouthearted, suspect. Bale's lot: his soldiers of fortune, his heart's highwaymen. Though this was a ruse, a bit of deception he had got up for his own benefit, something Foreign Legion, if not about their bona fides then about their character, left over in his head from a time he had gone to films. Almost telling them when they agreed to join him in his venture—thinking of it as "venture," too, "operation," "undertaking," the code words more satisfying to him than the "dream holiday" label the press had taken up—that they'd have to put by the hard stuff till they'd pulled this one off, that if he so much as smelled anything stronger than tea on their breath they'd be thrown out quicker than snap, and a severe warning that they'd have to lay off the birds—this last to a male nurse who'd tended Liam at the London Clinic and was almost certainly a poof. And nothing on the side, he would have warned: no private swindle, no skimming the cookie jar, no dipping into the private stock. One smutch on the escutcheon and out, he wanted to say. When they got back to England, he wanted to say, could barely keep himself from saying, they could do as they pleased. He was no parson himself; no one had elected *him* pope. They could go on a bender or fish pox in the stews, *he* didn't care. They could bash up old ladies or belt cripples about. (This to Nedra Carp, a woman who, briefly, had been Prince Andrew's nanny. He hadn't thought of bringing a nanny, just the private pediatric nurse and erstwhile casualty-ward physician—a pediatrician—he'd met when Liam had been a patient at Queen Mary's in Roehampton. He had the idea when he saw the woman on television. The children would like that, he thought, having the hero of the Falklands' personal nanny.) Oh, yeah, he wanted to say, they could talk low bosh or play the berk. They could turn bloody kosher as far as he was concerned, but one smutch, *one*, and he'd have their guts for garters and their bones for toothpicks. They'd never work with terminal kiddies again, not while Eddy Bale drew breath! And *hard* cases, bullies and killers from the bottom bins, psychopaths, sociopaths, enemies of the people, enemies of God! Bale's private fiction: Bale's desperado wheelmen and demolitions experts, his lookouts and strong-arm guys pitched against the human! (Almost telling them this rubbish, his own low bosh almost out of his mouth, a strange wickedness on the tip of his tongue, all he could do just to mask it at the last moment in the sober turns of his conversations with them. Because I am mad. Am I mad?)

Actually the group was practically blue-ribbon, worthy as

the blue-ribbon cash he had put together after the Queen had given him his seed money.

Colin Bible, the male nurse from the London Clinic, is a tallish, decorous, handsome man, his appearance in his impeccable hospital whites and almost slipperlike shoes oddly nautical, not so much jaunty as vaguely languorous, like the summery deck clothes of actors on private yachts in films. He has that same spoiled, fine blond hair and would look wind-blown, Eddy imagines, in sealed rooms. And a quality in his expression of some just-disturbed petulance, ruffled as his hair and as suddenly smoothed back, as if he is obliged to welcome surprise guests. Colin had been his son's favorite, breezy with the boy, exaggeratedly swish, his broad effeminacy laid on as an accent in a joke and designed, Bale and his wife were certain, to give the boy the impression that it was to Liam alone he spoke this way. It was Bible who insisted, even in the last week of Liam's life, that the boy required exercise and, when the doctors left—the technicians from Radiology to photograph his bones, from Hematology to draw his blood, from Nuclear Medicine to inject him with substances they would subsequently read tracings of on big, complicated machinery—he would pop into the kid's room, look comically round to see if anyone was left (managing in quick strobic glances to give the impression that even Ginny and Bale were gone, who were *always* there, who in that last week did not even return to their flat except to change into fresh clothes, even then never going back together, the one fetching for the other and, in the last days, not going back at all, taking their meals not in the Clinic's small coffee shop, or even from the vending machines, but ordering from the hospital kitchen, paying the same inflated prices—"They don't make their money," Ginny once joked, "on the operations and tests. They make it on the goddamn lunches and dinners"—choosing their next day's meals from the same menu the Clinic's dietician showed their dying child), and call out, first conspiratorially, then loudly, "Walkies, Liam. *Walk*ies, *walk*ies!"

("Colin says I mustn't invalid myself," Liam tells them, back, breathless, in bed.

("You're overextended, darling," Ginny says. "You must save your strength."

("What for?"

("It's just gone three," his father says. "Where have you been these past twenty-five minutes?"

("Colin took me to stand by the window. We looked out on Devonshire Place."

("Oh? What did you see?"

("The traffic," Liam says. "We counted two Humbers. There were Bentleys and Jags. Colin calls them doctor's cars. Morris-Minors, of course, and Ford Cortinas and Anglias. We saw ever so many Vauxhalls and Daimlers. And Colin says he saw a Hillman-Minx with its top rolled back in the phaeton position. I missed that one."

(He knew he was dying. He might have been talking about birds spotted in nature. He knew he was dying. He would have known this if he hadn't the evidence of his decaying body. The doctors had spoken guardedly when he'd asked if he'd ever leave hospital again. He knew he was dying. There was the pathetic testimony of his parents' vigil, their soured, close-quarters breath, Bale's stubble and the careless erosion of his mum's makeup. So he knew he was dying. Colin Bible had told him so. "It's only traffic down there, kiddo," the man had said. "They're just cars, not kangaroos. If Lord and Lady Muck let me, I'd have you off to Kew Gardens or Regent's Park zoo. We could pop by Madame Tussaud's for a look-see. Most of that lot's goners too, Liam." Liam shuddered. "What, you've seen 'em then? Ozymandias, Ozymandias, hey, kid? They look a grave and gray bunch now, I grant, but I'll say *this* much for 'em. They done their time, they done their time and they put on a show, the villains no less than the heroes and courtesans. Every mum's son, every dad's daughter. All the ancient and modern personages. Not one eager to die and, except for the crazies, p'raps, not one even willing. Not because they didn't know what they was getting into but because only a crazy don't appreciate what he's getting out of. So that's what you have in common with the moguls and presidents, Liam. Everybody wants to live. We all love the sunshine and we all love the rain. Only the nut case thinks life is hard. Hard? It's softer than silk pajamas."

("My life is hard."

("Oh? Then you're the one don't mind dying."

("Yes. Yes I do."

("There you go then."

("I'm twelve years old," Liam said.

("Yes, and you weren't always sick. You've kicked the football in your time, I'll be bound. You've jumped into the header." Liam smiled. "Sure. And I'll bet you the baby you know how to swim, that you've been to the baths, maybe even to the sea itself. Maybe even to Brighton."

("And Blackpool."

("Brighton *and* Blackpool! And you tell me life is hard. Oh, yes. *I* believe you but thousands wouldn't!"

("One time, on the pitch, I was bowling and knocked the bails clear off the stumps three times running," Liam remembers.

("You were a bowler, were you?"

("It wasn't a regu*la*tion cricket ground. Something me and my mates set up on the common."

("You've done it all," Colin Bible says.

("I never did," he tells him quietly, and looks at his nurse. The boy is tired, wishes the man would help him back to his room. On these occasions Colin rarely brings the child's wheelchair. He carries him when he's too weak to walk and sets him down on the hospital's deep window ledges. "I never did those things."

("What things, Liam?"

("That the ancient and modern personages did."

("That was my surprise," Colin says.

("*I* won't live long enough to do just even ordinary things. I'll never have my own bed-sitter."

("That's not so much," Colin Bible says. "What, a bed-sitter? There's less *there* than meets the eye. They're all moldy and dank, with patches of lino on the floor that never match. I think the Council has rules against it."

("I always wanted to live in one," the boy says. "That was my idea. To rent a bed-sitter and put my shillings in the electric fire. What surprise?"

("Well, you know, Liam, you really are a personage."

("What, *I* am?"

("A modern personage but a personage all the same," Colin tells him. "Maybe the most famous young personage in England."

("What, because I'm going to die, you mean?"

("Your picture's been in *News of the Day*. You've been on the telly. They've written about you in all the papers, even the *Times*. Just everyone knows you. You've been a poster boy. Famous people pray for you. Girls write for your autograph. They know you listen to Terry Wogan. They call him up and he dedicates songs to you. One Sunday in the flat my friend and I were listening to 'Melodies for You' and we heard your name. 'I know him,' I said. 'You know Liam Bale?' he asked. 'Sure,' I said, 'he's my patient.'

("I never did anything brave. The pain doesn't count. When it hurts I cry. I whine and I whimper. You've heard me, Colin."

("You've been to Madame Tussaud's, Liam," Colin Bible said. "It's not all Monty and Lord Nelson and Christ on the Cross. You've seen the noted criminals, you've seen the film stars. Of *course* you're a personage."

("Madame Tussaud's?"

("Well, that's what we've been talking about, isn't it? That's my surprise. I can't absolutely guarantee it, of course, but my friend is one of their top artists. He's Artistic Director, actually, and makes most of the decisions about who'll be showcased. When he heard I actually knew you he was very excited. He'd already made some marvelous sketches that he took from the papers. 'Hold on,' I said. 'I don't know if Liam even *wants* to be in your waxworks. Not everyone would, you know, Colin.'—my friend's name is Colin, too.—Well, he said he'd respect your wishes in the matter, of course. He doesn't have to. He's Artistic Director, and you're a public personage. Even if you weren't, once you're dead you'd be in the public domain anyway—I *think* that's the law—so he can pretty much do as he pleases, though he promised he'd respect your wishes. I said I'd check with you, Liam. Personally, I think it would be flippin' lovely, but it's your decision."

("Madame Tussaud's!" Liam says. "Me in Madame Tussaud's! That's a stunner. I mean, no boy *wants* to die, but that's a stunner. I can almost see the expression on my mates' faces when they see me."

("Well, you know, Liam, I told Colin I thought that might be the way you'd react when I told you. He's very good, Colin is. He doesn't make the actual molds. Those are done in France, mostly, but he does the preliminary sketches and determines the poses."

(Liam's face goes suddenly pale. Colin Bible grabs him from the window seat and carries the boy to a bench, where he lays him down gently. He raises his pajama top, warms the metal disk with breath from his mouth, and puts it against the child's skin. Liam starts to say something. "Shh, shh," the nurse says. "All right then," he says in a moment. "I want to take your pulse." Which is rapid but not alarming. He places a thermometer under Liam's tongue. Again the boy tries to speak. "Liam, please, you'll snap it in two. Then we'll both be at the Madame's."

("Uh *oj*esh," Liam says.

("In a minute," Colin says. The color has returned to Liam's face. "Not even normal," he scolds. "All right, Liam, what was *that* all about then?"

("The poses," Liam says, "the *poses!*"

("All right, the poses. What about the poses?"

("Not in a hospital bed! Sitting up in a chair, maybe, but not in a *hospital* bed! When you said that about the poses—"

("Was *that* all that was? Sure," Colin says, "I'll tell Colin. He'll have you in a chair. Reading, perhaps, or watching the telly. Looking out the window, seeing things far away or counting the Humbers. Don't worry, Liam. It will be as grand as any effigy there. Colin's a good friend. He'll do all of us proud."

(And these are almost his son's last words, the ones Bale had held back from the journalists when they'd turned out on the wet and nasty evening of Liam's last day, the words he'd hardly heard, could barely make out, when Liam pulled his father close, speaking from the fearful, terrible ecstasy of his dread: "Mamtooshawfsh."

("What, Liam? I'm sorry, son. I don't understand." Carefully, silently, signaling Ginny beside him, almost as if she is some Chief Inspector asked in a soft gesture to pick up an extension to hear a message from the kidnappers. "I'm sorry, Liam. Calmly. Calmly."

(The boy shakes his head, breathes deeply, seeks for mastery of himself, finds it, starts again slowly, as slowly, as patiently as if his parents are the ones in peril. "They," he says, "want," he says, "to put," he says, "my—" he says, and pauses, trying to recall the word, "—effigy, my *effigy*," he says, "in Madame Tussaud's," he says.

("*Never!*" his father reassures him.

("Of course not, sweetheart," his mother agrees.

("No," Liam pleads with them, bewildered, "you have to let them. Please," he says. "I want . . . I want it there. Promise me!" he says, and dies.)

The ex-casualty ward physician is Mr. Moorhead. He is not, as Eddy Bale vaguely wishes, a ship's doctor, someone ruined, a hardened stray from the China trade, the belowdecks, palmetto-fanned heats and ruthlessnesses of tubs and packets, the steamy African river routes, or the pack-ice Murmansk and Greenland ones—some drummed-out being, some tainted, weary wiz. (Why do I insist on this stuff? Bale wonders. Who will have young lives in his charge. Not even the just ordinary Boy Scouts and Girl Guides of summer's hold-hand organized wayfare but the real thing, some from-the-start-doomed-and-threatened expedition itself. So why do I insist on this stuff? My wife walked out on me. I lost a son. Ain't my life full enough already?) But far from being in disgrace, he is, despite Eddy Bale's garish dreams for him, an eminent man. (In less than the four years since Bale first met him, Moorhead had left the National Health, set up in private practice, and was now Senior Registrar in Internal Medicine at the Hospital for Sick Children in Great Ormond Street, an excellent, highly regarded doctor with a service at Sick Children's which was one of the most distinguished in Britain.) Secretly he wishes to be awarded an O.B.E. Editorial leaders in *Lancet* have favorably mentioned his name, and even respected colleagues, to whom he's never disclosed his ambitions, can't understand why he's overlooked while, year after year, rock stars, actors, TV journalists, designers, and others, less deserving and perhaps even less famous, are included. The omission has been noted and actually occasioned several letters to the *Times,* usually followed and sometimes accompanied by delicately worded, clearly embarrassed disclaimers from Moorhead himself. Who knows well enough, but will not of course state, the real reason he's been passed over. Just as he knows why he's chosen to go off with Bale and the children on their futile flying circus to Florida. Almost certainly, though he loves the sun, the heat, and regularly goes on holiday to Spain's Balearic Islands or Africa's west coast or even out on the banana boats, those fuming tubs and packets of Eddy Bale's imagination, it's a place he would never, as a tourist, enter on his own. It is the Jews. He is going to see the Jews. He has heard that there is an even higher concentration of them in Florida than there is in Israel. It is the Jews who have kept him off the Queen's Honors List, who for three years now have permitted him to attend the Queen's Garden Party but drawn the line when it came to sharing real privilege and power. All those Jews. It is for Moorhead alone the dream holiday.

They were in Eddy Bale's council flat in Putney. "Doct—" Bale, offering refreshment, started to say, then, correcting himself, named instead the inverted, oddly up-ante'd title of certain physicians. "*Mister* Moorhead?"

Eddy, fussing tea, opening in front of his guest, who had followed him into his small kitchen, the all-in selection from Sainsbury's dairy case, murmuring, apologizing for his surviving father's and bachelor's ready-to-wear arrangements, popping the tiny crustless sandwiches and little cakes into the gas range to take the chill off.

"It all looks quite delicious, Bale," Mr. Moorhead said.

"I know it isn't what you're accustomed to."

"It looks quite delicious."

"Well," Eddy said, "it's hardly what they serve at the Queen's Garden Party."

"You know the Queen's Garden Party?"

"I've been this fund raiser, this special pleader, for years now. I have the guest lists by heart. Well, I'd have to, wouldn't I? For the leads. Like an assurance broker or a customer's man in the City. I know my nobs. I know my hons."

"My dear Bale," the doctor said, "I don't think you know *me*. It's true I federate with the nobs and hons at Her Majesty's company picnic. I've even an eye out for the chain and collar. Which makes me as much customer's man as yourself, as anyone in bourse or bucket shop, but it all goes for the children in Great Ormond Street. If I climb it's for them I climb, more Sherpa than Hillary. Which could explain my presence on this long march of yours. Now," he said, "*about* these terminal kiddies, these goner spawn." And indicated an immense pile of folders on the sofa in Eddy's lounge.

And Mary Cottle, neither nanny nor nurse, a woman in her early thirties who'd lost neither husband nor child but fiancé, not to death, not even to a rival, and who would herself bear no children, who could conceive them readily enough and even carry them to term, but who wore a poisoned womb, a terrible necklace of tainted genes that could destroy any child, boy or girl, to whom she might give birth. Healthy herself, and quite beautiful, she suffered from the strangest disease of all. She was a carrier. Twice, once in her teens and again in her twenties, she had delivered ruined, stillborn babes. Two other times amniocentesis had revealed awful birth defect, chromosomes suffused with broad and latent deformity like too-bitter tea.

"There's something wrong," the doctor said. "Your children will be born blind. With cancer, measles, swollen glands. With canes in their little fists."

"We shall have to throw out the baby with the bathwater," the surgeon said who performed her second abortion.

"It's all bathwater," Mary said and broke off her engagement.

"It's crazy," her fiancé had said. "We don't have to have kids."

"No," Mary Cottle said.

"We could adopt."

"You don't understand," Mary Cottle said. "I could never sleep with you."

"That's ridiculous. What is it you're supposed to have?"

"Everything. I'm this Borgia madonna. I poison babies."

Since then she has not so much as kissed a man and kept herself equable by frequent and furious bouts of masturbation, each time wondering what unkempt, dreadful, sickened soups she stirred with her finger.

Although she was precisely the sort of self-exiled outcast Eddy wanted for his enterprise, Bale knew nothing of her history. She came to him with queer credentials: as a highly recommended gray lady, a candidate, in everybody's books, of unchurched sanctity, always peaceful—her sponsors knew nothing of her habits either, her steady state, orgasmic calm—always serene.

"Mary's a brick," the parents of dying children told him. "She's quite marvelous. I can't imagine where she gets her strength."

"We depend on Mary," her supporters said when he checked with them. "I don't think she has a nerve in her body."

"All she's supposed to have seen," Eddy confided to two trusted nurses at the London Clinic, "perhaps she's callous."

"Go on, she never is. It's more like—well, something spiritual. Isn't that what you'd call that far-off look in her eyes, Bert?"

"Spiritual, yes," Bert said. "I'd say so. That calm, spiritual quality."

"Always smiling. You know what she reminds me of? The Mona Lisa."

"She's an angel, is Mary."

"Angels don't smoke," Bale, who'd never seen her enter a room without a cigarette in her lips, said.

She was smoking one then, in Putney, on the day they chose their finalists.

"Sorry I'm late," Mary Cottle said, sitting down, and Eddy was struck by the lack of sorrow in her voice or on her beautiful, blissful face, which seemed never to have entertained the slightest anxiety. "What have I missed?"

"Mister Moorhead's been disposing of our case load," Colin Bible said, and pointed to about two dozen file folders at the physician's feet.

Nedra Carp had to laugh over that one, she said, and did, loudly, and Bale was reminded again of something he'd noticed all his life: that people, even quite humdrum people, often behave eccentrically in groups. He'd seen this in school, had observed it when he'd done his National Service, in the office when he'd held down a regular job. It was as if the laws of civility, which not only governed but actually controlled people in one-on-one situations, were repealed once individuals joined with others, as if sanity were only a sort of practiced shyness and that what they were, what they were *really*, their true colors, wild as the plumage of exotic birds, was permitted to glow only in association, all their nut-case gushers and bonanzas, all their moonstruck, batty doings flourishing in packs, fielded herds of the erratic.

Because on television she had seemed such a *nice* woman. On the phone she had. And although it was true what Colin Bible had suggested, that Moorhead had been behaving with peremptory flair, rummaging among the names Eddy had proposed for the dream holiday with something more like impatience than judgment, like a card player discarding anything not of immediate value to his hand, say, Bale supposed it was only what Moorhead, as the only physician there, supposed was expected of him. Perhaps he *did* think that, for when Colin Bible said what Nedra Carp had laughed about so loudly, Moorhead looked up sharply. "It isn't a contest, you know," he said. "None of these children has actually made application to come with us. This is only a sort of *triage*. Doctors do it in casualty wards all the time. On battlefields they do. What we're looking for here are those children who would most profit from our attentions."

"The deserving dead," Mary Cottle said. Nedra Carp shrieked.

"There are ethical considerations," Moorhead said.

"My friend Colin warned me this would happen," Colin Bible whispered to Mary Cottle. " 'Just take what comes,' he said. 'Regard the group, whatever its final makeup, as a sort of found sculpture.' "

"What ethical considerations?" Eddy Bale said.

"Well, if we chose a child whose parents can afford to make the trip on their own," Moorhead said.

"Say, that's right," Eddy said.

"And the children ought to be compatible."

"And what if they haven't taken in yet that they're going to die?" Mary Cottle asked equably. "Seeing some of their companions could come as a frightful shock."

"The trip will be exhausting. It could shorten their lives."

"That's right," Moorhead said.

"Then there's the whole question of taste," Colin Bible said.

"Taste?" said Eddy Bale.

"I'm sorry," Colin Bible said. "My roomie warned me to keep my nose out of this."

"Where's the Ladies'?" Mary Cottle wanted to know.

"Taste?"

"Well, there'll be all that media coverage, won't there?" Colin Bible said. "You know how the press exploits these kids, Mister Bale. Who better?"

"They trained their long lenses on us whenever we went on an outing," Nedra Carp said. "They could shoot right into Prince Andrew's picnic hamper."

"And medicine is more of an art than an exact science anyway."

"So?" Eddy Bale said.

"A doctor gives one child six months and another two years."

"So?"

"There's no guarantee the one with six months couldn't go two years."

"Or the one with two years die in a week."

"We have to be sure, you see," Nedra Carp said.

"That they're dying. That it's actually imminent."

"It's a nice question," Moorhead said.

"Like when brain death occurs."

"Lung death."

"Finger death," muttered Mary Cottle in the loo.

"There are many nice questions."

"There are many ethical considerations."

"Suppose one kid is religious?"

"That he believes in God?"

"Has hope of Heaven?"

"Is convinced of it."

"While the other kid isn't even a believer?"

"Thinks when you're dead you're dead."

"Or's Jewish."

"It wouldn't be fair."

"To the skeptic, atheist, agnostic kid."

"To the kosher boy."

"To the skeptic, atheist, agnost—?"

"Well, the religious kid would have it both ways, wouldn't he?"

"Disney World, and Heaven too."

"Or look at it the other way around."

"That's right."

"Should the believer be penalized for his beliefs?"

"There are all these nice questions. I shouldn't have thought we'd even scratched the surface."

"Ought they to spend their final weeks away from their family, friends, and pets?"

"If I wear my armband all the time," Bale reflected, "that could put them off."

"Perhaps something less ostentatious. Perhaps a button in your lapel."

"Well, you know, I never thought about the nice questions," Eddy Bale said. "All I thought about was the fellowship of the thing."

"See Naples and die."

"See Naples and die?"

"He means how you gonna keep 'em down on the farm."

"He means England and home might be a letdown."

"That they could go into a reactive depression."

"What's wrong with you?" Bale asked. "You parse good deeds. Lawyers, ambulance chasers. I don't know damn-all about the ethics and nice questions. Only ordinary human action. Nobody tells me 'Have a good day' anymore," he said.

They stared at him.

"The chief's right," Colin Bible said. "Let's get on with it."

Mary Cottle, rubbing her hands as if she'd just dried them but hadn't managed to get all the wetness off, came back into the room and smiled at them beatifically.

"Well," Moorhead said, and picked up the remaining folders.

"Spit-spot!" said the nanny, Nedra Carp.

Which was when he got the giddies. Could barely refrain from spouting his gibberish about the desperado backgrounds he was constantly sketching in for them, their base *curricula vitae* pasts. "Chief" had worked on him, on all of them, like an enchantment. Eddy couldn't help it, was as giddy with their gibberish and low bosh as with his own. Chief he'd never been, yet as soon as Bible spoke Bale perceived the change in the room, the simple fact of the matter. He was their chief, the responsible one in the bunch. The organizer. The enforcer. In their group madness they had, as madmen have always done—even those with delusions of grandeur—looked for someone at whose feet they could dump their delusions, fetching them to him with the pride of cats with dead mice, birds, cleverly preparing their loophole lunacy. While, just as cleverly (if with less good judgment), he saw what they were doing and accepted their nutty proposition, their singular single condition—that he be the one in charge.

So, like the good administrator he had just become, he delegated, who had himself been delegated, delegation smeared as perspective in a funhouse mirror—we're all mad now, he thought—and asked the doctor for a run-down. He wanted Moorhead's medical input, he said—he called him Moorhead; he said "input"—into a candidate's qualifications. He would entertain suggestions, he said, as to who might best benefit from such a trip. And was actually startled to see the doctor take up folders he had already discarded, names and case histories strewn at his feet like debris, like castoffs in card games, and listened attentively as the physician offered his careful Senior Registrar's considered advice, though not so much attentive—England's most famous beggar munificent for once—as patient, to the physician's latinate terms, expecting and getting his almost simultaneous layman's translation, a kind of due, a sort of deference, as if he were Head of Delegation at the U.N., say, feeling good about things—he crossed his legs—and finally neither so much attentive or patient as complacent—he felt the hair silver about his temples—interrupting only to ask his perfect administrator's breathtaking questions.

"Thank you, Mister Moorhead," he said politely when the doctor had finished. And turned smartly to Colin Bible. "And you, are you in concurrence, Sister?" he wickedly asked the poof nurse who would have had dead Liam stuffed and put on exhibit in a case.

"Oh, aye," Colin said. "There's nought we can do for the medulloblastomas. They quite put one off with their dizzy spells and fits of vomiting, their falling down and constant headache."

"Nanny?"

"They would me," Nedra Carp said.

"What about the Stepney lad with corrected transposition of the great vessels?"

"He's kind of cute," Mary Cottle said dreamily, looking at a photograph.

"Well," Colin Bible said, "as Doctor explained, their autopsies are interesting. Hearts like Spaghetti Junction. I say give him a pass."

Bale went round the room and gave each of them the opportunity to disqualify one or two victims out of hand. Mary

Cottle declined her turn sweetly and Eddy, his administrative eye on the logistics of the thing, reserved for himself the right to use her veto powers. In this way, in addition to Mr. Moorhead's exclusions and Colin Bible's of the boy from Stepney, they rid themselves of Dawson's, Tay-Sachs, Krabbe's I, Wilm's, and Cushing's disease, and were left with one case each of Gaucher's disease, tetralogy of Fallot, osteosarcoma, cystic fibrosis, dysgerminoma, Chédiak-Higashi syndrome, progeria, and lymphoblastic leukemia.

"Well," he said, standing up, "it seems all that remains to be done is to notify the parents and work out with the lawyers the wording of the disclaimer. Congratulations to you all and thank you. I'd say we've done rather a good day's work."

He believed it.

Then why, he asked himself when they left, do I feel like such a prick?

It was a nice question.

3

The kid with Chédiak-Higashi disease was dead. A newspaper reported the story of Eddy's group three days before its official release date. The child, recognizing Bale's name on the envelope that had been addressed to his parents, was so excited by the prospect of going on the dream holiday that he tore open the letter without thinking. The discrete paper cut he did not even feel at the time—he was that excited—but the big sandy granules that invaded his white blood cells, and made them ineffectual in fighting infection, did him in.

Janet Order also saw the letter before her parents did, and though she had a pretty good idea about its contents—like many of the diseased children, like Liam himself, she was exceptionally bright; she would, if she lived, be a teenager on her next birthday; her body had begun to fill out months before and already she'd had to abandon her training bra for the real thing; this didn't particularly embarrass her and, indeed, she quite accepted the idea of becoming a young lady, taking an interest in her puberty, rather proud of it actually, attending her monthlies with a modest though becoming interest, enjoying, if not the discomfort of her periods, at least the opportunity to minister to them, to care for herself, dressing in the queer new tampons and flushing herself with scentless, lightly medicated douches, evaluating not only the different painkillers on the market but their most effective dosages as well, taking an almost ecological interest in the crop of sparse, light brown hair which dusted her mons veneris, and generally presiding over and servicing the new blockbuster secretions of her glands with a solicitude she had a few years earlier shown for her dolls— she did not open it, preferring to wait for her parents, meanwhile practicing the new biofeedback techniques, stretching, and deep-breathing exercises her physical therapist had shown her. In a few minutes her pulse had returned to normal and her pressure, which she had been taught to take by herself, was not, for her, especially elevated.

Janet had a congenital heart disease, tetralogy of Fallot. In all other respects a bright and even beautiful child, she had been born with a hole in her heart and a transposed aorta, a heart like one of those spectacularly deformed vegetables one sometimes sees on Fair days: a potato in the shape of a white bread, say, or a cluster of Siamese-joined grapes. She was tall for her age, delicate but sturdily built, and had long, flaxen hair to her waist. In a black-and-white photograph one would have seen an unsmiling, even pouty, but remarkably attractive child. The pout was put on, a performance, not so much a sign of mood as, or so Janet thought, of character. She was, considering, a cheerful enough girl and sulked at the world only in those pictures, doing it, she liked to think, as a kind of truth in advertising, sending her sneers and sniffinesses, her frowns and scowls, to the people who would see these pictures, so as not to misrepresent herself; to discount her beauty or, rather, to signal its opposite, invisible in the black-and-white photographs. Because of her abnormality, the deficient oxygenation in her holed heart, the surgically attached aorta added on by the doctors like some displaced bit of afterthought architecture, she had been cyanotic from birth, her skin everywhere an even, dusky bluish color, dark as seawater.

Additional operations had, as her parents had been warned, as she had, only been remedial, not treatment so much as a flurry of activity, battles fought over the inopportune ground of her tampered chest.

Children teased her.

"Ooh," they might say, "dere goes a piece of der bloody sky."

"Yar. I've seen fledgling birds wot fly crost 'er face fer practice."

"Yar, well, dat's because dey fink she's one of deir own. Some great gawky bluebirdy her own self."

"Nah," they might say, "wot dey fink is dat she's a blueberry patch. Dey're looking to snack off her."

Janet Order viewed these occasions as opportunities to correct the kids, to make, as she saw it, the world a better place in which to live. "It's only a birth defect. You oughtn't to laugh at birth defects, children," she would say. "My skin is blue because when I was born my blood flowed through the hole in my heart to my body without first passing into my lungs. It's the lungs that tint the blood red by adding oxygen, boys and girls."

"Bleedin' 'eart 'ole!" they taunted. " 'Ere coom Janet Order wif er bleedin' 'eart 'ole!"

What most concerned her, though, was their fear. For each child who mocked her, there were a dozen who couldn't even look at her.

"No, no," she'd say, "don't be afraid, touch it. Go ahead, touch my skin. Oh, I know it looks icy but it isn't. It's as warm as your own. Go on, touch it. *I* don't mind."

And sometimes, occasionally, once in a while, a brave soul would. He would touch it gingerly, laying the back of his hand against her blue cheek while Janet took his own pink hand in her two blue ones and guided it along the length of her blue arm, her blue neck and blue shoulders, soothing him, comforting. "There," she'd say, "you see? It's not cold. It's blue like this because the lungs build up pressure and the patches burst where the surgeons keep sealing it and grafting blood vessels onto it like you'd patch an old tire. It could have been corrected, but they say I have this ventricular septal defect. You mustn't be afraid." But the child would think of Janet Order's blue defect and shudder involuntarily in her temperate blue grasp.

She had only grown kind. When she was smaller, and had played the secret games of childhood, the other children had been terrified of the blue surgical scars crisscrossing her chest like surfaced veins, of her blue behind and little blue mons. Wickedly, she'd teased them, cruel and comfortable in her blue power over them.

On the day of the letter, tears were rolling down her cheeks when her parents returned. "This letter came. I didn't open it but I think it's about my dream holiday." She handed the envelope to her father.

"It is," he said. "Oh, it's grand news, Janet. In two weeks you'll be leaving for Florida. Can we get her ready in time?" he asked his wife. "She'll need some summery dresses, I should think. And a new bathing suit. What do you think, Doris? Can we get her ready? Oh, ducks, *don't* cry. Don't *cry*, ducks."

"Our Janet's a big girl now," her mother explained. "Sometimes when they're extra especially happy the only way a big girl can show it is by crying." Then she turned to her daughter. "But please, Janet," her mother said, "you know it's not good for you to become emotional. Your lovely brown eyes have gone all blue."

"I'm not worthy, Mummy," her daughter whispered.

"Don't be silly, Janet. All those operations? You've been a dreadfully burdened little girl."

And then Janet Order confessed that her blueness had never been a burden and told her parents what she'd said to those little boys, whispered to them in those dank basements and dim potting sheds and in the obscure corners of the deserted common, frightening them, boasting of her blue bowels and blue pee, commanding their loyalty by the blue power of her blue tears.

Noah Cloth, confined to hospitals at a time in his life when other boys his age were in school, could not read well or do his maths. His history was weak, his geography, most of his subjects. Only in art had he done well, and now he'd lost his ability to draw. Nine times he'd been operated on for bone tumors: in his right wrist, along his left and right femurs, on both elbows, once at the base of his skull, and once for little garnetlike tumors around a necklace of collarbone. Twice they had cut into his left hand by the bones beneath the skin of his ring finger. The first operation had been successful, yielding tiny growths of a benign jewelry, but when the surgeons went back in a second time, they discovered the boy had severe osteosarcoma and had to amputate the finger. They told Noah's parents they must expect more malignancies, and a nice lady from a hospice came to explain what was what to the kid.

Noah argued with the woman, asserting that there were just hundreds of bones in the human body that were dispensable, the bone in his ring finger, for example. He told her he could live a normal life, not indefinitely, of course, no one lived forever, and probably not without some inconvenience, every once in a while sacrificing a really important poisoned bone or so, but what he really feared, he said, was that one of these days the poison would find its way into his leg and they'd have to amputate it and replace it with an artificial one—he saw what went on; he'd spent lots of time on the rehabilitation wards— and he'd have to walk with a cane. He laughed and said he guessed worse things had happened at sea, but what if it was the right leg they had to cut off?

"The right leg?" asked the lady from the hospice.

"Well, sure," he said, "then I'd really be knackered, wouldn't I? Well, I mean I spent all that time on the wards, didn't I? So I know about these things." She wasn't following him. "It's the opposite limb," Noah explained. "The cane goes in the hand opposite the wounded limb."

"I don't . . ."

"Oh, lady," Noah Cloth said, and held out the hand with the missing finger. "It's all right once you get accustomed, but how's a bloke supposed to rehabilitate himself into a wood leg if he can't even hold his cane proper? I mean, it's what happened with my drawing pens, isn't it?"

And only a few weeks before, he'd begun to detect a sharp pain along the length of his right shin. Uh-oh, he thought, but said nothing to his parents or the doctors, and nothing either to the busybody from the hospice, because he didn't want to give her the satisfaction and because, too, she only depressed him with her arguments.

"Don't you see, Noah," she told the eleven-year-old boy when she called round at his house to ask him to die, "you're denying the facts. Don't you see how typical your behavior is? Kübler-Ross tells us that denial, rage, bargaining, and acceptance is the classic pattern of people in your circumstance. *You* can't get past even the first stage. How do you expect to come to terms with your situation?"

"Well, if I don't," Noah Cloth said, "I won't die then, will I?"

"That's bargaining," the woman said, pouncing cheerfully.

"No," Noah Cloth said evenly, "it's rage."

The hospice woman left him a pamphlet.

Which, since he couldn't read, he threw to the corner of his bed, where his father found it when he came into Noah's room later that evening. The father picked the pamphlet up to examine. "You know what this is about?" he asked.

"No," Noah Cloth said.

"Do you want me to read it to you?"

"Is it a story?"

"No," his father said.

"Because there's better stories on the telly," Noah said.

"This isn't a story," his father said and cleared his throat while Noah quietly began to grieve and his mother came into the bedroom to listen as the father read to the son about letting go of life, tough talk about the child's fears, how it was important not to be ashamed to die. When his father finished he closed the book and looked at the boy.

"It was a story after all," Noah Cloth said, and drew a deep breath and felt a stitch. No bones there, he thought absently, ignorant still of what his disease might yet do to him—all its oyster irritabilities and abrasions, the little shards of malignant pearl piercing his lungs like studs, glowing like nacre, shining his breath like dew.

"Some dream holiday," Benny Maxine, the Gaucher's disease, complained to Rena Morgan, the cystic fibrosis.

"What's wrong with Disney World?"

"Well, nuffink if what you're into is rides and a bunch of dwarfs and down-and-out actors what can't get proper work all dressed up like animals wif their paws stuck out for a bit of graft every time you might want to take your picture wif dem. I'm at liberty to tell you dat's not *my* idea. Benjamin Maxine, luv. Benny to me mates. I don't fink I've 'ad the pleasure."

"Rena Morgan, Benjamin."

"Benny to me mates."

"Benny."

They shook hands solemnly.

"No, that's not *my* idea at all," Benny Maxine said. "Not of no *dream* holiday it ain't."

"Have you been there?"

"What, the *Wor*-ruld? No fear!"

"Well, maybe you'll be surprised. Perhaps you'll like it after all."

"Nah," Benny said. "It's some tarted-up Brighton, is all. Adventureland, Tomorrowland. The bloody Never-lands! Greasy great kid stuff is what I say!"

"The Netherlands?"

"What?" Benny Maxine said. "Oh. No, sweetheart. Never-Land. You know, where Peter Pansy flies his pals in the pantomime. Not the *coun*try, not the place wif the wood gym shoes and all the boot forests. You don't talk the bull's wool, do you, luv? Not to worry. We're all Englitch 'ere. Just little dying Englitch boys and girls. Which is why I fink we should 'ave been personally consulted, drawn into the discussions, like, before they shipped us all off to Florida and the Magic Kingdom to put us on the rides and expose us to the dangerous tropic sun.

("Don't look now, luv," Benny whispered, and indicated with a gesture of his chin where Janet Order was sitting, "but that one could *do* wif a bit o' old Sol!) I mean, how do *they* know where a poor little mortal loser like yours truly would like to take his dream holiday? No one sat on the side of *my* bed and listened to me talk in me sleep."

"Where would you?"

"What, take my dream holiday?"

"That's right."

"What, if I had the whole wide world to choose from?"

"Yes."

"Well, there's no contest then, is there? I mean, look what we got 'ere. Africa, South America, Australia. Asia. You can't forget Asia. There's Mother Russia and China, too, in Asia."

"Is that where you'd go, Asia?"

"Monte Carlo," Benny Maxine said.

"Why that's only in the south of France."

"Monaco. It's in Monaco."

The little girl giggled. "And isn't as big as Regent's Park, I shouldn't think."

"A choice seafront property," Benny Maxine said.

"What a queer place to choose," Rena said. "Whatever would you do there? Get your postcards franked?"

"Yeah, that's right. And send them off to you and Little Girl Blue over there in Mickey Mouseland. 'Yours truly,' I'd sign them. 'The Kid Who Broke the Bank at Monte Carlo!' "

"You wi-ish!"

"Hey, you're pretty lively for a snotnose, ain't you?"

For her giggle had shaken loose some of the immense reserves of Rena Morgan's clear, cystic fibrotic phlegm. Benny watched for a moment. "You got a bad cold there, luv," he said, offering his big clean handkerchief. Which, shaking her head, she declined, opening instead a rather large and attractive flowered canvas drawstring bag which, or so it seemed to Benny, appeared to contain nothing *but* handkerchiefs, men's handkerchiefs, bigger than his own, some of them already crumpled. She poked her hand into the depths of the bag, plunged her wrists past the wet linen, and withdrew an unused handkerchief. Then, taking hold of it by a corner, she flipped it once and the whole thing came unfolded, unfurling like a flag, rolled carpet, an umbrella. She didn't press the handkerchief to her face, she didn't even actually blow, but allowed it to pass under her nose in a continuous, unbroken movement, like someone sliding corn on the cob past her teeth, Benny thought, or like paper moving beneath the keys of a typewriter.

"Sorry," Rena Morgan said, crumpling the now-drenched handkerchief and dropping it into her bag. She seemed quite recovered.

"That's a great trick," Benny said. "How you unfolded that hanky."

"I secrete too much mucus. It's disgusting," she said. "I've cystic fibrosis."

"Well, we all got our cross, don't we, or we wouldn't be sitting here in de West bloody London Air Terminal waiting to be taken off to bleedin' Heathrow in the bloody limos like it was already our bleedin' funerals, would we?"

"You shouldn't curse."

"I'm fifteen years old."

"I don't think age has anything to do with it."

"Yeah, and *I* don't think age has anything to do with where a person would want to spend his dream holiday."

"Think?"

"Pardon?"

"You didn't say 'fink.' You can pronounce your th's."

"A diller, a dollar, a ten o'clock scholar."

"What's *your* cross?"

"Oh, *my* cross. *My* cross is the Magen David."

"I never know what you're talking about, Benny."

"I'm a yid. I've got this yid disease. Gaucher's, it's called.
I've got this big yid liver, this hulking hebe spleen. I've this mis-
shapen face and this big bloated belly. It's the chosen disease of
the chosen people."

"What does it do?"

"What does it *do*? It makes me beautiful and qualifies me
to meet Donald Duck in person."

"Does it hurt?"

"It's weird," he said. "It's very weird. Sugar accumulates in
my cells." He lowered his voice. "See my fingers?"

"You bite your nails."

"For a treat. I chew my thumbs. I lick my palms. I'm candy.
I squeeze sweetness out of the juice of my tongue; my saliva's
better than soda pop. Look." He unbuttoned his shirt sleeve.
Indistinct crescents of teeth mark made a random, mysterious
graffiti all along his arm. "I'm caramel, I'm cake, I'm syrup, I'm
mead. I'm treacle and jam, I'm bonbons and honey. It's incredible. I'm bloody fattening. But nah, it don't hurt. Only when
my bones break. I've got these peanut-brittle bones. Like tooth
decay, only in the marrow."

"Oh, that's horrible," Rena said.

"Yeah, well, we're all 'orrible 'ere. That blue kid? The one
that looks like someone's school colors? And what's'isname, Cloth,
the one with the cancer, that they keep sawing at and carving
on so that even if he lives he'll end up looking like a joint for
somebody's Sunday dinner?"

"You're terrible," Rena said.

"They put me off my feed, our crowd does," Benny Maxine said. "I don't think I could take one contented munch off
meself round this lot."

"Oh, Benny."

"You know what a tontine is?"

"A tontine?"

"It's this agreement, like. Usually geezers make it? Flyers
from the war, daft old boys, a particular chapter, say, of the
Baker Street Irregulars—people tied up in some dotty mutual
enterprise. And each puts something into the kitty, survivor take

all. That's what our bunch ought to do. Get up a tontine. We could have Mister Moorhead handicap us. Like underwriters do for the life assurance societies. We prorate what each puts in and—hey," Benny Maxine said, "hey, don't. Hey."

The girl was crying, her tears melding with the clear gelatins of her runny nose.

"What's happened?" her mother demanded, running from where she and the other parents had been talking with the staff. "Stop that, Rena! *Stop!* You *know* what crying does to you. Oh, Rena," she said, and held the child in her arms, dabbing at her daughter's nose with handkerchiefs from the drawstring bag, stabbing her mucus, blotting it up, stanching it as if it were some queer, devastating blood.

Bale feared they might never take off. Last-minute hitches. At this point almost a sign. Something might have been waving red flags at him, warning him off. Stand clear or be destroyed with them, his kids, his doomed collective charges. (Charges indeed. Bale's bombs. Rigged. Set. Eddy's timed tots. He felt like a sapper.) Ginny was there, Eddy waving and calling "Over here, over here," like a reconciliation in pictures, the kids looking as if a ringer had been snuck in on them, the wise-guy kid, Benny Maxine, rolling his eyes and nodding his Uh-oh's and What now's? as if he knew something. How do you like that kid? Bale wondered. Playing to the crowd, putting on his phony Cockney accent when the closest he'd been to Bow Bells was Michael Caine films; Eddy Bale spotting Ginny meanwhile and doing his own home movies in his head, crying and laughing like a loon in Heathrow's crowded departure lounge and singing "Over here, over here!" as if it were a railroad platform at Waterloo they stood on, both of them caught up in the indifferent traffic, swimming against the stream like salmon and Eddy already figuring out what to say. Ginny not even an apparition, not even someone who just looked like her, who wore her hair the same way or had similar tics. Ginny Ginny, and, worse luck, embarrassed. "Gee, Eddy, I didn't remember today was the big day." "What are you doing here then?" "Meeting a friend." "Oh," Eddy said. "Are those the children?" "What? Them? The saucy blue baggage who looks like she's been dipped in grape juice? The boy with no place to put his ring? That little tyke with the wig who looks like she's eight months pregnant? Or maybe you mean that idiot-looking nipper sucking chemotherapy from a bottle." "Oh, Eddy." "What friend?" "My lover friend, Eddy." "Your lover friend. Ri-ight." "I don't want to hold you up," she said. "Anyone I know?" "Oh, Eddy." "Is he?" "Yes." "You know something, Ginny? That's too bad. I mean it really is. That makes me sorry for you in a way. Because I can't, I mean try as I may, I brutal truthfully can't think of anyone we both know who can hold a candle to me in the way of friendship or anything like loyalty." The uproar in the lounge a welcome distraction by this time, a sound like the sudden appearance of celebrity, Eddy Bale looking over his shoulder.

"Oh, Jesus," he said. "It's the wiseacre."

Benny Maxine was talking to the media.

"After all this excitement, what's the first thing you mean to do when you get on that plane, Benny?"

"Hijack it to Monte Carlo. I've had an 'art-to-'art wif me mates an' we've decided dat Florider is a nice ernuff place ter be if you're a horange or a halligator, but Monte Carlo's where de action is for poor blokes wot are last-flinging it an' habout ter make deir mums an' das orfinks, as 'twere. Der red an' der black, Chemmy-de-fer an' de nude beaches, dat's de place fer us!" Benny Maxine said into their television cameras.

"You really mean to hijack that seven forty-seven, Benny?"

"You de bloke from de *Times*?"

"*Evening Standard.*"

"I want ter see de *Times* chap. De Queen takes de *Times*."

"I'm from the *Times*."

"Tell der Queen we're Englitchmen, loyal subjects one an' all. Tell 'er we go where we're sent. Tell 'em in Piccadilly, tell 'em in Leicester Square. Tell 'em on de playink fields de lent' an' bret' uh dis great kingdom. We're nought but poor terminal yunsters wot may be dying an' all, but true blue Englitch for all dat. Hip hip, haw haw!"

They stared at him.

"Too much?" Benny asked in his own voice.

Benny abandoned, the press off to take down the views of the more solemnly sick, getting Janet Order's blue opinions, Noah Cloth's amputate pearls, Rena Morgan's sob story, the wit and wisdom of Lydia Conscience and Charles Mudd-Gaddis and Tony Word.

"I make the best copy," Benny Maxine sulked to Bale. "I'm the character here."

"It isn't a contest, Benny," Eddy consoled. "Don't push so hard."

"Jimmy Cagney," Benny Maxine said. "I want to go out like those guys they used to send down that last mile to the chair. Chewing gum, cracking jokes. 'I know what you're up to, Fadda. You're a good Joe, but you're wasting your time. I guess I'm just this bad hardboiled egg, Fadda.' "

"Come on, Benny."

"I'm fifteen years old, Mr. Bale. Those other kids. Some of them are sicker than I am, but I don't think it's hit them yet. What's what. How they've been kissed off by God and medical science both. The nits are actually excited."

"Listen, Benny, don't get the idea you're here to set anyone straight. There's no timetable. It ain't British Rail. Leave them alone with your inside information."

And filling in the nanny, Nedra Carp, about Benny: "Use the spurs on that one, Miss Carp. He wants to tell ghost stories."

"Call me Nanny," Nedra Carp said. "Prince Philip called me Nanny. Her Highness did."

And Mr. Moorhead, who advised him that Ben was very likely in a manic phase just now and that they could expect a reactive depression to follow. Telling Eddy that while there wasn't much he could do medically for the child at this point, if his symptoms became more focused they could take certain steps. "Jesus," Bale said. "He's manic depressive too?"

"We can handle it. If he gets really low," said the physician, "I've some reds I can give him."

"Reds," Eddy said.

"Sure," the good doctor said, "and if he climbs too high we can put him on blues."

"Reds and blues," Eddy Bale said, staring at the medical man.

"Uppers and downers, Eddy," the doctor explained scientifically. "This could all have been avoided if we'd had extensive psychological profiles on these kids. Though it just might help if we kept him off sweets."

Eddy Bale thought of Benny Maxine's hi-cal fingernails.

Because the last-minute hitches were something more than the odd mislaid passport or their friends crowding round to see them off, their relatives' helpful hints, special-pleading the kids' tics and habits that they chose only at this last minute to disclose to Eddy, Eddy's staff, Eddy taking notes and going into a furious, extemporized version of a shorthand he would not later be entirely able to decipher, offering the benefit of their close, habituate knowledge, their eight- to fifteen-year-old front-line observation of their offspring, filling them in—even the hostesses, even the stewards, the pilot, the crew of the 747 who had come out to look at their special passengers—on everything they could think of, as if the children were temperamental doors that only they knew how to open, cars difficult to start unless you knew just how to turn the ignition—Eddy furiously writing, writing—or houses leased for a season to strangers, pressing on them, too, medications that would have to be chilled, chipped toys, broken dolls, scraps of blanket, swatches of garment: all the emergency rations of a crisis comfort. (Exactly as if they *were* mechanical, their disorders trying as someone else's machinery.) Or even the crush of the press. Not hitches, not even helpful hints, so much as a series of charms and spells. And Eddy trying to keep up, to get it all down. The real hitches his queer staff. Only Colin Bible quietly coping. Only Mary Cottle serene. The kids themselves in palace revolt, bloodless coup. Not noisy—they wouldn't be *noisy* children, giving loudness only to their pain, the klaxon fortissimos of alarm—but moving along vaguely forbidden routes, doing the water fountains excessively, the lever-operated ashtrays, the now dismantled television equipment, the mikes and lights, watching the planes land, pointing, their eyes peeled for catastrophe. The real hitch his staff, his caper-dreamed crew. (Bale taking notes furiously, abbreviating, jotting, underscoring, placing exclamation points like unsheathed daggers beside main points he would later puzzle over, wondering what they could possibly mean.)

Out of the side of Bale's mouth: "Get on them, please, Nanny."

"At once, sir," Nedra agreed, and Bale, even out of just the corner of his eye and even with only half an ear cocked and only a fraction of his already divided attentions, could tell at once the enormity of his mistake. She was solicitous and intimidated, her months with Prince Andrew no plus at all, a season of watered, undermined authority. (He should have demanded references from Her Majesty.) Eddy saw her for what she was more nursemaid than nanny, a tucker-inner, a pusher of perambulators and strollers, protective enough but incapable of anything but loyalty, by nature a fan, for Labor, he guessed, when Labor was in, a Tory under the Tories, on all Authority's impressive tit, effaced, invisible as a poor relation or maiden aunty. Wouldn't the children be happier in the airport's lovely, comfortable seats? she wondered. Would they like to look at some of our nation's lovely newspapers travelers were forever leaving behind? Perhaps a few of the bigger children could read some of the smaller children the news?

"Was that a crack?" Charles Mudd-Gaddis snarled.

"Of course not, Charles," Nedra Carp said. "I'm sorry if you took it that way."

"I may only be eight years old and three feet tall," he sneered, "and weigh only thirty-nine pounds, but I'm not 'some of the smaller children.' "

"Of course not."

"I've got progeria," he said bitterly.

"Yes."

"It's a condition," he grumbled.

"I know."

"It ages me prematurely," he complained.

"Tch-tch."

"It shrivels me up like a little old man," he groused sullenly.

"Of course it does," she said, and looked around desperately, studying Heathrow's lovely lever-operated ashtrays should she be taken ill.

"It wrinkles my skin and hardens my arteries and causes my hair to fall out," he whined.

"That's only natural," she said vaguely.

"No one knows the cause," he said acrimoniously. He pointed to the doctor. "That one, for example. *He* doesn't know the cause. He doesn't know the cure either," he grumped.

"I'm sure they're working on it," Nedra Carp offered brightly.

"Too rare," Mudd-Gaddis shot back crossly.

Her attention had wandered. She was looking at the airport's comfortable seats and wishing she were seated in one now, curled up with one of the nation's newspapers travelers were forever leaving behind. "Sorry?" she said, turning back to him.

"I said too *rare*. What's wrong with your ears, woman?" he asked irritably. "One in eight million births. *No* one's going to commit the research money to wipe out progeria when only one in eight million gets it," he growled.

Nedra Carp nodded.

"It constipates me and makes me cranky," he told her crankily.

"That's awful."

"I have to take prune juice," he said resentfully.

"I'll see there's some always on hand."

"But I've got all my faculties," he protested indignantly.

"Certainly," Nedra Carp said.

"Which I daresay is more than many can say," he added accusingly. "I can recall things that happened to me when I was two years old as if it were yesterday. I'm very alert for my age."

"What about yesterday?"

"I don't remember yesterday."

"I see."

He studied her carefully.

"Yes?" Nedra coaxed.

"Are you my uncle Phil?" he asked.

"I'm Nanny," Nanny said.

"That's right," Mudd-Gaddis said, and shuffled off, Nedra Carp looking after the little withered fellow in a sort of awe. Death was the authority here. Death was boss.

Bale, who'd overheard Benny Maxine offer to make book with the children about who'd get back alive, wanted a piece of the action. The kid quoted long odds for naming the deceased in a sort of daily double, suggested complicated bets—trifectas, quinellas. When they looked at him peculiarly he objected that there was nothing illegal about it, it was just like the pools. Eddy thought of going up to the boy. He'd have put Nedra Carp's name down beside his own.

Meanwhile, Ginny had come back into the lounge with a man who looked familiar, who rather resembled, except for his clothes, Tony, their old newsagent and tobacconist. A sport in a sort of savvy, modified trench coat television journalists sometimes wore in the field, he seemed absolutely at home in a world class airport like Heathrow and looked, in his cunning, elegant zippers, loops and epaulets, one hand rakishly tipped into what might have been a map pocket, every inch the double agent. He could almost have been holding a gun, was awash in gaiety and a kind of hysterical flush—joy?—and seemed as if he might be taken off any second now by a sort of apoplectic rapture.

"You remember Tony," Ginny said.

"How are you, Eddy?" Tony said, and withdrew the gun-toting hand from the depths of his trench coat. Bale wondered why all the men who broke up homes in Britain were named Tony. "Fine bunch of bairn," the anchorman added affably, indicating the terminally ill children. "You know, they don't seem all that sick?" he said.

"They don't?" Bale said.

"Well," Tony said, qualifying, "maybe the little preggers kid doesn't look quite strong enough to carry to term."

"The preggers kid."

Ginny's friend indicated wasted little Lydia Conscience, eleven, whose ovarian tumor had indeed punched up her belly to something like the appearance of a seventh- or eighth-month pregnancy.

"She has dysgerminoma," Eddy Bale said with great feigned dignity. "That's a tumor she's carrying to term."

"Hmm," the foreign correspondent said thoughtfully. "You know what gets me about all this?"

"What's that?"

He lowered his voice. "When they're that sick they go all emaciated, and it makes their eyes something enormous," he said. "That's because eyes don't grow. It's a fact. Eyes is full size at birth. Then, when the face comes down, it's pathetic. 'Windows of the soul,' eyes are. Big eyes touch a chord in Christians. Oxfam understands this. That's why you see all them great full-moon eyes in the adverts, Eddy." Bale widened his own eyes and looked at his wife. She hung on the fellow's arm, attached there like one more of the trench coat's accessories. Tony, intercepting Bale's glance, shrugged shyly. "It's odd and all, me calling you Eddy like this."

Eddy studied him. "Tell me something, would you?" he said at last.

"What's that?"

"Are you *really* our old tobacconist?"

"You don't recognize me?"

"Not without the cardigan, not without the loose buttons hanging by a thread. You pronging my wife, then, Tony?"

"That isn't a question a gentleman asks another gentleman," their newsagent said stiffly.

"Come on, old man. Are you?"

"I shouldn't have thought that was any of your bloody business," said their ice lolly monger.

"Too personal?"

"Yes," he said, poking about in his trench coat for a grenade, "*I'd* say too personal."

"*You'd* say too personal."

"*I'd* say so. Yes."

"I don't suppose it was too personal when you were selling us cigarettes!" Bale exploded. "I gather it wasn't too personal when we bought your damned newspapers!" he shouted senselessly. He saw Mary Cottle reappear from the Ladies'. She seemed to watch them from behind a thick, almost weighty tranquillity. He turned to his wife. "This is a joke, right? Showing up in the departure lounge like this?"

"A joke?"

"He's our tobacconist, for Christ's sake! He keeps house behind a yellow curtain. A bell rings when the door opens and he pops out to sell ten pence worth of sweets. How'd you get him to close the shop?"

"You know something, Eddy? You're a snob."

"Tony, I really *didn't* recognize you in that getup. Amateur theatricals, am I right? You're good. You're damned good. Isn't he good, Ginny? Hey, thanks for coming by to see us off. Both of you. Really, thanks. It's a grim occasion. And the fact is I *was* nervous. You took a lot of pressure off."

"Getup? *Getup?*"

"Listen," Bale said, "I appreciate it."

"Sure I prong her," Tony said. "Certainly I do. We prong each other. Turn and turn about. Behind the yellow curtain."

Ginny was tugging at the sleeve of Tony's coat. "Come on," she said, "we'll miss our plane."

Benny Maxine was taking it all in. Mary Cottle was. Colin Bible looked up for a moment from the bottle of chemically laced orange juice he was nursing past Tony Word's lips, and the nipple slid out of the little boy's mouth. Some juice squirted into the corner of the child's eye and he startled. "Watch what you're doing," the little boy said. "That stuff smarts."

"Don't grumble," Colin said. "That shows it's working."

"Isn't he too big to take medicine from a bottle?" Noah Cloth asked.

"It's nasty," Colin explained. "A spoonful of titty makes the medicine go down. Don't ask *me* why."

Noah Cloth ran off laughing to tell the others what Bible had said.

Mr. Moorhead was making a sort of Grand Rounds in the

departure lounge, almost abstractedly checking pulses, touching foreheads with the back of his hand, peering down throats and looking into eyes and ears, making jokes, soothing parents and children both with his big, complicated presence.

An airlines agent cleared his throat into a live microphone. "Well," Ginny said, holding her hand out for her husband to shake, "happy landings."

"Turn and turn about," Eddy Bale said, taking it.

"Good trip, Colin," she said, acknowledging her dead son's nurse. Bible nodded, and Ginny went off with her lover.

Parents were hugging their own, each other's kids. Colin Bible's roommate, who'd shown up just as the children and their caretakers were about to board, reached out and patted his friend's cheek and handed him what looked to be a brand-new Polaroid camera. Mary Cottle smiled dreamily as Lydia Conscience began to recite. "Now I lay me down to sleep," she recited, "and pray the Lord my soul to keep. And if I die before I wake, I pray the Lord my soul to take."

"It's just like they say," Benny Maxine said. "There ain't no atheists in foxholes." And Eddy Bale, boarding the airplane, wondered what he thought he was doing and, oddly, and not for the first time either, just what the hell went on behind that yellow curtain.

Mr. Moorhead needn't have worried. He'd been unable to sleep during the long flight across the Atlantic. Though he hadn't paid for a headset, he sat in the dark and watched a film he'd already seen, trying, with the aid of his memory and intense concentration, to read the actors' lips, even to bring back the theme music, grand and vaguely classical, to see if he could match his memory of the story to the mood of the weak and watery silent scene projected before him on a screen the size of a desk top. For some reason the exercise reminded him of his days as a medical student, when he'd spent entire nights getting up an exam. A close-up of the heroine brought back the obscure pathology of a wasting disease, a master shot of a city street

the sharp, deserted, shut-down memory of epidemic, an overview of a crowd scene the metallic taste and texture of plague.
He rarely took his eyes from the screen—once to adjust the vol-
ume on Tony Word's headset and again to find an additional
blanket for Lydia Conscience—and when the film was over Mr.
Moorhead had both a complicated sense of the film's mildly
melodramatic plot and the sour etiologies of a hundred diseases in his head.

What had upset him, however obscurely, what had forced
him to his strange effort to bring back an entire motion picture
he hadn't enjoyed when he'd seen it the first time, was the fear
that he might have to room with Colin Bible.

I'm not a bad man, Mr. Moorhead thought. I do no evil.
And, wondering whether he was a good doctor, he began
soundlessly to cry.

In the seat next to him Benny Maxine stirred, whimpered
in his sleep. The doctor carefully removed the shoes from the
boy's swollen feet and loosened the small airline blanket from
where it had become tangled, caught beneath his hips. He adjusted the pillow to a more comfortable angle and frowned in
the dim light at the Jew's oddly slacked jaw, the puffy, almost
flexible bone structure that gave Benny's head a queer mashed
quality. If he could he would have remolded the kid's face,
tamping, patting, massaging the bad bones back into phase,
packing the distended skin about them as he would have
trimmed wet sand about the pylons and fretwork of a beach
castle.

Mr. Moorhead had a vagrant impulse toward the chiro-
practic, an urge like some Pygmalion of the medical, a desire to
extract health, to grow it like a culture in a petri dish, to adjust,
as he'd adjusted Benny's blanket and pillow, drawing off all the
gnarled strings and matted clumps of illness and disease. At
university he had led his classes in anatomy, a wizard of parts,
an almost sculptor's instinct for muscle and bone, an almost geologist's or diviner's one for the shales and fluids of form. He
could tell at a glance the distortions on an anatomical chart and
all the split ends of an internal organ badly drawn. He had an

artist's eye for the human body and, in museums, would actually diagnose statues, excitedly explaining to astonished friends, even to strangers, which statues and pictures were modeled from life, which were only the sculptor's or painter's Platonic ideal. Michelangelo he thought a fraud. "If there'd been an actual model for David," he'd once told his professor, "he'd probably still be alive." And had a theory that her incipient goiter would, were she real, almost certainly have killed off the Mona Lisa before her thirtieth year.

And that was the rub. A pal to whom he'd explained his David idea was a student at the Royal Academy of Art. "But look here, Moorhead," his friend told him, "there really was. A model. Some kosher boy Michelangelo was sweet on. Genuine McCoy right down to his high holy circumcised pecker. There are life casts in the R.A. basement."

"Life casts."

His friend winked. "High times in sunny Italy. Signor Buonarroti liked them dripping in plaster, ooh la la."

Because he was smitten by an ideal of health and life, some full-moon notion of the hale and hearty. Of soundness, bloom, the body filled to its sunny, f-stop conditions of solstitial, absolute ripeness like a ship floating in water precisely between its measured load lines. Flowers in their brief perfection broke his heart. Healthy beasts did. All perfect specimens, male and female. All heedless vitality, all organisms generally unconscious of pain, unmindful of death. It was why he had become a doctor in the first place and chosen pediatrics as his specialty. It was what both appalled and fascinated him about Jews.

He was already a resident when he saw the photographs. Of the survivors. From the camps. Not men but devastated, stick-figured blueprints for men. The declined, obscene inversions of all those anatomical paradigms of the human he'd studied at university. And that overturned for him forever the near-flawless portraits of the sound and scatheless, the immaculately unblemished, all those slick, transparent graphics and overlays that had, almost without his thinking about it, instilled in him an idea of centrifugal man, the notion of health as a radiation outward from some fixed center, of the organs and glands, the gristles and guts, impacting their neighbors, transmitting actual electric life from some unseen, unseeable omphalos—pith? gist? soul?— as if body, body itself, were only a kind of archaeology, some careful pile of palimpsest arrangement, sequential as arithmetic. The photographs had been a revelation to him, astonishing not for what they revealed to him about what men were capable of doing to each other but for what they taught him about his trade. He had to revise all his old theories. Disease, not health, was at the core of things; his idea of pith and gist and soul obsolete for him now, revised downward to flaw, nubbin, rift; incipient sickness the seed which sent forth its contaged shoots raging through the poisoned circuits of being. He stuck a jeweler's loupe in his eye and examined, pored over, scrutinized, their busted constitutions. From loose and sunken skeletons, from hollows and craters beneath baggy skin ill-fitting as badly hung wallpaper, he dared spectacular diagnoses, astonishing prognoses. He must have seemed like some scholarly counterfeiter, double-, even triple-checking his plates, searching them for error and balls-up. Learning more from those terrible photographs than ever he had from the perfect meat in those idealized medical texts. He must have seemed crazy to his Jewish registrar, who caught him out, the loupe in his eye like a pawnbroker's and the pictures spread out before him like pornography.

But Colin Bible was a different story.

Colin Bible was a perfect specimen and Mr. Moorhead was flustered by him. He hadn't bargained for any Colin Bible. Most likely the male nurse was a fag and, already in love with the man's visible health, Moorhead bit his nails and worried that he'd have to share a room with him. He wished now he'd argued more persuasively with his wife, a comfortable, not unattractive woman, made safe to Moorhead's consciousness by the varicose veins in her calves, that she accompany him. Moorhead, who wished to be a good man, missed her. He was crying again, not soundlessly this time but openly sobbing.

Benny Maxine stirred and murmured in his sleep, and Moorhead leaned over to listen.

"If you can't afford to lose, don't gamble," Benny mumbled.

Lydia Conscience giggled. Of all the children on the plane—indeed, of all the sleeping children in the world at that moment, those in their beds for the night as well as those merely napping—she was the only one who happened to be dreaming of the Magic Kingdom. She knew this because there was no busy signal, no distracting burr to flatten and compromise the call. And, though she was a generous child, it was pleasant to have the dream to herself, not, as in hospital, to have always to share—the attentions of the nurses, treats, visitors, the ward's big telly—with the other patients.

The big park was not empty of visitors—that would have frightened her—but there were no long lines for the rides and shows and restaurants, no one in the clean rest rooms. There were a nurse and a doctor on duty in the cool, comfortable emergency tent but no one was there to cry out for first aid, not even a lost child to rumple a cot or mess the place up with candy wrappers, soft-drink bottles, an ice-cream cone, smashed and melting on the pavement. Except for the cheerful, efficient crew, Lydia had Captain Nemo's plush, handsomely appointed submarine practically to herself, a fine view through the big portholes of the fleet's other craft disporting like dolphins in the dark clear water—water, Lydia imagined, crisp and quenching in the throat as the ice in the packs that brought down her fevers and cooled her sleep.

Throughout the Magic Kingdom there was the same comfortable traffic, the thin, perfect crowds there only for scale, to set off the fantastic buildings and marvelous attractions, appearing, or so it seemed to Lydia, as they must have appeared in the original architectural sketches, well-groomed adults and their kempt, healthy children taking their ease on the wide benches and strolling at leisure through the park's beautiful pavilions, the cunning vistas and landscapes, the visitors—Lydia was the exception—like line drawings, attractive figures in a brochure, well-behaved as guests at a garden party. Lydia was

delighted by her unobstructed views, by her keen sense of privilege and status. On the river trip, for example, in the tiny
steamer that vaguely replicated the *African Queen* with its chuff-
ing, sputtering engine and its soiled and rumpled honorable
mate, Lydia was comfortable enough during even the small boat's
most treacherous passages down the winding jungle river to load
her camera, get exactly the right light reading, focus carefully,
and shoot only after she was satisfied with her composition. When
a fierce-looking hippopotamus submerged itself in the muddy
waters alongside the ship, Lydia had sufficient presence of mind
to ask the mate to turn off the engines so that she might get an
even better picture when he reemerged into the air.

"She," the mate said.

"Sir?" Lydia Conscience said quizzically.

"That hippo's a female, miss," the man informed her. "She
does that for her babies. It ain't playfulness, mademoiselle. The
fact is, hips hate water about as much as cats do. It's a hygiene
thing. She's setting an example for her cubs. They must be fairly
close by or she wouldn't have bothered. She'll come up two more
times, then make that noise they're so famous for, that special-
call noise that the cubs, no matter where they are and no matter what they're doing, have to come running when they hear
it. That's the picture you want, ma'am. I'll steer the boat over
to where the water's a bit clearer. You can get a shot of the cubs
sucking her teats."

"Really, Mister Bale!" Lydia said.

"It's how they breathe, Fräulein," the grizzled mate explained. "They get their air out of the cow's milk. Something
terrible is a hippopotamus's breath, but them little ones' lungs
is so tiny they'd drown otherwise."

"Nature is amazing," Lydia Conscience said.

"It's alarming, comrade. Me, I never went to no school,"
the man told her. "I learned all my lore here on the river." With
a broad sweep of his arm he indicated the rubber duckies floating on the surface of the water, the mechanically driven, wind-
up sharks, the needlework palm fronds along the banks.

Before the ride was finished and the conductor collected

her ticket, Lydia had several other opportunities for fine photographs. She got a rare close-up of Tarzan pruning his treehouse and an absolute stunner of a cannibal picnic. Once again the mate silenced the engine and, putting his fingers to his lips, indicated that Lydia be quiet. Together they listened to the cheery campfire songs the cannibals were singing.

"I like this," Lydia said when they were again under way. "Not being from a Third World country myself, it gives a London girl a grand opportunity to find out what really goes on."

The hoary mate with the sad, steely eyes nodded judiciously.

"Wait till you meet Mickey," he said.

"Mickey?"

"Mouse."

"Oh, will I actually get to meet Mickey Mouse?"

"A private audience, memsahib."

"A private audience!"

The mate lowered his voice. "Because you're the only one who really wanted to come on the dream holiday." It was true. Lydia Conscience had wanted to visit the Magic Kingdom for donkey's years. For fear of hurting his feelings, she couldn't tell the mate that Donald Duck and Goofy and Dumbo or even the 101 Dalmatians were her real favorites, but the shrewd old tramp, suspecting something of the sort, turned aside whatever objection she might have made. "He's very kind, really. Not at all as standoffish as his critics make out. And he has wonderful powers. If he takes a liking to a kid there ain't anything he wouldn't—" But before he could finish, busy signals had begun to interfere with the dream. They were coming in from Holland, they were coming in from Spain. They were coming in from a hundred countries where little children were being set down for their naps.

Lydia was a generous child and ordinarily wouldn't have minded. Disney World was a big enough place. It had been pleasant not to have to stand in line or deal with the crowds and, from a strictly practical standpoint, safer not to run the risk of bumping into people with her bloated, swollen belly, painful on sudden contact as a sore toe jammed in a door. And shameful, too. She was perfectly aware of how she must appear to strangers (P-R-E-G-G-E-R-S). And had long ago taken to wearing a cheap engagement and wedding ring so people wouldn't get the wrong idea (or so they would, she giggled). But it was too spooky-making just now to have to run into that little blue girl. What was her name? Oh, yes—Janet. Janet Order. Who was just now being handed aboard. So Lydia Conscience ran and hid, her big tumor painfully sloshing in the amnion that had grown up around it.

In the smoking section toward the back of the plane, Janet Order had finally slipped into sleep. Janet was a child who welcomed sleep. It was the dreams. Janet Order looked forward to her dreams. In these dreams she'd found an infinite number of ways in which she was able to take on a sort of protective coloration. Sometimes she was an ancient Briton, one of that old Celtic tribe who painted themselves blue, or she dreamed of Mardi Gras, fabulous celebrations, the holiday makers behind incredible disguises, her own blue skin almost ordinary among the brilliant hues and shades of the gaudy, garish celebrators. Or was a huntress, a warrior, the bright blue cosmetics of her pigmentation there for war paint and terror, the honorable, acceptable hues of murder. Or at court at masquerades, or gloved at beaux arts balls behind soft veils or holding a lorgnette against her eyes like a stiff, slim flag. And sometimes the actual blue flag at the ceremonies and state occasions of imaginary nations. Or even—this was tricky, thrilling—as she marched past a reviewing stand, waving a large, heavy Union Jack in front of her in such a way that the flag's staves and superimposed crosses hid her face while her body was protected behind the livid, rippling triangles of the blue field. She felt at these times quite like a fan dancer, quite like a tease. There were thousands of ways to protect herself. She dreamed of blue populations in blue towns and blue cities. She dreamed of herself cold and at peace in water, her lips and face blue in the temperature. Or exposed on a beach, blue and drowned.

At the precise moment that Lydia Conscience was hiding from the blue girl, Janet Order entered the dream. Lydia was nowhere about, nor did Janet know that Lydia—she was that neat—had ever occupied it. But noticed the water first off and dove into the stinging river downstream of the *African Queen*, the rumpled mate blowing warning whistles at her, cupping his hands and shouting directions she couldn't hear but perfectly understood when he threw a line to her. Which she wouldn't take. Preferring instead to wait until the water became chilly enough to justify her appearance. Only when she saw the hippo did she realize that it was a jungle river.

"Grab it," the mate shouted when the tiny steamer came abreast of the girl. "Grab the life preserver, kid." Blushing— the rosiness of her modesty added to her natural color and turned her a deep shade of purple—Janet Order dove under the dark, muddy water and swam away from the boat. There, along the warm bottom of the jungle river, in the soft medium of a swirling, rising mud, in broken earth's cloudy dissolution, through all erosion's rich rots and deltic rusts, Janet Order, her eyes adjusting to the decomposing silts and sediments and lees, all the fermenting dregs of all drenched dirt's loamy planetary brew, swam. The badly hearted child—she'd seen her x-rays, her blunt, boot-shaped heart, the mismanaged arteries and ventriculars like faulty wiring or badly tied shoelace—relieved of gravity, flew through the water, her breathing easy as a fish's, as the heavy hippo's or the two dreamy cubs, oblivious, abstracted, stuck at their mother's teats as at soda straws. She swam past the stalled propellers of the little steamer and came into an area not so much clearer as less perturbed than the one she had just come through. Here the mud and motes of the river bottom no longer swirled but lay fixed in the strata of water—she perceived that water was subtly stratified as rock or sky—as in aspic. Indeed, when she stuck out her finger to lick a particularly delicious-looking piece of mud-studded water, she seemed somehow to compromise the delicately balanced layers of the river. The water trembled, entire panes and levels of it smashing around her like so much glass. "Oh, my," Janet said, seeing too late the DO NOT

MOIL signs posted all about the warm jungle river. Everywhere fabulous creatures, their sleep disturbed if not by the intruder herself than by her thoughtless liberties, came out to see what had happened to upset the balance of nature. And although nothing was said, she sensed herself scolded by the coral, scorned and disparaged by the haughty sea horse, upright and stately as an initial on a towel. Microorganisms abused her: plankton and a tiny grain of sand which one day would irritate itself into a pearl and was just now slipping into the shell of an oyster. She was snubbed by great whales and silently upbraided by sharks. Reproach glittered like tears in the eyes of sirens and mermaids. Drowned sailors speechlessly gave her the rough side of their tongues.

"Excuse me, I'm sure!" said Janet Order indignantly, the syllables carried out of her mouth in bubbles that accommodated them like language in cartoons. Released, they dispersed, bumped by the current, buffeted, snagged, a random, wayward detritus, a debris babble. *I'm*, she read, *cuse sure! me Ex.*

Oh, dear, she thought, bothered that she'd been unable to make herself clear and seeing herself as they must see her, feeling a trespasser now, a poacher in this peaceable kingdom. But I didn't mean, she dreamed, holding her tongue, biting it so that the words could not escape only to reassemble into that frightful syntax.

Which was when the sea serpent swam up close to inspect her. Which was when the seals grazed her sides, the sea robins and orcs. Which was when the manatee brushed against her gently. Which was when Triton did, and the naiads and nereids. Which was when Leviathan smiled and Janet Order realized that of all these fabulous creatures it was she, the little blue girl, who was the most fabulous of all.

In the seat next to Janet's, Mary Cottle slipped a Gaulois from its pack and lit it, discharging the sweet, vaguely fecal smoke into the air about her. Mary Cottle enjoyed harsh cigarettes and often even treated herself to cheapish cigars in her Islington flat, rather enjoying the crossfire of fusty smells. She thought they made the place seem more lived-in somehow. She would smoke a pipe, too, at least until it was broken in, and, on holiday on the Continent, in Italy and Yugoslavia, in Spain and behind the Iron Curtain, was careful to observe what the peasants smoked, the old-timers she meant, their severe tobaccos—not the imports, not the better-grade domestic brands of the trendy teenagers and working-class young people in the cafés—and chose these, preferring to purchase them loose at the kiosk, even forty or fifty at a time, pleased by the street merchant's grimy hands, stained by newsprint, by the cheap colored inks of the magazines they handled, the diesel and industrial fumes to which they were exposed, selecting the rough burleys and dark, synthetic latakias and spiked, ersatz Virginias, dense, bitter, aromatic as mold. She might have smoked this sort of tobacco even more often—even the cigars, even the oppressive pipes—but discovered early on that that sort of thing made her oddly attractive to men, exciting them in some strange way, almost as if she gave off a musk, some suggestive, cabaretish spoor of Weimar, pre-war Berlin. And women, too. Thinking her butch, mistaking her serene expression for smug, dikey complacency.

Beside her the child stirred uneasily in her sleep and began to cough, gasp. Mary Cottle patted her gently awake while in her dream Janet Order, choking, reasoned that she'd been underwater too long and struggled to the surface, bruising past the astonished sea gods and monsters, past Triton and Poseidon and lovely, curious Amphitrite. It was fortunate, she thought, that it was only a dream. In real life she'd learned to float but never to swim, though on doctor's orders she was brought frequently to the public swimming baths for therapy, there to float in the water, lifted from gravity and all the ordinary exertions of life, while her mother or one of her brothers looked on from the side.

Because everything has a perfectly reasonable explanation. It was the smoke from Mary Cottle's cigarette which in Janet Order's dream had triggered the transposed bubble-speech and set off the choking of her jigsaw heart and wakened her.

Only after Janet was thoroughly roused from sleep did Lydia Conscience come out of hiding and return to the picturesque deck of the *African Queen*.

"Did you see her?" Lydia asked the mate.

"Who would that be, mama-san?" the crusty old sailor asked.

"The little girl."

"Blue kid?"

"That's right."

"Hell of a swimmer," the man said.

"Is she?"

"Oh, yeah," the mate said, "*hell* of a swimmer! I tried to throw her a line but she wouldn't take it."

You'd have had to look quickly to see Mary Cottle crush her cigarette out in the tiny ashtray built into the armrest of her seat on the 747 and fan away the smoke. And almost have had stroboscopic vision to have caught at all the momentary flicker of concern that passed across her face.

"Are you all right? Shall I fetch you some water?" she asked Janet when the little girl's coughing had begun to subside.

"Yes, please," Janet said. "That would be lovely."

The drinking water that came out of the taps was too tepid and the cups themselves too small, so Mary went forward to ask the stewardess for a glass and some ice. As she passed Rena Morgan she looked down at the sleeping child and felt a kind of gratitude to her for declaring straight off that if Mary was a smoker she thought she'd better change seats rather than run the risk of having her chest and sinuses fill with mucus. It would be better all round if she didn't have to sit in the smoking section, she'd added apologetically. And because Mary was upset—*everything* has a reasonable explanation—that Janet had so nearly choked in her sleep she decided to slip into the lav for a moment to relieve some of the tension.

Colin Bible watched Mary Cottle pass. I don't know what she thinks she's up to, he thought, but she's definitely not gay. Who had an eye, almost an instinct, for such things, blessed with a sort of perfect pitch for sexual preference, not one ever to be fooled by appearances, the drag shams of gender—bearing and behavior, effeminacy and manliness, only a sort of jewelry, Colin thought, only posture's and gesture's dress code. And who on more than one occasion had been spared embarrassment, rebuff, even beatings or arrests because of his gift. A sexual geologist, a sexual prospector who worked only the real veins and never wasted effort where it wouldn't pan out.

Thank God for Colin, Colin thought, pleased to be settled and *to* have settled, grateful for all the sedentary inducements and consolations of love, to be out of that rat race of the heart, grateful not to have to scrounge for companionship, done with flirting, dating, the extended, lifelong adolescence that was the mark and curse too of the single condition. He thought of his flatmate with a certain gratitude and feeling over and above their feelings for each other, and was aware, too, of a kind of unaccountable peace until he became conscious of the great speed at which they were traveling, their black, tremendous altitude, the dark, dangerous ocean beneath them. Always before, unless they were on holiday together, it had been his lover who had borne the risks of travel, who had been the flier, off to Paris for a conference with his artisans, to eastern Europe, to Africa—he'd spent two weeks in Uganda with Idi Amin to get that tough customer to agree to pose for his portrait in wax—to Utah to obtain for Madame Tussaud's the artistic rights to Gary Gilmore's execution by firing squad: all over the world arranging the compliance of principals, the cooperation of families. "Headhunting," Colin called these expeditions. Bible had remained behind. Like a fireman's wife, a cop's, like a war bride.

And though he was not really worried, it was nice once and again to be oneself at risk, there being a certain comfort in being the benefactor rather than the beneficiary. He had received with rather more humiliation than dread those policies, mailed from Heathrow and usually delivered the same day, that named him legatee in the event of Colin's death by misadventure. The pound that would get him a hundred thousand should his friend's plane crash and Colin die had seemed to make of their relationship a joke dependancy, and Colin's larky notes accompanying the instrument and usually scribbled across its faint third copy—*'Bye, darling, buy yourself a new dress!*—did not much mitigate Bible's feeling of having suffered an indignity, a flip deprecation. (Who knew well enough the terms of Colin's real will, the thicker-than-water arrangements of sedate and serious death. Who, indeed, had been a witness to the document. Everything to the sister in Birmingham, to her two boys should she precede them, to a network of uncles, aunts, and cousins, complicated as an aristocracy, should the nephews die, Colin himself bringing up the rear of a very long file.) He no longer bothered to open these envelopes, allowing them to stand at the bottom of the pile of correspondence which would accumulate during his friend's absences.

"Really, Colin," his friend scolded him on finding the unopened envelope, "you oughtn't be so cavalier. This is an important paper. Insurance on my life should my plane have gone down. You'd have stood to gain a hundred thousand."

"Ta," Colin Bible told him, "but if you really want to buy me a present, why don't you just get me a ticket on the pools?"

After that, the policies Colin sent from Heathrow became more and more elaborate. Not only did the premiums and benefits go up but the contingencies they covered became increasingly diverse. Not only would Colin collect if Colin were killed in an automobile accident, if he were taken from him in a train or bus crash, but if he died in a hotel fire, if his plane was hijacked, if he was kidnapped or poisoned or sustained injuries inflicted by terrorists. There was a triple indemnity clause if he died in a foreign hospital that was no longer accredited.

"Really, Colin," Colin said, "I don't understand you. I really don't. Do you know what a good all-in policy sets one back? Fifteen pounds! With the riders I take out it comes almost to twenty.

"And don't look so indifferent, dearie! Do you have any idea how they drive in some of those countries? Have you even the foggiest how volatile the wogs are? Just the sight of a white skin inflames them!"

"Me too," Colin said.

"It's no joke. I could go like that."

"Don't you dare go like that."

"Be a little more businesslike in future, please, Colin. There are real risks."

"Don't tell *me* about risks," Colin answered, angry now. "I'm a nurse. I work in hospital. Don't go all bogeyman on me and threaten me with your spoiled food and terrorists. You know why I don't open those envelopes? Your snide remarks. 'Get your hair done!' 'Towards a decent suit for the funeral!' Who do you think you are, talking to me that way?"

"My adorable floozy."

"Now *there's* a policy I'd treasure! Floozy insurance. Herpes riders."

"I don't cheat on you, Colin."

And he probably didn't, Colin thought. Like himself, Colin was a decorous man. Even before they'd found each other, neither had been a chaser. (That probably explained his lover's will—Colin's inability to put down in writing or acknowledge in law what had been an open secret for all the time they'd been together, that their arrangement was serious, a commitment, a pledge, a relationship, a devotion lacking in nothing save what would stand up in court. It explained the Birmingham sister, the nephews, the uncles and aunts and distant cousins, all Colin's trophies of vague, treasured legitimacy. Perhaps it even explained the ever more complicated travel insurance Colin took out each time he went away on business. Possibly he even intended, wanted, or was simply just willing to die out of town, as if the disasters he insured against, the bizarre deaths he underwrote in Heathrow, were only the ordinary extension of the sort of agreement undertaken by flatmates, like a side bet, say.) So Colin was no chaser. Indeed, it had only been Colin Bible's extraordinary sensitivity to the sexuality of other persons which had brought them together in the first place.

They'd met in hospital. Colin had come in for minor surgery but had been having a bad time of it: painful though not dangerous—thank God—complications. Colin Bible had been taken off the pediatric ward and transferred to orthopedics during a temporary shortage of nurses there. He recognized at once that the man was homosexual, and Colin, seeing how un-comfortable his new patient had become from being forced to lie in one position, asked if he would like a back rub.

He ejaculated while Colin was still applying the lotion. The nurse hastened to reassure him.

"Don't worry about it," Colin told the man. "It happens all the time."

"Extraordinary," his future lover explained hastily. "I haven't a clue why I should have behaved that way. That sort of thing has never happened to me. You must know special contact points—being a nurse and all. You must accidentally have rubbed against one of them."

"It's the skin," Colin lied. "The skin's especially responsive after trauma."

"You must have a very bad impression of me."

"No," he said, and did something he hadn't imagined him-self capable of. He violated his professional ethics. He leaned forward and kissed his patient. He stroked his hair. The man didn't move.

"I'm artistic," the man explained irrelevantly. "I work for Madame Tussaud's. I'm one of the new breed. Well, I suppose that sounds rather grand. All I mean is I've these bold ideas. Innovative," he added nervously.

"Madame Tussaud's was one of my favorite places when I was a kid," Colin said. "I haven't been there in donkey's years." He was still stroking his patient's hair.

"You wouldn't recognize the place. And once the new wing is in . . . do you recall the Chamber of Horrors?"

"*Do* I?" Colin Bible said. "I should say!"

"Jack the Ripper," his new friend said scornfully. "Burke and Hare!"

Colin Bible shuddered.

"No," the man said, "that's just the point. They were merely aberrant." He flushed reflexively. "I mean they had no *social* significance. What's the point? They put fellows like that on display to titillate. What I'm after is something else entirely. I mean, would you like to know my dream, my vision for the place? God, I mean, just listen to the way I'm talking!"

"Of course I would," Colin Bible said.

"Really? I mean you're not just humoring an old poof, are you?"

"Of course not."

"Well," he said, "those fellows, that lot, they were just our own parochial, historical sociopaths. Freak show, is all. Hydras and kraken. Rocs and manticores. Stuff that goes bump in the night. I mean, even Hitler—and there was a do just to get *him* in at all. I mean, can you imagine? The old-timers on the Board of Directors were dead against it. Even after they came round, they propped him up in full-dress regalia like an entirely proper führer. Why, he looks like a Caesar. *Hitler!*"

Colin Bible nodded.

"Well, what *is* the point? My notion is to show what he *did*. I want the Holocaust represented. I think that deserves a room all to itself. A *large* room. We could show the ovens, we could show the showers and the Jews, naked, their blue numbers burned into their wrists, not knowing what's going to happen to them. We could show the wasted survivors pressed against the barbed wire in their penal stripes. Their mountains of gold teeth, their piles of shoes.

"Hiroshima. Just one wall of a building still standing, a shadow of vaporized flesh imprinted on it like a double exposure.

"We should show cancer," the man said, tears in his eyes and the bent index finger of the hand that, seconds before, Colin had been holding pressed between his teeth. "And I'm not an old poof," he said.

"I know that," Colin Bible said.

"I'm *not*."

"I know," Colin said.

"Actually, sexually I've never been very active."

"I know it."

"I haven't."

"I haven't either," Colin Bible said.

"Oh, dear," his patient said.

What he told him was true, but when Colin was discharged from hospital Colin Bible moved in with him and they became lovers. They had been together almost four years.

Nevertheless, it was good to feel the odd sense of self-reliance imposed on him by the remote dangers of the speeding aircraft.

At Heathrow he'd been too busy with the children to give much thought to Colin—they did not accompany each other much to airports, and he'd been taken by surprise when his friend had shown up in the departure lounge at the last minute—and had come upon the flight insurance desk quite by accident. I really ought to take some out, he thought impatiently. Colin sets store in such things. He thinks he's sending you a dozen long-stemmed roses. The girl began to explain the various plans. "No, no," Colin Bible interrupted. "Just your basic 'My God, We're Going Into the Drink,' 'Three Hundred Feared Dead in Air Disaster!' coverage," he said. *Take care of yourself,* he scribbled hastily across the top of Colin's copy.

He could not account for it, but he was smiling.

The children slept, fitfully dreaming.

Little Tony Word, dying of leukocytes, of clear, white, colorless cells watering his blood and turning it pale, of petechia and purpura, the petty hemorrhages across his face like so many false freckles, of fatigue and fever and bone pain, of malignant cells buttering his marrow with contamination, of major and minor infections exploding inside his body like ordnance, of the inability of his blood to clot, of his outsized, improperly functioning organs, all the cheap cuts—his liver, his kidneys—of his compromised .meat—of leukemia—of the broad palette of chemicals with which his oncologists painted his blood, going over it, careful as art restorers, chipping away at the white smear that poisoned it, bringing back the brisk, original color from their tubes of vincristine and prednisone and asparaginase and dexamethasone and mercaptopurine and allopurinol and methotrexate and cyclophosphamide and doxorubicin and other assorted hues—dying, too, of time itself, of the five- and six- and seven-year survival rate (Tony is now two years beyond his last remission but freckles have begun to reappear along his jawline and his renal functions are in an early stage of fail- ure)—little Tony Word dreams of his low-salt meals, of the liq- uids and fruit juices he is forced to swallow, almost, or so it seems to him, by the pailful, of all the rind fruits he must eat, and which, because of the invisible germs and hidden dirts which might be on his mother's hands, he must peel himself—the sealed orange, the difficult apple, the impossible pear, the ordeal of a grape, which he handles with specially sterilized toothpicks, as he does everything, to avoid the accident of cuts which will not stanch—encouraged, too, to prepare his own well-balanced, nu- tritious meals (though he's not allowed to go near a stove), his boiled and scrubbed green leafy vegetables, washing lettuce, kale and cauliflower, broccoli, sprouts, cabbage; washing everything, eggplant and potatoes, shallots and mushrooms, then consum- ing the congealed pot liquor which he has to scrape from the side of the pot with a spoon and spread on toasted sandwiches (from which he first must tear away the crusts) just to be able to get it down, or drinking the broth, thick as barium, to get at the vitamins and minerals, and eating the flaccid vegetable flesh; preparing the meats, too, scrubbing (this much, at least, his own idea, the scared kid's) his veal and ham, his steaks and chops, his joints and shanks, so that everything he eats, or so he thinks, tastes of a light seasoning of dishwashing detergent, learning to cook even at four and already at ten an accomplished chef, teased for this, for this only, not for his weak and sickly ways, his in- ability at games (which he would not have been permitted to play anyway), or even his high anxiety as a spectator sitting well back in the stands in the gymnasium lest he be hit by a stray ball, or far away from the sidelines when what they would surely snicker at him for should he call them his mates went outdoors to play, but because they know he cooks, have heard him brag of it who has nothing else to boast of (save his pain, save his endurance, save the one or two or, at the outside, three years he has left to live perhaps, and which he has never mentioned), seen him in the lunchroom chewing his queer veggie remnant sandwiches with their vitamin slime and viscous mineral fillings, have seen him fastidiously peel his fruits and drink his juices, his quart of bottled water from which someone else has first to remove the cap and then pour into a paper cup lest Tony cut his finger on the saw-toothed cap or the bottle opener or the drinking glass he was not even permitted to use accidentally break. So the small dying boy tosses and turns, dreaming his breakfasts of champions, his athlete's meals, his health faddist's strict dietary laws, sated in sleep, stuffed, full as a glutton, who has never been hungry, dreaming of food who is not hungry now.

Charles Mudd-Gaddis, that little old man, dreams of his first birthday. He dreams the cake and dreams the candles, dreams the balloons and dreams the streamers; he dreams the toys, he dreams the clapping. And dreams he's three, the little boy, who would have been a man by now—twenty, twenty-one. Then dreams the girl, six, to him a woman. And now he's five and pushing forty. Ah, to be thirty-four again! he dreams. And dreams he's seven and confusion comes, that white aphasia of the heart and head. And dreams in awful clarity it's now, and can't recall how old he really is.

Rena Morgan can't tell if she's awake or sleeping. She'd sensed Miss Cottle pass down the aisle, the trace of tobacco scent clinging to her clothes and skin like an odor backed up in a cellar. In what is more likely sleep than not, she brings a hanky, which she is never without, up to her nostrils, and mildly blows, delicately, ladylike, folding the discharge into a dry patch of handkerchief as expertly as a magician hiding a coin. She has taught herself to make these passes at her face before actual mirrors, using as her model images she's picked up of tragic ladies dabbing at tears in the corners of their eyes, her fingertip eased along a groove of linen so that, when it works, as it al-

most always does now that she so perfectly executes the gesture, it isn't as if she were wiping tears away at all so much as
brushing cosmetics into her flesh or whisking flecks of mascara
and excess powder out of her vision—even in sleep there is exactly that look of concentrated dispassion on her face—doing
all the last-minute repairs and touch-ups of grace. Yet it is really
as tears that she thinks of her mucus, some vast reservoir of the
sorrowful, her sad pain treasury. She fills her hankies and dis-
poses of them in her sleep, folding them neatly into pockets,
putting them under pillows, a kind of controlled, sedentary
somnambulism, her tricky cardsharp slumber. She doesn't know
why she does this (or even how), though she supposes it a form
of pride, some maidenly self-governance, romantic even, the
hope-chest antics of the heart. But has no time for dreams and,
vigilant, ever on her toes, can never quite tell whether she dozes
or is wide awake.

In Monte Carlo, Benny Maxine held a bad hand and waited
for the croupier to scoop in his losses.

The amputee, Noah Cloth, held up his bad hand and
counted his losses.

This was the best time, thought Nedra Carp. The children
all tucked and making their bye-byes. She even enjoyed their
little snores. Hardly snores, really. Barely rustles. Just only some
tinny nasality of warmed air. In with the good, out with the bad.
Though she couldn't hear even this. Not over the husky drone
of the motors. (Engines, would they be?) Or, for that matter,
even see her charges. Only, on her right, Charles Mudd-Gaddis
and, on her left, Rena, who, in her sleep, raises hankies to her
eyes as though she dreams something sad, watching whatever
it is like some warmhearted little dear at a play or cinema. She
likes such tenderness, enjoys being with children who can't hold
back their tears when Bambi's mother dies or, at the pantomime, when Cinderella's wicked stepmother and stepsisters plot
against her. She doesn't care what they say, sentiment is the only

true breeding. Prince Andrew had shocked her when he'd been small and had watched with cool indifference and unalterably dry eyes the terrible sufferings of Hansel and Gretel when they finally realized that their father, that hen-pecked woodcutter, meant actually to abandon them in the forest just because his shrew of a wife told him there wasn't enough food to go round. It's a jolly good thing for the U.K., Nedra Carp thinks, that Andrew is so far removed from the succession. Monarchs ought to be properly compassionate, she feels, to understand that not all their subjects are as well-off as themselves. Ho. Not half, they aren't. (And wasn't that woodchopper's wife another stepmother? Though Nedra doesn't let the husband off so easily. The reconciliation at the end is all very well, but if she were those two she wouldn't have been so quick to jump back into his arms. Suppose times turned bad again. Suppose . . . Well. Once burned, twice sorry.)

Or even, when it comes down to it, tucked. Not properly anyway. Only a dusty old airline blanket thrown over them, smoothed about their shoulders and flowing loose about their torsos. Hardly like being in their own beds, though one does one's best. And recalls the healthy children she has tended. Nedra, reading them stories, stroking their heads, has almost absorbed their soporific comfort, that agreeable ease and comfy coze, their bodies' balmy thermometry and featherbed climate just so, like a snug tropic. Oh, yes, she knows well enough how they feel, their maiden, their bachelor laze and grand smug innocence and sometimes wonders if she takes this from them to bed with her, if the memory of that heavy rest that lies about her like perfume is not hers but the airy burr they exhale? Is all this, to her, to Nedra Carp, what their stuffed animals and bits of blanket and fingered cloth and crushed bunches of palmed wool are to them? She rejects the supposition. She stands *in loco parentis*, after all. Yes, she thinks grimly, like all those wicked stepmothers. Yet *she* is not wicked, if anything *too* tender, discipline not her strong suit, her lack of firmness a weakness. Ha ha, she laughs in her reverie, that's a good one; lack of firmness a weakness is a good one. Yet she knows the literature well enough, the stories of stern nannies, repressed, dried-up old crazies jealous of their privileged charges. Letting them howl their hunger, then tweaking them in the nursery, laying on sharp twists and pinches when no one important's about, gossiping in the parks among the sisterhood. Oh, well, they probably meant governesses. To the uninitiated, governesses gave nannies a bad name.

It's ironic, Nedra Carp thinks, but here I am, off to America, to Disney World, Florida, and feels a queer thrill. It was Mr. Disney and the Yanks that made Mary Poppins famous, a household name throughout the world, in all the climes and cultures, a comfort, a tonic. It's silly, she thinks, I'm no R.C., but Mary Poppins is practically my patron saint.

She was. Nedra Carp imagines Mary Poppins watching over her, not convinced of so much as comforted by the idea of her presence. She has seen the film seventeen times, and though she knows she is nothing like that mysterious woman, has neither her powers nor her flair, yet it is to Mary she turns when she's in trouble, to Mary to whom she flies now high above the watery rooftops and smoking chimney wisps of the clouded world. And thinks of Mary, that stout, good-natured voyager, of Mary of England and all the globey sky. And knows that it's because of Mary Poppins that she makes this trip, racing toward Disney World as to a sort of Lourdes, bringing, who has no talent even for changing a diaper and is probably embarrassed by it, no skill with even feverish children let alone dying ones, who cannot make even healthy children laugh or, for that matter, keep them entertained or, if you must know, make them behave, who has none of Mary Poppins's aptitudes but only her own dull gift of love, flying to Florida, to her patron there—maybe there—to pray before some very likely tarted-up, possibly animated saint. Off to Orlando, who is in the wrong profession and whose love of little children is unrequited, a repressed, dried-up old crazy herself, one *muy loco parentis* who can't bear to think of those characters she carries in her handbag like a packet of tame old love letters.

Nedra Carp, Nedra Carp thinks. With my name like a fish.

And though most of her employers these self-conscious, egal-
itarian days call her Mrs. Carp—the Queen herself did; lisping
Andrew, keeping his distance, did—she has never married. And
knows those aren't love letters she carries in her purse but only
her tepid warrants and credentials—she's peeked; she's read
them—like the lukewarm references of someone honest and even
diligent but uninspired. And knows, too, that if she *had* married it would probably have been to some widower with kids, *in
loco parentis* again, *in loco parentis* always who would never have
a place of her own. And also knows, as she knows she's never
gossiped about her charges or practiced any of the petty cruel-
ties of her trade, that she would starve rather than deny her
stepchildren even one morsel or talk behind their backs to the
woodchopper, that unlike Cinderella's stepmother she could play
no favorites, not she, she thinks proudly, not Nedra Carp, who
has, for good or ill, like a built-in murmur, her adoptive heart.

Because probably no one but Nedra and those involved
know that as a child she had had nannies herself and, as an older
child, a governess, or that she was herself a stepchild, her mother
having died when Nedra was four, her father remarried to a
woman with two children of her own. Hers had been kind
enough, nannies, governess, stepmother, stepsister, stepbrother, father, and, later, her half brother and half sister. But
then, when she was nine, it was her father who died and her
stepmother, not yet thirty-four, who remarried, a widower with
two daughters. And Nedra carries with her still a sad sense of
fragmentation and dissolved loyalties, a vague notion of having
grown up with distant and distancing cousins, who had two
stepsisters now, a new baby brother, a new baby sister, and a
confused notion of having been raised by aunts and uncles or
even just in-laws, all tenuously related and removed, too, by
marriage. Only she and the half brother and half sister were
Carps, and as much out of confusion as blood and love she
sought to make an alliance with them, which they did, but when
the last of the stepmother's children was born, he'd come to her,
the half brother. "I find I may no longer in good conscience
honor our special relationship," he said.

"Oh?" said Nedra.

"It would be unfair to my half brother, my new half sister."

"I see," Nedra said.

"This complicates things awfully," the only male Carp apologized.

"It does, rather," Nedra admitted.

"Though I shall always half love you," he said, and seemed to fade before her very eyes.

But then it was the stepmother who died and the double widower who remarried, the house filled now with steps and halves and quarters, an ever more fractioned tangle of thinned kinship, practically a decimalized one.

So it was to the nannies she'd turned. Perhaps because they understood even less than she who was who, the strange range of relation in the house. It would have taken a Debrett to work it all out. I was no poor relation, you understand, thinks Nedra Carp, but the only living child in that household of the true founders of the family. The very house in which we lived had belonged to my mother. So it was to the nannies I turned, as bonded and blooded to any of them as to any of the steps and halves and lesser fractions of alliance there, those amiable non-consanguineous sleep-in ladies: to them, to the nannies I turned, pitching in, pulling my oar, helping out with the smaller children, a Cinderella of the voluntary, who must have thought of me, if they regarded me at all, as some nanny apprentice or nanny greenhorn, whom though they—the nannies—did not scold, were yet without love, their trained, neutral hearts less in it—yes, and less called for, too—than their time.

Except, Nedra Carp thinks, that should never have been permitted. That was unforgivable. Someone should have corrected that when it first came up. My new stepmother, my diluted half brother, the double widower, the real nanny herself, somebody. My mother had owned that house. Those children had no right to call me Nanny.

Eddy Bale talks to his dead son, Liam, in his sleep addresses the boy in a hospital room he does not remember, cheered by that very fact, taking heart from the realization that it isn't just that he can't remember the room but, looking past Liam and out the boy's window, doesn't recall the view. It isn't London, it isn't even England. There's a park out there but the vegetation is unfamiliar, the cars going back and forth in the heavy traffic. They are not even of a design he recognizes, and trail from their tailpipes a faint, curious steam he does not recognize as ordinary exhaust. He wishes a nurse or doctor would drop by so he could see what race they are. He is too high above street level to make out the ethnic characteristics of the passersby, and he's unable to make out anything at all of the drivers in their oddball machines. Indeed, there's a curiously opaque quality to the window glass of the strange automobiles. What he really hopes, of course, is to have confirmed that he is somewhere he has never been, in a land of new breakthrough technologies, some boldly experimental hi-tech country where they have their priorities right. He would like to see, for example, one of those pie-shaped charts that tell where the tax dollars go: 25 percent for social services, 25 percent for R&D, 25 percent for entitlement programs, and 25 percent for a military so strong no country would dare challenge such a civilized power.

He can't ask Ginny. Ginny isn't around. But perhaps that's good news, too. Maybe the treatment here is so advanced that visitors are either nonexistent or only come out of some true sociability, as one might call on a pal in town overnight in his hotel room.

So he can't ask Ginny and won't ask the boy. For fear he might be interfering with some delicate therapeutic balance. And is heartened, too, by other things, small stuff, little touches not ordinarily associated with science but, or so runs his hunch, telling enough in a hospital room. There's the gas range, for example, and a larder stocked with bakery goods, with rich pâtés and cheeses. There is a small refrigerator with fine wines and various drugs lining its shelves. Beside it, on a laboratory table adjusted to what must be his son's height, is an assortment of pharmaceutical equipment: Bunsen burners, a good microscope, and, nearby, several covered petri dishes glowing with cultures as with bits of bread. There is a burette, sundry flasks, an old-fashioned mortar and pestle where his son probably ground his cunning nostrums and medications and coffee beans into a fine powder. Other instruments whose names he doesn't know. Also, there's a box of candy, a nice bowl of fruit.

"What I thought I'd explain to you, Liam," he says guardedly to the boy in the bed, "is this 'Dream Holiday' business. I'm trying to make it up to them, you see. For being so sick, I mean. For having these catastrophic diseases. For having to die before their time, you understand. Well if *you* don't understand, who would?" he adds, chuckling. "I mean, you've been there, son. You know how it is. Who better? I mean, you're that Indian whom no one may criticize until they walk a mile in your moccasins, my child.

"So it's like a reward is the way I look at it. *Entre nous,* kiddo," he whispers, "bonus pay for hazardous duty." He winks at the boy. "Just this little inducement, just this small 'consideration,' if you know what I mean," and rubs his thumb and forefinger together, and makes a sign as if he were greasing a palm. "Just this bit on the side, boy. Hey, son? Hey, Liam?" And shakes his head and slowly raises a finger to his lips. It's that delicate therapeutic balance again. That he doesn't want upset. So he paces the room. Diligently avoiding eye contact. Wondering to himself, How'm I doin'? How'm I doin'?

"It isn't as if this trip were your memo*rial* or anything. Of course not. What, are you kidding? A clambake in Florida? A binge on the roundabout? A spree at the fun fair? Your *memorial?* You think your mum and I would turn something like that into a great bloody red-letter day or go skylarking about like nits in the pump room? It's shocked I am you should think so, well and truly shocked. Come on, Liam, you know better!" But still won't look at the lad.

"Or *should. Should* know better. Because we've a proper memorial stone already picked out. Your favorite kind, kid. Pure solid marble. None of this newfangled 'composition' crap. Nothing ersatz, nothing trashy. With your name, address, dates, phone number, and grades cut in to last a thousand years. Could a father say fairer?

"Because we're proud of you, son. You bust our buttons.

Really, child, Daddy's pleased you're getting on so well. All this equipment. Whew! I wouldn't begin to know what to do with it, I'm sure. You mix this black sauce with the snotty green lumps all by yourself? P.U. . . . Smells nasty enough. What it must taste like, eh? It's the furry part *I* couldn't get down." And suddenly turns to look at his son directly. Though Liam's eyes are shut, his lids seem to follow Eddy wherever he goes in the room, like a trick of perspective in a portrait. "But then again you've taken plenty of punishment in your time. The x-rays and lasers, the invasive procedures, the pain and the nausea. Suffering was always your very particular speciality. I'd give you a first. I really would. I'm not just saying this because you're my son. Somebody ought to do something about all that vomit, though.

"Well, I'm sure it was very clever of the doctors to let you work out your cure for yourself. They seemed to be stymied there when *they* had a go at it, God knows. So what did it turn out to be? The breakthrough? What'd it turn out to be in the end? When all is said and done, I mean?"

This time he rushes his finger to his lips, admonishing Liam's silence. The gesture is like an awry slap.

"No," Eddy says. "Hush, Liam. Hush, son. Because if you really *are* dead—not that I think you are, you understand, not for a minute—but just in the event, on the outside chance, I don't want to hear about it. I *won't* hear about it. Nor will I listen to a word about bold cures and new breakthroughs. Not if you're dead, I won't.

"How'm I doin'?"

II

1

A light, fine snow was falling on the Magic Kingdom. It covered the streets and rooftops of the amusement province with a thin dry powder. The storm cell was totally unexpected and caught the weathermen on the TV and radio stations in Orlando completely by surprise. It was a freak storm in all its aspects. No one working in the park remembered its like, and though some of the citrus growers in the area could recall similar storms—there'd been one back in 1959, before the park opened, when the temperature had dropped forty degrees in less than seven hours, and the growers had had to arrange sheets over the crowns of the trees and burn smudge pots in an attempt to save their orchards—those had been in deep winter, not late October. In any event, it wasn't really that cold, the temperature only in the mid-thirties. That the snow didn't melt at all but collected on the ground, experts attributed to the fact—or speculation, rather—that it must have fallen from a very great height, possibly the stratosphere, pushed through—well, nothing, a sort of stalled, rare, and massive air pocket that just happened to coincide in its dimensions with the boundaries of the park itself.

Naturally the children were disappointed by the chilly weather, particularly after their surprise when, deplaning in Miami and bundled in heavy coats and scarves more convenient to wear than carry along with their cumbersome burden of toys and parcels, they had been hit full in the face with the warm, humid Florida air, an air—or so it seemed to Janet Order, or so it seemed to Lydia Conscience, or so it seemed to Charles Mudd-Gaddis, who back in those few days when he had been a young man had enjoyed going there—as sultry and earthy and steamy as the air in the big hothouse in Kew Gardens.

By the time they cleared Customs and made their connecting flight and used their transfers in Orlando and been registered in the hotel, it was already late afternoon and, with the time difference, well past their British bedtimes, and they were ordered to their rooms by Mr. Moorhead. So, although it was barely eight o'clock when it began to snow, they were asleep and only noticed the accumulation the following morning.

It looked like a scene shaken up in a crystal.

Snow was falling on Cinderella Castle, snow was falling on Main Street and Liberty Square. It was falling on Adventureland and on Fantasyland. It sheathed the spires on the Haunted Mansion and clung to the umbrellalike strutted sides of Space Mountain and looked grim and oddly bruised against the spiky red slopes of Big Thunder Mountain. It coated the crazed, bulging eyes of Captain Nemo's surfaced craft and collected as slush in the saucers of the Mad Tea Party and left powdery traces along the big ledges and sills of the Liberty Tree Tavern's wide leaded windows. Discrete drifts of the stuff were swept against the heavily weathered stockade fences of Frontierland and intensified the gleam of Tomorrowland's crisp concretes and metals and alloys. A fine powder dusted the notched and scalloped foliage along the banks of the steaming river that bent and flexed, hooked and curled past tropical rain forest and choked veldt, past the Asian jungle and the rich green growth of the Nile Valley. It filled in the pocked surfaces of Spaceship Earth and lent the entire park the look of some new, raw, terrible ice age.

From Top of the World, the hotel's fifteenth-floor restaurant, Nedra Carp and the children saw it cover the islands in Bay Lake and Seven Seas Lagoon and, beyond, watched horses on a distant ranch roll in the white stuff, startle, leap up, and furiously throw themselves over and over into the strange, cold element, stinging their skin and alarming their great horse hearts.

Nine stories below in Mr. Moorhead's room, which Benny Maxine had dubbed "the intensive care ward," the adults watched it fall on the roofs of the longhouses in the Polynesian Village. They watched it snag in the tops of the palm trees and cover the gleaming tracks of the park's monorails in a flat white.

It's . . . it's a . . . it's a mistake, Eddy Bale thought. And, despondent, realized he'd come all this way and raised all their hopes in a futile cause. Because it was almost gone eleven—never mind the freak storm or rapidly rising temperatures through which the flakes fell, losing their icy edge, their crystalline structures collapsing so that what dropped through the air seemed less like weather than some spilled aspect of the jettisoned, not a freak storm at all so much as a mid-course meteorological correction, and never mind either whatever of accidental, unintentioned beauty the storm, by way of the blind bizarre, happened, like paint in milk, to bring about—and the morning of the first day was damn near shot and the children hadn't even had their breakfasts. The storm not of account here either, though with other children it might have been (the guests caught short, the coffee shops and restaurants filling up, tables, food, tea, and cigarettes lingered over, no one in a hurry, the whole company of displaced persons thrown together like cheery flood victims), an excuse, certainly, but not of account, since what Bale had not taken into consideration (so busy with long-haul logistics, the finances, his caper crew and gleaned, short-listed candidates, his Heathrow-to-Miami arrangements, his Miami-to-Orlando ones, the room assignments worked out in advance) were the sluggish ways of the dying, their awful morning catarrhs and constipations, the wheezed wind of their snarled, tangled breathing, their stalled blood and aches and pains like an actual traffic in their bones, all the low-grade fevers of their stiff, bruised sleep. He'd forgotten Liam's nausea and given no thought to theirs—mouths stenchy as Beirut, stomachs floating a slick film of morning sickness, the torpid hangover of their medications. They groaned. They stumbled listlessly through their rooms or waited, hung in trance above shoes, buttons, expression denied their faces as if they lived in some lulled climate of withdrawn will.

Ah, it was terrible, Eddy Bale thought hopelessly. Time wasting and the doctor's hands tied and none of them able to organize anything as simple as breakfast. Only Nedra Carp up and about, standing behind the maid when that woman had let herself in with her passkey just after eight that morning, her surprise, if she was surprised, concealed, taking in himself, the sleeping Colin, and the two boys—the doctor had made the room assignments, Bale drawing Colin, Mudd-Gaddis, and Benny Maxine—with a kind of stoic patience, almost, it struck Eddy, a hotel policy, as if she knew their special circumstances, perhaps. She had whispered Bale a soft apology for having disturbed them and withdrew. But not before Nedra had appeared from behind her back like a surprise, a clutch of the park's pamphlets and a "Walt Disney World Newsletter" in her hand.

"Will the boys want to go to Mass? I didn't mention it last night and thought they'd be too worn out to disturb them this morning, but there's a lovely little chapel off what they call the Interstate Four, and transportation is quite convenient. I caught the brown-flagged bus outside the hotel and showed the driver the I.D. they gave us when we checked in."

"You've been to Mass, Miss Carp?"

"Not *proper* Mass, Mister Bale—I don't even know if the

chapel's consecrated—but there was something that looked like an altar, and pews and stained glass, and a priest comes on Sundays."

"Benny is Jewish. I don't know Mudd-Gaddis's affiliations, but I'll ask if he's interested."

"Oh, I nearly forgot," she said, and handed Bale the newsletter. "There's this lovely write-up about us in the paper. Quite tasteful, I think." Eddy read the notice. It was a modest story under a small headline on the back page: ENGLISH CHILDREN WIN TRIP TO VACATION KINGDOM. It recorded all their names and listed the children's ages but said nothing of the purpose of the trip. Death wasn't mentioned, disease wasn't. Mr. Moorhead wasn't identified as a doctor. "The big news is all about the weather," Nedra Carp said.

"The weather?" Bale had said, who'd not yet looked out the window and had forgotten the strange inclemency of the previous day.

"Oh, yes," Nedra Carp said, "there must be three or four inches of snow. The driver—he's called a 'cast member,' everyone who works here is; did you know that, Mister Bale?—was quite concerned he had no chains. Though not a flake's fallen outside the park."

Which was before the kids had awakened, Nedra drawing back the curtains and indicating the scene, unveiling and flourishing it like a commissioned portrait. And Bale, already fainthearted, despairing, worrying his—their—losses like a field marshal, awake even before the maid had let herself in, awake and despondent a full hour before first light, already brooding when he'd turned in, and in his dreamless sleep too, hopelessness like a cinder in his eye. (Though Bale was no dummy, though he knew himself well enough, or well enough to recognize his habits, the if-then sequences of his conditioned behavior. And reminded himself, Eddy, watch it; Eddy, don't let the part stand for the whole. You always go all sad-ass and sourpuss at finish lines and destinations. My God, man, there was a time when it broke your heart just to hear the bus conductor call out your stop. And reminded himself of the time when he'd allowed an unfavorable rate of exchange—so they'd have money in their pockets he'd traded a few quid for pesetas at the duty-free shop at Gatwick—almost to ruin their honeymoon on the Costa Brava. Ginny had tried to reassure him, had told him at least half a dozen times that the 20 percent premium they'd paid for the pesetas was irregular, that the banks in Spain would give them the official rate, but he continued to worry, the pound he'd lost on the deal multiplied in his head by a factor of five for all the pounds and Thomas Cook traveler's checks they carried on their persons, for all the drafts they would have yet to write on their bank at home to make up for the one-to-five deficiency, his poor, depleted, gutted lolly, their love stake; doing in his head, too, all the complicated projections of suddenly inflated meals, souvenirs, hotel bills, fares, sun creams, tabs at nightclubs, and mad money. Discounting their honeymoon to the Spaniards. And wouldn't leave the room for more than twenty-four hours—they had ten days—thinking: *If we don't go out they can't cheat us;* thinking: *But they already have, a day shot, one already 20 percent less precious day of our ten out the window.* Where he saw the sun shining 20 percent brighter than it had even on the brochure, the sea 20 percent bluer, the waves that much higher, too, conspiring by remaining in the room to recover: *They had ten days. If they had ten days and the ratio was four to one—five to one?—what would it be, 10 percent of their losses, but they had to make love, they had to sleep, they had to use the room, call it twelve out of the twenty-four hours anyway, so it would be more like 5 percent than 10 percent, and they were still 15 percent in the hole.* "There's this *bodega*," he'd told Ginny, "not a block from the hotel. We could get wine, we could get oranges and bread. Maybe they do Spanish sandwiches. We'll eat in the room tonight. We'll use the money they stuck us with at Gatwick. We'll stick *them* with it." Ginny accused him of being mean. Meanness had nothing to do with it, he said. And it didn't. He was no miser. He was a coward of the unaccustomed, raw, all thumbs, greenhorn fear in his bones and blood, in his nails and hair. He explained this to Ginny, his oblique vertigo. "Give me time," he said. "When the banks open"—they'd arrived too late, the banks had already closed—"and we get our proper rate, I'll be the last of the big-time spenders for you." Or choice. Burdened by choice. Overwhelmed. Dreading evenings on the town. Hating to read menus, picking a movie, choosing a play. And craven in taxis if he didn't know the route. Though forgetting this. Each time forgetting this. Hailing cabs with the authority and assurance of an M.P. until, inside, he felt the greenhorn paranoid temerity again, one eye on the meter, another looking not for landmark, since this would be, for him, *terra incognita*, but for some discoverable *logic* of the route, the principles of geography, and all the while listening to the cabby for clues, the chatty-seeming observation, the too-matey question, Bale figuring the hackman figuring him. The both of them lost in Willesden one time, looking for 14 Broalbrond Road because Bale, without actually saying so, had implied he'd been there before, practically old stamping grounds for Eddy, and had, to keep the driver honest, indicated with nothing much more than the mildest sarcastic thrust to his tone that such and such a building, standing, it had to be, since the Great War, must, it seemed to him, at least if they were anywhere near the Willesden *he* knew, *his* old stamping grounds, have gone up overnight. And in Johannesburg, with Liam for new aggressive treatment, the same dark curtains descending. In Beijing. Even in Lourdes. Especially in Lourdes. The beginnings of all expeditions the same sad business, jet lag in Eddy an actual disease. But not mean, no miser, no screw or scrimp. Not a lickpenny bone in his body. Abject at waste is all, a cringer for missed opportunity, abused life. And who could say he was wrong? Hadn't Ginny left him, hadn't Liam died? Wasn't he usually disappointed at the theater? Hadn't oysters Casino given him indigestion?) So he didn't wake Colin. So he didn't wake the children.

Who dropped out of sleep into wakefulness—Eddy watching through his lashes—like synchronized swimmers. A contagion of halt beginnings, the stuttered start of a new day. Colin Bible supervising from his rollaway, calling ablutions like stations of the Cross. "Brush your teeth, Benny. Move your bowels." Then, raising his voice for the little old man: *"Your* teeth are in the glass by the nightstand, Mudd-Gaddis. Don't forget to wear your sweater, don't forget to put on your scarf." Winking at Eddy past his shut eyes, past his lashes, piercing Bale's squeezed charade, a laser intrusion. Who wanted nothing more than to be done with it and wondered if it was as late as he hoped. And, looking for grievance, tried to resent the tone the nurse had taken with the little golden-ager, condescension loaded into his voice like a round of ammunition, tried to resent the implied conspiracy of the wink (who was, after all, found out, discovered as a shirker, known for what he was, could be, by a bloody pansy), tried and failed—struck finally only by the difference in their styles, Eddy not so much outraged as intimidated, orientalized by a holdover respect for his elders, the sense he had that Mudd-Gaddis's freaky years deserved a kind of honor, for—God, what was a bloke like him doing with folks like these?—it was, to Bale, almost as if Charles Mudd-Gaddis was the genuine article, a brittle scroll of a being, some actual ancient. Bale had to bite his lips to keep the deference out of his voice, and once had actually been on the verge of calling him "sir."

" 'Ello, 'ello," said Benny Maxine, coming out of the bathroom and spotting the snow outside their window. "Coo, la! Look at the weather, will you! What odds on something like that happening?"

The snow had already begun to melt. In the restaurant Nedra Carp and the children, joined by the rest of the adults, tried not to notice as Lydia Conscience, swept in the waves of her morning sickness, gagged bits of dry toast and gouts of grapefruit into her napkin.

"Must have gone down the wrong pipe," Lydia said, her face red.

"Here, dear," Rena Morgan said, offering Kleenex she'd slipped from a sleeve.

"Sorry, didn't think," Mary Cottle said, snuffing a Gitane into her saucer.

"Smokes like a man, that one," Benny Maxine whispered to Noah Cloth. "Bet she's les."

"Well," said Mr. Moorhead, again taking up the remarkable topic the children had been discussing when he, Bale, Bible, and the two ladies had first joined Nedra in the restaurant, "I don't agree."

"You only mean my disease," Charles Mudd-Gaddis said. He was seated at the head of the table, and it seemed to Eddy that a queer clarity had settled over the strange child. The waitress had handed him the check, and before Eddy could even reach for it, Mudd-Gaddis was already signing the back of the bill. "I want to be fair. What's fifteen percent of seventy-three dollars and forty-four cents? I can't think," he said in his reedy old voice.

"Leave eleven dollars," Mary Cottle said.

Mudd-Gaddis smiled up at the waitress. "Thank you, my dear," he said, and turned back to the doctor. "I really haven't. I've never felt special, I've never felt marked. Singled out, I mean. What I've lived was just"—and here the little geriatric paused, struggled for the exact words—"a life."

"Just a *life*, my dear fellow? *Just* a life?"

"Oh, you mean my symptoms," Mudd-Gaddis said. "You're a physician. Symptoms make a difference to you. I've my fingerprints, of course, and my eyes are probably their own shade of blue. And I sit on a different bum than the rest, my own special customized behind, but so does everyone."

"Charles!" Nedra Carp scolded.

But his hearing was bad. He was a little deaf and went on as if there'd been no interruption. "I mean we all know that bit about no two snowflakes, and when we first hear it it's news of a sort. Of a sort, it is. We think, we think, 'All this *stuff* in the world and no two leaves exactly alike? No two thumbs or signatures?' Make-work for the handwriting experts, the forgery detectives. But what difference does a difference make? A fine distinction? All right." He sighed. "Those three or four months back when I was a kid, I admit it, I do rather remember imagining I was wrapped in some mantle of the special. But *all* kids think that. It's a snare and a delusion."

He's wise, Eddy Bale thought. He's a wise old nipper. Like whoosis, Sam Jaffe, in *Lost Horizon*. One day I'll get him alone.

I'll pour out my soul. I'll ask about Liam, I'll ask about Ginny.

"What's Her Royal Highness's given name?" Moorhead asked suddenly.

"Her Royal Highness?"

"Her Royal Highness. The Queen. What's the Queen's given name?"

Mudd-Gaddis seemed confused. There was cloud cover in his eyes. "Wait," he said, "it's on the tip of my . . . on the tip of my . . . the tip of my . . ."

"I'll give odds he don't get it," Benny Maxine said.

Moorhead nodded encouragement, but the little pensioner could only look helplessly back at the physician.

It was Goofy and Pluto who broke the tension. They came up to the table clutching a brace of balloons in vaguely articulated paws, a cross, it seemed to Eddy, somewhere on the evolutionary scale between mittens and hands. Goofy grinned at the children behind his amiable overbite. Pluto, his long red tongue lolling like an oversize shoehorn, stared at them in perpetual pant, his tremendous, lidless eyes fixed in agreeable astonishment. Ears hung from the sides of their heads like narrow neckties.

"Hi, there," Rena Morgan said.

Goofy nodded.

"Ta," said Noah Cloth, choosing a purple balloon from the bunch like a great grape and taking it in his own modified mitt.

Janet Order patted the crouching Pluto, soft boluses of orange-brown nape in her blue hand. "Does that feel good? Does it? Do you like that, Pluto? Do you, boy?" The doggish creature turned its head, silently offering luxurious swatches of bright coat to her cyanotic nails. "Can you beg? Can you growl for me? Pluto? Can you beg?"

"They're not allowed to speak," Nedra Carp said. "It's a strict rule. I read it in the brochure."

"What? Like in the Guards, you mean?" Tony Word said.

"Outside Buckingham Palace?" Lydia Conscience said.

"That's right," Nedra Carp said. "They're trained."

"Ooh," said Benny Maxine, "*there's* a bet. *I'll* provoke them!"

"*Benny!*" Eddy Bale warned.

But it was too late. Maxine had stood up and was already holding Goofy's nose, round and black as a handball. "Bugger off," he said. "Go on, beat it."

The manlike animal—Goofy wore a kind of clothes, a bunting of vest, a signal of trousers, a streamer of shoes, over his body—just stood there. Perhaps he inclined his head a few degrees to the side, but if he had he still stood in a sort of plaintive, lockjaw serenity, his dim good humor stamped on his face, broad, deep and mute as a crocodile's.

"Think you're a hard case, do you? All right, all right, but I haven't shown you my best stuff yet. You ready, dogface?"

The creature brought its head to attention.

"Benny," Eddy Bale said, "*don't.*"

"What's this then," Benny Maxine said, and placed his hands on the spiky bristles stuck like splinters along the cusps of its jowls. "What's this then, *quills?* Call yourself a dog? You're a bleedin' *por*cupine."

"I told you they were trained," Nedra Carp said. "Well *done,* young man!"

"Cut it out, Benny," Eddy Bale said.

But the animal stood still, quite as the guardsmen he'd been compared to, his cheerfulness like an indifference.

"Oh, I ain't done wif *you* yet, young porcupine," Benny Maxine said, and laid hands on the tall bent-stovepipe hat pinned to its costume. "Ooh, 'ere's a doggy bone. What you want to put it on your head for? You hidin' it from the mutt? Suppose I throw it. Suppose you fetch."

"I mean it, Benny," Eddy Bale said. "If you expect to eat with us again, if you don't want to take the rest of your meals in the room . . ."

Benny Maxine carefully removed the first pin. "Steady, fellow, this could smart," he said, withdrawing a long second pin from Goofy's scalp.

"Benny," Rena shouted, "if you're going to be wicked I won't be your friend." She began to cry, her fluids and phlegms spilling from their reservoirs.

" 'Ere now, 'ere now," Benny Maxine said, "me and the Goof was only 'avin' a bit of fun. 'E enjoys it. Don't you enjoy it, Goof?" Though its expression of stony contentment hadn't at all changed, the animal seemed to shrink before its tormentor, its amusement subtly bruised, its bearing and demeanor at odds with the gorgeousness of its trusting smile, the Cheshire risibilities of its pleased teeth, almost as if its doggy expectations and hopes were frozen forever two and three beats behind its more clever limbs and more knowing body. Rena Morgan was pulling Kleenex and handkerchiefs from all their cunning places of concealment. "All right," Benny said, chastened. Carefully he replaced the first hatpin, weaving it through the hat and loose folds of Goofy's fabric scalp. Rena continued to sniffle and Benny handed over the second dangerous-looking pin to the contented, oddly dignified Goofy, who, though it was his own, bowed, stood to his full height, accepted it as if it were a surrender sword, and withdrew.

"*Tongue,*" Mudd-Gaddis cried triumphantly. "Tip of my *tongue!*"

"What is, Charles?" Moorhead asked. "What's on the tip of your tongue?"

The withered little youth seemed to collapse under the weight of his sweaters. He seemed shawled and slippered.

Benny Maxine looked accusingly at Eddy Bale and Nedra Carp. With Rena Morgan he seemed at once both apologetic and the injured party. "Why'd you want to go and make me lose my bet? What for? Why?"

"You didn't have a bet," Mary Cottle said. "No one took you up on one. You had no bet."

"Sure I did," he said. "With myself." And turned from them. And raising his voice, called after the retreating orange figures. "Hey!" he shouted. "Hey! I bet we don't die! Not one of us. I *bet* you. I bet we *don't* die!"

Embarrassed, all the adults and children except for Charles, Benny, and Rena, who was tamping at her now tapering mucus as if it were the last drippings about an ice-cream cone, watched

Goofy and Pluto distribute their balloons at a far table. They seemed restored, recovered, bright and tawny as mint lions.

"What's their relationship to each other, do you suppose?" Noah Cloth asked speculatively. "Is Pluto Goofy's son?"

"Is he its brother?" Tony Word said.

"I think he's its nephew," said Lydia Conscience.

"Maybe he's its dog," muttered Benny Maxine.

2

It was awkward. Even for Mary Cottle, flexible as a flag, practiced and accommodate to prevailing conditions as a windsock, it was awkward. Accustomed to quirk and anomaly as an old shoe—the expression "hand-in-glove" occurred to her, the expressions "square peg in a round hole," "finger in the pie" did—to all the oddball contingencies and weird one-in-a-million circumstances. And never caught out, never, not once in all the doomtime she'd put in since her second abortion, since her blood tests came back all stained, the workups and medical reports and dire prophecies which she'd accepted like a knowledgeable Oedipus, a more clever Macbeth, her eyes neither blinded to loopholes nor shut to them—"loophole" occurred to her—since she'd seen them at once, *she* had, even before the doctor had had a chance to outline her options: tubal ligation, even a hysterectomy. ("Listen," the surgeon said, "that's asking over the odds, a hysterectomy is. There isn't a useful doctor or doctorine in the Kingdom who'd hold the baby on this one. Why, your glory garden's all sweetness and light, untouched by tare, vetch, or pesky vermin. There ain't a mite, louse, or flea to trouble it. No earwig or locust, no beetle or bedbug. There are only very delightful faeries at the bottom of your garden, Miss Cottle. Your little polluted eggies aside, the carton is fit as a fiddle. So who would touch you, who would tamper? It's all 'Doctor Livingstone, I presume' with these wowser castor-oil artists and Tory flesh tailors." "Thank you, doctor, for your professional candor." "Hold the job," the surgeon said. "I didn't say *I* wouldn't perform it." "No, thank you." "Besides, it's preventive medicine. It takes down the odds on cancer." "No, thank you," she said, and blew thick fog from her cheap cigarettes in the doctor's direction. "It's like having your appendix out. You don't actually ne—" "No. Thank you." "So," the doctor said, "you're a tough customer. All right, luv, you're the doctor. If you prefer I tie granny knots in your strings, then granny knots it shall be. Hell, dearie, I'll do you braids and corn rows, bows and reef knots. I'll—" "No, thank you." Which was when he really let loose with his candor. "Go ahead, then," the physician said, "go get your second opinions. It won't make any difference. You carry chemistries so rancid you could poison wells. I do assure you, Miss Cottle, any child you have the misfortune to bear could have you up on charges. You can only bear monsters. Your kids would be kraken, children chimeras, and basilisk babes. Mummy to wyvern, to snark, and to sphinx. Generations of vipers, Miss Cottle." "Is that your professional opinion?" "The pill's no guarantee against conception. You're *on* the pill and have already had a couple of miscarriages, a pair of abortions. We don't yet understand why some women are less susceptible than others to its effects, but that's the way it is. I'm afraid you're one of those who can't afford to rely on the usual methods of birth control." "I shan't." "If you intend to live the life," he continued, without hearing her, "of a normal, healthy young woman, you'll almost certainly have to undergo one of the mildly radical procedures I've outlined." "No, thank you." "Oh, there are other surgeons. If you don't trust *me*, I'd be happy to put you on to one of them. I should think I might even be able to locate a quite upright man willing to perform the hysterectomy. I mean, once he knows the circumstances. . . ." "There'll be no hysterectomy, there'll be no procedures." "You know," he said, "I was having you on with that bit about those knots I was going to tie. It's a simple thing, really. I was teasing to cheer you up." "I know that." "So then," he said, "what's your decision? I don't mean to rush you, but the sooner we do something about all this the sooner you'll be able to resume your normal sexual activities." "I told you," she said, "there will be no procedures." The surgeon studied her. "Then I'm afraid I shall certainly have to inform the authorities," he said quietly. "It's a crime in this country willfully to bring a child into the world when it's known long enough in advance of its birth that it would suffer multiple and severe physical and mental disorders.") And the other loophole too. The one the surgeon hadn't mentioned. That she could have it off with men who were sterile. With men with vasectomies, even with men who were impotent, men with implants, with little rubber bulbs they squeezed in their palms to fill up their spurious erections with fluids, actually coming, ejaculating, shooting fluids, douche water, perfume, actual champagne, up her parts. She would have none of it. Hating arrangements, she would make none. Men lied. If you held out, if you told them you couldn't have children, if you explained, they could do you a song and dance, admit to sterility, vasectomy, even to impotence, even to implants, excusing themselves to show up next time with a syringe, the makeshift rubber tubing broken off from enema bags, bicycle pumps, doucheworks, sphygmomanometers, machineries from the chemist. She hated subterfuge, she hated being courted. The burdensome, elaborate, social choreographies embarrassed and depressed her. Gifts, flowers, love letters, telephone calls taken in bed late at night, home from a date, even the engagement ring her fiancé had given her. (And had agreed to marry him, to move in with him, and even been the one to suggest this, if only to get him to call off the courtship.) Because she was modest, refined, lustrate, nice. Because she was natty, spruce, spic-and-span. Because she was always morally well turned out. Pure, discreet, demure. Because she was picky, discriminating, dainty, shocked. Even squeamish, even shy. Because she had this honed sense of occasion, of nuance and nicety. Because she drew the line and split the hair. Because she was puritanical. Because she was tasteful. Because she was good. Because, finally, she was fastidious. This fastidious whack-off artist.

So of *course* it was awkward. Because she needed her relief—the strongest nicotines and harshest blends were almost useless to her now—and would, had she known she was to have been assigned three roommates—Moorhead had put her in 629 with Nedra Carp, Lydia, and Rena—willingly have paid for a single. (Of *course* her cigarettes were useless. With Rena Morgan around she didn't dare light one. The cystic fibrotic was even more sensitive to smoke, however mild, than Janet Order and was sent off into spasms of respiratory seizure if someone so much as struck a match within ten feet of her. Even now she toyed with the idea of taking a room of her own, on a different floor perhaps, a place where she could go off by herself if the strain became too great. And hesitated only because *that* would have been an arrangement.) Or brought along the three little steel balls she'd purchased at the sex shop on Shaftesbury Avenue. (Though she hadn't used them—a most hideous arrangement—except that one time, she still had them about somewhere, probably in her closet with the gifts her fiancé had given her. She had fit them between her legs, inserting them, deep, high up—the instructions had indicated that for best results she consult her gynecologist, but of course she'd been too discreet to do anything like that, and, though she played with the notion of going back to the smart-ass surgeon to teach him a thing or two about radical procedures, in the end, expert as she was, familiar as she was with her own sweet, rich territories, she decided to do it herself—and went about her apartment in a state of unrelieved ecstasy, her orgasms triggered by her own footsteps. Seven paces across the lounge to the geraniums in the flower pot on the window ledge and wow, oh God, oh, oh, oh Christ, *oh*, o, o, ooh! A few steps to the fridge in the kitchen to get out some veggies for supper and ooh, *ooh*, ahh, ahh, *ah*, mnn, mnnnn, ahh, ah, ah, *mnnnnnhnhuhh!* A short walk to the W.C. to wash her hands before dinner and she had to stuff her fists into her mouth to modulate her cries and yelps. No way for a nice, modest, refined, pure, natty, demure and dainty, spruce and lustrate lady like herself to behave.) So she'd left them at home. Along with the vibrator, neutrally enough shaped except for its roundish, bluntish tip, but covered in a tight, almost fleshlike plastic a little like the electrical wire on her stereo—on the whole Mary rather disapproved of music, it being itself something of an arrangement—and picked up in that same sex shop on that same day on Shaftesbury Avenue when she'd purchased the little stainless steel perpetual orgasm machine, ignoring the glances of the men—there were no other lone women in the shop—and genuinely indifferent to the clerk's sly leer, his callous, unprofessional remark—"Will madam be wanting these wrapped?"—handling him with that same brash refinement with which she'd almost undone the surgeon, still controlled, still prim even after his next remark, telling him, "If I were as ballsy as you seem to think I am, I wouldn't really need this shit, would I?" Used once and abandoned, leaving it home, perhaps in that same closet with the fiancé's porcelain presents (because shame, though she felt no shame, would be an arrangement too and lead to other arrangements—doing away with the "evidence," disguising it, dismantling it, burying it a piece at a time in the rubbish so even the dustman wouldn't recognize it). Her reasons this time having nothing to do with unrelieved ecstasy, the propriety of a bounded pleasure, or even the slight uneasiness she felt about the possibility of becoming wet enough and thrusting it deep enough actually to electrocute herself. No. It was that little arrangement of the manufacturer, that deference to fantasy. It was the lifelike skin. She needed relief, not fantasy. (She thought of nothing when she masturbated, nothing, her attention only on the mechanics of the thing or, in a tight spot like this one now, of strategies, planning ahead, *arrangements*.) Because, finally, she was high-strung and, like anyone who drills deportment like intaglio into her character, was subject to nerves, spells, jitters, all the gooseflesh of the hair, all the alarmist knee-knock of scene, flap and disorder. Valium only made her sleepy. Music she disapproved of. Reading took too long to get into and, in any event, was impractical on the wards. Needlepoint, cooking, and the crafts had their own built-in liabilities. Only orgasm calmed her, lined up the iron filings—this is how she thought of it, as tiny, piercing shrapnel—of her scattered spirit like a powerful magnet, restored her, and, wonderfully, could hold her for hours. So flexible Mary Cottle found herself climbing the walls who, in emergency, could bring herself off in under two minutes. (Because it wasn't fulfillment she needed any more than fantasy. Duration meant nothing to her, multiple orgasms didn't, and were incapable of extending her self-induced relief by as much as five minutes. This by empirical evidence. She'd needed to know. She'd experimented. Withdrawal had been an experiment, the occasional, deliberately willed fantasy, and other clever white noises of deflection and deferral. The steel balls were an experiment, the vibrator was.)

The monorail made its steady slot-car yardage. There'd been a balls-up. The Cottle woman had vanished, and now Colin Bible was bringing the boys back to the hotel by himself. After the rapid melt, in its way quite as astonishing as the freak snowstorm (and practically no trace of moisture left, as burned off as fog, as over and done as morning dew), there'd been a palpable rise in all their spirits. Even Moorhead, rubbing his hands (and thinking of Jews, anxious to be out among them), had seemed overcome by a pumped and racing enthusiasm that Colin (who'd nursed for the man, who'd followed his orders, who'd attended his low-keyed talks about the special needs of dying tykes—Moorhead's own odd and discrepant term—and who felt without particularly liking him a rapport that was almost a kind of affection that people of different castes in related fields often have for each other) had never seen. The doctor had practically burst into lecture.

"We're foreigners in a foreign land here, and it's only proper we begin by paying our respects to our hosts. That's what all those tourists are about tramping up and down Whitehall, you know. Taking each other's photographs with Parliament in the background and nosing out Number Ten. This isn't a seat of government, of course, but I've been studying the guides and I should say we ought to begin on Main Street, U.S.A."

Which the children had loved, which they all had. Falling in at once with the cobbled ambiance of the place, its pretty High Street shops and brisk Victorian roofs, touched by the gold-lettered nimbuses of the names in the second-story windows, by the horse-drawn trams and open double-deck buses, trim as sunlight, by the gaslights and the bandbox atmospherics of its boater feel, its emporiums and ice-cream parlors and all the sweet, from-scratch, holiday aromatics of its candy treasuries. They were overwhelmed by nostalgia, even the youngest, by the vague and unspoken consanguine textures of its British-seaside-resort equivalencies. They moved briskly, swept along by that boater feel and bunting mode, almost sensing wind at their backs, almost smelling taffy, almost sniffing salt. This could be Blackpool, some thought. This could be Brighton, thought others.

They'd enjoyed, too, the Hall of Presidents, sitting politely through the brief historical film that preceded the main show, even Mudd-Gaddis's aged cynicism in abeyance, even Benny Maxine's cultivated scorn suspended. "Shh," said Nedra. "Hush." Though she needn't have bothered. No one was making very much noise. For one thing, they were too comfortable, sitting back in the deep, soft seats, breathing the air conditioning like oxygen, all of them, the sick and the well, in that perfectly balanced state of absorption and anticipation, the easy doldrums that surround an entertainment and seem to fill time and make even the preparations and directions, soft warnings, and signals between the ushers and guides an organic part of the proceedings, as pleasant to watch, as interesting to overhear, as anything that follows, other people's work an extension of the performance.

Yet none was prepared when the patriotic film ended and the curtains rose on the automatons, the curiously detailed machines that were at once as stiff and fidgety as people caught in some fret of life, the shuffling and bitten-back coughs of a group photograph, say, a public ceremony.

"They're these androids," Nedra Carp said in a whisper. "They're not real."

"Actors," Tony Word said.

"They're actors," Noah Cloth conceded, "but like that frog actor you see on the telly they got over in France who plays like he's a machine."

"But there must be forty of them up there," Lydia Conscience said.

"Sure," Benny Maxine said, "it's a chorus line."

"They're robots. I think so," Janet Order said.

"They're these special computers," Rena Morgan said.

"They're real," Charles Mudd-Gaddis said with all the authority of his years.

"They're real? They're *real*?" Benny challenged. "Don't you read the papers, don't you keep up? That one's Ronald Reagan. There's Nixon, there's Carter. You think there's this band of statesmen, this troupe of artiste presidents engaged in theatrical entertainments?"

"They're real," Mudd-Gaddis repeated.

"Sure, Grandpa," Benny said, "they went all out."

And when Lincoln began speaking, Colin Bible could only feel shame for his friend back in England, for the pale dead figures in the pale dead waxworks, for all the pale unresurrected heroes and villains here mocked.

Remarkable anatomical detail, thought Mr. Moorhead. But how could anyone ever have thought that Roosevelt was Jewish, I wonder?

Let them wonder, thought Eddy Bale.

"They're *not* real," Colin Bible said, choking back his sob, as taken with the fret of life as any of the machinery on the stage. And moved, terribly moved. He never told me anything about this, Colin thought. He never told me because he loves me. The nit wanted me to be proud of him. And there, in the Hall of Presidents, in the solemn silence that had replaced the quiet debate that had buzzed throughout the auditorium, Colin *was*. Proud of being loved like that. He'd say nothing to Colin. He wouldn't mention the matter. And if *Colin* brought it up he'd make a joke. "What, *them?*" he'd say. "Circuits and circuitry. They were put together by electricians. They were turned out by Japanese," he would reassure him.

And even Eddy Bale, breathing easy because they'd come through the first morning and a piece of the first afternoon. They were doing it properly. Even lunch had been easy, a piece, thought Bale cheerfully, of cake. Moorhead had found a sort of juice bar, and the children had snacked on the juices of fresh fruits and vegetables. Two or three had had yogurt. So Bale, whatever it was that made him reluctant and kept him indoors, the old tourist misgivings that almost ruined his and Ginny's honeymoon on the Costa Brava and made him sit upright in cabs, his greenhorn temerity stilled, his sucker-oriented agoraphobia, actually—though Mr. Moorhead by simple dint of status outranked him, Eddy was still the leader of this expedition—made a decision. They would split up. It made more sense. More bang for the buck, as the Americans put it. (As Bale did. Putting "as the Americans put it" before even "more bang for the buck," drawing them in not with the slang so much as the Britishism, drawing them in, consolidating and federating them, reminding them in this southerly latitude on this thick spit of land if not who they were then at least where they were from.)

So Bale delegates Mary and Colin to lead Charles, Tony, Noah, and Ben to the Haunted Mansion. Which, it turns out, is not all that much unlike one of the lesser stately homes of England, more particularly Mr. Moorhead's. It is, surprisingly, the wizened little in-and-out memory-damaged Charles Mudd-Gaddis who points this out to the rest of them.

"It's the very place," Benny Maxine said.

"Well, not the *very* place," Colin Bible said.

"Awfully *like*," said Noah Cloth and out of habit held up a fingernail to bite which had been amputated along with the phantom finger it had grown from seven months before.

"It's sort of eighteenth-century," Mary Cottle said, "but it's Dutch."

"Mister Moorhead is Dutch," Tony Word said.

"Mister Moorhead is? How would you know something like that?" Colin asked.

"Well, he told me," Tony Word said. "That one time we went there."

"They were testing us," Benny Maxine said. "To see if we were compatible."

"Compatible?" Noah Cloth said.

"If we could get along," Benny said. "Be good companions."

"And he showed me these wooden shoes. That he said were his great-grandad's."

"We're compatible," Mudd-Gaddis cackled.

"Only I was afraid to touch them," said Tony Word.

"We're compatible," said Mudd-Gaddis, who was enjoying a respite, a period of lucidity.

"There could have been splinters."

"We're compatible. We're children who die," said Mudd-Gaddis in his hoarse, old-man's wheeze.

When Noah begins to cry, when Tony does. And Charles Mudd-Gaddis, his lucidity shining, his head clear as crystal, seeing the bright, sharp angles on causes, effects; restored, it could be, to his true, rightful age, seeing *every*thing, even that what he feels now, at this minute, the perfectly furnished ripeness of his eight seasoned years, might only be a trick; his sluiced and dancing chemicals misfiring, some neurological overload, some snapped and brittle synapse, his remission only some long-shot bit of coincident, collusive senescence, quite suddenly rips off his wig and hurls it to the ground. *"Yellow,"* he snarls. "I had brown hair. My hair was *brown!"* And begins to stamp on it.

Frightened Maxine reaching out to calm him, restore him, unaware of course that he is already restored, that his compatible, furious friend, kicking at the ripped yellow hair, tromping it, wiping his shoes on it as though it were a mat, stumbling on it in his aged, broken gait, is beyond reassurance.

"This won't do, old chap," Benny says, taking his arm. "No, this won't do at all. Come on, old boy. Come on, old fellow. This really won't do. Tell him, Miss Cottle," Benny says, imploring the woman, tears flowing now from his own eyes. "Please, Miss Cottle, can't you do something?"

Whose right hand covers her mouth in shock, in horror, whose left already clutches her crotch, palming a handful of fabric there, Colin Bible sees, as if she's had an accident.

They were quickly surrounded by cast members. (Mary Cottle, despising scenes as much as arrangements, thinking: They'd have come anyway. Having our number. They'd have come anyway. Something telltale about us even in repose. They'd have come anyway.)

The one in the black mourner's band—it's the Haunted Mansion—kindly offers to take them to the front of the line. While a handsome, well-built young man retrieves Mudd-Gaddis's wig and, brushing it off, hands it to Colin, who, Mary Cottle observes, seems touched by the gesture. A girl affectionately pats Charles's bald little head and, lifting him up, bypasses the people standing in line and carries him on her shoulders to a side door while the others follow, hustled along by the remaining cast members, openly winking, not at each other but at the children, at the two adults, flashing secret agreement, doling these out somehow—the winks—managing the delicate choreography of their high-sign arrangements so that no one is winked at twice by the same person or is even observed to have winked. Except that Mary Cottle sees the young man who had handed Colin Charles's hairpiece wink at Colin and Colin return it, giving as good as he got, better. She sees the kid flush. I'm admired, Colin thinks guiltily. In a country where AIDS is rampant.

Inside, they stand, could be, along the building's stitching,

shabby as a kitchen in a posh restaurant, as anything backstage
or where workers gather to punch out by time clocks. They can
hear a babble of recordings, just make out the winding, canted,
interlocking paths, vaguely like baggage carrousels in airports,
of other tour groups, the black, open trains that carry them.
They can see periodic flashes of special effects like a kind of
heat lightning, like phosphorent bursts of insect. Afterimage
burns along their retinas like wick: the laser bombardments, the
fireball theatrics of warfare, all the burnt-out guttering torches
and candles and tapers of haunted radiance.

The fellow in the armband signals a girl standing by a control board, who presses a button that halts the tour. She takes
a microphone down from the wall. "We have to stop now to take
on some 'late' "—she pauses, lowers a voice charged with joke
menace—"visitors." "Visitors" is pronounced like a question.

The machinery grinds down—it's as if some solemn, tender
armistice is taking place—and Colin, Mary, and the boys are
helped in the dark into an empty gondola, are settled into seats
that have some sort of built-in stereo arrangement. They begin
their tour. Which is rather enhanced than otherwise—something has been done to the air in here, a tampered humidity
like the wet, faint chill of a catacomb—by their having been
plucked from the bright sunlight into the damp darkness.

Their faces move against cobwebs, break them like phantom finishers in a phantom race. The same raven seems to appear over and over. Resisting death, a suit of armor, its old fierce
metals sweating, its hinges groaning, transcends rust, swells into
life. The eyes of night creatures blink on the wallpaper. A teapot pours a poisoned tea. Specters, translucent as the tea, move
in the air like laundry. A living woman is entombed in a crystal
ball. All about them they can hear the wails of the dead, insistent and hopeless as the demands of beggars. It's this note, the
noise of desperate petition, that causes the children more trouble than the conventional props of death: the bats, the coffins
set out like furniture. They're still upset. Mary Cottle senses it;
Colin Bible, still seeing the afterimage of the twenty-year-old boy
who'd winked at him, who'd touched his hand a fraction of a

section longer than he was required to when he'd handed him Charles's wig, does.

"They're trying to say something," Noah Cloth whispers to his companion, Tony Word. "What is it, you think, they're trying to say?"

"Dunno. It's like the lowing of cattle." Both boys shudder.

Only Charles Mudd-Gaddis's trapped, soft screams go almost unheard among these professional spookhouse shrieks and cries of actors, the funhouse arias of the dead. If the others are upset, Mudd-Gaddis is terrified; if they hear him at all they mistake the sound for the low-priority complaint of the infant dead. He has been whimpering like this since the strong tall girl had raised him to her shoulders and carried him into the mansion, and who sits beside him now, holding his hand, mindlessly squeezing his arthritic joints, amiably mashing them while she makes her own soft noises at him, noises which he not only cannot hear but which he will not listen to.

Because, in darkness, his ancient eyes are almost blind; and outdoors was riding—his back to them, too—so high up on the big girl's shoulders he dared not look down, did not pick up, and would not have accepted if he had, the hale fellow, sema-phore reassurances of the cast members. Indeed, he is barely aware that the girl who sits beside him now is the same young woman who had swooped down on him in his rage and lifted him from the ground he had been stamping on and kicking at only seconds before, raised him, removed him from earth, torn him off that lying, hideous yellow wig he had been trying to muddy back to the brown he remembered. He is not in remis-sion now, not enjoying a lucid moment, is uncertain, for that matter, where he is, and has the sense only that he's somewhere underground, riding along a narrow-gauge track in a coal mine, perhaps, or being pulled on a sled, though he's not cold, through the six-months' midnight of the Arctic Circle. He is not in re-mission, does not enjoy the crystal clarifics of only twenty min-utes before—though he remembers all that clearly enough, in perfect detail, in fact, not a single thing slipped or blurred, not one, even the at once humiliating and infuriating business of the wig as clear to him as if it happened years ago—and recalls the day he was seven years old. His whimpers a sort of nostalgia, his memory of the day so sharp and poignant the whimper becomes a snuffling, the snuffling a sob, the sob a cry.

"Oh, my lost youth!" he cries.

"Hush, cutie," the girl beside him says, "the tour's almost done. Another two minutes."

Charles Mudd-Gaddis begins to scream. Colin, the children, Mary, are frightened. He screams. He screams and screams.

"Another two minutes," the big girl says. "Two minutes. I promise."

He screams.

"*Stat!*" shouts the girl to cast members behind the scenes. Charles knows the word. Mary, Colin, all the children do. It is the code word for emergencies in hospitals. Mary, Colin, and the kids think something has happened to Charles. "*Stat! Stat!*" the girl shouts. The gondola stops abruptly.

"Hey!" a tourist jokes. "Whiplash!"

Cast members rush up with flashlights.

"What is it?"

"What's happened?"

"I think he's scared of the dark," the girl says.

Colin starts to climb over the seats to get to Charles.

"Please don't do that, sir. Please sit down. Arlene's got the boy."

"He's—"

"I'm going to have to ask you to sit down, sir. For your own safety. The little boy will be fine. We're going to evacuate him."

"He moves like he's a thousand," Benny Maxine says. "He'll fall and break his hip in the dark."

"There's an ample catwalk. He'll be all right."

All have scrambled out of the car; the children are led away by solicitous cast members. It's as if they're being guided through tear gas. Then lights come on through the Haunted Mansion like the stark auxiliary lights in theaters and hospitals, like emergency lights in subway cars. Props fade, patterns disappear from the bare canvas walls, the specters are snuffed out, the crystal ball is empty, the bats' eyes on the wallpaper are tiny light bulbs, the puppet teapot spills a ribbon of twisted, colored cellophane, the coffins and old chests seem only a reliable wood, the ravens some hinged taxidermy, the illusionary space they have been traveling through a sort of warehouse. Visitors to the mansion groan.

"Just look at this place," Noah Cloth grumbles. "I bet there's no such thing as ghosts."

"I guess not," Tony Word agrees dispiritedly.

"Dying blokes like us ain't got a snowball's chance in Hell," Benny Maxine says, moving along the pavement beside the curving tracks, the baffled architecture, up the trace inclines and down the indifferent slopes which, in the dark, had seemed so formidable.

"There's probably no such place as Hell," Noah says.

"No," says Tony Word.

"No," says Benny Maxine, "it's just an expression."

"Like Heaven."

"Let's don't tell the girls," Benny says.

And the three boys dissolve in tears.

Charles Mudd-Gaddis was inconsolable.

So was Mary Cottle, who, practically bleeding from the nerves by this time, her mile-high tensions actually giving her a sort of pain, managed to shake Colin, who received the four children at the same door through which they'd been admitted, accepting them like prisoners formally surrendered by the good-looking attendant who'd dusted off the boy's blond wig and handed it to the male nurse ("Still got the little fellow's yellow hat, Dad?" "Oh, I'm not their dad." "No?" "I'm just the nurse who travels with them." "Is that so?" "I'm nobody's dad." "Not the daddy type?" "Never have been, never will be." "Where you staying?" "At the Contemporary." "Swell health club at the Contemporary. You ought to check it out." "Maybe I will"), and extricated herself from the crowd on the ramp at the Transportation and Ticket Center, using it as a shield and positioning herself behind a lone gate on the platform, and now sits by herself in the dark, empty car on the same monorail on which Colin Bible and the four boys ride, her skirt hiked above her knees, her hand down in her panties and two fingers on her dry clit, pulling the till-now dependable flesh, ringing it like a bell, but distracted, her mind not quite blank this time (which, frankly, her body abandoned to a merely mechanical friction had always been an ally in this business) but filled with a whole catalogue of vagrant images (rather, she thinks, like the Haunted Mansion itself), from the could-be-trouble exchange between Colin and the tall, good-looking attendant to, for example, the skirt, the dresses she's packed, how proud she is of what can only have been a keen sense of her own character, a trained forethought, anticipating, she supposed, that there would be scenes, that there'd have to be, and so eschewing pants suits (though she had known that these, in all likelihood, would be the standard mode of dress, as indeed, they quite turned out to be) for the skirts and dresses which would be more convenient in emergency. So on the one hand—even the idiom distracts her, takes her still further from that state of mind, not desire, not lust, but merely the bleeding nerves, the mile-high tensions, the sort of pain—pleased, but on the other bothered, the absence of soap and water, for another example, being a damned nuisance just now, most inconvenient, for if she brings herself off or, for that matter, even if she doesn't, it won't do to touch any of the children without first washing her hands, so she'll have to continue to hide from them, duck into the Ladies', though none of this constitutes even a fraction of her real nervousness, for if she *is* able to bring herself off, why, she'll be cool as a cucumber, *able* to cope, but she's not so sure now she will. For one thing she hadn't paid close enough attention on the way out, can't recall how long it takes to get to the hotel, whether there's a stop. There is, at the Polynesian Village Resort Hotel, and though more people get off the monorail there than on, and absolutely no one comes into her car, the doors automatically open and Mary is forced to do some very fancy cape work with the skirt—thank God she's wearing one, otherwise she'd have had to stand, she'd never be able to get the pants up over her hips in time without becoming something of another attraction at Disney World, at least for the people passing by on the station platform—and now she's quite sure it's clear sailing back to their hotel and she might just be able to make it if only the recorded voices on the car's loudspeaker that keeps nattering on about Disney and the "imagineers" who built this place would just shut up for a minute, and if only she could get that damned vision of Colin Bible out of her head. The silly sod. The poof nurse *would* have to go making googoo eyes at the kid from the Haunted Mansion. Blast people who make scenes, she thinks.

As the train pulls into the big bright interior of the Contemporary Resort Hotel. And the doors open. And Mary Cottle, coming up empty, hastily lowers her skirt over her bare thighs and her awry panties and leaves the monorail.

Pretending to be searching for something she's dropped, she crouches behind the wide-flung doors and waits until Colin and the kids clear the platform, are out of sight.

Then she goes down to the desk and rents that room.

3

I dunno," Colin Bible said. "I dunno what happened. Maybe he's bent."

"He's a little kid. He was spooked. He was afraid of the ghosts," Bale said.

"It was before we ever got inside. It was before he ever even seen any ghosts. We was still in the queue."

"You waited in the queue?"

"They don't want special treatment, Mister Bale."

"Eddy," Eddy said.

"Jeez, 'Eddy's' hard, Mister Bale. No disrespect, but 'Eddy's' hard for me. You've got to remember that Liam was my patient."

"You don't think I remember that?"

"I've hurt your feelings."

"Nonsense."

"I've hurt your feelings. It was all right to call Liam by his first name. He was my patient but he was a kid. It's just not on to go all intimate with a patient's family. You can ask Mister Moorhead regarding the ethicals of all this."

"Mary Cottle calls me Eddy."

"If Liam had lived it'd be a different story."

"Oh? Yes?"

"If Liam had lived, you, me, and your missus could have gone off to the boozer, bought pints all around, tossed darts into the cork, and toasted one another's health. It'd've been, 'Here's to your health, Colin.' And turn and turn about I'd have picked up my mug and replied, 'And 'ere's to your own, Eddy!' And Liam's, of course. And Ginny's—Mrs. Bale as was. If Liam had lived."

"We could have been mates? If Liam had lived?"

"We'd have come through something important, don't you see."

"And of course, if Liam had lived, you'd have had no *reason* to keep your distance."

"I don't think of it as a question of distance, Mister Bale."

"Don't you? You know, Colin, I was rather surprised you let me recruit you on this enterprise. I should have thought you could have made more money if you'd stayed on in England."

"I'm paid well enough. Higher than regular."

"Still," Eddy said.

"What, didn't you know that?"

"Higher than higher than regular," Eddy said.

"Anyways, I wouldn't want you to think I'm here for the money. These kids, these kids are condemned and convicted. They've been found guilty. Mister Bale. They've been put on the index. There's a price on their heads. I'm a nurse. It's my professional duty. Still, if my friend hadn't given his blessing I shouldn't have come."

"Yes," Eddy said, "it's your 'friend' we've been talking about."

Which was when Eddy thought the now flushed, embarrassed, and unforgiven man seemed to lose his temper. Colin glared at him and Bale thought, Won't call me Eddy but'd strangle me easily enough. Though when he spoke, Colin's voice was meek, the put-upon tones of patient, humbled injury muffling it like carpet, heavy drapes. "I'm not aware," he said, "that we've ever discussed my friend, Mister Bale."

"Liam brought him up," Bale said.

"Liam? Liam did?"

"Oh, please," Eddy said, "I saw you hugging at Heathrow. I know all about it. How you promised my son he'd go into the waxworks when he died."

"I was cheering him up."

"Liam didn't believe you were cheering him up. Liam thought you meant every word. He believed it on his deathbed."

"He didn't seem a religious boy, our Liam. I was sounding him out like, Mister Bale. He seemed to take to the notion, so I encouraged him to believe I could arrange it."

"What? *To think he could be turned into some great wickless candle?*"

"*Candle? Candle?* We're talking about art, Mister Bale. That's art what my friend does."

"Oh, your *friend* again! That gave you his blessing. That told you, 'Certainly, Colin. Go for it, darling. Take the Brownie along, why don't you? Maybe we can get all of them in the picture.' "

"We *could!*" Colin snapped. "We never discussed it but we *could!* No one stands in the way of art. Oh, I don't say what you're doing isn't well meant, even heroic in some proper charlie sort of way, but if it's all to end up in the boneyard what difference does it make?"

"It calls attention."

"And wax doesn't? Wax *doesn't* call attention?"

"That's ridiculous."

"Why'd you hire me? Why'd you hire me then, you think I'm so bloody ridiculous?"

"Because mugs have no control," Bale said calmly. "Because sooner or later they get in over their heads. They become outrageous."

"Outrageous?"

"Outrageous. Oh, *yes*. Because sooner or later they're thinking Great Train Robbery. They're dreaming about tunneling under Lloyd's. They have Old Lady of Threadneedle Street schemes and hold opinions about Richard III, the babes in the Tower."

"You've been to the Madame's then?"

"They're *think*ing Madame Tussaud's! Oh, yes, outrageous. Some dreadful crèche of the infant dead. Because I thought you might pull something like this, that's why. That if you had enough rope . . . You never gave a thought to bad taste, did you? Or turned your mind to public opinion, invasion of privacy, the terrible consequences of going too far?"

"Not a bit of it," Colin Bible said. "Just as you never thought about what it means to be dead."

"What? What does it mean, Colin?"

"It means you've no longer any say in the matter," Colin Bible said. "According to my friend, who happens to be an expert in this particular area, it means public domain, Mister Bale."

"Eddy," Eddy Bale said.

Who was astonished but not displeased to be speaking as he'd meant to speak back in England, warning them away from their private fiddles, his quiet caper heart at last unburdened. Sorry only that it had to be Colin Bible, whom he liked and trusted more than the others, who took the brunt of his wild charges. Seeing he had set a fire under the man.

Then I *am* mad, he thought sadly.

Colin certainly was. Furious. All he'd meant was to take Bale aside and cite the woman's dereliction. Getting separated like that was unforgivable. He wanted it on the record. Now he couldn't remember whether they'd even spoken of it. And he was fond of Eddy. How had they gotten into such a foofaraw? However, they were in it. The man had implied just awful things about his friend. Poor Colin, Colin thought. And not without a blast of the same shame, stricken, embarrassed for his fuddy-duddy technology, he'd felt earlier that day in the Hall of Presidents when Lincoln had begun to speak. And felt again, only this time with the full force of an idea which earlier had been only the vaguest of notions and was to its implications and consequences what loose change in one's pocket might be to an idea of money, say. Now it was almost fully formed, beginning to take shape even as he'd tried to deflect Bale's wild charges, and still firming up, though what he was going to do already clear enough for him to begin to take the first dreadful steps.

Because she shared a room with them, Nedra Carp was partial to Lydia Conscience and Rena Morgan. If this was unfair to the rest of the children, if it excluded the boys or put a distance between Janet Order and herself, why, then, it couldn't be helped. It would have been a defiance of her nanny heart otherwise. A nanny—she could not, in conscience, endorse the justice of this, only vouch for it; it seemed an instinct, almost a condition, some less-than-neutral magnetism of the blood that drew her loyalties and turned her into some patriot of the propinquitous that carried with it all the convenient obligations of hired-hand love—she felt herself constitutionally unable (and disinclined, too) not so much of assuming responsibility—she was responsible by nature and would probably have put herself at risk without a second thought, throwing herself into burning buildings and heavy seas, though she feared fire above all else and was not a strong swimmer, if a young life were at stake—for the welfare of children not in her charge, as unable to work up any affection that had not actually been bought and paid for. It was a flaw in her character. She understood and even chided herself for this. She even tried to be better but knew she was incapable of an unauthorized love. What bothered her even more were her aversions, her view of other children, even these children—the boys, Janet Order—as threats and rivals, something "other" in them that put her off and made her uneasy, queasy, squeamish: rather, she thought, like some hungry, willful orthodox offered proscribed food. Objectively, she disapproved of this aspect of her character. She was nothing if not objective, professional objectivity being her strong suit, her stock in trade, and was prepared not only to do the fair thing but to perceive it, which was not always easy (*turns,* for example; not *whose* turn, necessarily, which was usually only a matter of simple reckoning, but the *quality* of a turn, too, its special boons or built-in deficiencies: if the wind was down and refused the kite, if the one pushing the swing was a slacker, if a child didn't fully understand the terms of a game; or *trades:* whether fraud was intended, whether a toy was damaged by abuse, accident, or through some basic defect in its construction; settling all manner of arguments and disputes right down to the thorny question of taste itself: what to do, for instance, if only yellow balloons remained to be distributed; who should get the caramel, who must take the toffee) and was, because she dealt with children who didn't have her fine perceptions and sensibilities and were without skill in weighing evidence or making her surgical distinctions, who had, in fact, nothing but their own supercharged egos to judge by and go on, and whose blind, barbaric self-interest lived in them like a weight in dice and was sometimes, even for Nedra, impossible, a judgment call. And not just her aversion to children who did not come under her immediate purview. Mary Cottle seemed a nice enough young woman— though Nedra could not have been more than four or five years older than Mary and quite possibly may even have been the same age, it was Nedra, in her capacity as nanny, who willingly took it upon herself to assume the seniority—yet to Nedra, Mary was just one more "other." Though she could hardly have meant "just" since she did not suffer others all that lightly. The fact was that Mary Cottle's presence in the room was nothing less than an affront. Nedra couldn't help it and even felt bad about her squeamish antipathies and unreasonable inimicals, but facts were facts. She was put off by the sight of the woman's toothbrush in the bathroom they shared, by the razor she used to shave her legs, the stench of her cigarettes, the hair in her comb, her nightgown on the hook on the back of the bathroom door, the sight of her soiled, unmade bed, the sound of her breathing when she'd fallen asleep. And if it was true what the children were saying, that Miss Cottle had become separated from Colin Bible and the youngsters on the way back to the hotel . . . ? Dereliction of duty made Nedra's skin crawl.

She knew her impatience was hardly the Mary Poppins ideal, but it did not do to betray one's character. She admitted when she was wrong. She was wrong in this instance. She admitted when she was wrong but she was all-forgiving. All right, she *did* play favorites, but she could have played God, come, were it required of her, to terrible determinations—who should live, who should die—and come to them, moreover, according to the same sound principles that permitted her to decide who should get the caramel, who must take the toffee.

She knew how she must appear to them, of course. People so loved their stereotypes. Living for others the sublimate life. They would put her down as a dried-up old maid. Quiet as a mouse and hung up in the love department on her male employers or, less flattering and more disgusting, her prepubescent charges. Playing with them, she suspected others suspected, in the tub, soaping and tickling their little thingummies till they stood up in the bathwater like periscopes. So she knew how she must appear to them. With a dried-up old pussy. More dust collector than sex organ. Nedra Carp giggled. The divine Mary Poppins had had her Bert, after all. Nedra was no libertine. Her juices happened not to flow in that direction, but she was no old maid. She'd had her ashes hauled, chim chim-i-ney, chim chim-i-ney, chim chim cheroo. It just wasn't that important, is all.

The nanny business was important, the nanny business was. And maybe, she thought, maybe you had to go around in a sort of disguise. Maybe other people's stereotypes protected you, kept you hidden, quiet, wrapped up in cotton wool and otherwise engaged.

Because all her life she'd never forgiven them for abandoning her, all her life picked at her resentment, worried her *loco parentis* history, nursed her injured-Gretel misgivings.

And all because of the formative years, Nedra thought bitterly. The formative years. That small, not even full handful of kiddie time when anything that was not already stuffed into the genes—and for Nedra, as for Mary, between nature and nurture it was no contest—must be packed into the child like a kind of tuck pointing. If, as the poet said, the child was father to the man, the stepmothers, governesses, step-relations, and nannies were worth all the rest of relation. Particularly the nannies. (Because children that small would not have heard about stereotypes yet, would, before memory kicked in, have taken their imprinting from the available, anyone near at hand, anyone bigger or older or stronger than oneself, *anyone*: a close distant cousin would do; the upstairs maid; the lad from the greengrocer's.) But particularly the nannies. Who drew, she recalled, the bath, and adjusted the temperature of the water, who came with towels of great thickness, the cozy naps and piles of love, who managed one's meat and, later, held one's small, still imperfect hands to the cutlery and guided one's movements over the joint, who gave lessons in spreading jam and buttering toast, who offered the hankie as if it were a rose, who rinsed the cut and kissed the bruise, who showed the picture books, all the abecedarian "A is for Apple, B is for Bird" lap tutorials, and read the storybooks in the safe and serious weather of the quilt or blanket, who did first for the body the stations of kindness and later, like choirmasters prompting hymn, mouthed the close and intimate terms of prayer (kindness here, too: some infant *noblesse oblige*, and even the names of rivals offered to God, of detractors and enemies, the by-now thinned and thinning not-even consanguineous and imperfectly understood merely legal relation). And, still later yet, ministered to the soul itself, explaining, explaining away, the sudden breaches of faith and inexplicable hostilities of once close distant cousins. Taking actual instruction from them, a sort of convert, a sort of catechumen—no Catholic, she attended Mass as often as possible; it wasn't the ceremony or the gorgeous trappings that attracted her, it was the absolute conviction and authority—it was to her nannies she turned whenever she felt confused, had run out of lessons she could apply to a new situation—Nedra was in command of many solutions and hundreds of explanations but few principles—seeking, though she didn't know this, hadn't learned it yet, neither explanations nor principles but only the old cocoa comforts. It was to a nanny she'd turned (though she'd outgrown them, no longer had one, was with the governesses now and had, since her own had left and this was a new girl, even lost the right to call her Nanny, though she did anyway, not realizing that in doing so—it was a different nanny who'd provided this explanation too, though to Nedra it would forever after seem a principle—she had unwittingly placed herself in a kind of authority over the girl, compromised the title, that only a present or former charge, employer, or fellow employee of the household retained that particular privilege—she said "privilege"—) to explain her period, a nanny who'd explained, explained away, her half brother's cold warning that they could no longer enjoy, once the twins were born and he had a new half sister and half brother of his own, their special relationship. ("He's sucking up to them, miss.") The nannies whom she relied on for comfort and depended upon for what she still thought of as love. Except that they moved on too, were, in that department at least, as unreliable and transient as real mothers and fathers. And was shocked to discover that they were actually paid, were in it for money, were not merely some distant sort of relation themselves, like a kind of Cinderella, say, two or three times removed. (And, although she'd be the first to admit—admit to herself since it was no one else's business and could only hurt others if it ever got out—that hers was hired-hand love too, Nedra Carp wasn't in it for the money. For one, she had money.)

Who now waited for others to turn to her. Assuming, on those rare occasions when they did, the very same poses and attitudes her own nannies had assumed. Vaguely abstracted, detached, as if she wore imaginary shawls about her shoulders and had been come upon knitting, an aura of an old-aunty love clinging to her like some musty, foolish dignity.

Rena Morgan looked up from the television set, turned low so as not to disturb Lydia Conscience's sleep.

"Was Prince Andrew brave?" she asked.

"Hmm?"

"Prince Andrew. Was he brave?"

"Oh, very brave, dear."

"Even when he was small?"

"A little hero."

"So you weren't surprised when he went off to fight the Argies?"

"I expected it."

"You did?"

"I was only surprised it took him so long."

"Bravery is important, isn't it, Nanny?"

"Quite important, dear. Valor is the *sine qua non* of gentlemen."

"Of ladies too. Anyway, I should have thought so."

"Bravery in men, patience in ladies."

"Do you think so?"

"Women, well-brought-up women, don't have the upper-body strength for true bravery."

"When push comes to shove, do you mean?"

"What a clever way to put it! What a very bright little girl you are!"

"Thank you, Nanny, but there are many things I don't understand."

"If something's troubling you, Rena dear, perhaps I can be of some help. Has that Janet Order been bothering you?"

"Janet Order?"

"She seems quite cheeky to me, and, though I shouldn't be the one to say it, her blue color does put one off so. I noticed that you just picked at your food today. Your four basic food groups are extremely important, you know. If it's Janet who's putting you off your feed, I think I can arrange with Mister Moorhead and Mister Bale for you and Lydia to take your meals separately."

"I like Janet."

"What a *charitable* girl as well!"

"As a matter of fact, Nanny, it's something you said just now."

"What? Something *I* said? I don't know what it could have been then, dear, I'm sure."

"That bit about bravery in men, patience in ladies."

"Calm endurance, dear. Tolerant imperturbability. Forebearance, resignation, and submission."

"Janet isn't in the least submissive, and I shouldn't have thought to have called her resigned."

"Ah, but I was talking about *ladies.*"

"Yes. Bravery in men, patience in ladies."

"Just so."

"I think Janet Order is brave," Rena said. "If I'd her complexion I think I should have it whitewashed, hide it away as I do my handkerchiefs."

"Show consideration for the feelings of others, yes."

"For myself, rather. People stare. She takes no notice."

"Cheeky."

"Courage."

"If you say so, dear," Nedra Carp said, returning to her imaginary knitting.

"I wonder if I could go down to the game room," Rena said after a while.

"What, the *game* room? At this time of night? It's almost gone nine. That Miss Cottle's nowhere about. Lydia's sleeping, but what if she should wake up? Of course I *could* leave a note."

"No," Rena said, "she might not find it."

"Oh, don't fear on that score. Nanny would leave it somewhere she'd be certain to find it."

"She's in a new place. She could panic. There might be something she needs."

"Mister Moorhead's just 'cross the hall. Mister Bale and that nurse are the next room over."

"Do you suppose she'd think of all that in those first moments of terror?"

"And thoughtful too! I like that in my girls."

"Nanny, I'm not thoughtful or considerate either. Nor charitable nor even all that clever."

"*And* modest!"

"When I asked you that about Prince Andrew before, about

his being brave—well, you know that's a quality I very much admire."

"What very lovely values you have, dear," Nedra Carp said.

"It's a quality I very much aspire to, Nanny," the child said.

"That's *very* noble."

"That's why I want to go down to the game room by myself."

"By *yourself?* By *yourself?* But you're dying, dear. It's quite out of the question."

"It's *because* I'm dying that I have to be brave. I've this awful cystic fibrosis which the doctors can't seem to control, and I go about with all this linen folded up my sleeves. I haven't the courage to be seen blowing my nose, Nanny. I just thought if I went down to the game room by myself for an hour or so and *let* people stare—they know us here, you know, they see us traveling with our caretakers like this clan of the doomed, and after that scene in the restaurant this morning, and whatever it was that happened to the boys at the Haunted Mansion—healthy kids, kids my own age: well, I just thought they might think better of us, and of me—of me, I admit it—if they saw us one at a time once in a while. Please, Nanny. *Please.*"

"You'd play those arcade games?"

"Yes," Rena said.

"They're very stimulating. You could become overexcited."

"I'll just have to learn to control it."

"What if someone teases you? Children can be quite cruel. It could bring on an attack."

Rena opened her purse, showed Nedra a single white handkerchief. "This will have to serve then, won't it?"

"Well." Nedra considered. "This *is* a situation. For my part I think you're already very brave. Thoughtful, charitable, considerate, clever. Lovely values, just lovely. You're doing this as much for the others as you are for yourself. You are, aren't you, Rena? You're showing the flag, aren't you, dear?"

"Yes, Nanny," the child said, looking down.

"It isn't an easy decision. I have to parse this," Nedra Carp said. "You're dangerously ill with a condition that makes you subject to devastating attacks. You mean deliberately to put yourself in harm's way. Knowing full well that people recognize you, you mean to encourage one of your attacks by going to a place which would tax the resistance of even a normal child. Moreover, rather than provide yourself with your usual aids— I didn't see your inhalator when you opened your purse just now, did I?—you mean to go down to that game room with a single handkerchief, one or two less than a child might carry who merely suffers from a common cold. Is that about it?"

"Yes, Nanny."

"It's a dangerous game you're playing, dear, a dangerous game indeed."

"But that's just the point of it, Nanny."

"Oh, I understand the point of it, child."

"Yes, Nanny."

"But do *you* understand that Nanny is responsible for you? Do *you* understand that if anything . . . well, untoward should happen to you during the course of this . . . adventure, Nanny could, and quite properly, be brought up on charges, and that almost certainly it would mean the end of the dream holiday?"

"Yes, Nanny."

"Yet you're still willing to put your friends' pleasure and your nanny in jeopardy—and yourself, yourself too—just to prove some quite abstract point that no one is ever likely to understand? I do not make exception of your dear parents. Do you see the ramifications of all this, Rena?"

"Yes, Nanny."

"Cause all that trouble all for the sake of a vague principle?"

"Yes, Nanny."

"An hour is out of the question. If you're not back in the room within forty-five minutes I shall have hotel security bring you back," Nedra Carp said.

"Thank you, Nanny."

"Well, spit-spot, child! Spit-spot! The clock is ticking," Nedra Carp said, and Rena Morgan, her inhalator banging against the pocket in her skirt and the rolled handkerchiefs she kept like magician's silks along the sleeves of her dress absorbing her perspiration, ran off to meet Benny Maxine, who was already waiting for her outside Spirit World, the liquor store where by prearrangement they had agreed to meet at nine.

Colin Bible lurked—lurked was the word for it—in the health club of the Contemporary Resort Hotel. He loitered by the urinals, skulked near the stalls, slunk along the washstands, and insinuated himself at the electric hand-dry machines. He looked, he supposed, like a madman, like someone, all dignity drained, in throes, the rapturous fits of a not entirely undivided abandon, as if, by avoiding eye contact, he preserved some last-minute, merely technical remnant of sanity. He knew his type, he thought uneasily, had often enough recognized it in the Gents' at the great Piccadilly and Baker Street, Knightsbridge and Oxford Circus underground stations. He did not even lack the obligatory newspaper, the peculiar faraway cast—put on, assumed as a disguise—to his expression. Nor did he bother to make a show of busying himself, heartily pretending to shake free the last drops of urine from his dick or noisily opening and slamming the stall doors as if he were all preoccupied urge and dither. Neither had he rolled up his shirt sleeves, his hands and forearms thickly lathered as a surgeon's. Or stood by the electric hand-dry machines, waving off excess water with all the brio of a symphony conductor imposing a downbeat. He was not happy to hide, didn't enjoy his stealthy camouflage, took no pleasure from his furtive tiptoe masquerade. It was only that he didn't have the nerve to make an overture of his own—unless turning himself into something coy and clandestine was itself an overture—and didn't believe the guy would recognize him. He thought, that is, that he would have to be picked up all over again, winked at again, his hand brushed a second time. This was the reason he made himself so suspicious looking, why he kept himself under wraps in his best suit among the men in their gym shorts and jogging outfits, posing in it as if it were a raincoat, why he leaned like a flirt beside the stationary bicycle, why he prowled surreptitiously between the Nautilus machines and pussyfooted along the treadmill and gym's small track. It was the reason he snuck back and forth by the weight bench, why he snooped in the sauna and inferred himself past the rowing machine. It was because he didn't think he'd be recognized that he so ostentatiously lay in ambush—lost and shrouded, a burrowed lay-low, a smoke screen, anonymous, covert, sequestered, disguised and reticenced and secluded, an inference, a stowaway.

He didn't even hear him when he came in.

"Hi, toots," the fellow said, "been waiting long?"

If you tried to guess what annoyed Noah Cloth most about having to die, in all likelihood you'd have been wrong. His parents, trying to guess what went on in their little boy's head, trying to poke past his terminally ill child's view of things, suspected it was pain or the flat-out fear of death itself, sensibly reading the fierce denial of his condition as simple terror but, with it, some sense of ideal justice insulted, sullied, outraged, his short-changed, short-circuited life a smear on his values, some ultimate slur of the ought, an aspersion on the otherwise. They saw him, that is, as noble, reading his reluctance to acknowledge symptoms or admit to pain as the reaction of a gentleman to that which was grossly one-sided and indefensibly unfair. They prized this in him, and though by keeping his complaints to himself for as long as he could he probably stymied their own and the doctor's best efforts to help him extend his life, they cherished this aspect of their child's character and doubled up on their losses, grieving an ever-escalated, ever-escalating grief, although they determined that when the time came they would try to be, must try to be, as good as their son, his match, for *his* sake his match. They would not be the sort of parents who turned their home into a shrine, preserving his pathetic bits and relics, his clothes, his pictures, his toys and braces and canes. It was their pledge to him—what they whispered in his ear when he boarded the plane at Heathrow—that they'd try to survive him with style, with tact and honor and class and grace, assuring him too that he'd not been wrong, that his fate was a quirk, almost apologizing, almost begging his pardon if it looked otherwise (indicating to Noah the line of wheelchairs, the special boarding procedures the airline insisted upon), assuring him that most children grew up to be adults, that most adults had children of their own and, after a reasonably long and happy life, did not survive them. Seeing his need and trying to comfort him. "It's a blot, Noah," his father said. "It's a slip-up, son." Noah, looking up at them from the wheelchair the airline would not allow them to push, trying to grasp his father's words as he walked along beside the boy being rolled down the jetway. "Dad's right, Noah," his mum said. "What's happened to you is a crook go, but in the long run, in the long run . . ." "Things average out, she's trying to say," his father finished. "They do, Noah," his mum said, "so you mustn't think it's not a democratic business. Because it is, ain't it, Dad?" "Oh, aye," the father said, "turn and turn about. It really is. You're the exception that proves the rule."

In some ways they were right about their son: the pain, the fear, the outrage. But it was more complicated than that.

In a real way it came down to the fact that he would not live to make money.

He was almost unschooled (the woman at the hospice, who was good, not a psychiatrist or even a psychologist but a grand listener, a genuine death expert, interested in all the messages of death, would have been able to explain it even to unschooled Noah, would have been able to give back his reasons to him, not to reconcile him, never to reconcile him, but to sharpen his rage); even for an eleven-year-old—so much time in hospital, so much time blasted by radiation and smothered by chemotherapy, so much time sedated, so much confused by painkillers—he was unschooled. He didn't read right, could barely follow the plot when people read stories to him, and looked for diversion in newspapers and their colored Sunday supplements, in the advertisements in magazines and on television shows, in the fat illustrations of picture books. It was this which had set him to drawing in the first place. He was not a natural artist or even a very dedicated one. He traced his drawings or

copied them with a care that was literally painstaking, the
crayons and drawing pens squeezed against his wounded joints,
putting pressure on his decomposing wrist. Had he been more
mobile he would have taken snapshots of the toasters and estate cars he drew, of the houses and cameras and lounge furniture, of the stocked shelves in the supermarkets, of the gas
ranges, fridges, and central heating systems, of the coats, shirts,
dresses, ties, and television sets, of the stereos, flatirons, cosmetics jars, of the boxes of candy and bottles of gin, of the
computers and shoes, of the packets of cigarettes and tubes of
toothpaste and all the other consumer goods that so fascinated
him. Because what he could follow who could not follow a simple story line was the news on television, the bleak steady theme
of growing unemployment, redundancies, angry men laid off,
entire shipyards shut down, assembly lines, factories shut, services reduced and the people who supplied them sent home,
and feared first for his father's job, then for his father, because
he was mortal too—gravestones he drew, monuments, wreaths—
and then, because he was unschooled, couldn't read well, do his
maths, wasn't getting the technical training so important to the
current generation of workers and so, as the news reader told
him almost every evening, absolutely indispensable to his own.
Because where would he get money who couldn't read, do his
maths, had no skills? Because where would he get money for
the foodstuffs he traced, for the fridge and cabinets which stored
them, for the range on which they were prepared? Because
where would he get money for the luxuries, the big-ticket items
of consolation? So he drew them, copied them down from advertisements. By magic homeopathy to have that which he would
never live to earn. "So," the lady in the hospice—who really *was*
good—would have comforted, "it isn't really death you fear. It's
getting well." "No," unschooled Noah, the easing cosmetics of
morphine withheld during these times when they spoke, would
have answered, all the acuity of his stiff, unblurred pain on him
like solid facts lined up and marshaled as the packages and
canned goods on those stocked supermarket shelves he used to
draw. "Not anymore. I hurt too much. The stitches from my

first operations, that finger they cut off, my bones and my buttons, the stuff drying in my handkerchief. The light that falls across my sheet from the bed lamp, the shadows. All, all of it hurts me. I'm not afraid," he would have said, "I'm not. May I please have my morphine now please?"

But that would have been then. An aspect of the conditional. Alternative time. But now, in the here-and-now of Disney World, he is perfectly delighted with the shops. It is, for him, rather like being plunked down in the very center of those colored supplements in the Sunday paper. (Because he has been rarely to shops. Even his clothes—it would have been too much of an ordeal for him to undress in changing rooms—have been first brought home by one of his parents for him to try on. He has been to the gift shop in hospital, of course, and has often enough been visited by the cart volunteers—he supposed they were volunteers: nurses laid off, people in maintenance, the National Health having no money to pay people to push the cart; he supposed they were volunteers—have brought to his ward with its meager inventory. He could count on his remaining fingers the times he has ever actually bought anything and to this day does not remember, if he ever knew, the correct posture for giving money or accepting change. Even in Heathrow, his first time in an airport, they hadn't let him browse W. H. Smith's immense stall and hustled him past the duty-free shop. Though he had his look, of course, spied in passing the window displays, cartons of cigarettes, bottles of liquor he recognized from the adverts, cameras he'd drawn the like of in his sketchbooks.)

"All right," Mr. Moorhead said, "if you think you're up to it."

"I do. I do think I'm up to it. Ta, sir. Ta, Mister Moorhead."

"What about you, Janet? How do *you* feel?"

"Shipshape," Janet Order said. Shipshape, she thought, the very color of the seas they ride upon.

"All right. As an experiment, then. But remember, you operate on the buddy system when you're by yourselves. Under no circumstances, *no circumstances,* may you leave the hotel. And no sweets. If you're thirsty you may take water. Have you money?"

"The twenty dollars you gave me in London, Mister Moorhead," Noah said.

"Well, that's quite a lot. You mustn't spend it all. We've another five days yet, plenty of time to think about what sort of souvenirs you'll be wanting to take home with you."

"When may we have the rest of our money, Mister Moorhead?" Noah asked timidly.

"Why, when I give it to you."

The children started toward the door.

"You're quite sure you'll be fine?"

"Yes, Mister Moorhead."

"Yes, Mister Moorhead."

"At the first sign of weakness, the *first,* you get word to me. Don't try to return to the room. You've your pills that I gave you?"

"Yes, Mister Moorhead."

"Yes, Mister Moorhead."

"You know each other's symptoms? You're alert to the danger signals I told you about?"

Janet Order nodded; unschooled Noah, uncertain about the words Moorhead had tried to teach him—stenosis, atresia, dyspnea, syncope—but who remembered in a general sort of way what bad things to look for in his blue buddy, did.

So for him it's like being plunked down right in the very center of those bright-colored supplements in the Sunday paper. He tells this to Janet Order.

"No smart remarks, nine knuckles," the little blue girl says.

"Look at it all," Noah says, and thinks with pride about the sort of customer he'd make.

"What, *this* junk?"

"My mum would love this."

"Film? Your mum would love a box of film?"

But he's not listening. He's lost not only in his first shopping spree but in the first experience he's ever had of any sort of shopping at all. Within ten minutes he has bought the box of film, a bottle of shampoo, an antihistamine he's seen advertised on television, a flea and tick collar, and a pair of infant's water wings. He has spent more than twelve dollars (and guessing incorrectly—he's not too embarrassed to ask Janet, he's too excited by the actual act of spending money to remember that she's even there: if she is struck by stenosis, atresia, dyspnea, or syncope just now she is almost certainly a goner—he waits for the clerk to take the money from his hand and almost forcibly wrenches his change from her own) but isn't bothered because he still has, in addition to the change from the twenty dollars that Moorhead advanced him out of the hundred each child has been promised for spending money, the fifty his dad had slipped to him at Heathrow and which he's not even mentioned to Moorhead. (It's the long-term and higher maths he can't do, those which perhaps even he knows he has no use for.) And returns to the same clerk five separate times, once for each of the five items he has purchased. Janet, beside him, is almost breathless. She's never seen anything like it, this frenzy, and wonders if she's in the presence of some seizure Mr. Moorhead has neglected to tell her about.

"Come away," she says. "Come away, Noah. Please, Noah. We'll find another shop. There are these other shops we can go to."

She feels her breathlessness—the dyspnea—and is almost prepared to squat down right there in the middle of the store. (Squatting sometimes restores her breathing, though it's an act that embarrasses her, conscious as she is that people seeing her will be listening for grunts, looking for little blue turds beneath her skirt when she rises.) She has her Inderal ready to hand when Noah can suddenly see her again.

"Other shops?"

Clumsily, he holds five paper bags, which another clerk, noticing his deformity, offers to put into a large plastic carrier that he can hold by its handle.

"Other shops?"

"Would you like me to take one of your parcels, Noah?"

"No," he says sharply, angrily, almost greedily. But though they're quite light he can't manage them very well and twice they have to stop while Noah rearranges his packages. Which he does with his nose, with his teeth, which he keeps in balance by bringing his hands up and moving the bags from side to side with his face, all the while thinking, who cannot read—Who *would* fardels bear? Before they have reached the next shop along the hotel's wide concourse, the sack with the shampoo drops to the hard floor and Noah starts to cry.

"Look, Noah," Janet Order tells him reassuringly, "the bottle's plastic. It didn't break. Why don't you let me carry this one for you?"

"You better not drop it if you know what's good for you."

And in the store, which is a sort of Disney boutique, Noah's strange frenzy returns. He seems neither irritable nor calm but somehow triumphant, rather, Janet supposes, the way explorers might look, discoverers at the headwaters of great rivers they have been tracing, men come upon new mountain ranges, waterfalls, archaeologists at digs yielding sudden, spectular treasures.

"Oh, Noah," Janet Order says, and watches him as he performs what she does not know are his entirely personal maths, his customized sums. He flicks price tags, turns over china figurines to see the prices on their base. (How did I know? he wonders. How did I even know that that's where they'd be?) He doesn't bother to add the odd cents but counts by two- and five- and seven- and ten-dollar units, rounding the figures off to the next highest dollar, the sums to their next highest even number, adding on taxes, too, all the old asterisk attachments he's seen beside the goods pictured in the adverts he's not only looked at but studied, drawn, copied. Even unschooled Noah, who can't read right, knows that's where the catch will lie, in the fine print, the asterisk not only a trap but fair warning that a trap exists: "plus V.A.T." and "Batteries Not Included" and "Allow Eight to Twelve Weeks for Delivery" like all smug arms-across-the-chest-folded caveat emptor. So adding on taxes too, adding on anything he can think of, not so much extravagant as preparing himself for disappointment who can't read right or do any but the personal maths and who is going to die. (Nor does he understand American money, seeing it for the first time not when his father had slipped fifty dollars to him at Heathrow, since that had been sealed in an envelope, and not even when Mr. Moorhead had advanced them the twenty out of the hundred that had been promised, since that had been sealed in an envelope too, and not even when he had torn the envelope open and patiently waited for the clerk to take the twenty-dollar bill out of his hand when he made that first purchase, but when he physically wrested his change out of the clerk's astonished grip, having no notion at all of a dollar, a dime, a nickel, a penny. He has a vague idea of the United States as a rich and powerful country—on the news this evening they never mentioned redundancies, shipyards shut down, factories closed—and so supposes the dollar is worth more than the pound. To him it even *looks* more valuable, the high numerical face values of the paper bills, the portraits of the nation's male rulers, that wicked-looking eagle, the green artillery of the arrows. Even the dull, flimsy coins suggest an indifferent sense of plenitude. And he has an impression of bounty, of infinite variety—the things in this shop that fall neither under the category of staple nor luxury and that seem to him products for which no real use exists—the Mickey Mouse candle holders, for example, the cartoon stamp books, their gauzy, transparent envelopes filled with pictures of Mowgli, Mr Toad, Bambi, Snow White, the dwarfs on gummed stamps.)

"Noah? What will you do with all this stuff? Noah?"

But he doesn't bother to answer and takes his purchases—he no longer pays for the items separately but waits until he's made all his selections before bringing them to the clerk, not because he's grown accustomed to shopping but because he sees that he has been wasting time, that it is more efficient this way—to the woman at the register.

By the time they enter the next shop Noah Cloth has spent sixty-two dollars and fourteen cents and, because it would be impossible otherwise, has agreed to accept the plastic carrier. In this, in addition to his original purchases, are two china figurines, one of the Mad Hatter, the other of the Cheshire Cat, a Dumbo quartz wristwatch, duplicate Mickey Mouse sweat shirts, and a deck of playing cards picturing Minnie as Queen, Mickey as King. There is also a set of wooden coasters in which are etched the faces of Donald Duck, his little duck nephews.

In the Contemporary Man, Noah buys casual beachwear for his dad: sandals, a bathing suit, sunglasses, a terry-cloth robe, a beach towel, a visored sun hat.

The bill comes to seventy-three dollars and change.

"Lend me money," he whispers to Janet Order. "I'll give it back to you when Moorhead pays up."

"Oh, Noah," she says, "I haven't that much."

"If you're staying in the hotel," says the salesman (who is no more salesman than Noah is customer; there is nothing even close to negotiation going on here, not transaction, not commerce, not even business; the merchandise, which is no more merchandise really than the salesman is salesman or Noah customer but only the counter or token, as is the money Noah exchanges it for, the to-him foreign denominations and queer seals and symbols scribbled across its face and back and which, however powerful, are merely power in some unfamiliar, unaccustomed language and thus unknown, unknowable, only the counter or token for the simple symbolic occasion of his old frozen dreams), "you can charge it to your room. All you have to do is show your guest card."

"I'm exhausted," Noah Cloth says.

"Do you want me to call Mister Moorhead?"

"I'm exhausted," he says. "I think I ought to sit down."

"I'll call Moorhead."

"I'll just sit down."

"Where's your phone? I have to call his doctor."

"This is better."

Janet Order feels Noah's head. His temperature doesn't seem to be elevated, his pulse is regular and strong.

The salesman has already packed the beachwear away.

"Yes, this is much better," Noah says, his legs up, stretched out and comfortable in the wood-and-canvas lawn chair the salesman has set up for Noah to sit in.

"Don't go off, Noah. Technically," she tells the salesman, "on the buddy system, you're not supposed to leave them alone."

"I'm fine."

You're daft, she thinks. My buddy is daft.

"What does a nice chair like this usually run?" Noah Cloth asks the man while Janet is off making her call.

I can charge it, he thinks when he hears the price, I can charge it to the room.

"He doesn't think it's anything," Janet Order tells Noah when she returns. "A little fatigue."

"I'm fine."

"Are you rested up enough to go back to the room?"

"I'm fine."

"All right," she says and holds her arm out to assist him in getting out of the chair. When they go back up in the elevator together she doesn't bother to tell him—he's just a bonkers, crackers kid—that she has spotted Benny Maxine with Rena Morgan. It looked to her as if they were up to something.

Lamar Kenny has spotted the little wise guy. He thinks maybe he'll have some fun with him.

With Tony Word asleep for the night and Noah and Janet gone off, Mr. Moorhead is left free to think about the Jew.

There is a kind of villain—Moorhead has spent too much time on sick wards not to have noticed the type on kid's cartoon shows; indeed, these scoundrels have actually been absorbed into the doctor's bedside manner, become a source of preliminary chat with his small patients, a device to trivialize the physician's presence—who seems to thrive on adversity, who again and again overestimates his own dark powers at the expense of his adversary's light and more potent ones. Every defeat suffered by one of this sort somehow becomes the occasion for a greater gloating, a nefarious gibe, an unruly, unfounded optimism. In a way,

Moorhead, who tries to steady himself by remembering that he's been wrong before, puts himself in mind of such fellows. For one, he shares their incredible enthusiasm, their sense of invulnerability. He recalls his days at university, his theories, the confidence with which he strolled art galleries, diagnosing the portraits and statues there, a kind of cocky Grand Rounds. He remembers why he chose medicine as his life's work, his aesthetic attraction to health, his old notion that children carried theirs as lightly as a man might his umbrella. Chiefly he recalls his cheerful, discarded overview: his old modeling-clay inclinations, his belief that health, not disease, sat at the core of life. Laid forever by those photos he'd seen of survivors from the camps, those too-intimate pictures, naked as surgery, of Jews, their maniac expressions and broken posture, bone projecting from bone in awry cantilever like an unkempt architecture of bruise and wound, their skin, slack as men's garments on the bodies of children, their almost perceptible joints and sockets ill fitting their faulty scaffolding, the predicament of their swollen-seeming bones like badly rigged pulley, stripped gear.

His idea was as simple as a before-and-after photograph. A superb diagnostician, he believed (as he believed he'd spotted the Mona Lisa's incipient goiter and explained the famous smile as nothing more than the bitter aftertaste of iodine gushing from her overactive thyroid) that almost all illness was chronic, even congenital. If the admiration of health and well-being was what sent him into pediatrics in the first place, it was those pictures from the camps which—except for his brief tour on the casualty wards, almost as good an opportunity as an autopsy for getting close to the human body—caused him to stay there. The child, he knew, was father to the man.

His mistake in the old days was that he'd put too much faith in those artists. They'd idealized their subjects as much as any of the blokes who illustrated those perfect organs—the perfect hearts and perfect livers—in the textbooks. (For all Moorhead knew, Da Vinci had probably reduced the Mona Lisa's goiter and trained to a mysterious smile what could already have been a grimace.) So what was wanted were photographs, the kind the

Germans had made, the kind the Allies had. Though what was *really* wanted was the complete record, photographs of the Jews *before* they were rounded up—it would already have been too late when they were in the camps, the debilitating ride in the cattle cars, the bad sanitation—family albums with their individual and group photographs taken in different, more relaxed settings: on the beach, at picnics and parties, at weddings, bar mitzvahs, baby's first picture, rabbis at their devotions, all the candids of the daily round. (But *still* a sucker for good health, at least its appearance, his mind stuffed with images of perfect specimens, of strong, beautifully tapered athletes, women as well as men. Which accounted, of course, for his shyness with Bible. Had he been thrown in with the man it would have been no time at all before he asked him to strip for an examination, auscultated his chest, palpated and poked the fellow till he was black and blue, then asked if he might examine the bruises. Once, just once, he wanted to feel the ostensibly healthy kidney, hear the report of the seemingly sound heart. Which would have created many misunderstandings.)

In the hands of a superior diagnostician, what he'd stumbled upon could be a great and useful tool. Working backward, and using follow-up studies of survivors from the camps as a control, he could test his theory about the latency of all pathologies. If he could lay his hands on those albums—he doubted the Germans would have let them keep them, but the Jews were a clannish people and surely early pictures of Jews who survived the camps were available in the albums of even distant family relations who'd never entered them—that would be perfect, but it was more important for him to find the survivors themselves, to take their medical histories and examine them, to see, finally, if their conditions jibed, as he was certain they would who could not understand the obstinacy of villains in children's cartoons but admitted up front that he sometimes shared it, with the diagnoses and prognoses—he didn't mean malnutrition except as it affected related, subsequent diseases; he didn't mean psychological disturbances unless they preceded and were exacerbated by their experience in the camps—

he'd made in his early holocaust studies. (New technologies were available now; he used blowups and computer enhancements of those grainy old photographs, bringing it all out, punching it all up, making all that latency and incipience stand out crisp as a scab, articulated as a rash.) Because there was no Registrar to answer to now and he had in his personal collection something over a thousand computer-enhanced blowups of men and women at the fences posing for their liberation, most of them right out of the front rows, too, along with some really wizard shots of their palms splayed out against the barbed wire, clumsily leaning against it to take the weight off their bodies, or their fingers clutching it, their distended knuckles and broken nails fine and well defined in his enhanced photographs as the features of knaves, queens, and kings on playing cards. Though it was a risky business, far riskier actually than asking Colin Bible to submit to an examination. (One day, for the sake of the sample, he would *have* to examine superior specimens, but he supposed that was still a way off.) Though there'd be no more garden parties if it ever got out. And he could kiss his position in Great Ormond Street good-bye. To say nothing of any O.B.E.'s. To say nothing. Not even his nefarious gibe.

In his joke he's completed the preliminary part of his studies. He delivers a paper: "Diagnoses and Prognoses of Some Jewish Survivors from the Concentration Camps." Afterward, during the question period, he's asked if he found no use for the photos of those victims who'd been gassed or shot. After all, his questioner says, the survivors had been clad. Those others had been commanded to strip, killed, then dumped into open graves. Surely their *naked* bodies could have been useful for his studies.

And he tells him, he says, he goes, "Yes, but only for the diagnosis!"

So he'd come to Florida.

And found his Jew.

Mary Cottle, looking rested, is standing outside Eddy Bale's door when he answers her knock.

"I'm told you've been asking about me."

"Oh. It was good of you to drop by. It's nothing important. Come in, why don't you?"

"Thank you. I seem to have lost the others at the monorail station."

"Colin said there'd been a mix-up."

"Yes. Quite stupid of me."

"No, no, of course not. No harm done. All present and accounted for."

"Who's that in the bed, Mudd-Gaddis?"

"Oh. Right. Well, accounted for, anyway. Benny Maxine seemed a little antsy. I thought I'd let him out for a bit. You know how kids love to explore hotels."

"I don't actually."

"Oh, yes. They're quite in ecstasy in lifts. They quite fancy pushing buttons and being allowed to call out the floors for the other guests."

"Do they? It just doesn't seem Benny's line of country somehow."

"No, I suppose not. He's—what?—fifteen. I guess he'd be more interested in hanging about the hotel's cocktail lounges. I reckon I was thinking more about my son."

"I'm awfully sorry. I don't think I ever offered my condolences."

"Well."

"It's just that one feels such a fool. One feels terrible, of course, but there's nothing to say."

"Well, that's very kind of you. I appreciate that."

"He seemed a nice kid."

"You knew Liam?"

"Well, more by reputation than otherwise, but I did help with his lunch one or two times."

"I'm sorry. I think I may have known that and forgotten."

"Of course."

"Would you care for a drink? There's not a *great* selection, but I have some lovely gin I bought in the duty-free shop. Or if you prefer I think I could organize some of Colin's sherry."

"Thank you. You go ahead. Cigarettes are my vice. I was never much of a drinker."

"Yes. I've noticed the smell of your tobacco."

"I know. It's a nasty habit."

"Not at all. I like the smell of foreign cigarettes. French, are they?"

"Sometimes. Sometimes French. Or Russian, Bulgarian. The Iron Curtain flavors."

"Aren't those rather harsh?"

"I decided long ago that if I was going to smoke I was going to smoke. In for a penny, in for a pound."

"Yes, I know what you mean. I hope you've stocked up. American brands are mild by comparison."

"I'm a bit of a smuggler, I'm afraid. I snuck two cartons past Customs."

"Good for you."

"Does your wife smoke?"

"She smokes our tobacconist."

"Sorry. That was stupid of me. I'd heard you'd separated."

"She separated."

"She'd been under a strain."

"It was my strain too."

"My God, Eddy—may I call you Eddy? That's right, you insist, we went through this at Moorhead's—it was all Britain's strain. Wales, Scotland, and Northern Ireland. The Isle of Man, the Isle of Wight. You fair gave all of us the hernia, Ed."

"Is something wrong? What's wrong? I lost my boy. What's wrong with you?"

"Me? Nothing. I'm this volunteer, I'm this paladin. I'm this lenient melt-mood Candy Striper."

"Shh."

"Old Mudd-Gaddis can really snore, can't he? I wonder if any air gets through all that."

"I'm working on my second lovely gin and you're the one who's one over the eight."

"Organize Colin's sherry, I'll join you."

"You're a smoker. You were never much of a drinker."

"You know I gave to all your campaigns?"

"What? Money, you mean?"

"Over the years probably more than a hundred quid."

"I'm afraid you made a bad investment, Mary."

"*Hey!* Watch that. Just who the bloody hell do you fucking think you are?"

"Jesus! Bloody hell is right. You've gone and spilled Colin's sherry all over the place. It looks like a massacre in here."

"That's not on. That's not *on*, I said!" Mary Cottle said, and stormed out of Eddy Bale's room.

Because everything has a perfectly reasonable explanation. Everything. Wars, earthquakes, and the self-contained individual disasters of men. Courage as well as cowardice. Generous acts out of left field and the conviction that one is put upon. Everything. Man's fallen condition and birth defect too, those San Andreas and Anatolian, Altyn Tagh, and Great Glen faults of the heart, of the ova and genes. They're working on it, working on all of it: theologians in their gloomy studies where the muted light falls distantly on their antique, closely printed texts, as distant as God (which, God's exorbitant aphelion, out-post, and mileage—the boondocks of God—also has a perfectly reasonable explanation); scientists in their bright laboratories where the light seems a kind of white and stunning grease.

Everything has a reasonable explanation.

So Charles Mudd-Gaddis in Bale's and Colin's, Lydia Con-science in the nanny's and Mary's, and Tony Word in Mr. Moorhead's room, meet in each other's sleep.

They gather on a Sunday afternoon in one of the public rooms in the Contemporary Resort Hotel, which Mudd-Gaddis believes to be a nursing home where he has been stashed by his family. By what, that is, Mudd-Gaddis guesses, is not the re-mains *of,* so much as in a certain sense accounts *for,* what is his family now, his family informed by time and evolution, an in-crement of new additional relation which, try as he may, as he *does,* he can't keep straight. Though he's certain it's all been ex-plained to him, and repeatedly too, and probably even patiently—they are not unkind here; stashed or no, this is no Dickensian charnel house and the doctors and staff are as pleasant as they are efficient; he's no complaints on *that* score, or on the other either, for that matter— the stashed business, he means; he's a man of the world, or anyway *was;* in their shoes he'd have done the same, because what *can* you do, what can you actually *do* when people get so old they can't take care of themselves any longer? When they get *so* old (talk about your second childhoods) they become incontinent and piss their pants and shit their sheets and move about (though it isn't as if they actually could—move about, that is—they can't, and have to be pushed in wheelchairs, lifted in and out of them like, like— what?—socks in a drawer, laundry in a hamper) under some stink of the personal, the inclement intimate? So old they can't cut meat or butter bread. Of *course* you stash and warehouse them, though he knows it's a waste of breath, of time and money. It's a joke, really. A joke and at the same time a tribute to the basic decency of people that they even *bother* to explain. All right, so they slow their normal speech patterns and maybe raise their voices. He can understand that too. Because what the devil would you expect? Would you expect otherwise? Would you talk Great Ideas with an infant? And if you did, if you could, but it was this hard-of-hearing infant, this *deaf* infant, wouldn't *you* raise *your* voice? It's a wonder to him how they find the patience. It's a wonder to him they don't go all shirty every once in a while and send up the old fart. "I'm Jim and that's Bill. You remember Bill, don't you, Dad? He was your fireman on your post-mistress's side. I'm your dustman on your papal nuncio's, nun-cle."

Which is not to say he doesn't have it coming. The defer-ence. The weekly visits. However uncomfortable they make him feel, whatever trouble they put him to. Well, all that fuss and bother. Having to endure the shave, the indignity of the double nappies if he shits where he shouldn't. All of it: the fresh shirt and starched collar (which gives him a rash like a bedsore; and *that's* another thing, having to sit before them in his wheelchair perched on his sheepskin as if his arsehole might take the cold), the ordeal of the tie which, even though it's no charnel house here and even though they're gentle, is still no protection from the orderly's breath which, even if it isn't bad, could still carry the germ—so close they get when they do your tie—which could give him pneumonia. All of it. Though he's the one who insists on this: the damn-fool mummery of the scents and talcums which, since his nose seems to be going along with everything else, he probably puts on, or rather that orderly puts on for him, too liberally. Which, face it, is maybe the one plus—he doesn't count having to be diapered—in the whole business, sensitized and able as he is to respond to the pats and tickles of flesh on flesh even though those pats and tickles are administered by a poof male orderly and even though, unless they hang old men, he'll never be tumescent again?

Because everything has a reasonable explanation and his visitors mustn't get wind of his old man's stench.

So he has these visits coming no matter that it's a basinful for all concerned, no matter that they banjaxed each other or that all of them—he doesn't exclude himself—usually just spend the afternoon sitting around and talking through the back of their necks.

It was quite a predicament. Being so old. So suspicious. Because maybe the real reason it's no charnel house, maybe the real reason they're so gentle and kind in this well-appointed palace of pensioners, is that they don't want to cross him, that with all his other functions and faculties deserting him, he still retains the power of the purse, can write them out of his will— what's left of his will?—with one stroke of the legal. Obviously they still believe him to be *compos*. Which may be the real reason he's so polite to *them*, so gracious and agreeable, which may even be the real reason why he consents to see them every Sunday.

Because how could it possibly be love?

On any of their parts?

My God, he doesn't even remember them from one week to the next!

And for their part, for their part, what was left of him to

love? A nappied, sheepskin-assed old man who stank on top of perfume flowers that never grew in nature, and of the compost which never grew them underneath.

Lydia Conscience begins.

"How are you today, Charles?"

And old Mudd-Gaddis thinking: So that's how it stands. Not Pop, not Granddad or Great-granddad either. So old. Not Uncle or Cousin-German. Charles. (Not *friends,* too young to be friends, never *friends.*) Relation reduced to the watered technicalities of lineage. So old. *So* old.

Tony Word sees the old boy's rheumy eyes inspect him.

"Yeah, Charles, how are you keeping?"

"I'm fine, thank you," Mudd-Gaddis tells them politely. "And yourself? Yourselves?"

Lydia Conscience rests her engagement and wedding rings across her belly. "Very well, thank you, Charles."

"No morning sickness?" he inquires alertly.

"My goodness no," she tells him gratefully. "That passes in about two months. I'm long into my awkward phase by now. My ankles are ever so swollen. I tell my friends I feel like a cow and must look like the full moon."

"No, of course not," he hastens to reassure her. "She looks . . ."—he tries to think of the word—"*radiant,* positively *radiant,*" he tells Tony Word.

Who nods noncommittally.

"And how are *you* feeling?"

"Me? No complaints, no letters to the *Times,*" Tony Word says. "As long as I stick to my diet."

Now Mudd-Gaddis, who has no idea what the little stick figure can possibly be talking about and who was just about to offer him some sweets out of the box he keeps for his Sunday visitors, nods and, covering his ass, adds, "Good, good. That's very important."

(Because with great age comes paranoia—so old, *so* old— and he knows he's already made one mistake when he asked his stupid question about morning sickness, not his finest hour, because he's given them something to jump on and maybe they think he can't remember his own wife's pregnancies, which he can't, or if he ever even had one, and he's on the verge of making another, a lulu, and it's all he can do to keep from making it because what he really wants to know, what he really wants to *do* is cut the crap altogether and demand of them straight out, "Just who in hell *are* you people?" They look like kids, for Christ's sake. Though to him, of course, everyone does these days. So old, *so* old. And why does the woman keep flashing those damned rings? *So* old. Still, he thinks, in the common dream the three of them share, it isn't as if I were a com*plete* twit. It's plain enough she's trying to remind me of something. My responsibilities, probably. I wish I'd better eyesight, though. From here the rings look like toys from the Cracker Jacks.)

"Oh, what lovely candy!" Lydia Conscience says.

"I'm sorry. Would you care for some?"

She takes two jaggery toffees and a chocolate caramel.

"It's positively shameless," Lydia Conscience says. "I'm eating for two now."

Though when she puts one of the sweets into her mouth she chews it without interest.

Mudd-Gaddis moves the box almost imperceptibly toward Tony Word. "How about you, old man? Unless the diet prevents, of course."

"I'd love to, ta very much. It's just that it would kill me."

"Of course."

"Though they look delicious."

"Yes, I'm told they're quite good," Mudd-Gaddis says. "I always try to have some on hand for my guests."

Tony Word nods, Lydia Conscience does.

"You have *many* guests then?"

The baggage! The little preggers baggage! Because suddenly he understands what this is all about.

How rich he must be!

And if it's not a charnel house here then it's because he, Mudd-Gaddis, must make it well worth their while for it not to be.

How rich he must be!

For all these poor relations to come trotting out here every Sunday—he feels himself in the country, Sussex, the Cotswolds—in their beat-up old Anglias and Ford Cortinas. And the ring business too, he understands the ring business. Which doesn't have damn all to do with reminding him of his responsibilities. It's semaphore, is all. Why the little light o' love is only signaling. The fat baggage was just making her manners. She was telling him that the contraband she carries in her breadbasket was legal now, that she and the little wimp—surely he can't be the father—were all conjugaled and properly wedlocked. She was only publishing the banns with those rings across her belly. And that question about his guests! So of *course* he understands what it's all about. It's a competition. To them he's just the goddamn pools!

Still, you can't be too careful. He doesn't know what claims they have on him, though he's certain they can't be great. Charles. Not Pop, Granddad, Great-granddad, Uncle, or Cousin. But *still* you can't be too careful. He sees he will have to continue to be rational, *compos*, polite, continue to chat them up, continue to endure them. So old, *so* old! They have some far-fetched stake of relationship, but it's a sure thing that however tenuous it may turn out to be it's enough to get him committed—because you don't get to be as wealthy as he is without knowing at least *something* about the law; a judge, one psychiatrist, and a neighbor's kid could probably do it—and if they're *that* greedy it won't be any well-appointed palace of pensioners next time but the true and genuine charnel house itself. And something else. If he's stashed, it was never any family did it to him. He has no family, only this attenuated bond of cousins, thinner than cheap paint. God knows why, but he's stashed himself. He's certain of it. He's self and voluntarily stashed!

Old. So old, so old, so old, so old. (Sold, sold, sold.)

"I say, do you have many guests then, Charles?"

"Oh. Beg pardon, dear, the hearing isn't what it used to be," Mudd-Gaddis tells her. (Because they can't commit you for deafness. He's thrown them a bone. It's the *compos* thing to do. And because he's canny now whom great age, subtracting faculties piecemeal, has managed to add only this, his almost volitionless cunning, to a character that always before had been strong enough to despise cunning. Just as, when he'd offered what's-his-name a confection, he'd taken none himself and automatically implied his dentures. Let them have deafness, let them have dentures. Let them see how far *those* will get them in Her Majesty's Courts!)

"I say, do you have many visitors?" repeats Lydia Conscience, raising her voice.

"Now and then. The odd male, the odd female."

"Benny Maxine?"

"Benny?"

"Maxine. The lumpy-faced Jewish boy."

He *does* recall a lad with a puffy face and thinks he recollects the voice, persistent, wheedling. He acknowledges Maxine's visits. But Jewish? Has he Jewish cousins?

"Janet Order?"

"Ye-es, I think so," Mudd-Gaddis says. "Dark girl."

"*Dark?*" Tony Word chimes in. "She's all over blue as a bruise."

"Well, my eyes," says Mudd-Gaddis, anteing his vision, throwing that in with his ears and his teeth.

"Does Noah Cloth come? Does Rena Morgan?"

"Noah's this finger amputee," Tony Word reminds. "Has a digit missing on his left hand. And Rena's nose runs. She's this phlegm faucet."

"My goodness," Mudd-Gaddis says and wonders about his time-informed, incremented, evolutionated family. A lump-faced Jew, a female bruise, a hand-gimp, and a Niagara nose. Plus these two. A wimp, a wimp's trollop. (And remembers now, has them sorted out. By their afflictions. And canny or no, believes he understands the real reason he keeps the box of sweets for them. It may be for no better reason than to please them.)

"Well, I *must* say," Lydia Conscience says. "It's no wonder to *me.*"

"What's that, dear?"

"Why they're not here today."

"Yes. We thought we'd see them," Tony Word says.

"*I* didn't."

"You didn't?"

"Of course not. And you wouldn't either if you'd been paying attention."

"I pay attention."

"Oh, yes," Lydia Conscience says.

"I pay attention, I do."

"To your diet."

"I have to. You know that."

Charles Mudd-Gaddis, who can't bear to witness lovers' quarrels, attempts to bring her back on track. "Why is it you're not surprised they're not here today, dear?"

Lydia Conscience looks from one to the other. Baffles seem to be hung about each of them in their common dream like curtains, like shunts and chutes, like traps in games, like all walled-off, buffered interveniency. They are discrete as people beneath earphones. None knows what the other is thinking. It's like one of those round robin petitions where signature is arranged in a circle to confuse the order of signing. How can Tony feign surprise, how can Charles stage ignorance?

"Well, the *buddy system*," she says. "They're never buddies. Whatever happened to the buddy system?" she demands anxiously.

"The buddy system," Mudd-Gaddis says.

"Boy/girl, boy/girl. It never had anything to do with rooms," she says.

"Rooms."

"Janet Order is off with Noah Cloth. Benny Maxine's off with Rena Morgan."

"I don't think I quite . . ."

"Tony heard Noah and Janet plotting. And I *knew* Rena was up to no good. All that taffy and rose water on the nanny. The poor bitch is quite barmy. The 'game room' indeed! I can quite imagine what games *those* two are up to. Anyway, Benny

Maxine is *my* buddy. I know his condition as well as I know my own. I was prepared for any contingency. *Any* contingency. *Tony's* Janet's buddy, Rena Morgan was supposed to be Noah's. We were assigned. It never had *anything* to do with rooms."

"Who's mine?" Mudd-Gaddis asks.

"Oh, Charles," she says brokenly, "you never had one. You couldn't remember the symptoms."

"You're out of my will!" Mudd-Gaddis roars at them suddenly.

"Oh, Charles," Tony Word says kindly, "were we in your will? That's awfully sweet of you, old man, but don't you think that's a wee foolish? I mean, I've this nasty case of leukemia to deal with. I haven't a chance of surviving you."

"Oh, Charles," Lydia Conscience says, "you've no will. You're a pauper. What could be in it? You're this charity boy, Charley. You're stony broke."

"I'm not rich?"

"Poor as a pebble," Lydia Conscience says.

"How do you explain all this, then?" He indicates the well-appointed public room.

"What, the hotel lobby?"

"It's a hotel lobby?"

"What'd you think it was, old-timer, the Albert Hall?" Tony Word asks, winking at Lydia.

"Why do you come then? Why do you all come every Sunday?"

"Oh, that was foolish," Lydia says. "Pique, I suppose. When I found out about the others, that they went off by themselves, I thought the three of us might try to do something about it. That maybe we could ally ourselves against them."

So it is love, Charles thinks. "We will," he declares. "All for one and one for all! The Three Musketeers!"

"Mouseketeers," Tony Word says cheerfully.

"We'll see," Lydia says.

So it is love. A kind of love. Love of a sort. At least friendship, the seesaw, shifting allegiance of mates.

Because everything has a reasonable explanation. Everything. They are dying. They sleep fitfully, tossing and turning on their symptoms, waking to the slightest disturbance, even to Nedra Carp's, Eddy Bale's, and Mr. Moorhead's light permissions.

1

By the end of the third day they'd been to all six of the lands in the Magic Kingdom. They'd been to Main Street, U.S.A. They'd been to Liberty Square, Adventureland, and Fantasyland. They'd been to Tomorrowland and to Frontierland and by now were tired of Benny's dark joke. " 'From whose bourne no traveler returns,' " he would say whenever the last two sections of the theme park were mentioned.

Moorhead permitted them to go on the tame rides only—the aerial tram, the little one-eighth-scale railroad, the trolleys, jitneys, and double-deck buses, the Jungle Cruise and Cinderella's Carousel, the paddle-wheelers and WEDway People-Mover. The Grand Prix Raceway, Big Thunder Mountain,

Starjets, and Space Mountain were off-limits to them. So were the Mad Tea Party, Mr. Toad's Wild Ride, Mission to Mars, and Peter Pan's Flight. "Thrills and chills," Benny would warn the others, sizing up a ride from its description in his guidebook and shaking his head, anticipating Moorhead's decision. Thus a good part of their days was taken up in being shuttled from one part of the park to the other, simple sightseers. Even at that, four of the children—Lydia, Charles, and Tony Word were exceptions—had balked at riding the double-deckers. Again, Maxine had been their spokesman. "We're Brits," he called up to the driver and argued with Bale, "and didn't cross the sea to the New World to ride no double-deck bus, which besides what it ain't authentic in the first place it don't even have no wog for a conductor in the second!"

They spent a lot of their time watching shows and riding in cars that ran along tracks past special effects of one sort or another. It was all rather like being in a kind of passive museum. Only Colin still seemed fascinated by the audio-animatronics, and when some of the children (by this time a little embarrassed at being always moved to the head of the line—as a precaution Moorhead had ordered Tony Word and Janet Order into wheelchairs—but unable to stand for more than fifteen or twenty minutes at a time) objected to the queues, it was Bible who volunteered to stand in for them. Mudd-Gaddis, Lydia Conscience, and Noah waited on benches or on chairs under awnings at outdoor cafés—usually at these times Moorhead went off to scout other attractions for them while Eddy Bale and Mary Cottle pushed Tony and Janet in the wheelchairs and Benny and Rena, still eager to take advantage of their invalid status, accompanied them—and Nedra Carp shuffled back and forth between Colin and the children, alerting them to the status of the queue.

"How was it, Benny?" Noah asked when Maxine and the others came out of It's A Small World.

"Thrills and chills," Benny Maxine said.

"Was it, Benny? Was it?"

"Nah," Benny said. "I guess it were all right, mate. There was all these little dolls from the U.N. singin' an' dancin'."

"Fascinating," Colin said.

"Cor," Benny said, pointing to Janet and Tony in their chairs. "If we got to keep looking at this stuff it won't be wheelchairs we'll need, it'll be glasses."

They went to Tropical Serenade; they went to Country Bear Jamboree. They spent time in theaters watching movies—something called Circle-Vision 360 wrapped them in the spanking, startling imagery of the world: Tivoli, New York, the Alps and Rome and the Valley of the Nile, Jerusalem's old stones and India and more—and looking at the exhibits of big corporate sponsors: Kodak, Eastern Airlines, RCA, McDonnell-Douglas.

And they were getting edgy.

"Don't you wish *you* had a wheelchair?" Lydia teased Noah.

"Yeah, I wish I had one to roll *you* about in."

"Bitch!" Lydia Conscience hissed at him under her breath.

"Pimp!" he breathed back.

"Mister Moorhead," said Lydia Conscience one afternoon, "may I have a new buddy for the buddy system? I don't think Benny remembers my symptoms. I mean I think I'd feel better if I switched with Janet."

"If you switched with Janet it would throw everything off," Moorhead objected.

"What if I have an attack? I don't think he's responsible," she whispered.

"Those assignments were made with great care," Moorhead said.

"There ought to be a drill then," she said, and, to calm her, Moorhead reluctantly agreed. He called Benny over to explain the situation.

"Lydia's upset," he said. "She doesn't think you'd know what to do in an emergency."

Lydia feigned an exacerbation and Benny Maxine moved to her side. He undid the buttons at her collar. He moistened a handkerchief and applied it to her forehead, her temples.

"He hurt my stomach."

"I didn't even touch it."

"He hurt my stomach, Mister Moorhead."

Because they were not only edgy but fragmented now as well. Some in wheelchairs, others out, the rides forbidden them, their staggered attendance at performances, the snacks they took at different times, and the separate memories of the world they'd seen projected, thrown up around them like a wall.

Only Lydia still suffering an aftertaste of the dream; Charles, who'd shared it, musing only that life was a lot more interesting to him asleep than awake; and Tony Word recalling with not a little pride that he'd not come off badly at all, that in fact he'd acquitted himself pretty well, considering. (The others, who not only had not been in the dream but who hadn't even been sleeping at the time, nevertheless went about for upwards of a day, a day and a half, with the queer conviction that someone—a person or persons unknown—had been talking about them behind their backs.)

Because Eddy Bale had been right. Kids *do* love to explore hotels. They *are* in ecstasy in elevators, they *do* fancy pushing buttons.

And it had begun just that innocently, Benny Maxine choosing Rena Morgan for no better reason than that she seemed game—a jolly good sort, a damned decent chap. (And, of all the children, quite frankly seemed the strongest, maybe the only one who could keep up with him.)

And even suggested that she bring her passport along. Just in case.

"Just in case what, Benny?"

"Better safe than sorry, luv." And showed her his, tapping the dark blue document as if it were a letter of credit, some official carte-blanche ace-in-the-hole talisman.

He was a fifteen-year-old boy, still a child, still a kid, and for all his bluster, for all the pains he took to sound street-wise— "Street-wise and city-foolish" he would admit later, sheepishly—he had never done any of the things he had wanted to do. Only his sickness had ever happened to him, and he lived the realest of lives in a condition of hope and fantasy.

For the first five or ten minutes they really did push buttons, taking turns, Rena up and Benny down, and politely asking "Floor, please?" in their most distinguished British accents of everyone who came into the elevator.

"Oh, aren't you kind?" a woman said. "Are you enjoying our country?"

"Yes, ma'am," Benny said, "but we're not tourists."

"You're not?"

"My partner and I"—here he indicated Rena, who had all she could do to keep a straight face and was desperately trying to suppress laughter and the vast reservoirs of mucus that she held in check by sheer will (because a giggle could trigger horrors)—"are with the Disney organization, actually."

"You are?"

"We were the two little children in the film version of *Mary Poppins.* Did you happen to see that particular film? Would you like our autographs?"

"But that was *years* back," the woman said. "You'd have to be close to thirty."

"Yes, ma'am," Benny said, "we're small for our age. The Disney organization is giving us a chance to make a comeback on the lift."

"This is my floor," the woman said.

"Yes, ma'am, they're good people. They take care of their own."

"Oh, Benny," Rena said when the woman got off, "what a thing to say! She never believed you."

"She did."

"No."

"Absolutely. On the Queen's life. I swear it."

"Would you swear on your own?"

"Sure," Benny said, "I swear on *my* life."

"Oh, *your* life," Rena said.

And on the way up—Rena was working the elevator—Benny

deliberately cut a great noisy fart. The crowd—there were perhaps a half dozen people on board—pretended to ignore it.

"I say," Benny said, "bad gas."

Which they also ignored.

"P.U.!" Benny said. "Jolly stinko bad gas, that. *Jolly* bad!"

That innocent. Still amused by the jokes hiding in smells
and by all the body's punch lines.

And explorers. Finding the banquet and meeting rooms and
special hospitality suites, bumping through the great maze of
the hotel, through its guts, taking service elevators whenever they
could, penetrating its laundry and maintenance plant, where they
were shooed away by a guard to whom Benny insisted on showing his U.K. passport.

"We get 'em from all over," the guard said. "We get 'em
from Tulsa, we get 'em from Indiana."

Through its restaurants and cocktail bars—outside one of
which Benny invited Rena to dance—its swimming pools, looking in on the game room, the caricaturist there offering to do
them together—"Please, Benny? Just to keep us honest," Rena
had said, and Benny, air in his cheeks, all his lumpish, lop-
sided, potholed face puckering, "Yeah, too right," he said—and
then returning to one of the restaurants, where Benny told the
hostess that friends were waiting and, taking Rena's arm, strode
businesslike—they were that innocent, innocent enough to believe they had to carry themselves in some special way—past her
and on into the kitchen.

"Our compliments to the chef!" Benny announced grandly.

Three men in tall hats looked up.

"To all of you," he said.

"Yes, everything was delicious," Rena said.

"Except the ice," Benny said.

They stared at the two children.

"The ice was tasteless. Tasteless ice. Didn't you think so, my
darling?"

"Get outa here," one of the men said.

And stopped outside the Spa, the health club where at that

very moment the chap from the Haunted Mansion was ambling up to Colin Bible.

"It's not open to the ladies at this hour," Benny said, reading the notice on the door.

"You go, Benny, I'll wait. You can tell me about it."

"What, go into a health spa? *Me?* Not bloody likely. I could be sued."

"Oh, Benny," Rena Morgan said.

It wasn't until they'd been gone nearly an hour that he remembered Mary Cottle. Even then, even as he introduced the idea to Rena, even then he was playing.

He said he thought he'd seen her that very afternoon at the hotel's monorail station.

"Crouching behind the automatic doors, she was."

He hadn't said anything. Not because Colin and the boys—not Mudd-Gaddis; Mudd-Gaddis was still out of it, lost in whatever private nightmare had set him off—hadn't noticed her absence or expressed concern, but because, even if it wasn't calculated on his part, information was information, fed edge, and gave a punter like Benny—and this wasn't calculated either, merely that same combination of hope, fantasy, and the real which drove his life—the whip hand should anyone go the gamble with him. Besides, he wasn't sure it was she. And he'd had to pee, was moving along full lick at the time.

And he didn't say anything now, only that bit about the doors. (Because he was that innocent as well, on his best behavior with his new pal, striding past his own misgivings as he'd stridden past the hostess in the restaurant. He had to be wrong not to have mentioned a thing like that. And that calculating. Even though he never suspected it. He wasn't giving *anything* away.)

Indeed, he wouldn't have brought it up at all except that suddenly he added two and two together.

Because Bale had split them up that afternoon and because of what happened at the Haunted Mansion, they had had to return to the hotel early.

They had lost Mary Cottle. Moorhead and the Carp woman had not come back yet with the girls. Colin Bible had no key to Tony's room, and the children hadn't been entrusted with one. They'd come all the way up to their floor before anyone realized there was a problem. When Colin told them they had to go back down again, they groaned. "Can't be helped," Colin said. "You're going to have to shower, then I want you all in bed. You can't stay by yourselves. We'll have to go back and get a key to Miss Cottle's room."

"That's the adjoining room," Benny said. "I bet it's unlocked."

"You're on, sport. I'll give you odds."

"What's the odds then?" He hadn't even peed yet.

"*You* say."

Benny considered. "No bet, Colin," he said. "It's that Miss Carp's room too."

"You're learning."

"But I can watch them," Benny said. "There's nothing to it."

"Where am I?" Mudd-Gaddis asked.

"Ta, mate," Benny said, and went off to the W.C. to relieve himself.

Which was just as well, because while Colin was explaining the situation to the room clerk at one end of the long counter, Benny thought he spotted Mary Cottle accepting a key from one of the registration clerks at the other.

He couldn't be sure. A bus had discharged a load of holiday makers who were just now registering and who literally surrounded her. If it was her.

"Come on, then," Colin had said, "we can go up now. I've got it." He never got a second look, but twenty minutes later she still hadn't come back.

"Let's find out what she's up to," he said now to Rena, making a mystery where even he wouldn't have taken the heaviest odds there was one.

"Miss Mary Cottle's room, please?" he asked the room clerk.

"You'll have to use a house phone."

"Benny," Rena Morgan said.

"A house phone?"

The clerk told him where to find one.

"Benny?"

"I have to use a house phone," Benny Maxine explained.

"May I please have Miss Mary Cottle's room number?" he asked the operator.

"Benny."

"Just a minute," he said, "she's getting it for me."

"Benny, look at the time. I was supposed to be back half an hour ago."

"No, not six twenty-nine, the other one," he said.

"I'm going back," she said.

He covered the mouthpiece. "Wait, will you!" he almost hissed.

Because he was beginning to believe now. In the mystery, the adventure.

Rena Morgan was crying.

"Oh, Jesus," Benny said. "All *right!* Oh, *Je*sus!" he said, and replaced the telephone.

And was still trying to calm her down when Lamar Kenny spotted them.

"Is something wrong?" he asked with a concern that was almost soothing and put his suitcase down before the open elevator door. "Is there anything *I* can do?"

"No," Benny said, "my friend just has this truly disastrous allergy is all there's to it. That's why her eyes is all funny. She'll be fine once she gets back to her room and can take her pill."

"I'll be fine," Rena managed, sobbing and already pulling lengths of rolled handkerchief from her rigged magician's person. She was all over herself, tapping and pulling and patting, conducting herself like an orchestra, playing herself like a shell game. If her left hand shot forward, a handkerchief might suddenly appear in her right. If her right hand moved, her left might already have disposed of the handkerchief Lamar Kenny had not yet even seen there. Her fingers, quick as a pickpocket's, moved across her body like a loom. She made lightning passes across her face and seemed to dab, to pluck at the corners of her eyes, drawing the juices away from her nose as one might tap a tree. One couldn't tell what she did with her hankies, whether they went into the big purse she carried or back up her sleeves.

And she's working me close up, Lamar Kenny thought.

It was only because he was trained as an actor and accustomed to quick bursts of sudden but misleading dexterity that he could tell not how she did it (or even what she did) but that she was doing anything out of the ordinary at all. To someone else she might simply have seemed nervous, fidgety, even flighty. But he was in the business. (And understood he had a name like a lounge act. It was no news to him. Few people believed it, but Lamar Kenny was his real name. Even his agent had tried to get him to change it. "It's my name," Lamar told him, "I won't change it. Maybe I'll switch it around, call myself Kenny Lamar. Then you can get me gigs introducing strippers, make me an M.C. at industrial shows." But he wouldn't have done that either. It was the name, he felt, which pointed him toward show business in the first place, the glamorous name which had become his fate.)

"You're pretty good," he told the girl.

"That's right," she said. "I'm fine."

"No, no. That stuff you do."

"I get this way," she told him. "I'm fluidal."

"Fluidal. Christ, yes. Fluidal," he said. "Like the burning Ganges, like old man river, like Victoria Falls. Christ, yes, fluidal."

"Hey," Benny Maxine said, stepping forward, almost tripping over the man's suitcase. They did not understand each other.

Kenny was referring to her moves with the handkerchiefs and didn't know about her fluids, could tell only that she was upset: her tears, her puffy red eyes.

"Please, Benny," she said and started around Lamar Kenny toward the elevator.

"I'm coming," he said.

The moves were from his old sheep-dog routine and, like the girl's, were based upon principles of misdirection and distraction. Soon the wise-guy kid was stumbling all over himself as Lamar imperceptibly shifted the suitcase with the merest touch of his shoe or by seeming to brush against it with a trouser leg or by picking it up and, with the aid of his body's exact compensatory movements, apparently replacing it again in its original and identical position—caviar for the general, thought the trained actor—although it was actually in an entirely new relation to the wise-guy kid or, conversely, though it seemed to have been set down inches or even feet from where he'd picked it up, was really in the same spot. (He didn't even *need* the suitcase. It was an impediment, circus, athletics, mere footwork, and added nothing to the routine, maybe even detracted from it, necessary only as a sort of grace note or drum roll, as superfluous and minor, finally, as the inspection of an escape artist's locks and chains. Even Lamar Kenny's extended helping hand an exquisite mockery, as blind and stammered as a fall, a plunge to balance. Even his bitten, embittered "Sorry"s and "Excuse me"s.)

Lamar Kenny's flexible face—all this would have been beyond any Kenny Lamar—mirrored Benny's own. "Timing" was too simple a term; what Lamar did was a sort of reverse ventriloquy, carefully monitoring Benny Maxine's face and body, picking up signals the boy was not even aware he was sending (almost literally putting himself in the other's place). It demanded incredible concentration. It was high and subtle art, but go tell *that* to the yahoos who thought they were seeing only the familiar clumsy choreography of two people stuck in each other's way, slapstick, ordinary doorway-and-sidewalk contretemps, when what it actually was was one man dueling for two, parrying all the wise-guy kid's progressively embarrassed, astonished, and finally terrified smiles. Mimicry so high and subtle it was no longer mimicry but an actual act of possession.

They might have stayed there forever, feinting and lunging and parrying, in eternal stand-off and locked as stars in each other's gravity and orbit. Because Lamar Kenny knew that the only way the victim/volunteer from his audiences could ever get away was actually to turn and flee. Indeed, it was that that he watched and waited for, not just for the moment when an adversary would do it but, looking in his eyes, watching and concentrating, thinking ahead—thinking ahead, that was the secret—examining him until the precise moment not when he would do it but when it first *occurred* to him that he would do it, when Lamar Kenny would break it off himself, when *he* would turn and flee, running the five or six steps to the side of the small stages where he used to work, to turn and bow to the stunned and generally silent audience.

"Come on, Robin," Lamar Kenny said, "see can you get past Friar Tuck."

Could Kenny Lamar do this stuff? Lamar Kenny wondered, and gave the suitcase a violent, peremptory kick, clearing the ground between them, himself and the wise-guy kid, as if defying him, upping the ante of his mockery now, as if to say, "There. That's gone. You won't have to worry about *that* anymore, about tripping or stumbling over it. Now all you've got to worry about is me." And looked up at the wise-guy kid to resume their impositioned parity and stalemate, dead-heat dance. Only he was staring at the grip, the wise-guy kid, seeing it for the first time perhaps, noticing its smooth unscathed leather, its unused, untagged, oddly mileless condition.

"Come on," Lamar Kenny said. "Come on, let's go."

But Kenny was distracted too. Something had broken his concentration. It wasn't the banging of the elevator door, its timed attempts to close, its short mechanical temper as the grace periods when it retracted itself once its long rubber safety plate had been touched became shorter and shorter until it literally whined and ground itself against the resisting arm or thigh of whoever pressed the plate—he'd allowed for that, he'd picked the spot for his performance and allowed for that—nor even the strident, outright claims of the little girl, her insistent, importunate, and even terrified "Benny! *Benny!*"—he'd allowed for that too—but the sight he had of her out of the corner of his eye. She had stopped the business with the handkerchiefs and was staring at him, her face enormous, enlarged, magnified to him behind the clear mask of her mucus.

"Is she all right?"

Benny rushed the door.

"Hey, listen," Lamar Kenny said, leaning all his weight against the elevator door, "we were only fooling around, right? Hey," he said, "listen."

Benny Maxine plunged his hands past the wet and crumpled handkerchiefs in her bag and found Kleenex. He wiped her face, grooming her, picking away long strands of the jellied flow, bruising her, doing clumsily all the delicate currycomb frictions for the penalized child.

They never talked about it. He didn't even know what cystic fibrosis was. Noah Cloth was her buddy, the osteosarcoma.

"What am I supposed to do?" Benny said.

"I'm so embarrassed," she wheezed.

"Rena, what should I do?"

"What's wrong? What's she got?" Kenny asked.

Her breathing was labored, rasped, catching and coming out of her like the cry of stripped gears, like a knock in an engine.

"We're broken," Benny cried.

"Please," she whispered, "can we go up now?"

"We have to go up," Benny Maxine said.

"Hey," the actor said, "I'm off," and left the elevator and picked up the unmarked bag, the light luggage with his Pluto suit in it.

Moorhead said her system hadn't sustained a real "insult." That it hadn't been an "event." Only, he'd said, a minor "episode." Doctors always said stuff like that, using words about what happened to their bodies that could almost have been dispatches from the front.

Benny was relieved, of course. He didn't want anything bad to happen to any of them, particularly not on *his* watch. Dying kids don't need any more responsibility than they already had. Which was why Benny had misgivings about this buddy-system business. *He* hadn't signed on as anybody's nurse. And, for his part, he hoped it wouldn't be Lydia Conscience's eyes he looked into when *his* time came. Hoped, that is, he wouldn't be caught short by death, amongst amateurs; that ambulances would be standing by, doctors and nurses and all the close relations shaved and dressed and saying their farewells on full stomachs; that his emergency would come during proper business hours, after lunch, say, the weather and the day auspicious. That he'd have time to make a few phone calls.

Though he didn't really believe in the possibility of a *terribly* premature death. Not *really*. Benny was a gambler, wise to the ways—at least he thought so—of house odds. Certainly fifteen-year-olds died. They died in car and plane wrecks, they were picked off by snipers, battered about by crazies in the streets, and some of them, he supposed, succumbed to Gaucher's disease. Ashkenazi Jews. But what even *was* an Ashkenazi Jew? Other than somebody who came from central or eastern Europe, he wasn't sure. *His* family had been in the U.K. for almost two hundred years. Benny wasn't even bar mitzvah. Whatever Ashkenazi acts, whatever Ashkenazi practices, whatever indigenous Ashkenazi dyes in the clothing and prayer shawls or Ashkenazi nutrients hung about in the Ashkenazi diet ought surely to have bleached out by now. Which was, Benny figured, where the house odds came in. Because after almost two hundred years surely it would have boiled down to half-life. What, hoist by some already rare, already attenuated and degraded and deflated gene? Snagged on some pathetic scrag of theological, geographical one? Not, for all his symptoms, for all his great liver and burgeoning spleen, not, for all the high sugar content in his cells, the sweet deposits there lining his blood like dessert, not, for all his bruised and brittle bones, bloody likely!

Benny was a true gambler. He lived with hope.

So when Moorhead said no damage had been done, that was good enough for Benny Maxine. He had his plan. The following morning it was a simple thing to ditch the tour, return to his room, and complete the call that Rena with her troubles and scruples had interrupted the night before.

He told a hotel operator that it was Mr. Maxine calling from 627 and said that though he'd written it down when she gave it to him he'd somehow managed to misplace Mary Cottle's room number. Putting a low wink in his voice, he impressed the fact upon her that it wasn't the 629 registration he was interested in but the other one. He'd hold while she looked it up. When she came back on the line and said she wasn't permitted to give that one out, Benny chuckled. "What," he said, taking his voice as deep as it would go, "an unpublished hotel room? What the devil, eh?" He said he thought he might just possibly have left it in his pants pocket and let it go out with the dry cleaning. Or, the more fool he, in the pocket of his pajama top, perhaps, and hinted at the great frantic pressures of dishevelment and abandon. "You know how it is, eh? *You* know how it is, I'll be bound."

"I can connect you with laundry service," the telephone operator told him coolly.

Benny said that was damned decent but that now it seemed to him that that's not what had happened at all. He rather remembered having scribbled it down on the financial pages of yesterday's paper. Perhaps the girl who made the room up . . . ?

"I'm sorry," she said. "When a guest says that we can't give a number out, we can't give the number out."

"Oh, absolutely," Benny Maxine said. "I quite understand; it goes back to the English common law," and took the operator into the conspiracy. "Miss Cottle and I are engaged, actually. I wanted to surprise her with this great bouquet of flowers just. I'm holding them now. They should be popped into water at once, but without my fiancée's room number, of course . . ."

"Just pop over to six twenty-nine, why don't you just?" she said.

"Well, the thing of it is," Benny explained, "she's staying there with her great brute old Aunt Nedra, who doesn't know about our engagement yet, and—" The line went dead.

I'm smart, Benny thought, but I have to admit, there's a lot I don't know. He went over and over what he'd said to the woman, remembering his gaffes like a good dealer recalling every card already played.

Still, he knew now he was on to something, and before they left the hotel that morning he turned gumshoe and, at a discreet distance, tailed Mary Cottle everywhere she went. She went window shopping on the big concourse. She went to get sunglasses. She went to the newsstand for a paper.

If he hadn't gotten on an up elevator he thought was going down, he might not have found it. The car was crowded. And when Benny looked at the panel above the elevator doors he saw that it would be stopping at every floor. It was very crowded. People pressed against his enlarged liver, his vulnerable bones. "Sorry," he said, "sorry," and got off on eight. Maids were making the rooms up, their big carts unguarded in the wide corridors. He went up and was about to take some extra soaps and shoe cloths from one when the housekeeper suddenly emerged from 822. She was emptying trash: gray and black cigarette butts, yellow tobacco the color of sick dog shit loose in the bottoms of the ashtrays, even the ashes odd, not entirely consumed by fire, balled, thick as slag, the crumpled packet of those cheap, stinking second- and third-world cigarettes she smoked only the final proof.

Bingo! thought the good and lucky gambler, Benny Maxine. *I've found it! I've found her hidey-hole!*

2

When the rash appeared on his arm, an even circle about two inches high that wrapped around his biceps like a red and gaudy garter, Eddy Bale removed the mourner's band—to spare its sight from the children, he'd been wearing it under his left shirt sleeve like a blood pressure cuff—and, folding the cloth, put it into the pocket of his trousers. It was the third time he'd repositioned it, taking it in an inch or so when he'd transferred it that first time from his mackintosh to his suit coat on the day after the funeral, and taking it in again to place directly against his flesh. His shifting, meandering grief like an old river, his deferential hideout sorrow on the lam in his pants.

The rash still hadn't gone away even after he had begun to

carry the carefully folded brassard about with him in his pockets. (Moving it about even then, each day relocating the dark cloth, positioning it first in this pocket, then in that, carrying it in his back pocket, in the pockets where he carried his handkerchief, his room key, his change.) The rash didn't itch. It was adiabatic, neutral to the touch as the circle of cloth itself. It didn't bother him at all, really, and each morning when he shaved, when he showered, it always came to him as a surprise to see that it was still there at all. The rash itself was of a piece—no tiny blossoms erupted there; the skin neither bubbled with texture nor tingled with impression the way a head sometimes recalls a hat one has already removed—smooth as the hairless space it occupied on his upper arm, the discoloration of the lingering wide red ring like some healed graft of complexion. He would have asked Colin Bible to take a look except that he assumed the nurse assumed they were on the outs. He might have asked Moorhead, but there was usually something or other to take care of when they were together and he forgot. Or had second thoughts, at the last minute more protective than otherwise of his ruby garter of grief, insensitive as idle genitals, undisturbed private parts. (Knowing that the other one, the black, already frayed and fraying mourner's band, of which the bloodshot rash was only the raddled ghost, would dissolve, decompose, return as broken fiber, a ball of dark fragmented lint, the uncremated ash of Liam's memory that would stick to his pants and shirt pockets, lining his clothes like a stain that would not come out.)

He missed him. He missed the Liam of those last and awful weeks when he and Ginny knew it was all up with their dying and now plainly suffering child, when they could hear his medication on his tongue, smell it on his breath, the drying, parched relief of his only mitigated pain. He missed that Liam because he had almost forgotten the other. (Because what you remember, Eddy Bale thought, what sticks to the ribs and drives everything else out, as the tune you're hearing drives out all other tunes or the taste of your food all other taste, is neither pleasure nor pain but only the heavy saliency of things. Liam's condition had come upon him and been diagnosed when the boy was eight years old. He died when he was twelve. Two thirds of his boy's life was lived in the remission of ordinary childhood, yet Bale found it almost impossible to remember those things. They must have happened, they had to have happened; Liam himself, recalling his own happy salience, had reminded him, dozens of times, of occasions they had gone on outings, of movies they'd seen together, trips to museums, treats they had taken in restaurants, picture books they'd read to him when he was small, stories Eddy told him at bedtime, the afternoon which, oddly, Bale has no memory of at all, when Liam claims Eddy had taught him to fly a kite on Hampstead Heath—total recall for the father/son sports—and, at this remove, can't even be sure what, when healthy, his kid's character had been like.) Knowing only—it's certainly not memory, it isn't actually knowledge, perhaps it isn't even love but only some shadow in the blood, or maybe the bones of his weighted, sunken heart—Liam's negative presence.

Indeed, it may have been for grief of Liam that Eddy felt the dream holiday was not going as it should. The children hadn't complained, none of the adults had said anything, but Bale had the feeling he'd made mistakes, that decorum had broken down, that something militated against honor here. Ginny wouldn't have approved, but that wasn't it. (And wasn't it odd that Eddy gave almost no thought at all to Ginny's own negative presence?) Perhaps, by splitting them into two groups that first day, it had been possible for Bale to think of Liam as being with the other group, the children who'd gone off with Colin and Mary Cottle to the Haunted Mansion. It was even possible to think of him as being in one of the other rooms, assigned, say, to Moorhead's contingent or to Mary and Nedra's. (It wasn't as if he wished to be reminded. He'd deliberately left Liam's scrapbook at home. Or perhaps Ginny had taken it with her when she left him. He hadn't looked for it. The photos were chiefly of the ill Liam, clipped from newspapers, most of them. He well enough remembered the ill Liam. That was the head-bandaged boy he vaguely thought of as being in those other rooms, the negative presence, as available to him as his rash.

Idle minds, he thought, devil's workshop.

He has to think about, then alter, whatever it is that's amiss—that busted decorum which was maybe only the weals, flaws, blots, and smears of their maculate, tarnished lives. The riot that festered in all despair. That flourished in Bale's manipulative, arranged fun. Because already order has broken down. He has caught reports—not even reports, hints and high signs, the excited, febrile signals of their encoded deceits. There have been goings-on in the lifts, scenes and sprees. He is embarrassed for his dying charges. The children are uninhibited in the restaurants, flaunting their illnesses, boasting their extremis. (And now a sort of rivalry has sprung up. Disney World has become a sort of Mecca for such children, a kind of reverse Lourdes. Each day Eddy, the kids, see other damaged children: Americans, of course, but there is a family from Spain, a contingent from South America. There are African kids with devastating tropical diseases. He's heard that a leper or two is in the park. It's a sort of Death's Invitational here. Eddy isn't the only one to have had the idea. Organizations have sprung up. The new style is to grant the wishes of terminally ill children, to deal reality the blows of fantasy.) Nedra Carp thinks Benny Maxine may be spying on the girls. At fifteen he's the oldest of the children—unless Mudd-Gaddis is—and annoys her with his needs. She wants the door connecting their adjoining rooms kept locked.

"We can't do that. Suppose Colin Bible has to get in there?"

"He's beastly. He's a nasty, beastly boy. He tells them smutty stories."

"He's a pubescent kid. He's showing off. What's the harm? He probably has a crush on them."

"His conversation is all double entendre. He teases my girls. He milks his zits and tells them there's sperm in his pores. That they could become pregnant if he touched them."

"He's flirting. Don't you think they need someone to flirt with them?"

"Those little girls are dying, Mister Bale."

"What would you like me to do, Miss Carp?"

"We're responsible for these children. Surely you could speak to him."

"And tell him what? That he not only has to accept his death but his virginity too?"

(And remembers that Liam had begun to masturbate two months before he died.)

"You think I'm an old maid."

"No. Of course not."

"You do. Yes. You think I'm picturesque. You think I'm this quaint, picturesque spinster. That's why you invited me."

"Not at all."

"Not at all? You believe you smell cedar chest on me. Sachet, laundry soap, and an old hygiene."

"I'll say something to Benny."

"I know about bodies," Nedra Carp said.

"About bodies."

"I *know* about bodies!" she said.

He did say something to Benny. It was embarrassing for him, but it was hardly a man-to-man talk. He didn't give him the birds and the bees. Benny would already have the birds and the bees. He didn't make Nedra Carp's crisp case for the unseemliness of the boy's position. He didn't even warn Benny off, lay down the law, or try to appeal to the kid's sense of the special vulnerability of doomed girls. What he did in effect was to tell Benny what he hadn't dared to tell Liam. What he did in effect, to forestall anxiety and allay fear, and out of neither makeshift bonhomie nor Dutch-uncle, scout-master love, was to apologize to Benny Maxine on behalf of everyone who would be surviving him.

"You'll be missing out."

"So it's all it's cracked up to be, is it?"

"I'm afraid so," Eddy Bale admitted.

"I thought it might be," Benny Maxine said. "Where there's smoke there's fire."

"Five-alarm."

"Fantastic," Benny Maxine said.

When the child tried to draw him out about which parts of a woman's anatomy Eddy preferred, the breasts, the behind, or the quim, Bale blushed and said he supposed it was a matter of individual taste.

Benny smiled and nudged Bale in the side with his elbow.

"You know what gets *me?*" he said.

"Perhaps I oughtn't to be talking to you like this."

"Their pelt."

"Perhaps these things might more properly be discussed in the home environme—"

"Their pelt, their fleece, their fell, their fur," Benny went on happily. "Their miniver, their feathers."

"Yes, well," Eddy said.

"Ask you a *ques*tion?"

Bale stared at the boy.

"It's personal, but you're the one brung it up."

"In for a penny, in for a pound," Bale said ruefully.

"Well," Benny Maxine said, "what it is then is . . . it's just only it's a bit awkward, me putting it, like."

"Look," Eddy said, "not on my account. I mean, if you're at all uncomfortable about this, you don't have to—"

"In for a penny, in for a pound," the child reminded him.

"Right," said Eddy.

"I'm still pretty much virgo intacta and all," Benny told him. "Well," he said, "you must *know* that or we wouldn't be having this conversation, would we?"

"Hey," Eddy reassured him, "at your age I was pretty virgo intacta myself. You make too much of it."

"Of virginity?"

He recalled Benny's list. The miniver, the feathers. "Of birds," Bale said.

"Well, it ain't the birds exactly."

"Maybe you should talk to Mister Moorhead," Eddy said quickly. "He's the physician on board. He could advise you on these things better than I. If this is anything at all to do with the effects of self-abuse on your condition, I'm sure he can fill you in on what's what."

"Nah, if I die, I die," Benny said and glared at Bale, accusing him with the full force of his doom. "*Are* you in for a pound?" he asked at last. "Are you even in for a penny even?"

"Sure," Eddy said. "I told you."

"Why won't you let me get it out then?"

"What is it?" Eddy asked.

"You sure it's okay?"

"Yes," he said, "certainly."

"All right," Benny said, "so so far I'm this yid vestal, this kid monk. I'm this fifteen-year-old virgin with this fifteen-year-old virgin maidenhead. Fifteen years, and it ain't any sure-thing, lead-pipe, dead-cert cinch I'll ever make sweet sixteen. So what I need to know is how long."

"How long?"

"It lasts. How long it lasts. That the chemicals work. That a chap can do it. That given the clean bill of health, the normal drives, and what the actuaries say, how long a party can keep his pecker up, Mister Bale."

Eddy was confused. "Sustain an orgasm?"

"Sustain an orgasm?" Benny said. "No, of course not. I *know* how long a chap can come off. It's the other I'm not sure of. How long the power's there for, I mean. How long he has till his knackers go off on him."

"How long? How old he is?"

"Yeah," Benny said. "How old he is."

"Oh, well," Bale said, "that all depends, I should think. They say we're sexual until the day we die."

"Right," Benny said.

"Oh, Benny," Eddy said.

"What? Oh," he said, "is that what you're thinking? Forget it," he said, "that ain't in it. I mean I can subtract fifteen or sixteen from three score and ten and get the difference. I can take away the subtrahend from the whoosihend well enough. That's not what bothers me. So I miss out on whatever it is, the fifty-four or fifty-five years of what you haul me in here to tell me the shouting's all about. No big deal, no Commonwealth case. Nah," Benny Maxine said, "that don't bother Benny Maxine."

"What does bother you?"

"That slyboots. That old son of a bitch," Benny says, almost to himself.

"What?"

"The crafty old bastard."

"I don't—"

"Mudd-Gaddis. Here I schlepp him from room to room giving him gazes, giving him ganders, and at his age the little geezer has probably nineteen dozen times my own experience. Pushed his wheelchair, I did. Took him for a ride. Showed him the sights. And him under his shawls and lap robes with his hand in the heather. *Ooh,* he's the sly one!"

"Benny," Eddy Bale says quietly, "it's *not* what the shouting's all about. Benny, it isn't."

"Yeah, well," Benny Maxine says, "thanks for the grand bloke-to-bloke chat."

And, when Maxine has gone, Eddy Bale wondering aloud, and not for the first time, "Am I mad? Am I mad?"

(Because he was bursting with it: his discovery. Because, if his hunch was right, he figured he'd found the *real* Magic Kingdom. And, should they be caught, the ancient kid making such a good front and all. And because he thought the old boy was past it anyway. Wouldn't remember. Certainly not where he'd taken him. Not where they'd been.

(And his hunch *had* been right.

(And Benny blessing his god-given, gambler's gifts: his luck, his attention to detail, all his boon instincts.

(So the unlikely pair, the one, dying from some Old Testament curse which, since he wasn't bar mitzvah, he couldn't even begin to understand, pushing the chair down the hotel corridor, and the other, riding in it, dying of all his squeezed and heaped natural causes, nattering away from the depths of his old-age-pensioner's, unpredictable, golden-aged, senior citizen's cumulative heart. "Ahh," Mudd-Gaddis had said from his congested chest, taking the air, "I do love a stroll about the decks of a morning. Thank you so very much for inviting me, Maxine."

("What's a shipmate for?" Benny had said.

("The stabilizers these days, you'd hardly suspect there's a sea under you."

("Steady as she goes."

(Mudd-Gaddis had chuckled. "Quite good, that. 'Steady as she goes.' Not like the old days," he added wistfully.

("No," Benny had said.

("No. Not at all like the old days."

("No."

("Not like any HMS *I* ever sailed aboard."

("I'll be bound," Benny had said.

("Not like the East India Company days. Not like the tubs H.M. sent us out in to encounter the Spanish Armada."

("Really."

(" 'Rule Britannia, Britannia rule the waves,' " Charles Mudd-Gaddis had sung in his high, reedy voice.

("You could probably have used stabilizers like these on the *Titanic*," Benny had said, "or when you went off with Captain Cook to discover the Hawaiian Islands."

(Mudd-Gaddis gave Benny Maxine a sharp look. "I never sailed with Jim Cook," he told him quietly.

("No, of course not. After your time," Benny mumbled, wondering if the little petrified man was having him on.

("Still," Mudd-Gaddis said, "it's not *all* progress. The sea air, for example. The sea air doesn't seem quite as bracing as it used to." Through his thick glasses Mudd-Gaddis stared at the corridor's blue walls. "Indeed, it seems rather close out here. Even a little stuffy, in fact."

("Not like the old days."

("No. Not at all."

("It *is* stuffy," Benny Maxine said suddenly. "Say, why don't we duck into this lounge for a bit? It's probably air-conditioned." They had come to room 822. Benny knocked forcefully on the door and, hearing no answer, folded Mudd-Gaddis's chair and hid it beyond the fire doors at the end of the corridor. Returning to 822 and working with one of the cunning tools on his Swiss Army knife, Benny had made short, clever work of jimmying the door.

("Quick," he said, "in back of the drapes."

("Behind the arras?"

(Benny glanced at his little wizened buddy. "Ri-i-ight," he said.

("It's stuffy here too," his old friend complained.

(Though, as it turned out, they didn't have long to wait. Hardly any time at all. But something as outside the range of ordinary luck—though Benny recognized a roll when he saw one—as the two boys were beyond the range of ordinary children. His gambler's gift for pattern, design. His feel for all the low and high tides of special circumstance, his adaptive, compensatory fortune. All opportune juncture's auspicious luck levers, its favorable, propitious, sweet nick-of- and all-due-time sweepstakes: its bust-the-bank, godsend mercies and jackpot bonanza obligations. No fluke, Benny had thought, only what's coming, only what's owed. And Benny blessing his money-where-his-mouth-was heart.

(And when Benny Maxine heard Mary Cottle at the door he didn't even have to shush Mudd-Gaddis. Who'd evidently been, to judge from his transformed eyes, beyond an arras or two himself in his time.

(She came into her hotel room—she seemed nervous, she seemed irritable—shut the door behind her, and dropped her purse on a chair.

(It wasn't stripping. It wasn't even undressing. It was divestment, divestiture. Orderly and compelled as the speeded-up toilet of some fireman in reverse, or the practiced discipline of sailors whistled to battle stations, say. There was nothing of panic in it, nothing even of haste, just that same compelled, rehearsed efficiency of all mastered routine, just that workmanlike, functional competency, know-how, tact, skill, grace, and craft of adroit forte. Just that same shipshape, green-thumbed, known-rope knack and aptitude of all veteran prowess. She might have been pouring her morning tea or buttering her morning toast or returning home along a route she'd taken years.

(And Benny, both children, amazed who'd only meant to spy on her, astonished who at the outside could only have hoped to trap her in—again, at the outside—some only stiff and formal tryst, some only stilted, silly dalliance with Colin Bible or

Eddy Bale or Mr. Moorhead; or, more like it, to catch her smoking what she oughtn't, in privacy; phoning a boyfriend in England or ordering liquor from room service or bingeing on ice cream, on sweets, and on biscuits; stunned who all along could have hoped only to gather the familiar gossip of their imaginations or, behind the closed bathroom door, to have heard her tinkle, heard her poop. Who hadn't expected, who, counting only on the auspicious and favorable, the opportune and propitious, even *could* have expected, this gusher of bonanza, this ship-come-in, sweet-sweep-staked, bank-broke, jackpot boon. They were flies on the very walls of mystery, and this went beyond what was coming, beyond what was owed. This was out-and-out hallmark fluke!

(Later Benny wouldn't even remember the order in which her clothes had come off. Only that blur of no-nonsense, businesslike efficiency. One moment she had dropped her purse on a chair, the next her clothes were hanging neatly in the closet—and when had she removed her panties or, folding them, laid them carefully on the chair beside her purse? and when had she kicked off her shoes? rolled down her hose and set them across the back of the chair?—and she was completely stripped, uncovered, bare, naked, nude, starkers. She stood before them without a stitch, in the buff, the raw—it was, Benny thought, an apt word; she looked in her nakedness nude as meat in a butcher shop—and he was struck by the rare, pink baldness of her body, by its unsuspected curves and fullnesses—and, oddly, oddly because he would never actually remember seeing her like this, she would become a paradigm for all women, up to her thighs in silk stocking, sitting on underwear, a buried treasure of lace and garter belt, all the lovely, invisible bondages of flesh, her pubic hair bulging her panties like a dark triangle of reinforced silk, her sex like a box of unoffered candy, hoarded fruit—and they see her breasts, they see her cunt. She lies down nude on top of the still made bed. She raises her long legs, spreads them.

(Then she rolls over on her side, turning away from them. They can't see what she's doing but they see her ass. Her left arm goes down, over and across her body, and it looks from their angle as if she's clutching a second pillow to her, getting ready for a nap. They watch her behind as it pumps back and forth on top of the bedspread. She's nestling in all comfy for her bye-byes, thinks Benny Maxine. She's 'aving a bit of a lie-down. The two boys stare at her ass, study its dark vertical, the two discrete, hollow, brown shadows within her cheeks like halved darning eggs, like healed burns, like hairy stains.

(She is quickly done, shivers all along her body, and bounds from the bed. In the bathroom—she leaves the door open; they can see part of her reflection in the full-length mirror—she sits to pee, pulls a few sheets of toilet paper from the roll, and wipes herself. She washes her hands, slaps water on her face, and, when she returns to the room, she seems completely restored. Even her eyes seem restored too, returned to some neutral condition of peace.

("I've heard of this," Benny Maxine mouths to Charles Mudd-Gaddis, explaining. "World-class, champion speed sleep."

(The old gnome frowns at him. The entire time they watch her dress she is still businesslike, still efficient, but now, putting on her clothes, it is almost as if she is posing. As she is, though Benny doesn't realize this. She is posing for the clothes themselves, moving her body into perfect alignment with her apparel, adjusting straps and cups, seams and undergarments to all those unsuspected boluses of flesh. They get an eyeful. They see her from the side, from the rear, from the front. As she rests a leg on the bed and leans forward to leverage a stocking up along her thigh, they get a brief, unobstructed view of her sex, of her bunched and weighted breasts. But she moves too rapidly.

(Benny doesn't know where to look first and, worried about any telltale arthritic creaks, glances at Mudd-Gaddis, meaning to steady him, to forestall the chirping of his old companion's joints, the snap and crackle of his burned bones. But even Mudd-Gaddis's eyes barely move, his fierce old countenance as absolved of desire and edge as Mary Cottle's own.

(Which was when he first thought *slyboots, crafty bastard!* And when he first formulated the questions he did not even know yet he would ever get to ask. Not only the one about how long it lasted, when he might reasonably expect surcease, relief, to be disburdened of what he already knew and recognized was to be just one more additional symptom of his life, but the one about preference too, especially the one about preference, offering pelt as he might ante a chip in a game of chance and despising Mudd-Gaddis, the old roué lech and sated boulevardier, who did not even have to trouble to crane his neck or even to move his eyes about, who'd already seen and presumably done it all in his time, who'd had only to wait there in ambush for something wondrous and delicious to come into view, the old bastard sedate and smug as an assassin behind his cross-hairs, settled in his sexual nostalgia—not having to choose, maybe not even *having* a preference, because the old fart knew that choice was a mug's game—as that woman in her own arms on the bed, and only poor fifteen-year-old virgin Benny burdened forever by his fifteen-year-old turned-stone maidenhead, not knowing the odds but having to place his bet down anyway, the red or the black, declaring for quim, declaring for tush, declaring for boobs or pelt, and hoping, though he knew better, that tush or boobs would come up winners because, let's face it, if he was ever going to get in the game it could only be by copping a feel. When he knew all along. When he by God knew all along where he had to be, where—for him—the real action was, but until this morning hadn't even known the geography existed: *the darning eggs, those elliptical hollows, those two discrete dark shadows, the twin burns, those stinking stains inside the fold of each buttock!*

(She is dressed and out, not looking toward the drapes once, not looking anywhere, not even checking—as everyone does, as even Benny does, as even Mudd-Gaddis must do, tapping their pockets or looking into their purses, for gum, for keys or comb or handkerchief or change—the hotel room she is about to leave. Is gone. Totally collected and moving through the room and out of it, as through with and out of any indifferent space, as assured and confident and possessed as she might be passing from one room to another in her flat.

(And though in many ways it has been a great morning for him, a real eye-opener, the things he's seen trapped in his head as on a photographic plate, Benny is nervous, jealous and convinced as he is—he'd looked at Mudd-Gaddis from time to time, even during her performance, glancing at him as much for confirmation that this was all happening as for the respect he felt was owed him for actually finding the place—that this, so new and exciting to him, was just old familiar stuff to his wise and jaded comrade.

(Who could at least—thank God for small favors—share the discovery Benny was busting with, temper *that* burden, at least, his spilled, cup-run-over excitement, but who wouldn't remember, who couldn't remember lunch and thus wouldn't be able, the forgetful good front and past-it boulevardier, kid-ancient old boy, to ruin a good thing for him, something he would almost certainly want to look in on again and again, or to give him away.)

"Yes," Charles Mudd-Gaddis said to Tony Word and Lydia Conscience on one occasion, and to Janet Order, Rena Morgan, and Noah Cloth on three others, "Mary Cottle. She's taken a room in the hotel just for herself. Room eight twenty-two. Somewhat smaller than any of ours but quite well furnished. A deep, oblong affair with a dark olive-colored dresser, Danish modern, I think, with three long, faintly louvered drawers. A circular table of similar shade about one and a third meters in diameter stands in the southeast corner with two matching generic Scandinavian armchairs. There's a somewhat larger chair off to the side of her Trimline Sylvania TV. The drapes are a patternless brown about the color of damp bark, and the rug is a soft acrylic and wool shag, treated with a somewhat glossy fire retardant. There are four ashtrays rather than the customary three: one on each bedstand and the others on the dresser and table. I suppose she *may* have taken the one on the dresser from the W.C., though my guess—you know how she smokes—is she probably asked Housekeeping for the extra. There were seven fag-ends in only two of the trays, two in the one on the dresser, and five in the one on the bedstand by the beige telephone to the right of the queen-sized bed. I liked her bedspread, incidentally, a sort of burnt sienna. Instead of the usual stylized map of Disney World that hangs in these rooms, there's a quite nice portrait of the old Mickey Mouse. Black and white and from the early days when he was still Steamboat Willy.

"On my way out I happened to notice that the Orlando telephone directory on the dresser was turned to page forty-three."

"Did you mention any of this to Benny?" Rena Morgan asked.

"Benny?" the little gerontological case said uncertainly.

Because everything has a reasonable explanation.

It was Janet Order who reported to Nedra Carp that Mary Cottle had taken room 822. She was still sore because Mary had been thoughtless enough to light that cigarette and caused her to cough and choke and wake from her dream the evening of their airplane ride to Florida. She still remembered the circumstances, the difficulty she'd had falling asleep in the first place—the little blue girl who welcomed sleep if only for the dreams, the disguises she found there, and who, forget special circumstances, forget need, had to wait right along with everyone else for the hour or so to pass before REM sleep came with its marvelously cunning camouflage solutions—and the even greater difficulty she had falling back asleep after she was awake, though she remembered dozing, fitful naps, and recalled, too, her lively suspicions, thinking, She's seen my file, she knows my case, how it is with me. She did that on purpose. And thinking too, Now even if I *do* get to sleep again I'll probably have to go to the bathroom. In any case I'll have to be out just getting my rest a whole other hour or so, or hour and a half or so, before I ever get to dream again. And even if she *didn't* do it on purpose, even if she just needed a cigarette, I know how smokers are. They're addicted as alcoholics. She'll wait an hour—isn't that just what she did in the first place?—or an hour and a half or so, and then, when she thinks I'm sleeping deeply, just go ahead and light up again!

So that's why Janet told on her.

And why she'd asked to be put in with Mr. Moorhead and the boys, even though she'd have preferred to stay with Rena and even with Lydia, so standoffish in the dream, and whose presence there, despite her neatness, picking and cleaning up after herself as she had, wiping away all she could find of her dead-giveaway spoor and all the traces of her prior tenancy, Janet had somehow suspected anyway. (All the dead-giveaway spoor she *could* find!) And why, of all the adults along on the holiday, it was to Nedra Carp she chose to spill the beans. Because the child, with her heightened awareness of other people's aversion to her, could sense *all* aversion a mile off, had this gift the way certain animals were said to have an olfactory knowledge of fear. And why shouldn't she? Wasn't she blue? Wasn't she the blue girl? (No wonder I knew she'd been there, she thought—in the dream. It was my doggy instincts.) And chose Nedra out of some still higher sense of the squeamish, not just the ordinary vibes of simple blue racism this time but even her peculiar sense of caste. Not only had she sensed that Nedra had no use for her, she sensed the reason too. It was simply because she inhabited a different room. It was simply because she was not officially her charge. Not because she was blue and disgusting but because she was not one of Nedra's girls. As soon as she realized this she felt her heart buckle, the strange new symptom of love. So she chose Nedra, almost shy, almost nervous, bringing her the news—first checking the information by attempting to put a call through to 822 (if Miss Cottle answered she'd have hung up), only to be told by the hotel operator that the guest in 822 had instructed the hotel that she would accept no calls ("She," Janet said, *"she?"* "The guest," the operator replied coolly)—like a suitor. Sucking up, Janet thought, I'm sucking up. And didn't mind at all, who wouldn't have minded even if she hadn't picked up all those other vibes as well, the sixth, seventh, and maybe even eighth senses that told her of Nedra's antipathy to the other woman before she so much as mentioned her name. Or the other thing. That the woman she'd chosen to love did not love her back. And not only didn't love her back but probably had an aversion to her greater even than the one she had for Mary Cottle, but whose aversion, whose squeamishness even, was not based on Janet Order's blueness but only on that simple stupid business—her beloved nanny was stupid—that she lived across the hall with Mr. Moorhead and Noah Cloth and Tony Word and so was an affront to her.

"Oh, what a lovely room," she began. "I do so wish I lived here with you and the other girls, Nanny," Janet Order said.

Nedra Carp, knowing it would get back to her employer without her being the one to trouble the dear and troubled man, told Colin Bible.

Who was encouraged, almost buoyed, by the promising ease with which the fellow—Matthew Gale; his name was Matthew Gale—had been able to obtain the key. Turf, Colin Bible thought. The perks of turf. On mine, had I wished to, I could have witnessed the historic operations, met the famous sick, seen their charts and x-rays, the sheiks' and prime ministers' and movie stars' who were always popping into the clinic with their secret under-the-table diseases. I could have had second helpings in the restaurant, access to the drug larders even.

Encouraged, but only almost buoyed. Too nervous still. And guilty, who still felt the humiliation of being so easily spotted and who recalled Gale's knowing wink as forcefully as if it had been a slap. Who'd never flaunted it (and daunted by this vulgar man who did), who didn't in even these compromised circumstances flaunt it now, and who might, so neutrally had they—the two Colins—behaved with each other in public, in the pubs they frequented, the theaters and concert halls they attended, have been taken for second cousins or businessmen or two distant acquaintances thrown together for the evening by the simple innocent agency of one or the other of them's being in possession of an extra ticket. And even more humiliated by the memory of his own outrageous behavior at the health club, by his decoy ambush at the urinals, his skulking camouflage by the toilet stalls, by all his bad play-actor's raving, put-on nonchalance: his prowled, clandestine presence near the equipment, covered in layers of stealth and insinuation as in a raincoat. So amusing to Matthew. Who'd called him "toots" and asked if he'd been waiting long.

He'd had second thoughts, but they'd been as much for poor old obsolescent Colin as for himself, and even after their encounter at the Spa he'd stalled Gale for two days now.

"You know what I think?" Matthew had said. "I think you're a cock-tease."

"No, I'm not," Colin said. "That's an awful thing to say."

"What is it then, dearie, your time of month?"

"Please," Colin said, "don't be common."

"Am I wasting my time with you, sailor? What sort of crap is this?"

"Can't we get to know each other?" Colin said. "Can't we just get to be friends first?"

"I know enough people. I've friends up the wazoo."

"I told you," Colin said, "I'm no light o' love."

"You sure ain't. You're the Blue Balls Kid."

"I told you," Colin mumbled, "I've this very special friend back in England."

"Yeah, you told me. I just want you to know something, sister. I'm getting a little bit tired of these damned Coke dates of ours. I'm a certified faggot, I don't believe in long courtships." Matthew was off duty. They were sitting together at a table outside a café waiting for the fireworks to begin.

"You have to give me more time." He sounded like a foolish girl. Even to himself.

"You know something? You're one naive bimbo. What, you think you're the only married man ever to have gone out of town? The only bespoke hubby at the convention? One-night stands are great. Foxy old grampas do it leaning against the rusted porcelain in tearooms."

"I'm not a foxy old grandpa."

"You're telling me." Matthew smiled, appraising him. "You're one bitch chick."

"Please," Colin said. "Don't talk like that."

"How do you expect me to talk, Miss Priss? I'm coming on. I'm paying you compliments. I'm no Lord What'shisname. I see a skirt I go for, I have to interrupt the programs. It's just my way." An umbrella of fireworks opened up over the Magic Kingdom, the red, blue, and green reflections running down their faces like greasepaint. "Ooh, ahh, eh, Doris?" Matthew Gale said.

Colin wouldn't look at him.

"All right," Gale had said, "all right, I'll respect you in the morning. Anything. All I want is to get you in bed. You're driving me nuts, you know that?"

"Poofs," Colin said.

"I'm not so bad," Matthew Gale said.

"Oh, no," Colin Bible said, "you're terrible."

"I'm not terrible," Matthew Gale said. "You want vulnerability? I'm vulnerable. Gentle sensitivity? I'm sensitive as dick. I'm telling you the truth, old girl. What do you think, I draw graffiti on the walls? I don't even have a pencil."

"Some recommendation that is," Colin said.

"Oh, boy," he said, "she talks dirty."

"How old are you?" Colin asked.

"Twenty-six. Why?"

"You don't look it."

"A fag's fate," Matthew said, "his baby-face genes. Why?"

"You look like a teenager."

"Oh," Matthew said, "I get it. You're afraid you might be contributing to the delinquency of a minor. Forget it. Be easy on that score. Thousands have given at the office."

"You're really twenty-six?"

"I'm fucking thirty, man," Matthew said.

Because it was a test. Because he knew about the room now. "Listen," he said, "I won't leave the park. I shouldn't even be out *here* with you."

Under the table Matthew covered Colin's crotch with his hand. "You'll never believe what you've been missing," he said. "You haven't been blown till you've been blown by a Gale."

Colin pushed his hand away. "I won't do it in automobiles," he said. "I won't do it in holes and corners."

"You limeys have class."

"I mean it," Colin warned.

"You want to get a room?"

"No," he said. (Because it was still the test.)

"You want *me* to?" Matthew asked. "I mean I will if you want, though that could be risky. I mean I don't mind about the money. It's just that you say you won't leave the park. And they know me at the Contemporary; they know me at the Polynesian and the Walt Disney World Village. I mean if you want *me* to sign in and then leave a note for you in a bottle, okay, I'll do it, but this is a company town and if it ever gets back I'll never haunt another mansion."

"No," he'd said, "you wouldn't have to register."

And Colin Bible told Matthew Gale about room 822.

So it was the ease with which Matthew passed the test and was able to produce a key to Mary Cottle's room that enabled Colin to go through with it finally.

He waited until they were both naked until he asked him.

"What are you," Matthew Gale said, "some kind of industrial spy?"

"Never mind about that," Colin said, "can you do it?"

"I don't know. I don't even know what I'm supposed to do."

"You know what you're supposed to do. I just told you."

"Manuals," Matthew Gale said.

"That's right."

"Repair manuals."

"And anything else you can get."

"What do you think, I'm a mechanical engineer? I'm this good-looking fag with a charming manner and a winning smile. I couldn't recognize *blue*prints. Animatronics! *Jesus!*"

"Just the repair manuals then. He's very clever, Colin is. He could work backward from them."

"God!" Matthew Gale said. "If you weren't so well built . . . boy, oh, boy. What I did for love!"

"What we all did," Colin said.

"I don't even *work* at the Hall of Presidents!"

"I've no doubt you've your friends," Colin said sweetly.

And then, without so much as even threatening him with exposure if he failed, Colin Bible, who was confident he wouldn't, who believed in and accepted on trust the existence of a sort of spirit of freemasonry among them, a given, never-to-be-abused loyalty that was not only understood but actually available, actually advocated and depended upon between all the kinds and conditions of homohood, admitted Matthew Gale into Mary Cottle's bed.

3

The acronym in Epcot Center stood for "experimental prototype community of tomorrow," and the place itself was divided into two parts: Future World and World Showcase. Eddy Bale, who'd scouted it, didn't think it was going to be much fun for the dying kids.

Something to do with that emphasis on the future, of course, but not entirely, not even chiefly.

He had, after all, some experience in these matters. Liam was eight when his disease was diagnosed and, while he was nervous about his long-term prospects from the first, it wasn't until he was ten that he suspected he was going to die, and not until he was eleven that he knew he was. And not until those last awful months, Bale remembered, that he actually looked forward to it. His mostly not-forward-looking son.

And that's the point, isn't it, Bale thought. That not once in all the four years of his child's awful disease, or the one or two or of his terrible knowledge, had the boy openly expressed or—or so Bale, who knew the kid, believed—secretly harbored opinions about either the world's or his own future. At six he'd wanted to be a fireman, a pilot, a singer, a cop. At seven his imagination had briefly entertained the notion of becoming a film star. And at nine he wanted, to the extent that he extrapolated a life at all, simply to grow up. After he knew how ill he was he never mentioned it. As closed to the idea of a future as it to him.

They would go, of course. There had been too much hype about the Magic Kingdom's new wing for them not to. So they would go. And have twinges, privately or distanced by their bad public jokes. Some fleeting regrets, some reverse nostalgia for the yet-to-be, but not all that stronger, finally, than his own. Bale wasn't forty yet and, although he expected to live another thirty or thirty-five years, he didn't believe that even in his lifetime (for the moment forgetting the sixty or sixty-five years his dream-holiday kids would probably have lived had they not become ill) the world's cities would blossom into those tall, slim, futuristic forms projected by the park's planners and engineers: cityscapes, Bale thought, like nothing so much as the special effects in science fiction movies, the smooth, permeate Lego acrylics of starships or the capital cities of distant planets, glowing on some night in the future blue as runway lights or the color of water on maps.

But they would go. They'd go—this was hard for Eddy to admit—because there wasn't that much left for them to do. He supposed they had enjoyed their time at Disney World. He had misgivings—his unclear notion of a busted decorum—but on the whole Bale felt it had been a good visit. What they had for health—Moorhead had chosen wisely—had so far held up, and they all seemed to get along better than anyone had probably had a right to expect. Colin's hostility had marred the ointment, but that was personal. Otherwise the fellow performed his job conscientiously, as they all did—Eddy had chosen wisely too—and had made no stir in front of the children.

So as far as Eddy was concerned, it wasn't any abstract anxiety at not being around when the time came for the world to change and put on its new hi-tech face. Posterity did not much trouble them. As much mourn not being on the scene when history happened. As much mourn the Middle Ages, the Renaissance, all the glorious red-letter days one had missed out on, the hour before one was born and time began. Posterity would have its hands full too, even, he suspected, its own incurables. So it wasn't envy. Envy didn't stand much chance when the object of the envy was still thirty or thirty-five—he still hadn't remembered the children's if-all-had-gone-well sixty or sixty-five—years down the road.

It was the other part about which Bale had his doubts. The World Showcase which made him nervous.

For one, he didn't think they'd be entertained. With its boutiques and expensive restaurants it was more like some shopping mall than the stage on which one acted out last flings. For another, the pavilions (points-of-interest, highlights like the obligatory views on postal cards—in the Paris street scene Bale spotted, reduced for perspective, the tapered, graceful top of the Eiffel Tower blooming from the roof of the building on which it had been set up like a potted plant—stage set, tableaux, backdrop like a sort of world vaudeville) of the nine represented countries (Canada, the U.K., France, Japan, the U.S., Italy, Germany, China, Mexico) had been built around the shore of a man-made lagoon, and the effect, at least for Eddy, was disconcerting, surreal. Indeed, it was rather like moving in a dream. China was sandwiched in between Mexico and Germany, America between Italy and Japan. Canada just down the road from the U.K. It was, finally, like Heaven. Convenient, about the same size, without obstacle or climate, and laid out like the aisles in a department store. It was like Heaven and it scared him. It would scare the kids too. They would see that there really *was* a China, that there really *was* a France. That

Germany was not made up. That Italy was no invention, improbable Mexico, unlikely Japan. (All, all real, the scale, toy, gussied-up lands as genuine—wasn't the evidence of the U.K. pavilion with its High Street and pub, its Tudor and Georgian and Victorian styles, its chimneys and timbers and thatch, or even its costers with their pearly plate like a soft, obsolete armor, proof enough?—as the great engines their tiny models merely stood for. All, all real, alas.) It could put them off. Such knowledge. Reminding them of the simple symbolism of their arrangements, that what they did now had to last them, forcing their hands who should have spent their lives like drunken sailors, like there was no tomorrow. (And speaking of history, Eddy Bale thought, of red-letter days and death at time's other end like a counterweight, hadn't Liam himself had a rough go on his birthdays, on Christmas? All holidays, really, those on which no gifts were exchanged as well as those on which they were? Anniversary sodden as bad air. Hadn't Ginny? Hadn't Eddy? The presents coming in his boy's last years not only cardless and unwrapped but unpackaged too, out of their boxes, and, at last, as if they'd been fetched from home in paper bags along with his clean pajamas and his fresh tube of toothpaste. Which would probably outlast him. And queer, he thought, that Liam's voice had begun to change just a couple of months before he died. Queer. An additional blow. "This is what I would've sounded like, ain't it, Dad?" his son had asked. And Bale had lied. "You've a frog in your throat," he said. "If it's all right with the doctor, Colin can bring you lozenges for that." And, terrified, broached the subject of Liam's puberty with the man. "You're being silly," the physician said. "No," Bale said, "he's too weak. A wet dream could kill him," Bale said. And tried to keep up the pretense even after he'd found out that Liam had begun masturbating. Liam dutifully sucking the lozenges Bale brought. Their conversations coated by the vapors of eucalyptus, of cherry and honey and lemon. So that, for Eddy, the effect was that the boy might have come down with nothing more bothersome than a bad sore throat, a seriously stuffed nose. That he slept in a room with a vaporizer, with camphor-coated cloths about his neck. Till the doctor brought Eddy up sharp. "What's that in his mouth?" "A Hall's," Liam said. "Take it out. Don't you know that menthol could upset your stomach?" But a few weeks had passed. Liam's voice was changed now. And, Bale hoped, he might have forgotten he ever sounded any different. Till Liam brought him up sharp. "I'll never have another sore throat, will I?" he said. The anniversaries and special occasions coming thick and fast now. "It's the full moon tonight. I hope I remember to look at it when they wake me for my medication," he said. One day, a week or so before he died, he and Ginny, having stepped out into the corridor for a cigarette, returned to the room. Their son was crying. "What is it, Liam? What is it, dear?" "The shipyards are shut down," he told them. "I heard on the news that the builders have gone out on strike." They were in a country where no more ships would be built while he lived, he meant. And it was another anniversary of sorts—— Liam's milestone yardage. Because the centennials and jubilees, the birthdays and holidays and seasons were closing in, becoming the monthly and fortnightly and weekly, becoming the daily, all periodicity and fixed interval shrinking through the wide, rotational tidal toward some ever-diminished, diminishing now. Which was about when Colin began to come in to take him to look at the cars down on Devonshire Place. And every day red-letter. Speaking of history.)

But the children weren't put off. That didn't happen, at least. Bale's fears, his theme-park notions of Heaven, his awry orientation and sense of the surreal didn't send them into decline. And if they shared his misgivings about the place's skewed geography, if it offended their sense of the orderly that Italy was a stone's throw from Asia or that China shared a border with Mexico, they never let on. The mutualized climate didn't bother them. That they didn't have to deal with mountains or cross seas seemed not to trouble them. Nothing seemed to trouble them. They were not upset, or even perhaps aware, of the simple symbolism of their arrangements. They spent their lives like sober sailors.

And if they seemed less excited than they'd been, Eddy put it down not to boredom—they *weren't* bored—but to something like the mildest loss of innocence, becoming acclimated perhaps to being in a new country, their jet lag smoothed over, their travelers' up-front awe cleared up.

The fact was that they were concerned about getting to, or getting back to, Mary Cottle's room.

Except for Eddy, who didn't know about it, they were on their best behavior, the adults as well as the children, at the peak of their conscientiousness. Working, though not all of them knew this—Eddy, of course; Mary Cottle herself—as a group without even knowing it.

For the first time, buddy aligned with buddy without being reminded. Janet Order and Tony Word, Rena Morgan and Noah Cloth, Benny Maxine and Lydia Conscience formed into pairs. On line, they held each other's hands tight as tickets. And Eddy Bale, touched, wondered what he'd been worrying about. They seemed sweet, totally without airs, like school children on field trips, their diseases oddly muffled by their patience and courtesy, something faintly disadvantaged about them still, long-suffering but not fatal, reduced to a sort of poverty, perhaps, some vaguely respectful, intimidated sense of the out-of-their-element clinging to them. They might have been on queue at the water fountain or waiting to board a bus. Whatever, they seemed subdued, serious as beggars making their manners. They didn't so much as whisper among themselves, let alone bray out the loud public jokes Bale had half expected. That they were physically mismatched—Janet and Rena towered over their tiny charges—only managed to make them seem even more settled, almost married, as if the difference in their ages and heights signified some acute mutual acceptance, the way a wife guiding a blind husband seems somehow even more intimately connected to her partner than if the man were sighted. It was the same with Lydia Conscience and Benny Maxine. The underage, gorbelly girl, pregnant-seeming behind her great tumor, and the teenage boy looked like joined, hand-in-hand lovers, overwhelmed, perhaps, and certainly too young for their circumstances, but as bonded and content as youthful, dangerous killers on a spree.

Behind the children, watching over them, Nedra Carp and

Colin stood beside each other while Mr. Moorhead went bustling from pair to pair, checking, but decorous and proper as a maître d'.

And, looking all of them over as they waited to be handed into the cars that would carry them up the seventeen stories of Spaceship Earth (Future World's great landmark, a huge sphere, pocked as an immense golf ball), Eddy Bale felt a strange pride in the odd group. It's because they're taking it so well, he thought.

Careful not to become separated—they recalled the fuss when they had—the children instinctively gave way, voluntarily allowing others to precede them even if it was not their turn.

My, Eddy thought, watching in the theatrical gloom, his congratulatory pride incremented by the dark, by expectation and a suffusion of love. My, Eddy thought, flooded with his curious content, his madness peaking now, spiking like a fever, how good they all are!

He was pleased even by the serendipitous symmetry of the arrangements. One adult to each pair of buddies—Nedra sat between Janet Order and Tony Word while Colin Bible took his place in the cars with Rena and Noah, and Benny and Lydia Conscience were with Mr. Moorhead—the partners seemed less disadvantaged now, neither ill nor poor nor out of place. It was the adults, he thought, that lent them force, a scant air of there being something premeditated about their quiet good manners, not long-suffering as he had thought but placid, vaguely exhibitionist. And then he had it. Why, he thought, they might be Saturday's children, here by court order, official decree, sentenced by a judge and their own mixed loyalties, perfecting their expressions, balancing them like books, all the smoky nonchalance of the indifferently loved, rehearsing the customs of visitation and doing God knows what secret sums of custody in their heads, sneaking glances at their watches, timing what was left of the morning, the long afternoon, and wondering if it was time yet to go to the restaurant, how long the line would be at the movies.

Eddy Bale, comforted by his imagination—divorce was a

better doom than doom—moved beside Mary Cottle, who'd taken charge of Charles Mudd-Gaddis in his wheelchair, pushing it along the platform like a child's stroller each time the line inched forward and new people climbed into the cars. In the dim light he accidentally brushed her hip and asked if he could take the tour with them. Mary shrugged and he got into the tram with Mudd-Gaddis and Miss Cottle. Snug, he felt snug. The two grown-ups, the little boy, made a cozy family.

The tram pulled away from the platform, began its long climb, while Eddy speculated about their collective calm, their take-what-came inscrutability.

He didn't know, couldn't have known, that they were disinterested, being pulled past the highlights in this palace of highlights, being drawn up the mammoth geosphere as up a well, the history of civilization illuminated on either side like river views from an open boat, like Paris shoreline gliding across the vision in a *bateau mouche*.

He did not know, could not know, their indifference, absolute now—only Mudd-Gaddis pointed, only Mudd-Gaddis, alternately delighted and fearful, squealed—to humanity's transitionless breakthrough breakthroughs, detached, drifting through time as across the panels of a comic strip, seeming to slow down for each milestone as if they were pulling into a familiar train station along their route home, sliding past the cave paintings, beasts stylized as jewelry, primitives squatting over their Neanderthal fire like low gamblers at dice. They moved alongside Egyptians chiseling hieroglyphs like great strange keys and, farther up, caught glimpses of ancient Greece's legitimate theater, its antique declamated tragedies. They traveled Rome's blocky old roads and saw the great libraries of ruined empires. They saw monasteries where medieval monks, like secretaries taking painstaking dictation, copied out gospel. They passed Gutenberg's print shop—and didn't know, couldn't know, Colin Bible's held-tongue, bite-bullet pangs at each special effect: the movable type on Gutenberg's press—and pressed on into the glories of the Renaissance. And were plunged into the twentieth century as into din. A telegraph clicked like a castanet. They saw the stop-press banner hieroglyphs of newspapers. Radio was in it now, TV, computers. And, still climbing, rose into space, the comfortable room temperature of the heavens, galactic swamps swirling above them like fingerprints of starlight, space platforms like futuristic chandeliers.

At Journey Into Imagination they watched a sort of electronic puppet show—to him, they seemed riveted; how could he know?—and saw rainbows stripped as you'd strip paint, and led electronic orchestras, and walked across a floor that turned their footsteps into music, and stared, his distorted kids, into distorting mirrors. He watched a 3-D movie with them and saw them draw back as objects leaped out at them from the screen.

So how could he, how *could* he know whose uncompromised oohs and ahhs, like someone watching birthday candles being blown out, came from the heart? Or that Colin Bible stifled his injury-nursed gasps and carefully suppressed sighs and whimpers as he stared down from Epcot Computer Central's glassed-in balcony at the massive and complicated control boards that handled it all?

Or that Nedra Carp, seated between Janet Order and Tony Word, wondered why Mr. Moorhead hadn't assigned her to a car with children who were her official responsibility rather than hustling her in with strangers? (Did she know the contents of their pockets, what awful contraband candy they might have brought with them? Had they had a B.M. today? Who'd made sure they'd tinkled before permitting them to come out?) And a bit angry with the children, too, or put off—she was not the sort to lose her temper with children, not like that woman Mary Cottle, who used to run off to the bathroom for a sulk whenever things didn't go entirely spit-spot and now disappeared altogether whenever the poor dears fussed or grew cranky (and now she knew where, didn't she, and maybe it was something more than a bit of a sulk, and perhaps, if she'd wanted Mr. Bale to find out, it had been something of a mistake to have entrusted Colin Bible, who'd probably known it anyway, with the information, birds of a feather and all that)—because they hadn't protested, and had abandoned her without so much as a by-your-leave to finicky Tony Word with his peculiar tastes and foul vegetable breath, a boy, she suspected, who, had it been left to him, would actually have gotten down on the ground and rooted for potatoes, carrots, onions, the level radish and asparagus and pumpkin, the foreign zucchini and eggplant and broccoli, eating them from the soil, the earth itself; and that disgusting Janet Order, whose blue dreadfulness, even in the dark, was palpable to her, awful as vein, livid as beetle or basilisk. Or that she could not stop thinking about the woman?

Or that Benny Maxine couldn't either, or of the two discrete and darkened hollows in her ass, larger, sweeter than dimples?

Or that Mr. Moorhead, having removed his watch and put it in the pocket of his jacket and, out of earshot of the others, inquired of semitic-looking tourists for the one hundred and sixty-eighth time the time of day—he was a scientist, trial-and-error was part of his training, watching their wrists as they raised their arms to within inches of their eyes—— and, hypothesis too, they would have at least to be in their late middle age (the youngest among them would have been almost fifty by now) or, more likely, elderly, in their sixties, or, most probable of all, old, in their seventies, nearsighted, waited—patient observation was— and watched for the bookkeeping to appear on their skin, the fadeless, telltale numbers, the careful tattoo audit, and listened also—there could have been shame; they might have been wearing their watches on the opposite arm or worn a timepiece about their neck—auscultating their accents, and had found his Jew?

Or that Lydia Conscience no longer believed she was fooling anyone with her cheap rings and big belly? (That was made quite clear in that dream she'd shared with Mudd-Gaddis and Tony Word. They'd only been patronizing her. Mudd-Gaddis pretending Tony Word was the father! *Tony Word!* The remarks about morning sickness, her own bitter comments about the buddy system when all she meant, she supposed, was that she didn't want anyone to know her details. Better to be known for a loose under-age slut than for a terminal! And people stared when they were with her. Mr. Bible sometimes wearing that white nurse's jacket! Outrageous! Might as well take out an advert. As if Mudd-Gaddis weren't advert enough. Or Rena Morgan, thinking she fooled anyone with her dumb hidden hankies. Didn't the twit realize that the wet spots showed when she slipped them up her sleeve again? Or bald Tony Word, who didn't even have the decency to wear a wig! Or blue-skinned Janet Order, who invaded her dream on the plane. "I dream of Janet with the light blue skin," she sang to herself in her head. Or bloated Benny with his puffy face, and stupid Noah who couldn't read and, now he was losing his fingers, couldn't even count right!) And that was why she still wore the rings even though she knew they didn't fool anyone anymore and, twice removed—once to make people think she was preggers and now to keep them from knowing just *what* the hell she was—merely masked the details she couldn't bear anyone to know? Or that ever since she'd heard about Mary Cottle's private room she'd been trying to work up the nerve to tell her she hadn't spent any of her money and to ask her that, if she paid her fair share, could she use it just to get away once in a while?

Or that Noah Cloth, remembering the lady who'd visited him at home that time and recalling what she'd told him about denial, rage, bargaining, and acceptance—hadn't the compulsive shopping been, at least partly, a kind of bargaining? if that were so, then even if he couldn't recollect the denial and rage parts, he was almost gone—wondered whether, if she'd let him, maybe he could use Miss Cottle's room as a sort of hospice?

Or that Janet Order had grown tired of her camouflage, the permutations of all those blue dreamed force fields that had shielded her, hidden her like so much dun-colored predator, dun-colored prey, like birds indistinguishable from the trees they perch in, or soldiers in the always-too-flat Indian summer drabs of battle dress? Because the fact was that blue, quite apart from the cyanotics of her illness, was her favorite color. And hadn't she, in the ocean depths and sky heights of those blue dreams, at the balls and celebrations, the coronations, inaugurals, and masques, all the dress-blue ceremonials, lost against the royal-

and midnight- and navy-blue buntings, against the sleep-wrought hyacinthine drapes and wall hangings, or hovering over the peacock- and robin's-egg-blue napery, *all* the blue arrangements, all the deep cobalts of sparkling, spanking accessory, the sapphire studs, the violet eyeshadow, clothed in all the forget-me-not hues of her blue-jeweled skin, loved, even admired, above all else, herself? And now wants, actually needs, suddenly, quite simply, privacy—the bathroom's too small (Tony's and Noah's medications, her own, Mr. Moorhead's digestives and shaving equipment, all their toothbrushes, toothpastes, shampoos, and special soaps clutter the sink, its deep, wide counter); the children are suspicious of her in the toilet; if she runs the shower to cover the sounds of her inspections, the mirror clouds over—and longs to sneak into 822, wants, needs, to examine herself, at leisure to pry her blue behind, her budding cornflower breasts, her Prussian blue nipples?

Or that leukemic Tony Word, fearful because he's not been eating properly, suspicious of the scraped strained vegetables he's served, of the mashed, crushed potatoes, the creamed carrots and pea purées, the smashed beets and thrice-diced watery cauliflower, the brothy fruits and minced greens, beneath their staring, the kids' and adults' and waiters', yields, discards what is not even the menu but only some rote-recalled menu of the head and asks what baby food they have, orders it, and feels anyway this sinful dietary guilt, vaguely religious, aware that he chews (and knowing that he needn't, it's like chewing soup), thoughtful and careful as any Jew or Muslim, profane food, as if, if he's careful enough, he might be able to trap and spit out lumps of preservative and additive like bits of pork? Or that he is worn out by their curiosity (baby food? a kid his age?), dreads their attention at meals, and wishes to go back to the old regime, doing for himself (which would have been impossible of course until Mudd-Gaddis told him and he'd had the idea, now his dream), and thinks that if he can only get their permission he can use his food allowance, make up from cash whatever the difference comes to, and, specifying exactly the ingredients he needs, instructing the kitchen how long each must be boiled, what wood tools, what pots he requires, he could use Mary Cottle's telephone and order his dinner from room service?

Or that Charles Mudd-Gaddis, snagged on some shard of memory—is it personal or just more ancient history?—vague as the scattered fragments of a dream (how terrible to grow so old, infirm and invalid, to feel summer like a chill, trapped not only in skeleton—brittle as archaeology—and flesh—brittle as skeleton—but hobbled by crochet, got up like furniture, all the doily cerements of the old, the caps and shawls and lap robes—and a thousand years ago, it seems, worked out his answer, waits only for the question to be asked, the secret formula of his geologic life, will tell the smart-ass kid whose assignment he will be, will tell, if he can still remember his own remarks, will tell, will say, "Masochism. You've got to love pain and worship humiliation"—to be permitted such a long, forced-march lifetime), tries, as if he were trying, working about the obstacles of pain, all the pangs, nips, cramps, and bruises of his land-mined steeplechase being, to draw a very deep breath, to grasp and hold it? Pleasure was in it. He'd been a sort of witness. Shared the witness. With. A baby? How could that be? Since the baby had spoken. He distinctly remembered. Well, distinctly. But they were all babies to him, to a man of his years. The nurses and attendants. So not *literally* a baby. And there was something illicit. A display or performance. All right, some secret display or performance which had given him, them, himself and the child, pleasure. They'd gone to see some show. On an outing. But without the others in the Home and not to some museum of ancient history like this one today, where all there'd been to look at were some old-fashioned space platforms and obsolete computers like faded daguerreotypes. His nurse. Of course. His nurse. The one who smelled of that foreign tobacco. Whom he sat next to. He'd, they'd—himself and the other old-timer—spied on his nurse. Or that he had the memory now, only couldn't make sense of that comment afterward, the ancient mariner's, who'd asked him, "How about them hidey-holes in her hidey-hole, Charley?"

Or that Rena Morgan was exhausted?

Or that Mary Cottle, out of the starting gate serene, her laundered nerve endings smooth as fresh sheets, has begun to feel not the oppression again (which hadn't been there even in that tunnel-of-love rideup time or even under the circumstances of their imposed coze—— the kids calm, sedate, almost contemplative, their attentions absorbed, whatever preoccupied them releasing them for once from whatever had preoccupied them, their pull of obsession, the steady-state tensions of their defective bodies, because, face it, these children, why she bothered with them, who was, after all, the improbable party here, less probable than Nedra Carp, less probable than Bale, were, for her, projections not of the two stillborn fetuses which she did not have or even of the two aborted amniocentesisized fetuses which she did, the two wounded full-term babes themselves, damaged goods, those little suffering citizens whose sealed, suspected tantrums and soft exacerbated lives triggered, probably in inverse ratio, her own violent encounters with herself, her furious fixes) but still an itch, pastel, softer than she's accustomed to, even tender, locked in the wavelengths and frequencies of something like courtship—*nothing* alien is alien to her—some strange and lovely magnetism of skin, the compulsive yearning of the centrifugals along the tumbling, degraded orbit of her life, her interests focused for once on the conventional forks, playing catch-up who'd been hung up on fastidy and reserve but who knew her G-spot like the back of her hand, what the fuss was all about; this woman, lusty as a sailor, a fleet, a navy, bringing the spilled beans of her fevers and kindling points like all the pressed and faded roses of love, not barbarians at her gates now but blander, more unsuspected things, not the wired protocols of flesh or her body's steamy skirmishes and star wars so much as the politics of etiquette and love, all the gossip of the heart and head, of some brand-new flower style like those dumb sexual displays in nature, the bright bandings on birds, say, who do not even know that what they're wearing is instinct and evolution; *that* innocent, *that* naive, up to her ass in guilt and underwear and outraged as someone trying to clear her name, wanting, needing frill and circumstance, some all-the-trimmings life she hadn't ever lived and hadn't even known she'd longed to live, her lust diffused, broad and scattered as cloud cover? Or that the old gaffer seated between them, Mudd-Gaddis, could just as easily be patriarch as child, *is* patriarch, some ancient totem of relation who monitored behavior and whom they had to impress to please, wanting, she who had never wanted anything from men, some soft service, the honorable, ancient courtesies of pleasure: flowers and candy boxes in Romance's turnstile, toll-booth doorways, vino, gypsy violins, and, later, the more inventive stuff: pet names and pretty speeches, billet-doux, the rose beneath the windscreen wiper, a star of one's own, sonnets initialed as handkerchiefs, gems in the picnic hamper, cars sent, orchestras bribed, baths drawn—— all Soft Soap's pretty handouts, all Love's free lunch? Or that wholesome, afferent affections shot from the juiced peripheries of her heart to collect and gather like pooled blood beneath the little old gaffer, child-totem-patriarch's and Cupid-kid's dim scrutinies?

So how could Eddy, who could not sort his own, have made anything at all of the jumble of mixed motives and crossed purposes, ordinary and routine as heavy traffic, or seen design in their snarl of wills, feelings, and intentions, asynchronous and asyndeton as timber soaking in a logjam?

W ell, Colin Bible had seen enough. He'd a feeling he'd disgraced himself. He'd been had. But was in no position to cast aspersions. The guy was as good as his word (though, just as well, not that great in bed). The repair manuals were waiting for him in an outsized manila envelope when he checked his and Bale's box the next day. There were even some blueprints Matthew had been able to lay his hands on, even a few diagrams of what Colin supposed—he was no mechanical illiterate, after all; he was a nurse, could make a certain sense of x-rays and cardiograms, plug in I.V.'s and administer shots, and just generally knew his way around the human body (oh, yes, he thought, remembering and flushing), which was as complicated as any piece of just machinery—were schemata for wiring, for fire alarm systems, burglar.

But, he saw, the Empire was finished, over, dead. The future, certainly the present, was with the superpowers and the go-getter Nips. They had the nuclears and lasers, they had the highest tech and the microchips and the animatronics. One day soon there wouldn't be an up-to-date, decent, self-respecting tourist attraction left anywhere between America and the U.S.S.R. Everything else was just scenery—yes, and they had the wilderness areas, the deepest canyons and longest rivers; they had the sunsets; they had the climates—and thrill rides. There'd be nowhere else a dying kid could go.

But his real gloom, his real patriotism, he reserved for Colin back in Blighty in his obsolete waxworks. (We have the wax.) Poor Colin, Colin thought, and could not have said which one of them he had in mind.

No, by disgrace he meant he'd allowed his desperation to show and knew that, in his position, Mary Cottle would not have permitted herself the luxury. He admired the woman, and if he tried to snitch on her that time she'd become separated from the group, that had only been duty. The desperation was something else. Everyone's desperate, he knew, Mary Cottle included. It was giving oneself permission to reveal it that was off. Like the poet said, most blokes lead lives of quiet desperation, but the poet was wrong. Most blokes shouted it from the rooftops, they shouted and shouted it till the rafters rang. He yearned for the days of his former silence, for the old-time, stiff-upper-lip qualities that made him British and had kept him in the closet. He wanted his quiet desperation back. (It was too late, of course. If they hadn't maintained such a sterile field in this place—you could practically operate here—his name would be spray-painted all over the lavs by now.) It had been Mary Cottle's room they'd used, Mary Cottle's bed—his nursing skills had come in handy when he remade it; Matthew marveled at his hospital corners— and the least he owed her was his silence. He hadn't told Gale it was not his room. He didn't know what she was up to in hiring a hall—he'd cut Nedra off when she offered her theories after telling him of its existence—but desperation was bound to be in it. He'd leave her to Heaven. She could be one of the blokes to lead the quiet desperation life. While he, now *he* was in it, would have to continue to make his unseemly noises.

So the first chance he had he took his manuals and sought Gale out.

"What do you mean?" Gale said. "You've got William Henry Harrison there. You've got Dwight Eisenhower and Martin Van Buren. Warren Harding, James Knox Polk. You've got Republicans and Democrats. I gave you a Whig! I made up a nice assortment."

"A lovely assortment."

"I picked it out myself," Matthew said.

Fags, Colin thought, and had a vagrant image of Matthew Gale's toes curled in his shoes, smitten, shy and sly beneath the shoelace line. The penny-loafer line, he corrected, and realized Gale was in love, and wondered again if he were holding out on him.

"Matthew?" Colin said.

"What?"

"Are you holding out on me?"

"Holding out? Did I last night?"

"I'm not talking about last night."

"Whatever *are* you talking about?"

Fags, he thought. High-minded fag-aristocrat syntax-flourish. "I'm talking about the manuals. Really, Matthew! 'The Lowdown on Central Heating in the Magic Kingdom!' 'Secrets of Mickey Mouse's Loo Revealed!' "

"Do you know what would happen if they found out I was giving this stuff away?"

"Trading it," Colin Bible said.

"Oh," Matthew Gale said, "we're KGB, are we? We're CIA, we're MI-Five."

"No, Matthew," he said, "we're only a nurse in love."

"You going to turn state's evidence?" Matthew wondered gloomily.

"Who, me? What believes in all that allegiance and loyalty? No fear."

"What are you talking about now?"

"The brotherhood. That old spirit of freemasonry among all the kinds and conditions of homohood," he said wearily, deciding, Nah, he doesn't have the goods. "Hey, Matthew?"

"What?"

"You were right. I'd never been blown till I'd been blown by a Gale," Colin told him kindly as he moved off.

Because everything has a reasonable explanation. Because Colin Bible had seen enough and was ready to try a different tack.

"Come, children," Colin said.

"We already seen that parade," said Benny Maxine.

"I want you to see it again."

"Where are you taking them?" Nedra Carp asked.

"You needn't come, Miss Carp, if you don't wish to."

"Oh, I couldn't let you go by yourself. Who'd push the girl's wheelchair?"

"I'll push it. Benny can handle Mudd-Gaddis's."

Maxine looked at the nurse.

"Anyway, I don't see what the rush is. The parade don't start for nearly an hour yet," he said.

There were frequent parades in the Magic Kingdom. Mr. Moorhead had given them permission to stay up one night to watch the Main Street Electrical Parade, a procession of floats outlined in lights like the lights strung along the cables, piers, spans, and towers of suspension bridges. There were daily "character" parades in which the heroes and heroines of various Disney films posed on floats, Alice perched on her mushroom like the stem on fruit; Pinocchio in his avatar as a boy, his strings fallen away, absent as shed cocoon; Snow White flanked by her dwarfs; Donald Duck, his sailor-suited, nautical nephews. They'd seen this one, too. There'd been high school marching bands, drum majors, majorettes, pom-pom girls, drill teams like a Swiss Guard. Tall, rube-looking bears worked the crowd like advance men, parade marshals. Some carried balloons in the form of Mickey Mouse's trefoil-shaped head, vaguely like the club on a playing card. (Pluto marched by, a Mickey Mouse pennant over his right shoulder like a rifle. "Dog soldier!" Benny Maxine had shouted through his cupped hands. The mutt turned its head and, in spite of its look of pleased, wide-eyed, and fixed astonishment, had seemed to glare at him.) Everywhere there were Mickey Mouse banners, guidons, pennants, flags, color pikes, devices, and standards, the flash heraldics of all blazoned envoy livery. Music blared from the floats, from the high-stepping tootlers: Disney's greatest hits, bouncy and martial as anthems. It could almost have been a triumph, the bears, ducks, dogs, and dwarfs like slaves, like already convert captives from exotic far-flung lands and battlefields. The Mouse stood like a Caesar in raised and isolate imperiality on a bandbox like a decorated cake. He was got up like a bandmaster in his bright red jacket with its thick gold braid, his white, red-striped trousers. His white gloves were held stiff and high as a downbeat against his tall, white-and-red shako. His subjects cheered as he passed. (You wouldn't have guessed that Minnie was his concubine. In her polka-dot dress that looked almost like homespun, and riding along on a lower level of a lesser float, she could have been another pom-pom girl.)

It was toward this parade they thought they were headed.

But Main Street was practically deserted.

"What was the rush?" Nedra Carp asked.

"Yeah, where's the fire?" said Benny Maxine.

"Hang on," Colin Bible told them. "You'll see."

"It's another half hour yet," Lydia Conscience said.

"Are we just going to stand around?" Janet Order asked from her wheelchair.

"We could be back in our rooms resting," Rena Morgan said.

"We can sit over there," Colin said. He pointed across Main Street to the tiny commons. Old-fashioned wood benches were placed outside a low iron railing that ran about a fenced green.

"We sit here we won't see a thing once it starts," Noah Cloth said.

"He's right," Tony Word said. "People will line up along the curb and block out just everything."

"Hang on," Colin Bible said. "You'll see."

About twenty minutes before the parade was scheduled to start, a few people began to take up positions along the parade route.

"Look there," Colin said.

"Where, Colin?" Janet said.

"There," he said, "the young berk crossing the street, coming toward us." He was pointing to an odd-looking man with a wide thin mustache, macho and curved along his lip like a ring around a bathtub. His dark thick sideburns came down to a level just below his mouth. "They're dyed, you know," Colin whispered. "They're polished with bootblack."

"How would you know that, Colin?" Noah asked.

"Well, not to blind you with science, I'm a nurse, aren't I? And 'aven't a nurse eyes, 'aven't a nurse 'air? When you seen stuff so inky? There ain't such darkness collected together in all the dark holes."

"All the dark holes," Benny Maxine repeated, pretending to swoon.

"Look alive, mate," Colin scolded, "we're on a field trip, a scientifical investigation."

"We're only waiting for the parade to begin," Lydia said.

"A parade we already seen."

"Two times."

"By day and by night."

"M-I-C K-E-Y M-O-U-S-E."

"Can't we give the parade a pass?"

"*This*," Colin hissed, "*this* is the parade! This is the parade and you've *never* seen it! All you seen is the cuddlies, all you seen is the front runner, excellent dolls, happy as Larry and streets ahead of life."

"Really, Mister Bible," Nedra Carp said, "such slangy language!"

"Lie doggo, dearie, please. Keep your breath to cool your porridge, Miss Carp."

"I don't think this is distinguished, Mister Bible," Miss Carp said.

"Jack it in," he told her sharply. "Distinguished? *Distinguished?* I'm showing them the popsies, I'm showing them the poppets. I'm displaying the nits and flourishing the nut cases. The bleeders and bloods, the yobbos and stooges. I'm furnishing them mokes and bringing them muggins. All the mutton dressed as lamb. No one has yet, God knows, so old Joe Soap will must."

"Why?"

"Ask me another," he said.

"Why?"

"They've got to find out how many beans make five, don't they? It's only your ordinary level pegging, merely keeping abreast. There's a ton of niff in this world, you know. There's just lashings and lashings of death. Hark!" He broke off. *"Watch what you think you're going to miss.* Hush! Squint!" The man with the mustache and sideburns was passing in front of them.

And now you couldn't have dragged them away. You couldn't have rolled Janet Order's or Mudd-Gaddis's wheelchair downhill.

"Uh-oh," Colin Bible said, "we've been sold a pup."

"Snookered!" said one of the children.

"Skinned!" said another.

"Socked!"

"Some mothers have 'em," Benny Maxine said.

Because they saw that Colin had been wrong.

The man was not young, after all. He could have been in his fifties. He wore cowboy boots, the cheap imitation leather not so much worn as peeling, chipped as paint and mealy and rotten as spoiled fruit. His high raised heels were of a cloudy translucent plastic. Flecks of gold-colored foil were embedded in them like sparks painted on a loud tie. Up close he had the queer, pale, lone, and fragile look of men who cut themselves shaving. Of short-order cooks, of men wakened in drunk tanks or beaten in fights. A bolo tie, like undone laces, hung about a bright pink rayon shirt that fit over a discrete paunch tight and heavy as muscle. A chain that ran through a wallet in the back pocket of his pants was attached to his belt.

Nor were his broad sideburns dyed. They were tattooed along his ears and down his cheeks. His mustache was tattooed. The actual gloss and sheen tattooed too—like highlights in a landscape. Everything only indelible, deep driven inks among the raised scars of his illustrated whiskers.

They were gathering, coming together quickly now, lining up along the curbs, building a crowd, rapidly taking up the best vantage points like people filling a theater. "See 'em? They look like fans at the all-in wrestling," Colin said wickedly. And they did. Something not so much supportive as impatient and partisan about them. Apple Annies of style, Typhoid Marys of spirit, the men as well as the women, they could have been carriers, not of disease but of vague, pandemic strains on the psyche, on tastes not depleted but somehow made accommodate to the surrender terms of their lives and conditions. As though they'd survived their dreams, even their lives, only to find a need to be at a parade of cartoon characters at Disney World.

It was different with the children, their parents. Oddly in the minority, Colin barely made mention of them, as though most lives came with a grace period, thirty or thirty-five years, say, some fifty-thousand-mile guarantee of the agreeable and routine. It was the widows traveling together he pointed out, the senior citizens up from Miami or down from such places as Detroit or Cleveland on package tours. It was the retirees, the couples unescorted by kids. They were casually dressed, the women in pants suits or sometimes in shorts—it was a mild fall day—the men in Bermudas, in slacks the color of artificial fruit flavors, in white shoes, in billed caps with fishermen's patches. (Cinderella Castle, towering above them in the background, made them seem more like subjects than ever, reasonably content, well-off, even, but with a whiff of the indentured about them, of an obligated loyalty.)

"Look there!" Colin Bible said. "And *there*. Look at those over there!"

There was a couple with the lined, bloated, and satisfied heads of midgets. Wens were sprinkled across their faces like a kind of loose change of flesh.

There was a potbellied, slack-breasted man, his wife with bad skin, wrinkled, scarred, pitted as scrotum. They had smooth, fat fingers, and their hands were balled into the ineffectual, hairless fists of babies.

"Look, look there, how ugly!" Colin said.

An angry woman with long dark hair, her back to the street, stood near the couple with the wens. Her hair, tied beneath her chin, looked like a babushka. She stared back at Colin and the children, her black, thick eyebrows exactly the color and shape of leeches above eyes set so deep in her skull they seemed separated from her face, hidden as eyes behind a mask or holes cut from portraits in horror films. A set of tiny lips, Kewpie-doll, bow-shaped, red and glossy as wet paint, and superimposed, grafted onto her real lips like a botched bookkeeping or clumsy work in a child's coloring book, tinted an additional ferocity into her scrutiny.

"It breaks your heart," Colin said. "Imperfection everywhere, everywhere. Not like in nature. What, you think stars show their age? Oceans, the sky? No fear! Only in man, only in woman. Trees never look a day older. The mountains are better off for each million years. Everywhere, everywhere. Bodies mismanaged, malfeasanced, gone off. Like styles, like fashions gone off. It's this piecemeal surrender to time, kids. You can't hold on to your baby teeth. Scissors cut paper, paper covers rock, rock smashes scissors. A bite of candy causes tooth decay, and jawlines that were once firm slip off like shoreline lost to the sea. Noses balloon, amok as a cancer. Bellies swell up and muscles go down. Hips and thighs widen like jodhpurs. My God, children, we look like we're dressed for the horseback! (And everywhere, everywhere, there's this clumsy imbalance. You see these old, sluggish bodies on thin-looking legs, like folk carrying packages piled too high. Or like birds puffed out, skewed, out of sorts with their foundations.) And hair. Hair thins, recedes, is gone. Bodies fall away from true. I don't know. It's as if we've been nickel-and-dimed by the elements: by erosion, by wind and water, by the pull of gravity and the oxidation of the very air. Look! Look there!"

A middle-aged woman in a print dress waited in house slippers for the parade to begin. She was crying. Tears pushed over the ledges of her eyes. A clear mucus filled a corner of one nostril.

A dowager's hump draped a pretty young woman's shoulders and back like a shawl.

They saw the details of a man's face, the stubble, lines, cleft, dimples, and pores, sharp and clarified as closeups in black-and-white photographs.

Sunglasses in the form of swans, masks, butterflies, or random as the forms of costume jewelry. Odd-shaped wigs and hairdos sat on people's heads like a queer gardening, a strange botany. And, everywhere, penciled eyebrows, painted lips, like so many prostheses of the cosmetic.

It had begun now, the parade. A well-dressed man in a business suit stood at attention as the floats passed by. He held his hat over his heart. (And sanity, sanity too, marred, scuffed as a shoe, wrinkled as laundry.) It had begun now, but the children weren't watching. They couldn't take their eyes off the crowd. ("*This, this* is the parade!") They stared at the special area the park had provided for guests in wheelchairs, at the old men and women who sat in them, bundled against some internal chill on even this warm day, wrapped in blankets that tucked over their feet, in sweaters, in scarves, in wool gloves and mittens, covered by hats, by caps, Mickey Mouse's eared beanies, dark as *yarmulkes*, on top of their other headgear; at, among them, an ancient woman in a rubber Frankenstein mask for warmth; at her nurse, feeding her cigarettes, venting her smoke through a gap in the monster's wired jaws. At other women, depleted, tired, who sat on benches, their dresses hiked well above their knees, their legs (in heavy stockings the color of miscegenetic, coffee-creamed flesh) not so much spread as forgotten, separated, guided by the collapsing, melted lines of their thighs. At their husbands (or maybe just the men they lived with, for convenience, for company, for making the welfare checks go farther), their hands in their laps, incurious as people who have just folded in poker. (And *everywhere* those dark glasses. "It ain't for the glare," Colin told them, "it's for the warmth!") At grown men and women wearing the souvenirs of the Magic Kingdom: sweat shirts, T-shirts, with Eeyore, with Mickey Mouse, with Jiminy Cricket, Alice-in-Wonderland pinafores, Minnie Mouse dresses, carryalls with Dumbo and Tigger and Tramp. At a woman in her sixties, inexplicably wearing a boa, a turban, a veil of wide, loose black mesh; at hands and arms and shoulders blotched by liver spots; at a man in baggy pants suspiciously, unscrupulously bulging. At a man in shorts, the enlarged veins on his legs like wax dripping down Chianti bottles in Italian restaurants.

At a woman with oily skin and pores like a sort of gooseflesh, visible as the apertures of chickens where their pinfeathers have been plucked. At a still handsome woman with bare, shapely, but hairy legs (hair even on the tops of her feet), but carefully trimmed as sideburns or rolled as stockings two inches below her knees; at a powerfully built man in his sixties whose chest hair, visible through his sheer tank top, had been as lovingly, patiently groomed as a high school boy's. (Everywhere, everywhere hair—the strange feeling they had that they were among birds, the wigs, the boa, the babushka of hair beneath the woman's chin, the piled hairdos, the thinning hair, the penciled eyebrows, the tattooed mustache and sideburns of the strange Westerner. Mudd-Gaddis's own baldness and the chemotherapeutic fuzz of several of the children. Because everything has a reasonable explanation, and almost all had heard that hair didn't stop growing after you died. Because everything has a reasonable explanation and hair was the gnawed, tenuous rope by which they hung on to immortality.)

Everywhere there were peculiar couples. A boy and a girl who couldn't have been more than twelve but looked in their runt intimacy as if they could have been married. The boy held his arm protectively about the girl's shoulder, his free hand in the pocket of his three-quarter-length trench coat as though he fondled a gun. He wore a jacket, a shirt, and a tie. His floods, honed as a knife along their permanent crease, rose above sharp, snazzy shoes. The girl, shorter than her small boyfriend, in a decent wool coat that looked as if it had been bought at a back-to-school sale, smiled wanly. Her black full hair showed signs of gray and she seemed a little nervous, wary, even long-suffering, beneath the arm of her protector, as if she knew his faults, perhaps, his diseases—which weren't diseases in her book—his excessive drinking, his compulsive gambling, his quick fists and rude abuse.

And stared openly at the mismatched couples: at the big, powerful girls next to undersized men and the men large as football players beside bloodless, scrawny women, at the couples widely discrepant in age in open attitudes of love and regard, handholding or clutching butts, the men's fingers casually resting along breasts as if they lolled in water. Or their arms thrown abruptly across each other's shoulders. Sending the smug signals of secret satisfactions, like the wealthy, perhaps, like people in drag.

And at a closely supervised group of the retarded, oddly ageless, the males in overalls, the females in loose, shapeless dresses and rolled stockings, clutching one another with their short fat fingers, their strange, pleased eyes fixed in their happy Smile Faces like raisins in cakes, beaming above their neglected teeth, beaming, beaming beneath their close-cropped hair on their broad, short skulls.

(Yet most were not defective, merely aging or old, or anyway beyond that thirty- or thirty-five-year grace period that seemed to come with most lives.)

Not even needing Colin now to direct their attention, to point things out. In it themselves now, raising their voices, like people outbidding each other in some hot contest, not even listening; or, if listening, then listening for the break in the other's discourse, for that opportune moment when they could have their say, get in their licks; or, if listening, then listening not just for the other to finish but for some generalized cue, some more or less specific tag on which they could build, add, like players of dominoes, say, or card games that followed strict suit. But generally too excited even for that. Only half listening, really, less, fractionally, marginally, seeing how it was with them and concentrating only on the essence, pith, and gist of what they would say, thinking in a sort of deliberate and polite headlines but settling finally into a kind of conversation and still using the language of that other kingdom, the one they'd come from to get to this one.

"Lord love a duck!" said Janet Order. "Just clap eyes on these gaffers."

"My word, Janet! They're for it, I'd say so," Rena Morgan agreed.

"Lamb turning to mutton." Janet sighed.

"Fright fish."

"Blood puddles."

"Lawks!" said Benny Maxine. "Look at the bint with the healthy arse. I'm gone dead nuts on that fanny."

"Ooh, it's walloping big, ain't it?" Tony Word said.

"If it ever let off it wouldn't 'alf make a pongy pooh," Benny asserted.

"Like Billy-O!" Tony said.

"Good gracious me!" said Lydia Conscience. "Say what you will, my heart goes out to the old biddy what looks like someone put her in the pudding club."

"Yar, ain't she dishy? There's one in every village."

Tony Word considered. "No," he said. "She's just put on the nose bag. It's simply a case of your lumping, right grotty greedguts."

"Only loads of grub then, you think?" Lydia asked.

"Oh, yes," said Tony. "Oodles of inner man. Tub and tuck."

"Jesus weeps!" said illiterate Noah Cloth, looking about, his gaze settling on the little group of the retarded. "He weeps for all the potty, pig-ignorant prats off their chumps, for all the slow-coach clots and dead-from-the-neck-up dimbos, and wonky, puddled coots and gits, goofs and goons, for all his chuckle-headed, loopy muggins and passengers past praying for."

"Put a sock in it, old man," Benny Maxine said softly.

"For all the nanas," Noah said, crying now. "For all the bright specimens."

"Many's the nosh-up gone down that cake hole," Tony Word said, his eye fixed on the fat woman Lydia Conscience had thought pregnant. "Many's the porky pots of tram-stopper scoff and thundering stodge through that podge's gob," he said without appetite.

"She's chesty," Rena Morgan said, weeping, of a woman who coughed. "She should put by the gaspers."

"She's had her day," said Janet Order.

"Coo! Who ain't?" Rena, sobbing, wanted to know. "Which of us, hey? Which of them?"

"Are they all on the dream holiday then?" Charles Mudd-Gaddis asked.

"All, old son, and no mistake," Lydia Conscience said wearily.

"A shame," he said. "Letting themselves go like that. And them with their whole lives in front of them."

And, at last, just rudely pointing. (They could have been mutes waving at entrées, aiming at desserts in a cafeteria line.) Whirling, indiscriminate, flailing about in some random "*J'accuse*" of the spontaneous. Whining, wailing, whimpering, weeping.

Because everything has a reasonable explanation. They lived in England's cold climate. They came from a place where clothes made their men and their women. They were unaccustomed to sportswear, to shorts and the casual lightweights and washables of the near tropics. They were unaccustomed, that is, to the actual shapes of people and simply did not know that what they saw was just the ordinary let-hung-out wear and tear of years, of meals, of good times and comforts and all the body's thoughtless kindnesses to itself. So that when Colin said what he said they believed him.

"I tell you," he told them, "that's you in a few years, never mind those three-score-and-ten you thought was your birthright. All that soured flesh, all those bitched and bollixed bodies. You see? You see what you thought you were missing?"

"Bodies," Nedra Carp said. "Don't tell me about bodies. I *know* about bodies."

"I've got them!" Colin Bible shouted, bursting into the room he shared with Bale, with Mudd-Gaddis and Benny. *"I've got their consents in my pocket!"*

5

So Nedra Carp knew about bodies.

If nothing else, her duties as a nanny had given her expertise in that department. (Hadn't she bathed and toweled dozens of children? Hadn't she helped bathe and actually dress all those step- and less-than-step—"stair relation," she called them—brothers and sisters of her early years?) And if her expertise was largely limited to the bodies of children, why, weren't the bodies of children bodies in their purest form? Didn't children wear the sharp, original shape of form itself? Hairless, without extrusion or eyesore, the blemish of sex? (She was no prude. She did not mean blemish. She only meant the body distracted from itself, allowed to drift from its intentions, from the air-

230

and skin-tight condition of bone in its bearings: the baroque scroll and ornament of palimpsest flesh.) She had rub-a-dub-dubbed girls and boys for almost as long as she could remember and, seated on stools and chairs for leverage, drawn their bodies to her within the open V of her legs (and as little pederast as prude), vigorously scrubbing, rubbing, grooming them—for bed, for parties—as if they'd been poodles in shows, the texture of their skins and every inch and hollow of their bodies known to her even beneath the thick, rough nap of the towels and soft, slippery film and feel of the soap, discounting the misleading temperature of the water. Practicing on all that devolutionary line, her mitigated steps and halves (the two stepchildren, the stepbrother and stepsister, the half sister, the half brother, the three—what?—cousin sisters and her half brother's sister, half brother and half sister and two stepsisters by the double widower, so that for the rest of her life she feels she stands—she doesn't know *where* she stands—as much in *sororal parentis* as *loco*), the way some other little girl might play with dolls.

So, without ever having had any very particular interest in them, she knew about bodies. At least was accustomed to them, the little boys and girls just so much neutral doll stuff to her. Knew, that is, their surfaces, their skins, polishing them, buffing their luster like firearms for inspection. As long ago, or for the child long ago (when she was five, when she was six, when she was seven and eight and nine), she had once buffed her own, slipping out of her bed when Nanny had read her her book, when, the child feigning sleep, the woman had leaned over her and made one last adjustment of the bedclothes, the little girl's hair, and tiptoed out of the room, Nedra listening for her steps to fade before leaving the bed to go to the wardrobe, where, if it was during the warm months, she looked inside the sleeve of her thick winter coat or, during the cold, the sleeve of her lightweight summer one for the carefully rolled towel she hid there, returning not to the bed but to the full-length mirror that stood, out of sight of the window, in the corner of her room, there to remove the pretty nightdress and to examine her chest where she could not remember when she did not know one day breasts would grow, to see if the small, discrete port-wine stain, no larger and not unlike the partial ring that might be made by a damp glass set down on a wooden surface, was still there.

Which it always was, of course.

Using the towel, but only in those warm months first lubricating its edge with her spittle or with water from the glass on her night table (because a little wetness would not leave a mark on the grand, thick winter wool, whereas the light summer one easily spotted), at first patiently rubbing at it for as long as ten minutes, as if she wished to make it shine perhaps rather than disappear (and only in the cold months applying the elbow grease, using the material like an eraser rubber, scratching at it with the dry towel, abrading, scouring, swiping at it as one would strike a match against a strip of friction, actually scraping it until it bled—although never with her nails, though she longed to tear at it and was held back only by scruple, some prohibition she'd heard of against self-mutilation—raising welts, raising galls, bruising her bruise), only then switching from damp end to dry, going at it for ten more minutes or so but still gently—it was summer, it was close in the room, effort raised perspiration, and Nedra could not tolerate the smell of her own sweat, as she could not tolerate any of her imperfections—still with that same craftsman's restrained and delicate patience. (So maybe it was the warm months that saved her, that kept her from raising a cancer too, that reprieved her from the English climate with its three-to-one ratio of cool to warm like a recipe for a pitcher of martinis.)

Though her nanny could see the results when she bathed her.

"Are you still playing with that thing on your chest?"

"I don't play with it."

"You do. One day you're going to develop a nice case of blood poisoning from that nasty tic."

But the nanny was wrong. It wasn't a tic. What she did wasn't unconscious, in no way like biting her nails or fooling with her hair, although she had neither of these habits. All she wanted was to be rid of the thing, to have it whitewashed away by her furious frictions. (And, sometimes—this would have been during the warm months, past her bedtime, the pale sunlight coming into her bedroom window, mixing with the light from the ceiling fixture, the lamp on her night table, or during the cold months, the night slamming against the window glass, the room's only light coming off the dim wattage of the fixture on the ceiling and the lamp on the night table—she believed that the thing was actually fading.)

The doctor saw it when she went for examinations.

"Does it hurt?"

"No."

"Does it itch?"

"No."

"Then why fool with it? You're just irritating it, you know. You're going to end up with a bad infection. I'll give her a salve for that thing. I want this put on the area every night after her bath for five days. Now, Nedra," the doctor said, "this medicine is very strong. It's a steroid ointment and you mustn't scrape at it. You have to let the ointment do its work."

Which Nanny applied and which Nedra, misunderstanding, and seeing that so far the salve had merely helped to take down the rawness without doing anything to the stain itself, and believing that the doctor was afraid of dispensing it in too strong a dose—she'd lost a mum; she knew about dosages, strong drugs, the reluctance doctors had to let a patient have them even when they were clearly helping; her mum's morphine, for example, which the doctor told her mum she could take every four hours but which she needed again after two—continued to apply herself for another week, until, in fact, there was no more left in the tube and she had developed an ugly rash all over her body. The doctor told her she was allergic to steroids and no longer prescribed them. The rash cleared up in a while but the stain was still there.

Which she knew the name for now—stigma—and looked up in her father's dictionary. Learning that the purplish, iridescent flaw she wore like a piece of costume jewelry branded into her skin was, variously, "a mark burned into the skin of a

criminal or slave; a mark or token of infamy, disgrace, or reproach"; and, under Medicine, "a mark on the skin that bleeds
as a symptom of hysteria; a mark indicative of a history of a
disease or abnormality"; and, far down, at the end of the list,
past its biological definitions—"the respiratory spiracle of an insect or an eyespot in algae"—and botanical ones, she read that
stigmata were "sores corresponding to and resembling the cru-
cifixion wounds of Jesus"—not hers, which more closely resembled a crescent moon stamped by that hypothetical glass of beer,
say, left to dry on that hypothetical bar—"and sometimes impressed on certain persons in a state of religious ecstasy or hysteria."

Not, she felt, a lot to choose from: the sores of hysterics;
the tokens of infamy, disgrace, reproach; the marks of the abnormal; the brands on criminals and slaves. (She was marked.
She was a marked little girl. She would become a marked
woman.) She settled for slave and turned to the nannies.

A mother's helper's helper. Apprenticed herself to the
nannies.

Who by this time, her mother's house almost completely
populated now—she was ten, her mum had died when Nedra
was four, her dad when she was nine, her stepmother had remarried the widower and would within two years be dead herself, leaving the double widower free to marry, to bring his bride,
herself a widow with two children, into their little club—as sol-
idly booked as a reputable bed-and-breakfast, not only welcomed her but probably would actively have enlisted her if she
hadn't asked first. Transferring her old reflexive rub-a-dub-
dub—she'd ceased swiping at the thing on her chest, the stigma—
to the babies, all those doll substitutes whom she bathed and
toweled almost as roughly as she'd done herself. The nannies
attempting to make her ease off, to lighten up. "Nedra, don't
flay them so." Taking the washcloth from her, the soap, giving
her lessons in the soft, trying to. "You're not whittling wood,
Nedra dear. You must be more gentle with them." And who
would probably have given up on her altogether if it hadn't been
for all those deaths, the possibilities they continued to create for

the marriages of the survivors to more widows, more widowers, with their own complement of kids. (They were shortsighted—she thought of the succession of nannies that came into her mother's home as "they," thought there probably was never more than one nanny in the place at any one time—and didn't understand what was really happening. It's only the deaths of the adults, Nedra thought, that keeps things manageable here at all.) And who at last, seeing that she would never learn, did not have the touch with babies, sent her on to the toddlers. Who—if only because they were bigger, stronger, had larger lung capacities, if only because they'd been around longer, had developed a frame of reference against which they could measure their treatment in Nedra's hands against what they had received in the less dockwalloper ones of the real nannies, if only because they had begun to develop at least the inklings of a sense of indignation—made even more fuss than the babies.

So she was off toddlers now too and (because they saw that there was nothing actually mean about her and that her fury was without rancor and was probably only a sort of dedication, and something more, perhaps, something they recognized from their own old apprenticeships, just the helpless and maybe even just wanton sign of her accession and assent to her vocation, her nanny calling) promoted (who hadn't properly graduated either infants *or* toddlers) to out-and-out children.

She would have been about eleven, she would have been about twelve. There would have been, not counting herself, around eight kids in her mother's house by now. Nine when the double widower and the new stepmother once removed had a child of their own.

This was the pool from which the nannies had to choose. And if Nedra were twelve now and had already gone through all the infants and toddlers with whom they dared entrust her, then the only out-and-out children around—the stepsister and stepbrother were just a year or two younger—were her half sister and half brother, the only other Carps in the house.

They tried her out on the half sister, but the little girl was frail and could not stand up to Nedra's furious drubbings.

They gave her one last chance. They sent her into the bathroom to eight-year-old Gregory.

She saw him through the steam. He saw her as she moved toward him through the vaporish idiom of the damp tiles, the slippery marble. He was startled and, up to his chin in a lather of bubble bath, at a disadvantage.

"Hoicks! Yoicks and hoicks! What are *you* doing here?"

"I'm supposed to help bath you."

"What, help bath *me?*"

"Come on, Gregory, give me the washcloth, please."

"What for?"

"Hand it over, Gregory. I haven't all day."

"What are you, daft? You think I'm going to let some *girl?* No hope!"

"Don't be silly, Gregory. Nanny's bathed you for years."

"Yeah, well, that's Nanny, i'n' it? You're different pickles, ain't you?"

"I'm your sister." Her response to his offended modesty was obvious, even logical, but it was lame. Both knew that. There'd been little casual intimacy in this house. For all that the various issue of the strange, relay-race relationships and liaisons between their various parents lived and played together, took meals on the same schedules, had more or less the same bedtimes, shared the same clothes, lived behind the same unlocked doors, and, as they grew into it, were even at the same liberty to move at will about the same rooms and halls—her mother's rooms, her mother's halls—they hadn't often, and Nedra never, run into each other in even only ordinary familial propinquity's catch-as-catch-can dishabille. She didn't know why, or how it had happened, but it was a little like being guests living in the same hotel. The occasional compromised glimpse of another was simply not in the cards. There were, simply, no embarrassing moments. Nedra's forays into child management had permitted her certain privileged "views," even a kind of hands-on experience, but she was so busily engaged at these times—so furiously, some would have said—that she barely regarded the sex of whomever it was she was bathing.

"Go on," Gregory Carp said. "Get out of here. *G'wan!*"

"Not till I've done you."

"Yeah, well, I've heard you like that sort of thing. Sorry," he said and, partially raising himself, tried to pull the shower curtain around the tub. Nedra grabbed it away—he was her last chance, the nannies had told her so—and folded the curtain high up over the shower rod. Gregory looked at her. "Oh, yes," he said, "a regular bruiser's what I hear. Jack the Ripper, they call you in nursery. Scrub the spots off a leopard. You're queen of the queer-o's, you are, Nedra."

"You're wasting time, young man." She was on her knees, her sleeves rolled. She reached into the bathtub, searching with her hands for the washcloth. She pulled it from under his thigh.

"Go on, get away from me! Stop that! *You better stop that!*"

"You want them to hear you scream?"

"Too right I do!"

She rubbed his arms with the soapy cloth. He suddenly lay back in the water. "Sit up," she told him and he raised up a bit, the bubbles clinging to his chest like a soft chain mail. She scrubbed under his arm. He was ticklish. He began to giggle. "Don't be silly, Gregory. Gregory, don't be so silly." Her half brother was laughing uncontrollably now. He grabbed a handful of bubbles and threw them at her. Something about their weightless trajectory amused her. She smiled and scooped up some of the bubbles herself. It was a little like trying to throw feathers. Indeed, all of this was like some weightless, glorious pillow fight. They slapped at each other with thousand-faceted airy boluses of bubble bath. The stuff was on her clothes, on her face, in her hair. Then her brother pushed himself all the way up in the water and began splashing her. He shoved sheets of it at her, pushing the water away from his chest with his palms.

Which was when she first noticed it, saw it.

It was, of course, the thing, the port-wine stain, the partial ring, the costume-jewelry crescent, the iridescent purple flaw brand bruise stigma, the hysterical abnormal infamy skin token. He had one too. He was marked too. And now she saw what it really looked like. It looked like a lip.

It was right there on her half brother's chest, exactly, though reversed, where it was on her own, placed just so, where she could not remember when she had not known that one day breasts would grow.

It was at this time that Nedra began to work on their alliance, bringing into it, too, because she thought it was what Gregory would have wanted, Gregory's sister, offering the little girl special relationship, favored-nation status; not suspecting that, except for their own, there *were* no special relationships in that house, that blood didn't matter, neither full brotherhood, the fractured, fractioned fellowship of the descending halves and steps, nor any of the shadowy stair relation there: that nothing counted, not even normal friendship; not knowing that everything was exactly as her metaphor had it, that the others were no closer than guests staying in the same hotel (soon enough dropping the sister, when her half brother lightly mentioned his indifference to the child, feeling worse about it than he did), sitting on her own appetites to feed his, bringing him treats, saving him her desserts, reserving part of her allowance and, when they had gotten rid of the sister, the frail little girl who couldn't stand up to her drubbings, adding to it that part of the tithe—it amounted to a tithe, the little girl's portion—which Nedra (because she still believed in his goodwill, his generosity, sometimes actually chastising the boy for being too free with his— that is to say, Nedra's—money, spending too much on the cheap toys bought with coins held back from her own reserves and which otherwise would have been added to what she held back, still from her own reserves, to spend on Gregory) had withheld from Gregory's—she thought of it as Gregory's—money.

Because all she wanted to do was look at it, study it (not even touch it, actually ceasing to bathe him, not because he was too big, which he was, but because she did not want to fall again into her old patterns, did not wish ever again to inflict pain, even helplessly, even unconsciously, did not wish to administer—she had thrown the towel away—any of those at once thoughtless and obsessive rub-downs with which she had once raised welts on her own body and brought tears to the eyes of her clear-skinned halves, steps, and stairs), not even mentioning to him, though she wanted to, that she had one too.

They played. She was four years his senior. They played his games.

They played Fish, they played Old Maid. They pinned the tail on the donkey and fought wars with lead soldiers. She pushed him on the swing, she pulled him on the roundabout. She gave him piggyback rides. (She thought she could feel its heat through his jacket, through his shirt and undershirt, through her blouse and sweater and her own undershirt, the hot indelibles of his skin radiating through the half-dozen layers of fabric that separated them and warming her somewhere behind her heart at the contact point where he jounced against her.)

"You know, Nedra," he said one day, "I've almost gone ten. I'm big for my age, as big as you are. It looks daft, your hauling me about."

"You're light as a feather," she said.

"No," he said. "I feel quite silly." She had been about to carry him across the common, where quite recently she had begun to teach him to play rounders, where they leaned into each other in clumsy two-man rugby scrimmages, where they played a sort of hockey together, where they kicked the football about that Nedra had bought for him. They would have headed toward the small playground, where she still pushed him on the swing, where she still pulled him on the roundabout.

"All right then," she said. "You carry me."

Because she still hadn't shown him, hadn't told him. Not because it was a secret but because she was saving it, squirreling it away against the time when she would need it—perhaps the time had come, perhaps his misgivings about the piggyback rides was its presage—to bond him to her as she had been bonded to him for almost two years now. Her pretexts had begun to seem threadbare even to Nedra; the rough games they played and which had been her idea, the girl's, who knew nothing about boys' sports, not really, who had neither taste nor aptitude for them and had forced herself to bone up, to learn them from the rule books, and who practiced by herself in what spare time she had the fundamentals of football, of rugby and rounders and hockey, whose only game prior to the time she needed to know them had been washing children, playing nursemaid, and who had actually become quite competent at them, the rough games, if only so she could show them to him, keep him with her, keep him entertained. And who hadn't known at the time that the pretext of teaching him sports would develop subsequent pretexts, that the sweat he worked up would become a pretext to get him to take off his shirt, to wipe him down. So that she could stare at it, study it, see if it was still there.

So his misgivings about the piggyback rides weren't entirely unwelcome. She could see the advantages, all her served purposes. Which was why she didn't put up a fight, why she was so quick to suggest that they trade places and the boy carry her. Because she hadn't told him yet, and because she really didn't know how to tell him even if the time *was* right.

"I won't be too heavy for you, will I?" the fourteen-year-old girl asked the almost ten-year-old boy.

"No," he said as she climbed on his back.

Because perhaps he'll feel it, she thought. Because perhaps he'll feel it and know from the heat and I won't have to tell him.

But he said nothing when he put her down.

He's shy, she thought. He's just like me.

"Did you feel anything strange?" she asked him.

"You've got sharp tits," he said. "You've got tits like tenpenny nails."

What could I expect? she thought. He's *too* shy. I should never have asked him that.

So she waited until they got home. She didn't point out that he was perspiring, that he was overheated. She took him directly to her room and closed the door.

"You can't expect to go down to the table looking like that," she said. "Take your shirt off."

"*Ne*dra," he said.

"I'm not fooling, young man. Take it off."

And because he perfectly well understood that blood didn't matter in that house, special relationships, friendship, and knew where his treats were coming from, the desserts and the gifts and the extra money and his lessons in games, he agreed. He took his shirt and undershirt off and dutifully extended them to his queen of the queer-o's bonkers half sister. Who took them from him and let them drop to the floor.

"Don't you want to wipe me off? What are you doing? Hey," he said, "what's going on?"

"Look," she said. "See?"

"Jesus, sis," he said, "this is the best treat of all!"

And stood perfectly still as she came toward him and touched what at that moment Nedra didn't even realize were the breasts which she could not remember when she had not known one day would grow, to the iridescent purple flaw on his chest, locking their matching jigsaw stigmata, pressing her costume jewelry nether lip to his pouting, port-wine-stained, crescent upper one.

He was full ten when he came to her. She remembered because he was wearing the handsome tweed touring cap she had given him on his birthday.

He cleared his throat, making it seem that he'd come upon her unaware and, out of honor, was not only signaling her attention but giving her an opportunity to collect herself, pretending not his invisibility but hers.

"Gregory," she said.

"I find," her half brother said, "I may no longer in good conscience honor our special relationship."

"Oh?"

"Though I shall always half love you."

Janet Order, Nedra Carp suddenly finds herself thinking, Janet Order, Janet Order. Livid Janet Order, Little Girl Blue, she thinks, who seems to defy Nedra's longtime policies of bought-and-paid-for hired-hand love—it was, she acknowledged, a flaw—and old propinquitous patriotics and aversives, her dependence, for example, on the authorized and her slavish regard for her charges, the affront, for example, she took at just plain pure otherness, shared toilets and someone else's hair in the comb, boxes of other women's tampons and all the mnemonics of alternative being—it was a flaw, it was a flaw—her queasy antipatheticals and squeamish inimicals flaws (who would have resented Mary Cottle, for example, for no other reason than that she carried the Poppins baptismal name), her xenophobics and the coin's other side, her played favorites flaws, flaws, her old pagan Thumbs Up, Thumbs Down determinations flaws, flaws, flaws.

But forgiving herself by the light and shine of her turned new leaf, Nedra feels sympathy for the girl who went both of them one better. *Janet Order*, she thinks, quite simply, quite suddenly awed. *Janet Order. Janet Order.* Who was herself a bruise, her entire body one brute blue stigma.

While in Mary Cottle's room, Mr. Moorhead examined his Jew.

Because he was enough of a social animal never to volunteer at parties and gatherings that he was a pediatrician, or even an ex-casualty-ward physician. (But not courageous enough an egoist to proclaim himself, though he believed himself to be—and may in fact have been—one of the best diagnosticians in the world. And *never* mentioned what he absolutely knew to be the case: that what he really was was the finest prognostician ever to have lived. And though he may have wanted, at one of the Queen's garden parties, say, to blurt this out to those stuffy O.B.E.'s, he knew well enough what the upshot would be—they would put him down as demented—and held his tongue. But give him credit, Mr. Moorhead thought. It was out of neither modesty *nor* fear that he failed to offer his strong suit. It was good, honest prudence. The fact was, his gift was a curse. He knew outcomes. He knew when people would die. He handicapped death. And while he might have been no master of the social graces, he knew enough about human nature to realize that unless a person was a pretty good sport, reeling off his mortality table might be too off-putting. They'd mark him down, he giggled, as a wet blanket at Her Majesty's garden parties!

(Once he had. It was the first time he'd been asked to one, and he was a little squiffed. He'd boasted his forte to an eminent philanthropist. The man had been fascinated, telling the physician his medical history, leading him on to that point in the conversation where he was about to ask the awful question. Moorhead saw it coming—he was, after all, a prognostician— but there was no way to stop him. "I've told you," he said at last, "more than a little bit about myself. So what do you think? What do you think, eh?" Sometimes knowing that a thing will happen provides the opportunity to deal with it when it does— he was, after all, a doctor—and he was ready for him. "Sir," Moorhead told him indignantly, "I'm neither spiritualist, for-tuneteller, nor flim-flam man. I'm a scientist. I will not perform parlor tricks for you!" And nervously awaited the millionaire's reaction, which even to Moorhead's half-slewed mind was a beat too long in coming. The fellow looked round slowly, taking in Buckingham Palace's lush grounds, the ceremonial costumes of the guards, the fringed extravagant tents standing like Came-lot. "Some parlor," he said as Moorhead moved off. He was a pediatrician and knew a thing or two about childishness as well as about children and wasn't surprised to see the man looking after him, Moorhead trying to lose himself among the other guests when the old boy came up to him again and actually ig-noring him when he—he was a full-fledged Sir, one of the wealthiest men in England, and, in Mr. Moorhead's best professional judgment, would not last two years—tried to in-trude on the pediatrician and his new companions.) So when they asked, he simply told them "physician," letting it go at that, knowing human nature well enough to understand that every-one wanted to learn about his symptoms, offering up their bod-ies like patriots, volunteers, recruits of their own raw mortality.

He didn't mind these intrusions. He didn't mind people picking his brains. In fact, he welcomed it. But he needed data. These weren't data. They were anecdotal evidence, loose, quick-draw evaluations made at parties and never followed up by ex-aminations and tests, the obituaries he sometimes spotted in the papers the only corroboration of his findings.

So when he asked the woman the time—he'd been hanging about the fringes of the queue looking impatient, as if he'd been stood up—and saw the bracelet of tattooed numbers on her arm, he shrugged his disgust at other people's unreliability and drifted into line beside her. He offered small talk about the queue's progress—he said "queue," hoping she'd pick up on the foreign-sounding word—about the park's attractions, his accommodations, about, finally, what he was doing in Florida. An international medical convention in Miami, he said.

"You're a doctor?"

"Yes," he said, "a physician. Yes. I am. From England."

"From *Eng*land," she said. "I lived in England. In Liverpool."

"*Did* you?" he said. "I had a surgery in Liverpool after I came down from university. This would have been around '57. There were still refugees about. From the camps."

He had to raise his voice over the ruckus of the Country Bear Jamboree. After the show his colleague had still not shown up, and he asked if she cared to join him for lunch at the Liberty Tree Tavern. They could have a *schnaps,* he said.

The woman—he judged her to be about the same age he was, perhaps a year or two older; she would have been eighteen or nineteen after the war—declined and said she was tired and thought she would return to her room for a nap.

He walked along beside her for a while in silence.

"Look," he said at last, "I don't mean to pry, but has anyone ever triangulated those cysts on your face?"

So now, two days later, she is lying on Mary Cottle's bed in her slip. She has complaints but Moorhead has shushed her, explaining that too much has been made lately of patient feedback, that a diagnosis independently arrived at is more likely to be sound than one in which the patient leads her doctor around by the nose.

He finishes his examination and is returning his instruments to the black leather bag.

"You may put your clothes on," he says and hands the woman her dress. He goes into Mary Cottle's bathroom and washes his hands in Mary Cottle's sink.

"So what's the story?" she asks when he's back in the room. "Will I live?"

Mr. Moorhead frowns. "Obviously"—he indicates the room— "the facilities in here— Tell me, Mama, have you any family pictures?"

"Pictures."

"Family pictures."

"To tell you the truth, Doc, I don't make a move without my snaps, but no one ever asked before."

"I'm looking for possible genetic pathologies."

"Oh," she says, "genetic pathologies," and hunts about in her big purse. She digs out a large blue plastic holder like an oversized wallet. It is held together by rubber bands and is stuffed with photographs.

Mr. Moorhead takes a ballpoint pen from Mary Cottle's desk drawer, some hotel stationery, seats himself at the desk, turns on the three-way lamp to its highest position, pulls a chair over for the woman, and inserts the jeweler's loupe in his eye.

"Hand them to me one at a time and tell me their relation to you."

"That's Danny, my grandson," she says and shows him a color photograph of a spoiled-looking little boy playing a computer game in a finished basement in Shaker Heights, Ohio. "The little girl is Debbie, Danny's sister."

"I meant—" he says.

She shoves another photograph under his loupe. "That's my son Ben. That's his wife, Susan." They are sitting in an open Chrysler convertible.

"Those are Ben and Susan's twins, Sheila and Sharon. Ben and Susan can't have children. They're adopted."

She shows him dozens of photos. They are all in color and have a matte finish. They are of birthday parties in paneled rec rooms. They are of affairs in hotels—weddings, bar mitzvahs—with great flower centerpieces on the tables. She identifies all the guests.

"There's my other son, Ron. Danny and Debbie's father."

"I don't see any resemblance," Mr. Moorhead says.

"Any resemblance."

"Between you and your grandkids. Between you and your sons."

"They favor my husband."

"Who resembles you?"

"Sharon does. Sheila."

"But they're adopted."

She shrugs.

"Was there some medical reason—is it Ben? Ben. Ben and your daughter-in-law couldn't have kids?"

"Ben had a vasectomy."

"Oh," says the physician.

"He says it's wrong to bring your own children into this kind of world."

She points to a photo of another son, Donald, a draper in California. Donald is also childless. "He says to me, 'Ma, you want your grandchildren to grow up under the Shadow?' This is what he calls it—the Shadow."

"He means the Bomb?"

"He lives in Mill Valley. He means the San Andreas fault."

He sees a picture wrapped in cellophane. It's of Mack, her dead husband.

"Was it his second stroke that killed him?"

She looks frightened. "How did you know?"

"His grin doesn't cross to the left side of his face."

"Boy," she said, "you know your onions." She fingered the small, light-colored cysts on her face.

"I'd like to get your family history," Mr. Moorhead told her. "Your parents, your grandparents, your brothers and sisters. Blood aunts and blood uncles, their children."

She nodded.

"Are we talking about a large family?"

"Yes," she said.

"And you people are from—?"

"Poland."

"Much history of cancer?"

"No c-a-n-c-e-r," she said.

"Heart disease? Stroke?"

"Counting Mack?"

"Mack was your husband," Moorhead said. "He's not related."

"No," she said.

"Diabetes?"

"No," she said.

"There's a high incidence of diabetes among Polish Jews."

"Not by us," she said.

There was no abdominal pain; there had been no cirrhosis, no anemia, no arthritis, no asthma, no back pain.

"Gallbladder? Gallstones?"

"Absolutely not."

"Convulsions? Colon difficulties?"

"Feh!"

There'd been no pulmonary history, no pleurisy, no pneumonia.

"What about depression?"

"All in your head."

"How about gonorrhea, how about syphilis?"

"Say," she said, "who do you think you're talking to?"

"Diverticulitis."

"Knock on wood, no."

He asked about edema. She shook her head. He asked her about gastroenteritis. She shook her head.

"Microcephaly? Hyperplasia? Hypocolemia? Hemoptysis? Syncope? Ischemia or transient ischemic attack syndrome?"

"Bite your tongue."

Mr. Moorhead put down his pencil. "We are talking about a large family, you said."

"Oh," she said, "enormous."

He picked his pencil up again. "Vascular dysfunction?"

She shook her head. As she did when he asked her if anyone in her family had ever had hemorrhoids or palpitations or varicose veins or vertigo or an infection of the urinary tract. As she did when he asked about scabies or hepatitis or lupus or Parkinson's disease.

"Tuberculosis, poison ivy?"

"Out of the question."

As, it turned out, it was all out of the question: hernia and obesity and rectal bleeding and hyperthyroid and blisters and osteoporosis and renal failure and senile dementia and paresis and paresthesia and effusions of the pleurae and vaginitis and thyroid. Disease itself was out of the question, and all pathologies.

But still she has her complaints. Which Moorhead, dispirited and out of touch with his own theories, who can't even summarize them now, who can't say why he needed photographs, the old gemütlich formal sepia poses and black-and-white candids, only halfheartedly hears.

"Well," she says, "you're English. Socialized medicine, the National Health. Didn't I live after the war two years there? When my papers came through in five months? And I could have gone anywhere? The whole world to choose from? But stayed on to finish my pronunciation studies, my enunciation lessons? And don't forget, I already knew a little English. Enough to get by. But how can a Jew get by with an accent? A yid, a mockie, a hymie, a kike. So this is my fear, doctor. What's upsetting me so. It could come back. The accent. Sometimes I hear it. So vut if dere's trouble? Vut den? Vut vill be? Vut den vut vill be?"

"Please," he says. Moorhead presses her again. "Please, I *beg* you."

"Nu," she says, "he begs me. He begs me, de docteh."

And, on the waters behind the Contemporary, Colin Bible, his spirits revitalized by prospects he has brought about himself—it's neither immoral nor a particularly big deal for someone who negotiates with the sick, up to here in other people's pain and disease, to seem to take on an aspect of exceptional health, this bonus of well-being, this juxtaposed by-contrast aura of splendid, shining, booming energy, his scale immortality a perk, like loose change snapped up after the show by ushers, say—toodles about Bay Lake looking for a port of call. Mary

Cottle waits with the children at the marina. She gazes out as if to sea, her eyes peeled for Colin's tiny speedboat.

" 'Scuse me, if a poor death-blemished lad might 'ave a word wif da nice healfy lady."

"I'm sorry, Benny, are you talking to me?"

"Well, only tryin', you might say. Only makin' the odd modest effort." He winks at Mudd-Gaddis. He winks at Rena.

"What is it, Benny? If something's on your mind, be good enough to say what it is, please. I'm a bit browned with your indirection. Goodness, boy, you talk just like an informer lately. You do. You really do. Like a copper's nark. All these light kicks and promptings. I only speak like this," she adds, "because I love you."

"Oh, aye," says Benny, snorting, "*browned*."

"Are you out to ruin what may turn out to be the loveliest day we've had here?" Mary Cottle asks, almost as if she knows what he's talking about.

"It puts me in mind of a song, all this," Benny says. " 'It does, Benny?' " he says. "Yar, it really do," he answers himself. " 'Go on,' " he says, " 'sing it. Sing away, Ben boy.' " "I've no voice." " 'Go on,' " he insists. "Don't say I didn't warn you." " 'We want Ben-ny, we want Ben-ny,' " he chants. He cups his hands. " 'Were that the song then?' " he calls through them. "Nah," he says, "that were just the softening him up." " 'The song, the song,' " he demands. "Right, then," he says, "which it goes something like this." He looks toward Mary Cottle. " 'I cover the waterfront,' " he sings.

Mary Cottle is right about the day. At least about the weather. It's 80 degrees. The humidity can't be a quarter that. There is the breeze of dreams. Slapping confidence like balm on their skins. The sky's a perfect blue. The clouds are like topping.

"Ahoy, ahoy," Colin says conversationally up at them from the Water Sprite.

"What'd you find out?" calls Benny Maxine.

"Mate," Colin tells Benny softly, glancing toward the chap in the rental booth, "would you be so kind as to avast your voice there? Would you have the good manners to dim the running lights on your mouth?"

"What do you think?" Noah asks. "Do you think we'll be able to do it?"

"Oh, will we, Colin?" Lydia asks. "Will we?"

"Well," Colin says, "if you'll give me a minute to discuss with the admiral there"—he indicates the young man at the boat rental—"I'll get back to you." He hops out of the little speedboat and wriggles out of his life jacket.

"Listen," he tells the guy, "I don't want the tykes to hear me."

"Yes, sir?"

"That's why I'm talking low like this."

"Yes, sir?"

"You read about these little'uns?" he asks. "The Seven Dwarfs with Snow White over there."

The fellow—he's still in his teens, Colin judges, and a looker—glances in the kids' direction. "Read about them?" he says.

"Don't *stare*, man!"

"Was I staring?"

"People do, you know. That or look away. One or the other. Well, we don't know how to deal with celebrity, do we? We're not that much at home in fame."

"Are they on television?"

"They're on the news."

"Really? The news?"

"Not so loud."

"What did they do?"

"They haven't quite managed to do it yet."

"When they do," the boat-rental kid says, "what will it be?"

Colin lowers his voice still further. "Well," he says, "they're going to die,"

The young man nods. "Yes," he says sadly, "we get a lot of that here."

"Not at *this* concession! Not in *these* numbers!"

"No, I guess not here so much."

"There you go," Colin says.

"What have they got?"

"The little blue babe?" He moves his eyes in Janet Order's direction.

"Yes?"

"That's our Janet. You play a musical instrument?"

"Sax a little."

"The reeds in her heart are shot. Her valves and stops are queered."

"And the heavy girl?"

"Forty pounds of tumor."

"Gee."

"This"—he indicates Bay Lake, he indicates the sunshine, he indicates the blue sky and the lovely day—"would be unusual? Even for around here, even for Florida, am I right?"

"A little unusual."

"I'll be bound, 'a little.' Well," Colin says, "and the lump-faced kid is Benny Maxine. Benny's dying of his baggy great liver and his sizey spleen. And little Tony Word and wee Noah Cloth of leukemia and osteosarcoma. Those are your nagging cancers of the blood and the big bad bones."

"Oh, wow."

"That's how it is," Colin says.

"Awful."

"The other little girl is Rena Morgan. Rena is our cystic fibrosis."

"And the old-looking guy?"

"Charles Mudd-Gaddis. Charles can't tell you whether it's Tuesday morning or 1066. Not enough oxygen to his brain and belly button, to his organs and toenails."

"Really?"

"The Bible tells you so." The concessionaire looks at the children and shakes his head. "Don't stare," Colin says.

"Sorry."

"So I promised them this treat," he says, taking his voice so low the young man has to strain to hear him. "Well, to tell you the truth—they never said this, they're too polite—I think they're a little burned out on all the rides and exhibits, on the hi tech and brass bands. I thought a little time on the water, a little fun in the sun, you see what I mean?"

"Sure."

"Right. We'll take two of the Sprites. We'll take the Sunfish and one of those motorized pontoon boats."

"We don't rent to anyone under twelve. Even with an accompanying adult they're not allowed to drive. I'm sorry."

"Your passport please, Benny," Colin called. "Rena, yours? Benny's fifteen. Rena's a teenager."

"But these kids are dying," the boy objected.

"They'll wear life jackets."

"Really, mister," the young man said. "I mean, I don't see how I can do this. I mean it's irresponsible. Suppose something should happen? I mean, it could. Something could. They start up with each other, things get out of hand and they capsize. I mean, something awful could happen."

"You're right. It would be better if you closed the shop while we're out. Not lease your other boats. I mean, the heavier the traffic, the more likely something bad could happen."

"Not lease my boats?"

"Well, that's part of the treat too, you see. To let the kids have the lake to themselves, to fix it so that for once—look," he said, "you're a native, right?"

"A native?"

"A native, a local. You're from around here."

"From Orlando."

"All right. You're this local native Orlando boy. Tell me, how many days do you remember out of your whole life when the weather's been like this? Did I say weather? This isn't weather. This is Nature. How many? A dozen? Less? Could you count them on two hands? On one? I'm twice your age and don't recall any. All right, I'm not from Orlando or even from Florida, but I'm no stranger to the planet. I go on holiday to the sun coasts. I've been to Mediterranea. I've come back tan. But this, this is a special dispensation. This is God's odds." And now his voice is not lowered. The children can hear him chatting freely about their deaths, about the great disappointment their lives have been to them, about what he calls the day's miraculous reprieve—time's and temperature's deliverance. (Because he's flirting. He doesn't have to speak to him like this, doesn't have to mention their deaths or speak their names, doesn't have to bring up the day's rarity or say anything about not renting the other boats. Because—there's nothing in it for him; he wants nothing from this looker but his attention—he's flirting, waving his fine and fetching fettle like a braggart's flag. Because he's in high humor, has what he hadn't known he'd come for. Because he is flirting, floating the raised, willful waftage of his spirit. Flirting with the boat-rental boy, with Mary, even with his doomed and helpless charges.)

In minutes they are arranged in the boats. Colin is in a Sunfish with Tony Word, Benny in a Sprite with Lydia, and Mary Cottle and Noah Cloth are in a second Sprite. Rena Morgan is to drive Janet Order and Charles Mudd-Gaddis in the pontoon boat. The young fellow at the boat rental has agreed to close his booth and rent no more boats.

Colin, who looks like a good sailor, is. Somehow he maneuvers the sailboat between the two small speedboats and steers beside Rena's blocky, raftlike launch. He keeps them all in line with his high spirits, towing them with his extraordinary cheer.

"Men," he calls to Rena and Lydia, to Charles and to Tony, to Benny and Noah and Mary Cottle and Janet Order, "it's dear old Dunkerque all over again! Hail Britannia, how about it?" he roars. "Hail Britannia."

(It's like having money to spend. Like being a customer. Yes, like having an advantage over the clerk who serves him; and his decisions and his whims, still in reserve, are like having the clerk's commission in his pocket. Alternately yielding and withholding at will, this is his flirtatiousness, his playboy's devil-may-care airs on him like perfume.)

And leads his strange armada to Discovery Island. Surveillant. The expert here. Signaling their distance, instructing them to cut their engines while he, working with nothing but air—it isn't strong or concentrated enough to offer itself as wind—seems to take on their stalled and idling energies, to play the Sunfish like a surfboard, his arms and his shoulders, his body and head shifting and busy as a boxer's.

"Over there," Benny Maxine says, turning the key in the little boat's ignition and looking toward the dock.

"Use your head, Ben," Colin says. "We can't berth there."

"Why not?"

"That's where the boats come in to drop off the tourists. It won't do. It's bespoke."

"Ooh," Benny says, "which way then?"

"To the other island."

Ignoring the macaws and cockatoos, the ibis and rheas, ignoring the trumpeter swans, the cranes and white peacocks, ignoring the flamingos and pelicans, ignoring the eagles, they are towed by his chatter and cheer and make land in a cove like the underedge of a key where Colin Bible supervises their disembarkation, still pitching his mood at them as he helps them out of the boats. "And ain't it?" he asks again. "Ain't it old Dunkerque? Ain't it in a way? What was the dear old Dunker anyway if not just about the grandest last stand and evacuation of all time? Talk about your quality time, talk about your finest hours. Am I right? You know it."

"Where are we, Colin?"

"Shipwreck Marsh, Janet, it's called on the map."

"I wonder if there's snakes," Noah says.

"Snakes don't bother you," Benny says, "if you don't bother them."

"They say that about everything. Sharks and tigers and rabid dogs."

"It's true. That's why they say it."

"How would you know?"

"I been on outings. Before I was sick. I went to just dozens of rambles."

" 'Before I was sick.' That's rich. 'Before I was sick.' When would that have been?"

"You don't think I ever was healthy? You want to bet me? You want to?"

"Congenital. You're congenital."

"Oh, *I'm* congenital? *I* am?"

"Congenital and chronic."

"Did you hear that, Colin? She says I'm congenital."

"And chronic."

"Did you hear that, Miss Cottle?"

Mary Cottle, downwind of Janet and Rena, takes a smoke from a fresh pack of East African cigarettes and lights it.

"You suppose I could have one of those?" Benny asks.

"Strictly speaking, Ben boy, you oughtn't to smoke."

"The nerve," Lydia Conscience says. "After the way he spoke to her before."

"May I please?"

"Certainly not," Mary Cottle says.

"Shipwreck Marsh," Rena Morgan says. "It's not very pretty."

"It's quite suitable," Colin Bible says.

"*I* think it should do," Janet Order says.

"For our purposes."

"But it's *not* very pretty."

"Unspoiled," Colin Bible says, "it's unspoiled."

"Just what does *that* mean, Colin?"

"That the landscapers haven't been by yet. To put the macaws and cockatoos into the trees. The ibis and rheas. The trumpeter swans."

"Well?" Mary Cottle says.

"Well what?"

"I was thinking of our famous purposes."

"What's the hurry?"

"Where's the fire?"

"If I'm old enough to die," Benny sulks, "I'm old enough to smoke."

"It *looks* like a marsh."

"It *looks* like a shipwreck."

"That stuff isn't sand. Is that stuff sand?"

"It's some kind of cement, I think."

"The basic building blocks of life."

"This place must be crawling with poison ivy."

"Poison sumac."

"Deadly nightshade."

"Bloody pokeweed."

"Leaves of rhubarb."

"Seeds of castor."

"Whoever ain't game let him go back to the boats."

"Charles?"

"Ask the ladies."

"Janet?"

"Ask the blokes."

"Blokes?"

"All right then," Colin says. "You've a grand day for it."

So they split up. So they paired off. Charles, Tony, Noah, and Ben with Colin. Lydia and Janet and Rena Morgan with Mary. Not even thinking about swimming. Swimming not only out of the question but never even in it, as boating had never been in it either. Making their way in opposite directions across the spare, low, man-made island in the wide, blue man-made lake, stepping through the stunted thickets of mangrove and out into a sort of twin clearing, each group, perhaps not even consciously, seeking purchase, the advantaged, leveraged high ground, running silent as salmon all the traps and steeps (and this not only in opposite directions but with their backs to each other, and not only with their backs to each other but in actual stride-for-stride company with their tall leaders) of inconvenience.

They could have been duelists pacing off their combat like a piece of property.

"I guess this is as good a place as any," Colin Bible hears Mary Cottle settle.

"Right here's all right," Mary Cottle hears Colin Bible approve.

"Okay?"

"All right?"

The boys and girls scramble out of their clothes and lie down to their sun baths in the negligible humidity, in the balmy breeze across the perfect blue sky with its clouds like topping.

"Won't you be joining us, Miss Cottle?"

"I'm fine. I'm smoking my cigarettes."

"Colin? This is lovely. It's really super, Colin. It really is."

"That's all right. You go ahead. I'll keep an eye peeled in case the kid at the marina goes back on his word."

Separated by perhaps a hundred feet, the two groups lie about on hummocks of earth and rock at skewed, awry angles. Tony Word and Lydia Conscience lie in nests of their own clothes. It is really too great a distance to distinguish features, to make out the still only incipient shapes and chevrons of genitalia. They stare across the distance that separates them and have, each and collectively, a gorgeous impression of flesh. They are skinny-dipping in the air and leer across space in wonder and agape.

"That's enough, Rena. Put your clothes on. You don't want to burn."

"Five more minutes. Please, Miss Cottle? Just five more minutes. *Please*?"

"All right," she says and the boys get five more minutes to study her indistinct pinkness, the girls to note the fragile pallor of the boys.

And it was wondrous in the negligible humidity how they gawked across the perfect air, how, stunned by the helices and all the parabolas of grace, they gasped, they sighed, these short-timers who even at *their* young age could not buy insurance at any price, not even if the premiums were paid in the rare rich elements, in pearls clustered as grapes, in buckets of bullion, in trellises of diamonds, how, glad to be alive, they stared at each other and caught their breath.

6

Oh," said Matthew Gale when Mary Cottle, thinking it would be the housekeeper with her towels, answered his knock and opened the door to the hidey-hole, "excuse me. I must have the wrong room. I was looking for eight twenty-two. Oh," he said, "this *is* eight twenty-two."

"May I help you?"

"No, no. No problem. My friend used to have this room, but he's obviously checked out and gone back to England. Sorry to have bothered you."

"To England?"

"Gee," Matthew Gale said, "you're British too. Just like Colin. Well," he said, "enjoy your stay."

"Like Colin?" Mary Cottle said. "You were here with Colin?"

"Uh-oh," Matthew Gale said. "I've gone and put my foot in it, haven't I?"

"Colin brought you here." Because now she recognizes him. He's the young man who had helped them that time at the Haunted Mansion and whose exchange of winks with Colin she'd intercepted back in those now-dead live-and-let-live days of their arrival. It hadn't been he, of course, but the boiling circumstances of which he'd been a part that had turned her nerves into so many fuses waiting to be ignited and had caused her—who hated all arrangements in the first place—to—in the first place—take the room at all.

"Listen," he said, who, being no dummy and having a feel for the strange displacements of the ordinary and sizing up the situation, its unspeakable ramifications, and wondering, for example, just what Mrs. Bible was herself doing on the night in question, sought to give comfort where comfort may or may not have been due, "who knows what goes on in another person's marriage? In another person's life? May I come in?"

"You may not."

"I have no problem with that. I can say my piece right out here in the hall and let the neighbors think whatever they want to. I'm not going to tell you we're two consenting adults and there's the end of it. Because I'm beginning to suspect that in these particular circumstances two consenting adults wouldn't even begin to get the job done. No, ma'am. I'm beginning to suspect that to be fair to all the parties we're dealing with here would require a general goddamn election, a whole entire plebiscite. Well, there's you, of course, and that other one, the master industrial spy, the London, England Colin, and Lord knows who else, the man, woman, or child with whom you yourself may have been disporting on the fateful evening. . . . Look, if I'm the least bit out of line, blow the whistle on me, please. *Prom*ise now.

"He's really quite charming, your Colin. He even made me come up with the key to this place. I'm certain it was a test. Well, *you* know the sort of thing I mean. The little negotiations we do with the fates. . . . If such-and-so is meant to be, let a purple chicken come around that corner pulling a red wagon. Religion!—No, thank you, I'm perfectly fine, thank you very much; it's not a *bit* drafty out here—But, well, frankly, though it's *not* my business, it's just I *like* your Colin so. He has his faults, of course. Who's perfect? Certainly not *me*. Well, I'm sure you know that. Colin probably told you all about it. Well, why not? say I. What's an open marriage *for* if the party of the first part ain't free to lay it all out for the party of the second? How*ever* disgusting, degrading, and humiliating it may turn out to be for the poor hick son-bitch party of the third, fourth, fifth, or sixth! Am I getting warm?"

"I haven't a clue regarding whatever it is you're talking about," Mary Cottle said.

"No," Matthew Gale said, smiling prettily, "of course not."

She started to close the door in his face. Gale resisted at first, then stepped suddenly back, drawing her off balance, sending her stumbling to the door, her left cheek awkwardly pressed against it.

"I don't know," Matthew Gale said loudly from the other side of the door, "just what it is, what nasty sting operation you people are up to, but under the circumstances I feel obliged to warn you that what we've been funning with here isn't your standard, ordinary point-of-interest or your regular, everyday, five-star, not-to-be-missed, absolute *Must*, so much as the almighty God's almighty own country itself! *Can I get an Amen, somebody?*"

"Amen," said somebody.

"And why not," Gale said (and she had the impression he was whispering now, that whatever he said he might have been saying into the grain of the wooden door), "why? This is Disney World! This is the basic universal G-for-good, G-for-goodness, main attraction and main event. You're fucking with Disney World! *Lady, la*dy, do you appreciate what that means? That means, if it came right down to it, they could do you legal as apple pie if they wanted. They not only got the guns, the Bomb, and the animatronics, but the Ten Commandments and the

Onward Christian Soldiers too! They're connected high up with important principles: with Safety First and Handicap Access. With double sinks and orthopedic mattresses. With convenience, clean accommodations, and fair value understood. With public temperance and a Lost and Found like the secret fucking service! With clever mice and friendly bears, with reluctant dragons and horticultural bulls. With Nature in sweet tooth and claw, as it were. With— *Are you listening to me?*" he demanded.

"Yes," she said. Her hand was in her pants.

"With *family*, I mean! With grampas that fish and fathers that golf. With moms who drive car pools and look great in jeans. With brothers and sisses who'd be lost if they left each other's corner for even a minute. With pets who'd lay down their lives for any of them. This is the picture. Are you getting the picture?"

"Yes," she said. Was separating her pubic mat like a curtain and pushing a finger up into her cleft.

"I'm talking about a tone. Judgmental calls. Because it really *is* a small world after all. The high energy of high righteousness and fervency. All the us/them dichotomies. Not just capitalism, not just free enterprise. Not even just morality, finally, but something larger, grander, more important. Efficiency! That's it. That's all. Efficiency. More bang for the buck. It's simple as that. Efficiency. Everything else is moral turpitude. *Everything* else. This is still the picture. This is still the picture. Who ain't in it?"

"Who?"

"Colin ain't in it."

"Colin," she said.

"And you," he said. *"You* ain't in it."

"Are you in it?"

"I'm a different story," he said. "I'm behind the scenes."

"I know who you are," she said calmly. For she was herself again. Because she'd come now. Was restored to herself, in control, her nerves' temperature normal, like fever broken in a crisis.

"What?"

"I know who you are."

"Sure, sure," he said. "Colin let on. That's just the way of it with wise, experienced, double-dealing old fags."

"I saw you at the Haunted Mansion."

"Housekeeping," a woman said. "I've brought you your towels."

And when Mary opened the door he was gone.

Careful to let any guest, even a child, pass through first, he left the elevator and got off on the lobby floor. Gale high-signed his fellow cast members—we're tight, he thought, we're tight as skycaps passing in airports—and called out their names. He must have known almost everyone who worked at the Contemporary. Well, he hung out at the Spa so much. Which wasn't, he thought, in the least suspicious. He was just using the facilities. As he'd seen bellboys and desk clerks at the Haunted Mansion during their lunch breaks. Only part of the perks.

What was suspicious, of course, was his use of the elevators. Being caught on the guest floors, coming down into the lobby at midnight, at one in the morning. What *was* suspicious was the flimsy cover story he put out that he was a gambler, that he went up to their rooms to take their money in poker and crap games. They thought they knew better, his bellboy and desk clerk cronies. So he grinned and aw-shucks'd them, and toed awkward circles in the pile carpets and marble floors, as if he were barefoot or wore straws in his mouth.

"Better give it a rest, Gale, or you're going to lose it for certain."

"Let it come up for air once in a while."

"That's right, Matthew. It's going to burn out on you. It's going to disappear like a wick."

"Who was it this time?"

"Ten thirty-three?"

"Seven-oh-four?"

"The *blonde?* The one with the humongous mammaritos and the sweetheart great ass?"

"A fellow don't kiss and tell."

"You *kissed* them?"

"Man, you know what'll happen to you if the manager finds out?"

"Yeah, you better off if her daddy finds out."

"You'd believe all those workouts in the health club might slow him down a bit."

"They do! You think any of them gals would still be alive otherwise?"

So they kidded him, joshed into heroic farmboy studship the familiar creature from the tearooms of central Florida.

"Some lover," the bell captain said. "I saw you step into that elevator not fifteen minutes ago."

"Maybe it stopped on the fifth floor," he said. "Maybe that's where a certain redheaded Cuban spitfire got on board. Maybe she threatened to dance all over me with her spike heels if I didn't lock it from the inside. Maybe I serviced her right there in the box. Maybe that's all the time we needed. How you doin', Andy?"

"Pretty fair, Matthew. Yourself?"

"Be an ungrateful liar if I complained."

"Be seeing you, Matt."

"Be seeing you, Andrew."

And spotted the dog, Pluto, surrounded by kids and holding the brace of Mickey Mouse balloons he always carried but so sparingly gave out.

("Jesus, Lamar, you'd think you paid for them yourself," he'd said.

("No, but I have to fill them with helium. Do you know I have to blow up Goofy's as well as my own?"

("Really?"

("He outranks me."

("No shit?"

("Sure, and I'll tell you something else. That son-of-a-bitch dog is one hard taskmaster."

("You know something? You had me going. You break me up, Lamar."

("Well, shit, I'm a pro.")

Who owed him one. Probably more than one. For sometimes spelling Kenny whenever he drove over to Orlando or Winter Park or Daytona Beach or Kissimmee for an audition. ("Jesus, kid," he'd said, after returning from one of these auditions and coming up dry, "you've given away every fucking balloon I had. I'll be a year blowing the mothers up again. Show business!")

So then and there Matthew Gale decided to call in his marker. He ambled over to the besieged pup and gave what always before had been Lamar Kenny's overture, their secret silent signal. (Silent because as one of the characters he'd been forbidden all speech, not permitted even a growl. "Kid," he'd say afterward, "they've muzzled old Pluto.") He made the gesture with his hand. Kenny saw him but shook his head like a pitcher declining a sign. Matthew did the thing with his left hand again. The dog looked at him quizzically. (So comical, Gale thought. Damn, he's good! Matthew had no idea why Lamar never landed those jobs. He was a wonderful actor.) So Matthew stepped up to him and did it again. Again the pooch shook it off and again Matthew repeated the signal. Pluto shrugged and released the balloons he held in his paw. They floated up out of the reach of the children, who jumped to grab at their strings. In the confusion Matthew Gale sidled up to his friend. "Meet me," he said. "It's important!"

Pluto looked up sadly after the balloons. He didn't break character by so much as a whimper, but Gale could tell that anyone looking at him, every kid in the place, could read his mind, the expression written plain as day across his doggy jowls. Fuck damn, he was thinking, now I'll have to blow up twenty more of these mouseshit balloons!

They were standing by his locker. Not until he'd removed the last of his Pluto suit and hung it neatly away did Lamar Kenny say anything at all. He pointed to the locker. "Is that the dressing room of a star or is that the dressing room of a star?"

"What do you think, Lamar?"

"I think it's the dressing room of some assembly-line guy, a U.S. Steel worker, an A. F. of L."

"About the gig."

"Leave them to Heaven."

"Come on, Lamar, what do you say?"

"I say it's nuts. I say if you're looking to get us fired you've struck pay dirt."

Gale rubbed his finger across the locker's dusty metal shelves. "I think it's the dressing room of some assembly-line guy too."

"That's the way," Kenny said. "Play up to the trouper in me."

"I am. I want to. Didn't I come to you with my proposal?"

"Some proposal."

"Admit it, Lamar. It's a great gig. Admit that much."

"Don't say 'gig.' You've got no right to say 'gig.' "

"Sorry."

"Do I say 'rough trade'? Do I say 'butch'?"

"I didn't mean to offend, Lamar."

"I don't know," he said. "I don't know why I'm so touchy. I'm in a profession; we live, we let live. You're right," he said, "it's a hell of a part. Nah," he said, "they'd turn us in. They'd call Security. We'd be lucky if all that happened was we lost our jobs."

"They won't turn us in. The guy, Colin, is in too deep. Forget about the bed part. The bed part's the least of it. He has sensitive manuals in his possession."

"You gave him sensitive manuals?"

"You think I know what I gave him? I don't *know* what I gave him. I threw some stuff together. He played it down. He made out like it was nothing. Naturally I'm suspicious."

"And the wife?"

"There's something strange there."

"Strange."

"She's got this *at*titude."

"You," Mary Cottle commanded Colin Bible, "stay out of my room!" And reminded him of her good name and demanded to know how he'd found out.

It was astonishing, really. How the bottom of things lay at the bottom of things like the lowest rung on a ladder. But how, beneath that, there was a still lower level, that open area of the air, some apron of the underneath, mysterious, inexplicable. Colin sent her to Nedra Carp. Who put her on to Janet Order. Who implicated Mudd-Gaddis.

She went to him.

"Charles?" she said.

"Yes, lady?"

"Do you know who I am?"

"The Angel of Death?"

"No," she said.

"Do I get another turn?"

She stared at him.

"Are you living?"

"Of *course* I'm living!"

"Are you bigger than a breadbasket?"

"Mudd-Gaddis!"

"How many is that?"

"*Mudd-Gaddis!*"

"Do you reside in eastern Europe west of the Odra?"

"*I'm Mary Cottle!*" she said.

"That was my next question." He looked at her. "Yes, Miss Cottle?"

"Nothing," she said.

Because everything has a reasonable explanation.

She didn't really care about getting to the bottom of things. She didn't care about the mystery. She wasn't even protecting her good name. She was protecting that room.

"She's proper pissed," Mudd-Gaddis said.

"I've never even seen the room," Lydia Conscience said.

"Neither have I," said Rena Morgan.

Noah and Tony hadn't. Nor had Janet Order. Benny, of course, couldn't wait to get back there but knew there would be little point if anyone else came along.

They turned to Benny. He was the oldest. He had the Swiss Army knife that could get them in.

"It'd be breaking and entering," Benny said.

"But not for the first time," Rena Morgan said.

"What's that supposed to mean?"

"It means," Rena said, "that by now you're so practiced all the risk is removed. It isn't as if it were anything *stealthy*."

"Anything furtive," Lydia Conscience said.

"Clandestine," said Janet Order.

"Anything hugger-mugger."

"Hole-and-corner."

Benny Maxine looked from one girl to the other. "What's going on?" he asked. If they had told him "sorority" he wouldn't have known what they meant. They wouldn't themselves. They were friends now, close as they'd been that day on the island, closer than their mortality could take them. (Closer than Tony and Noah, who slept in the intensive care ward together and made sure they sat next to each other at every meal and on all the rides. Who regarded each other as best friends. Closer than that.)

"What could be *in* there?" Lydia Conscience said.

"Something important," Janet Order said.

"Do you think she has a lover?" asked Rena Morgan.

"A lover? Why would she have a lover?" Benny said angrily. "What do you mean do you think she has a lover?"

"That maybe she's in love," Rena said.

"She's not in love," Benny said.

"How would *you* know *what* people are?" Rena said.

"Come on," Benny said. "She's not in love."

"What's *in* that room?"

"Take us. Please? *Do* let's go see."

"Come on, Benny."

"*Please.*"

"It's crazy," he said.

"We've been on all the *other* rides."

"There's nothing there."

"She's proper pissed, Ben."

"There's nothing there," he said again.

Though of course there was. Her human geography. At least his memory of it. The sexual topography of those elliptical hollows, the two dark shadows, those twin stained darning eggs in her ass. At least there'd be the bedspread on which she'd lain.

So if he agreed to take them it was to honor the memory of those delicious relics.

7

They went at night.

They didn't tell anyone where they were going and didn't take the trouble to work out elaborate alibis. What happened was they simply managed to peel off individually from their respective groups. They'd handled themselves, Noah suggested, rather like flying aces in an aerobatic squadron. When one of them left, the ones who remained took up the slack and made just that much more noise, that much more fuss, neither adding nor detracting one whit from the general collective level of demand that any seven terminally ill children might put up under a similar set of dream holiday conditions. And really, when you came to think of it, it was quite a performance, one of the best-yet illusions in the magical kingdom. They weren't missed until after they were missing.

Any one of them could have told you straight off about 822's appeal. As soon as they saw it, it became for them what it was supposed to have been for Miss Cottle: a hidey-hole, a sort of clubhouse. Perhaps this was one of the reasons they were so neat. They managed to lie about the room, to fill its three chairs— four if you counted Mudd-Gaddis's wheelchair—and queen-sized bed—at once the girls had taken it for their own—and even— the boys—put their feet up on the wide round table, to use, in fact, all the long, deep olive oblong room with its dark modern furniture without sullying the least of its pristine from-the-hands- of-housekeeping appearance. There were tricks. Rena Morgan directed the fellows to shut flush each drawer in the bed tables, each louvered drawer in the dresser. Lydia Conscience told them they must keep the sound off if they turned on the TV. And Janet Order, their third expert in camouflage, suggested that all the advertising cards be removed from the top of the trim- line TV and hidden away, that they untangle the cord on the telephone and draw the patternless brown drapes.

So they sat, lay about in this curious rowdy tidiness—well, they were dying—and trim, discounted cleanliness and order. Very much at home. Very much at ease. They might have been snug and dry in a treehouse in rain. They watched the sound- less images on TV as if they were logs on a hearth.

Each felt restored, returned to some precious condition of privacy they'd almost forgotten.

"When do you think they'll think to look for us here?" one of them asked at last.

"They've already thought it," Janet Order said.

"Too right," said Benny.

"Oh," said Rena Morgan, "then why haven't they caught us?"

"Because they're embarrassed," Lydia said.

"Embarrassed."

"Well, they are," Benny Maxine said.

"Sure," Rena said. "I suppose they're afraid they'll bust in and catch us out in some big orgy."

"That's not what they think," Tony Word said.

"*You* know a lot about it."

"Rena, it's not."

"No," Noah Cloth said, "they're embarrassed for Miss Cottle."

"Or scared of her," Benny said.

"Because she lowered the boom on them."

"The room boom."

"Probably they'll call first."

"No," Rena said, "they'll never be able to get the number out of the hotel switchboard. Isn't that right, Benny? They don't give out unpublished numbers? Isn't that what you said?"

"For God's sake, Rena," Janet Order said, "once they have the *room* number they have the phone number too."

"Little old daftie me," Rena Morgan said.

"They won't expect us to answer," Benny said, "but probably they *will* call first. Give us time to clear out."

"Of course we mustn't answer," Rena said, glaring at Janet. "What, and tangle the phone cord?"

"Ladies!" Charles Mudd-Gaddis said.

Rena patted the bedspread beside her. "Want to come up here, Noah, and rest by my side? There's acres of room. Noah? Noey?"

"I'm fine."

"What about you, Tony? Tonah?"

"Of course maybe they won't realize most of us have figured it out and they'll *expect* us to answer," Lydia Conscience said. "I mean, maybe our friends haven't figured it out themselves. Or maybe they're just not the ladies and gentlemen you give them credit for, Ben."

"Maybe," Benny said. "I don't think we can take the chance. If the phone rings we scarper."

"I agree with Benny," Rena Morgan said. She looked around the clubhouse. "Shall we put it to a vote? Who'll make a motion?"

"Rena, for Christ's sake," Janet Order said.

"What is this, Rena?" Lydia asked.

"Well *what?*" Rena shot back. "Isn't this our all-purpose, syndicalist, council-in-the-treehouse synod and social club? Aren't we supposed to make motions? How do we occupy ourselves when we're finished with old business? Or is the only thing on our plate what to do if the phone rings?"

"Rena's got a bug up her ass."

"*Ladies!*"

Benny Maxine punched off the television. "Who's up for a ghost story?"

"A ghost story?"

"You got a better idea?"

"I love a good ghost story."

"So do I."

"Lots of gore."

"Gobs of guts hanging about, decorating the room like strings of popcorn."

"Moans. Howls of pain."

"I love a good ghost story."

"Takes me mind off things."

"Who'll go first?"

"Benny."

"It was his idea."

"That's what I'm saying."

"You go first, Ben?"

"How do I know you won't cry?"

"I won't."

"Suppose it's so terrible you can't help yourself?"

"I won't cry."

"You give me a forfeit if you do?"

"What forfeit?"

"Your money?"

"*Benny!*"

"You *know* what money means to Noah."

"I'm only trying to make it interesting. I'm trying to make it interesting for us all. You bet too. Bet me my ghost story can't make him cry."

"Wait a minute," Noah said. "What do I get if it doesn't? What do *you* forfeit?"

Maxine considered. "Forty dollars," he said. "And I'll lay you two-to-one odds."

"Noah?"

"Go ahead," Noah said, "he can't do it."

"They laid their bets down and Benny began.

"Once upon a time," he said, "there was this lad name of Noah Cloth—"

"Benny!"

"—*lad* name of Noah *Cloth*. Now Noah was a fine little fellow in all respects save one. He was even quite properly named, Noah was, for he had a disease and ripped real easy. Easy as *cloth!* The disease was called osteosarcoma, a deadly cancer, and it was the single most common bone tumor in children. There was only one way to deal with it, and that was to amputate. Wherever it showed up, that's where Noah's doctors had to cut. If it showed up in a finger they would chop off the finger; if it showed up in a leg the leg would come off."

"No fair."

"No fair?"

"No, no fair. You said a ghost story."

"What's no fair? He dies," Benny argued reasonably. "I kill him, he dies. The bone cancer gets him. He dies. He dies and comes back. He appears to his poor grieving parents, his sorrowful mum, his heartbusted dad." He glanced over at Noah to gauge the boy's reaction. The kid was chewing his lips, but Benny couldn't tell whether he was on the verge of tears or laughter. "It's not too late to back out," he said. "You want to back out?" The boy shook his head. Benny continued his tale.

"Though the cancer took a long time to tear through Cloth, Noah wasn't even into his teens when he passed. When he finally died there almost wasn't enough left of him to put in the ground. I mean, he was that cut up. All they could put together for his little casket—from its size you'd think they were burying a small dog—were the pieces of his face and head they hadn't had to saw on yet: some of his jawbone, the long bone that supports his nose, the bony socket of his left eye like the mounting for a missing jewel, pieces of skull like bits of pottery. And the remains of his diseased frame all wired up like the dinosaur in the museum. There was an elbow like a patch on a jacket. There was some shin, a fragment of ankle, maybe a sixth of his spine. There was his pelvis all eaten away and looking like a hive and, curiously, most of the toes on his right foot."

Benny Maxine looked sharply at Noah Cloth. It wasn't pleasant what he had to do next, but his honor as a gambler was at stake. Still, if the kid had shown him only the merest sign of submission he would have called it off. He stared at Noah. It wasn't laughter *or* tears that struggled for supremacy. Terror sat in his face like a tic.

Benny took a deep breath, rose from the chair in which he'd been sitting, and slowly paced along the wall as he spoke.

"Noah Cloth died on an operating table in a hospital in Surrey on the Tuesday following his twelfth birthday."

The children gasped and Benny Maxine went on.

"The undertakers had to work on him harder than ever the surgeons did just to make him acceptable for Christian burial. They did him with wax and with wire, working from the photographs of infants as their model. They wrapped him in a shroud and, obedient to the wishes of Mr. and Mrs. Cloth, buried him at midnight in an unmarked grave away from the sight of men. No one was permitted to come to the funeral. Even the Cloths stayed away.

"His cerements decayed in the damp grave. The wax that held him together dissolved and returned to the earth. The wires that ran through what was left of his bones rusted and became a part of the generalized tetanus of the world, and Noah Cloth was reduced, shrunken, boiled down, distilled into a sort of pointless dice. He was no longer, if he ever had been, a part of the respectable dead. Terminally ill from the day he was born, chipped away at and chipped away at by disease, nickel-and-dimed by the scalpels and hacksaws of his doctors, he was as unfit for the grave as he was for the world, and his spirit, caged now in that scant handful of spared, untouched bone like the undiscarded remnant marble of the sculptor's intention, rose up from the vast lake of the dead and returned one night to his parents' flat, there to bury itself in the bed he'd slept in as a boy, in the small room which, when he'd not been in hospital, had been his grave in life!

"It was Mrs. Cloth who first heard the macabre rattle of his bones. She was in bed and very frightened and tried to rouse her husband, for the queer click sounds that Noah made in death were not unlike the sounds her boy had made in life. She shook him and shook him but he would not rouse. 'Husband,' she hissed in his ear, 'husband, wake up! There are noises coming from Noah's room!' But his son's life and his son's death had taken so much from the poor man that he slept as one dead himself. So Mrs. Cloth got out of bed and followed the queer chattering sounds like the frozen blood-barren noises of men exposed to the cold.

"She reached her son's room and snapped on the light."

Benny paused, his back against the wall, studying Noah. Noah watched him, not daring to breathe. "Noah?" Benny called in a perfect rendition of a ruined mother's cracked old voice. "Noah, is that you?" And seemed in very fright and weakness to swoon, his back and neck buckling, in that precise instant catching the master switch that controlled the electricity in the room and with one smart swift convulsion plunged 822 into total darkness.

Here is what happened.

Janet Order and Lydia Conscience screamed.

Benny Maxine got his cry out of Noah Cloth.

Tony Word bit his tongue and wondered if he'd infected himself.

Charles Mudd-Gaddis thought for a moment that he had fallen asleep.

Rena Morgan caught her breath and marveled at Benny Maxine's timing.

Mickey Mouse materialized on the ceiling in full color.

Pluto stood behind the Mouse's shoulder staring down at the children.

Because everything has a reasonable explanation.

In complete darkness—the tightly drawn drapes, the light-proof rubberized curtains behind them, the room's somber-toned, dark-olive furniture, the plastic cards removed from the top of the television, the very thickness and density of the children themselves—the hidey-hole functioned exactly like a sort of camera obscura.

Because *everything* has a reasonable explanation.

The protective peephole in the door through which guests could observe their callers before admitting them had, in 822, been inadvertently reversed, installed in concave rather than convex relation to a guest's eye (not only a reasonable explanation, but a positively scientific one), the glazed, grommetlike eyepiece turned into a sort of light-collecting lens.

Everything.

In a normal camera obscura the image would have been projected onto a facing surface, the patternless brown drapes. That's what should have happened in 822. So why the ceiling? Because it was a room in a major hotel catering to guests not only from all over the country but from all over the world, to guests of different social, ethnic, and religious backgrounds, to smokers and nonsmokers, to people who lit votive candles, to romantics on their first honeymoons or even on their second or third, to men and women not on honeymoons at all but quite as romantic as the just-marrieds, who took their meals from room-service carts by the light of flickering candles, to adolescents and a range of the mystic-inclined who would not live in an unmediated environment and burned incense at the altar of their senses. So, in a way, Mickey and Pluto were on the ceiling rather than on the drapes because of the fire regulations and the insurance premiums, the thin layer of slightly glossy fire retardant on the drapes, which, just out of plumb from vertical true, canted their images down onto the retardant-soaked rug, which bounced the light off the floor and refracted it onto the ceiling. That's why.

All this happening too quickly to account for. Everything happening too quickly to account for. The children squealing, the girls and the boys, scurrying for cover, almost knocking Mudd-Gaddis out of his wheelchair in the ensuing melee. Holding their hands over their heads for protection, the way, one imagines, their remote ancestors might have responded to comets in the sky, portents.

"Jesus!" they screamed.

"Oh, my God!"

"Help!"

Benny Maxine, no less frightened than the others (indeed, if anything, more so; in their wild, blind wake, brushed by their dark stampede, his tender, battered organs touched, rubbed, pushed, and pained by the adiabatic conflagrancies of their blacked-out skirmishes), wheeled about, found the wall switch, and fumbled light into the room.

Mickey and Pluto disappeared at once and, seconds later, there was a loud knock on the door.

"It's them," Lydia said. "They didn't call after all."

"Hah!" Rena Morgan said.

"Well, we'd best get it over with," Benny said, and opened the door.

The Mouse and the Dog were standing there.

"Hi, kids," said Mickey Mouse in his high clear voice like a reed instrument, like music toward the top of a clarinet. "We're the good guys. We're"—he raised his strange hand, like a fielder's mitt with its four stump digits, against the side of his fixed grin—"these Moonies, sort of. But wholesome. Really, kids. Wholesome. I think so, anyway. Forty-eight highway, thirty-two city. Your mileage may vary. It probably does."

He started to tell them more or less what Matthew Gale had told Mary Cottle. And was warming to his theme when he was interrupted by the dog pulling on his master's arm, pumping it up and down as if he were raising bridges or flagging trains.

"I don't see the lady of the house anywhere about," Pluto said.

"It's all right," Mickey said, retrieving his arm, watching Rena and Benny and recognizing the girl magician and the wise-guy kid, rubbing both fielders' mitts together. "These are nice girls and boys. Just our meat. Or mine, anyway. Mickey meat, you might say. Let's stay on a bit, Plute."

"Or the master neither," said the dog.

"He thinks too much on masters and mistresses," Mickey explained. "That's his nature, of course, but sometimes you can overdo."

"You can overdo your nature?" Mudd-Gaddis asked.

The Mouse looked him over. Terrific, he thought. A roomful of wise-guy kids. "Well, certainly, old man," he said. "Ain't that what makes tragedy? When we haven't sense enough to get out of the way of our characters?"

Lydia Conscience and Tony Word were whispering together.

"What?" Mickey demanded. Tony Word looked down at his feet. "No, what?" repeated the Mouse. "Come on," he said, "won't you share with the rest of us? No? Don't you know it's rude to have secrets? No more whispering campaigns," he scolded. "Is that understood?"

"He wants to know how you got on the ceiling," Lydia said.

So part of it at least was a misunderstanding, a garble, a gloss. A little, that is, was farce, all the knockabout calisthenics of cross-purpose. Just so much was misconstrued, lost in translation. The children, the Dog and the Mouse, misunderstood each other. (Sure, they could be smeared across the ceiling like a slide show but they couldn't see through walls, could they?) And then there was Kenny's theatrical orientation. He was an actor. He'd had the floor. Of course he was angry. Boiling mad, actually.

Already boiling mad when the shill opened the door and Lamar recognized him, as well as the girl on the bed, the snot-nosed charmer from the elevator, so fast—better than the Vegas mechanics he'd seen, so fast, a little quick-draw artist—with her hands, which (he was a fair man) he didn't begrudge her in the least. Only wondering whether Matthew Gale, sweating, he trusted—anyway, hoped—in Lamar's Pluto suit there was in on it too. Some cast member, he thought ungenerously. (He *hoped* sweating. He hoped fucking *melting*, f'chrissake. Because it really *was* an art, being in that suit was, a question of breathing, like the difference between the singers who played the lounges and the ones who played Vegas's biggest, most important rooms: only

a matter of breathing, of phrasing. What separated the men from
the boys, the sheep from the goats. So if Matt *was* in on it, if all
this was happening in any way, shape, or form to set him up,
he hoped to God the lousy faggot was turning to tiger butter
inside the Pluto suit.) So he really *didn't* begrudge her. He respected her, if you wanted to know. Or her skills, anyway. The
ends she put them to was something else. The ends she put them
to was another story altogether. Scaring the shit out of people
was. What kind of a way was that? This was entertainment?
Thanks but no thanks.

So, already angry when he walked in the door and saw them.
Snappish and primed.

Not realizing, of course, or anyway realizing the wrong
things because the nature of misunderstanding, of farce (without which there would be no ball game), is that you don't know
that that's what it is. If someone had been there who could see
all sides, it would have been a different story, but there was no
one. Matthew Gale didn't remember them from the Haunted
Mansion. (The girls hadn't been there anyway, and only Mudd-
Gaddis, so excited then, now so sedate, would have made any
impression at all.) He saw so many tantrums during the course
of a day it's doubtful he could have remembered anything.
Oddly, Mudd-Gaddis might have if Gale hadn't been hidden by
Lamar's Pluto suit, warm and moist now as a greenhouse, incidentally, and growing gamier by the minute. Or Benny Maxine, who'd had a run-in with Goofy and Pluto in the restaurant,
who'd squeezed Goofy's nose and pulled the bristles in his jowls
and messed with his hat and, on behalf of his comrades, even
bet the pooches that none of them would die. (Talk, he might
have thought, about your Mississippi riverboat gamblers! *I'm* a
bleeding sport!) But who'd either forgotten the incident or didn't
recognize in the whipped and cringing mutt right there in front
of him—from itself cringing, from its close and closing circumstances—anything of the aloof, valorous pup of that first encounter. So there was no one. Lydia's remark about the ceiling
gobbledygook to the general, Lamar Kenny's rage not only inexplicable but not even picked up. (The whispering, of course—

he was an actor, he had the floor; you don't whisper when an actor has the floor; why, that's worse than heckling him—Mudd-Gaddis's remark, which he took to be a sly dig about his acting; the little girl on the bed— Of the three girls, only Rena had failed to get up when the Mouse and Dog appeared on the ceiling.)

And spotting the wise-guy kid straight off, *that* was a treat. Who'd heckled hell out of his breakfast show that time, who'd made a scene at the fried eggs and balloons.

(Which was what was so great about being a human being, thought Mickey Mouse and the girls, Mickey Mouse and the boys—— the reasons, the fine tracery of the reasons. The swirl of motive. Like snowflakes we are, thought Benny Maxine, like fingerprint and tooth record.)

But chiefly scaring the shit out of people, the difference in their artistic temperaments. (Artistic differences, they had artistic differences. Gee, thought Lamar Kenny, still comparatively new in the business and already I got artistic differences!) Yet, however impressed, even flattered, he may have been that they existed, it was their artistic differences that ticked him off most. For openers, he thought, he didn't have a handle on just what he was dealing with here. The kids were a new wrinkle. That was clear enough. But fad or trend? Flash in the pan or wave of the future? He didn't really know what was going on. From the time the original wise-guy kid had first given him the business, he'd been asking around. No one seemed to know if anything was up or not, though all had remarked the influx of terminally ill kiddies. He supposed the park was involved in some sort of market research and imagined that this group had *some-thing* to do with it. He'd heard, for example, that someone fitting the description of the odd little lame duck over there in the wheelchair had made a fuss at the Haunted Mansion the other day. (Though not from Matthew, you may be sure, who was almost certainly in on it, whatever it was, and who he hoped had not only turned to tiger butter but was rancid as well, gone off inside the pup tent like a bomb.)

Because he didn't need the aggravation. Your death acts—

here today and gone tomorrow—his hunch was, would never catch on, though he couldn't deny the outrageousness of the concept. Only where was the art? What did it take, after all, to display the dying? If you asked him, it was a little like public hangings. Sure, the poet was right on the money and there was nothing new under the sun. As a matter of fact, if you asked him it wasn't even in very good taste. Though he certainly saw the point, what they were getting at. The old triumph-of-the-human-spirit bit. Folks showing their lesions and cancers, exposing their stumps, sniffing their gangrene. There really was no business like show business. Well.

The first thing, he supposed, was to check them out, find out if they were for real. (Because didn't it stink, at least a little, of fraud and freak show?) He knew what the girl could do, of course, the one on the bed, but now he'd find out about the rest of them too, what the shouting was all about.

He turned to Janet Order.

"All right," he said, "let's just see if that shit comes off!" He tossed her a damp washcloth. "Oh, please," Mickey Mouse said, "you couldn't get chalk off a blackboard with such half-hearted efforts."

"I'm halfhearted," said the hole-hearted child.

"Here, let me," said the Mouse, taking the cloth back from the kid, vigorously rubbing her blue skin with it.

"You'd lay hands on a customer?" Pluto growled. "On a *customer?*"

"And how about you?" the Mouse shot back. "How about you, Mister Magic Fingers? You hypocritical dog, you!" Who was steamed anyway, who knew he'd been had the minute he walked into the room. Calling in his marker, Gale had said. For the times he'd pulled guard duty for him when Lamar had gone off to talk to the clubs. Calling in his marker. Calling in his *mark* was more like it! Telling him it was just to get his own back, furious because Colin had set him up, because, or so he'd said, the woman was in on it too. To get his own back, and maybe those manuals. Merely to devil them with implication and outrage, to bear down on the two of them with the full moral authority of

Mickey Mouse and his faithful friend. (Faithful friend was a good touch. Faithful friend had a bit of genius to it, what, he supposed, had ultimately sold him.) Though why hadn't he thought to ask him what he hadn't thought to ask him? Why hadn't he thought to ask him, "Then why not bring Minnie?" Because maybe Gale was no dummy. Because maybe he would probably have come right out and said what was on all their minds anyway: that Mickey and Minnie weren't married, that there was something a touch suspicious if not outright unsavory about that relationship. That if they slept together—and after a fifty-year engagement who could doubt it? a Mouse wasn't made of steel—without benefit of clergy, how could they hope to have any sort of moral edge over Colin and the woman? Anyway, he hadn't even thought to bring it up. And understood he'd been had as soon as the wise-guy kid opened the door for them, as soon as he'd taken in—or been taken in by—all the wise-guy kid's wise-guy cohorts, that little league of the year-to-live.

So what was he doing here? That still unfigured. (Which *was* what was so great about being a human being! Oh, how he thrived on it! Reason and motive. —Not unlike his act, really, the thinking ahead, one man dueling for two.— Life like the crossword. Nine down, fourteen across, and the unpuzzled life not worth living. So what? Above all, was this an opportunity or not? Was Matthew his friend after all, or was he one of the company men he knew thrived in these parts? Running his abscams, baiting his entrapments and setting them? What if he was only posing as a *faygeleh*? To sucker his trust? If so, it might be an opportunity. Maybe 822 was his very own Schwab's Drugstore; maybe Matthew Gale was that secret talent scout he'd always been on the lookout for. If not . . . well, if not, it was all up with him anyway. He was impersonating a Mickey Mouse. Dressed up in the Mouse's own official Mickey Mouse clothes, the vaguely impresarial tuxedo Mickey frequently wore these days. How many years could you get for that? Perhaps life, maybe the chair. (God, what it said for the star system, for perks and privilege! He'd heard, and would have suspected even if he hadn't—the cast was pretty tight-mouthed about their salaries—that the matinee rodent made tons more money than he did, or the other characters either, of course, and knew for a fact that the Mouse didn't, unless he was in a good mood, always speak to the rest of them, sometimes not even giving Min herself the time of day, arbitrary and temperamental as a soprano, which he was. So why hadn't they gone all out? Why didn't they provide Mickey with a separate dressing room? Was this management's way of keeping their star attraction in line? Why else would they make it so easy for Lamar to get into the Mouse's locker, with its rinky-dink high-school-gym-locker lock? Why, of course, Lamar thought: not to keep him in line but to impose that same moral authority that seemed to emanate from the Kingdom's every pore. Mousketeers didn't steal. Not from each other. Not from anyone. They were clean, reverent, helpful, loyal, and brave. Mousketeers were the cat's pajamas morality-wise. It was what lent them their terrible authority. Not only why they didn't speak but why, except for the younger children, most of the guests seemed to clam up in their presence.)

So what was expected? What? If he wasn't being set up? (Which, increasingly, beginning to feel at home in 822, he felt he wasn't.) What was expected? Ah, thought the trained actor, recalling Pluto's words. "You'd lay hands on a customer? On a *customer?*" Was this an admonishment? Some secret cautionary? (And he *wasn't* rank, hadn't turned into tiger butter; nor, now he thought of it, had the Pluto suit ever stunk on any of those occasions when Matthew had worn it to cover one of Lamar's absences. He knew for a fact Matthew admired him as an actor. And he wasn't rank! Maybe he knew how to breathe, too.) "You'd lay hands on a customer? On a *customer?*" If that wasn't a paraphrase of the ghost's warning to Hamlet to spare Gertrude, why then *he'd* never heard one! So what? *What?* Something to do with death, he bet. (Because something of what they did here was always a *little* slanted toward death. The Haunted Mansion where Matthew worked, for example. All the nostalgia: Main Street, U.S.A., with its gas lamps and hitching posts, its nickelodions and penny arcades and horse-drawn trolleys.

Liberty Square with its colonial modes. Frontierland with its stockade and squirrel-cap ones. Most of it fucking Yesteryearland, if you asked him. Even Tomorrowland. The past and the hereafter. And what about Snow White herself? Old buried-alive Snow White in her glass casket like those hatbox-shaped containers that keep pies fresh, doughnuts and sweet rolls, on counters in restaurants? And how about those Seven Dwarfs? Yeah, how about them? Sneezy, Dopey, Grumpy, Happy, Sleepy, Bashful, and Doc. Cholers and pathologies. Wasn't there an analogue to be discovered between the dwarfs and these wise-guy kids? He'd seen what she could do with a handkerchief, what, out of the corner of his eye, he could see she was doing now. The girl on the bed was a shoo-in for Sneezy. And the kids who'd been whispering together, the girl with the belly and the boy who'd stared at his shoes when they'd been caught out, who'd let the belly speak up for him. The guy was a clear Bashful. Lamar couldn't quite figure the little shaver in the wheelchair. His question about overdoing one's nature had clearly been hostile. On the other hand, despite the commotion, he seemed to have dozed off. A sure Sleepy! And it seemed to Lamar there was something a bit vacant about the stare of the kid with the amputated fingers. A probable Dopey. The original wise-guy kid, the officious creep who'd mouthed off in the restaurant and with whom he'd had the run-in at the elevator: a distinct and definite Doc. The little girl who looked like she'd gotten herself knocked up? Happy? Which left the blue kid, who'd given him that sullen, halfhearted response and who, more importantly, was the very color of choler. Grumpy to the life!) So *something* to do with death.

Only he must be careful to follow old Plute's cryptic warnings, his tricky, understated guidelines. If not, he could kiss his opportunities good-bye. If not he'd be out on the street without even the mangy old doggy suit to cover him. Remember, then, it was strictly hands off the customers. It was absolutely gentle as she goes.

He glanced from Matthew in the Pluto suit to the Kingdom's sickly new clientele, then moved smoothly into his audition in his soaring countertenor.

"You guys are something else," said Mickey Mouse. " 'The Fated Follies.' I love it!" He pointed to Tony Word. "How long they give you to live?"

Tony shrugged.

"Hey," said Benny Maxine.

"An hour? A day?" Mickey insisted.

Tony shrugged.

"Hey!"

"Because if it's less than a day you can forget about Rome. Know why?"

"Hey," Benny said, *"you!"*

Tony Word shrugged.

"Because Rome wasn't built in a day!" roared the Mouse.

"Is he crazy? Why's he saying these things?"

"Why's he bullying sick children?"

"The Mouse is a rat."

"All right," Mickey Mouse said, "let's see a show of hands. Who wants to be cremated? What, nobody? All right, who's for being planted? Hands? Not anyone? Buried at sea then? Recycled? We're running out of options here. Boy, you're some tough kids to please."

Pluto seemed to have slipped away. Mickey hadn't heard him leave. Perhaps he was listening in the bathroom.

"Alone at last," said the Mouse. "Let's see, where were we? Right, we were discussing what's to become of you. Or *I* was. You all seem a little shy about the subject. Oh, I know why, of course. This particular mouse wasn't born yesterday. He's been around the block a time or two. I'll tell you the truth, though. I was never really into tragedy. Control was always my thing, my gift. My special talent, you might say. Well, I never had any enemies to speak of. Popeye has enemies; Road Runner, Bugs Bunny, Tom and Jerry, Tweetie-Pie. Heckel and Jeckel have enemies. The Pink Panther. But not old Mickey the Mouse. I *never* had enemies. And neither do the people I hang with. My duckies and doggies. Life's too short. Hey, no offense." He looked around at the unsmiling children. "All right, all right," he said, "enough about me. What would you have wanted to be if you'd lived?" Doc, Dopey, Sleepy, Grumpy, Bashful, Happy, and Sneezy stared at him, their ancient humors clogged, choked, stymied as ice, their deflected phlegms and cholers, their thickened bloods and biles subsumed in stupefied wonder. "Tch tch tch," said the Mouse. "you kids, you poor kids. I don't think I ever saw such losers. Where'd you grow up—— on Fuck Street?"

Pluto tittered in the toilet. "On Fuck Street. Fuck Street! That's some mouse!"

"This is terrific for the nervous system," Lydia Conscience said.

"Oh?" said Janet.

"It makes it nervous."

"Because really," Mickey Mouse said, "I mean, it's a raw deal. What, are you kidding? I mean, *all* the King's horses, *all* the King's men?" He stared directly at Benny. "Those are some odds. Still," he said, "I suppose there's advantages, silver linings in the shit. Sure. Of course. Why not? Run amok. Break a law. Pillage and plunder. Smoke if you got 'em. I mean, what's to worry? Today *is* the first day of the rest of your life! You may never see Fuck Street again."

"They may never see Fuck Street again," echoed Pluto, laughing.

"You know, it's strange," the Mouse said philosophically. "It is. It really is. What goes on, I mean. I mean, people really *do* die. Your age. I mean there you are, you're going along taking pretty good care of yourself. You look both ways before crossing, you don't accept rides from strangers, you brush after each meal, then whammo! Whammo and blammo! Whammo and blammo and pow and zap! Kerboom and kerflooey, I mean. Mayday, I mean! But who's going to hear you? And what good would it do if they could? No one can help. All right, maybe they take up a collection, maybe you get to be guests of honor at the watering place of your choice. Lourdes, the Magic Kingdom.

"But what's strange, what's really strange, is that after the melodrama, after all the best efforts and good offices of the go-betweens, the mediators, the maids of honor, the honest brokers, and best men, after the prayers and after the sacrifices, after the candles and after the offerings, worse comes to worse anyway. The unthinkable happens, the out-of-the-question occurs, all the unabashed, unvarnished unwarranted, all the unjustifiable unhappy, all the unwieldy unbearable. The unbelievable, the uncivil, the uncharitable, the uncalled-for. The undivided, undignified uncouth. The unkempt, unkind unendurable. The uncontrollably uncomfortable. All that unethical, unbridled, unconditional undoing. All the ungodly unhinged, all the unfriendly unnatural. The unpleasant, the unimaginable, the unprincipled. The unfit, the unsavory, the unforeseen. The unsurpassed, unsightly unruly. The untimely unsuitable, the unwelcome unutterable. The undertaker, I mean."

"Untrue," Mudd-Gaddis objected. (Because everything has a reasonable explanation, and Charles felt so old, time like some plummeting second-per-second weight in free fall, time like the incremental, famous dragged-out absences of love, the seconds minutes, the minutes hours, the hours days, weeks, that he no longer believed in even the possibility of death.)

"But unusual," said Benny Maxine.

"I have to admit," Mudd-Gaddis said.

Which is when the uprising started, the commotion. (Though it still wasn't too late. All that was needed was someone who could have seen all sides.) Because most of them were filling the room now with their "Heys!" and their outrage. They'd been in Florida almost a week. Bombarded with special effects, with lasers, with 3-D like a geometry of the literal and a rounded stereophonics that sought the projections and deeps of the ear like a sort of liquid, they had seen science and engineering enlisted in passive play, at the service of the lesser wonders and mocking, it sometimes seemed to them, the priorities. By now they were accustomed to the little miracles as, two hours or so into their overseas flight, they had already adjusted to the idea of great speed, to eating in the sky, to pissing in it, to flying itself, and were offended—they needed someone to see round their corners—that the Mouse would betray them, that he had not come with a message of hope for them—they hadn't expected him, after all, hadn't even asked for him—showering dispensation, strewing reprieve. And offended by Pluto. Madder at the mutt, perhaps, than at the Mouse. Who'd failed to stand up for them, who'd slunk off to the bathroom when Mickey's monologue had turned embarrassing. He had—there'd been no opportunity to speak of this; to a certain extent at least they were thinking collectively, were in touch with the protocols and instincts of death—betrayed the dumb goodwill of his lampoon loyalty.

Now Pluto, drawn perhaps by their racket, by their promising clamor, was back. He had shambled into the room and was glancing from one to the other with his fixed and serviceable expression, universal, one-size-fits-all.

"Where've *you* been?" Mickey Mouse asked.

"Been in the washroom," said the Dog.

"Made a mess, have you?" the Mouse said, thinking they were into a different routine now, hoping they were, knowing as he did that he'd bombed with the first one. "Well, have you?"

"Have I what?"

"Made puppy poop."

"Made *puppy* poop? *Me*?"

"What about it, kids? Think the ka-ka maker here has done doo-doo?"

"Why not?" Lydia Conscience asked levelly. "England expects every man to do his doo-doo."

"Ohh," groaned Rena Morgan.

"Pretty good," Mickey acknowledged. First Sneezy, the speedy little magicianess sprawled out on the bed, then the original wise-guy kid, then Sleepy, then Happy Belly making with the puns. They're ringers, he thought. They ain't even sick. They're just these healthy all-pro ringers. Them little dwarfs is show-biz giants. I'm a goner, I'm done for. The Fated Follies. I love it. Yeah yeah yeah.

The heart gone out of him now. Not in the mood any longer to take up the challenge. Unresponsive, depleted. (Or not *even* someone who could look through walls, see all sides. Maybe just someone who could see straight. Maybe just anyone who wasn't depleted, who still had some of his wits about him. Though in the long run it probably wouldn't have mattered. Or even in the short one. Just enough run for all of them to get out with their honor intact, cover their ass, make it home free, not have to apologize for anything, not go buy trouble.) Figuring he'd lost out, blown this gig too, his big break, his chance of a lifetime, his opportunity to play what he now understood would probably have been a series of command performances, limited engagements to kids who were themselves limitedly engaged, showing his stuff, special death material—and didn't he have to hand it to the market research boys, though? they didn't miss a trick—as if the dying-children trade were only another sort of convention, another sort of industrial show, using his falsetto still, but as protective coloration pure and simple, as once, he remembered, he'd refused to come out of its rear end when he and a partner had played a rag horse in a class play. Some career, thought the depleted actor. Horses, dogs, mice.

Because the commotion, the uproar, was not only still going on but gathering momentum.

Noah Cloth, hurt and frightened by the Mouse's dark prophesies, had begun to cry. "Unbearable," he sobbed. "Unkind. Uncomfortable. Unendurable. Unpleasant. How true, how true."

"Get Cloth's buddy," Lydia Conscience said. "Who's his buddy? The kid's throwing a tantrum. Get his buddy over here. Janet?"

"I've nothing to do with it. I'm Tony's buddy," Janet Order said.

"Well, *I'm* not his buddy. I'm Benny's buddy," Lydia said.

"I'm telling," Tony Word said darkly.

"Well, who *is* his damn buddy? He's falling apart. He'll wake the whole hotel."

"Maybe Mudd-Gaddis."

"Mudd-Gaddis wasn't *assigned* a buddy. You think they'd assign Mudd-Gaddis a buddy? My God, he practically doesn't even come with a shadow practically."

"I'm telling."

"Maybe Tony's his buddy," Benny suggested.

"How can Tony be his buddy?" Janet asked. "What's wrong with you, don't you listen? I already said Tony's *my* buddy."

"Who are you, saying, 'What's wrong with you?' *Who?* Just who in *hell* are you, saying, 'Don't you listen?'"

"Big man!"

"I never had any complaints."

"Big man!"

"I am, I'm telling."

Noah was howling now.

"You *bet*, big man!"

Practically screaming.

"What, *what* are you telling?" Lydia shouted.

"That's what's wrong with our system," Mudd-Gaddis observed to Pluto. "We can't always remember who our buddies are when we need them."

"Does this have something to do with my religion?"

"What does your religion have to do with anything, Christ-killer?"

"This is what you think they want," Mickey said, appealing to the Dog, "din and squabble?"

"Rena Morgan!" Mudd-Gaddis said suddenly.

"Rena Morgan what?"

"Rena Morgan is Noah's buddy."

Lydia Conscience was all over Noah Cloth like a mother hen. Janet joined her, cajoling, consoling, the two girls' attentions vaguely suggestive.

"I'm telling that no one can help," Tony Word said, and burst into tears.

"Well, yeah, I see it," the Mouse said. "Really. I do. It has this certain—how shall one put it?—this certain . . . oh, Grand Guignol charm."

They led Noah to the bed and laid him down gently.

"There you go," Lydia said. "That's right. Right beside Rena. He's a little upset, Reenie," she said. "See if you can quiet him down. Are you going to be all right, Noah? Are you going to stop getting on everyone's N-E-R-V-E-S?"

"As a concept it's brilliant," Mickey Mouse said. "Right up there with, oh, say, signing Shakespeare for the deaf."

"You mustn't mind what Janet says," Lydia Conscience whispered to her buddy, Benny. "She's a bitch and a ballbreaker." And turned to the blue girl. "In case you haven't noticed," she said, "Tony's acting up."

"Take care of it yourself," she said. "Can't you see I've my hands full?"

Mickey Mouse could. On the bed Sneezy was flailing about, her windmill hands going like crazy, missing the probable Dopey lying next to her, who'd covered his ears but didn't seem inclined to roll out of her way. Together they managed to give the impression of a helpless, ignorant piglet and a vicious sow inside a farrowing house. Blue Grumpy had all she could do to try to guide the dangerous Sneezer's flying hands back down to her sides.

It's part of the show, was the Mouse's professional opinion. He looked over at the talent scout in his Pluto suit to gauge his reaction. The Dog seemed worried behind his one-size-fits-all permanent stare. Clearly such niceties were either over his head or he was building the tip with his phony rim-shot concern. Probably the former and, if anyone cared to ask *him*, it would be over the heads, too, of most of her potential audiences. If they noticed anything going on at all, chances were it would just be a jumble of meaningless tics to them. Would they understand, or even see, for that matter, that she was shifting rolled handkerchiefs from one place on her person to another? If they did, would they notice that she sacrificed the advantage of leverage and not only worked them close up but lying down? Would they appreciate the Grumpess's subtle contribution or at all take in that by laying hands on her, or attempting to, the result was the equivalent of working blindfold without a net, defying all ringmaster convention and actually *inviting* impedance rather than appealing for silence before a particularly difficult turn? Dulled, dying kids? It had to be lost on them. God, she was good. He had to admit it, suddenly as generous as one stand-up comic scrutinizing the performance of another. If it was lost it was lost. The children in her audiences had about twelve minutes to live. They *deserved* the best.

Then he saw that something had changed. She'd run out

of props, the long furl of handkerchiefs she'd managed to conceal—so that what she did passed beyond the realm of entertainment and entered art—hiding this one here, that one there, all the while making discreet, even delicate, passes at her nose—*because she actually used them,* the Mouse saw—had all been filled and returned to their hiding places, all the while continuing to maintain by misdirection and the feints of her grand and flighty fidget the complicated illusion that nothing was there. (Which by now, of course, nothing was.) What she did took the trained actor's breath away, and he looked again in the direction of the faggot Dog. Who seemed, talent scout or no, more than a little bored. Mickey Mouse shook his head in disgust at even this appearance of indifference and turned back to the girl on the bed. Who had gone into her labored breathing, the hacksaw rasps of her sawn and strangled weather. It was, essentially, the same big, terrifying finish she'd used on him in the elevator.

Her arms dropped to her sides and she flailed across the entire width of the bed, using all her body now, her torso, her arms, and her legs, digging into the bedspread with her face, trying to bite it away from the sheets with her teeth, very nearly smothering Noah before Lydia and one or two of the others thought to pull him away.

I'm wrong, thought the Mouse, it's an even bigger finish, and burst into applause. "Bravo, bravo!" Mickey Mouse cried. "Most bravissimo bravo!"

She'd worked the bedspread free. Great dollops of black congestion dropped from her nose, from her mouth.

"Ring our rooms!" Benny Maxine shouted. "Get Colin, get Moorhead!"

"What, actually go *near* her, you mean? Isn't that the buddy's job?" said Janet Order.

"The buddy's indisposed," Benny said. "Shit," he said, and picked the phone up, just inches from Rena's head, himself.

There was no answer in 627. He dialed the other rooms.

"Why haven't they called? I thought they were going to call." (But everything has a reasonable explanation.

(It hadn't occurred to the adults that the kids would be in

the hidey-hole. They'd looked for them throughout the hotel, in the shops, in the game room and restaurants. High and low. Recalling their splendid afternoon on Shipwreck Marsh, Mary and Colin believed they might have gone there. The marina closed in the late afternoon, but the more they thought about it, the more Colin and Mary were convinced that they'd taken a boat out, perhaps even stolen one. The marina man (who lived in Orlando and had to be called at home and told to drive the twenty or so miles back to the park) said that while he didn't think any boats were missing he couldn't be sure because at any given time there were always a few in the shop for maintenance. He'd a record of these in his notebook, of course, but hadn't thought to bring it with him when he'd driven in. He was sorry. Rather than return to Orlando and lose precious time, he took a Water Sprite and suggested Colin follow in a big slow canopy boat, the only craft large enough to carry them all back together should they be found. They looked for them on Shipwreck Marsh and, failing to find them there, went on to Discovery Island.

(Meanwhile, Eddy Bale and Nedra Carp went with the search party—Security had been called in—through the half-dozen lands of the Magic Kingdom, and Moorhead and Mary, attaching themselves to some of the park's policemen, trailed along with them through Epcot Center. Security, taking the disappearance seriously, alerted the transportation system: the buses and riverboats and monorails.

(So they never thought of the room. Because everything, everything, has a reasonable explanation and none of the adults ever understood why seven kids would want to coop themselves up in a stuffy hotel room.)

"You think we should go down?"

"I don't know. Ought we to move her?"

"Maybe one or two of us could go down and wait in the room in case they return."

"Take the kids then," Lydia Conscience said.

"Not you, Benny," Rena pleaded through her choking. "Please not you."

"Maybe we all ought to stay put."

"Get Tony out of here, at least."

Now that Noah had calmed a bit, relieved to be out of harm's way perhaps, Tony had taken up his friend's war cries. He bellowed like one at the stake.

"Tony, darling," Janet said, "I'm *your* buddy and you're *my* buddy. We're each *other's* buddies and have got to make sure that nothing happens to either of us. Clearly it isn't a one-for-all, all-for-one situation we have here. You wouldn't want something to happen to me, would you? I know you wouldn't. Yet all your screaming is giving me the heebie-jeebies. Do you know what the heebie-jeebies are, Tony darling?"

"The Hebrew jeebies?" he pouted.

"That's right, sweetheart," she said, ignoring Maxine's glare. "The Hebrew jeebies are these dangerous palpitations, this shortness of breath and angina. They're my symptoms. You don't want your buddy to die on you, do you, Tony?"

"No."

"Then please shut up," Janet Order said.

Rena reached out for Benny Maxine's hand.

"I beg your pardon," Pluto said timidly. "Just who is it you were expecting to call?"

There was so much talent in the world, Mickey Mouse thought. Even Matthew. His friend's panic couldn't entirely have been an attribute of the cunning mask. He had to admit: The Dog got a lot more out of the Pluto suit than he ever did. Gee, he thought sadly, remembering other auditions he'd blown up and down central Florida, maybe I'm not nearly the theatrical champ I'm cracked up to be.

"Benny?"

"Righty-o," Maxine said, "hit's our Benjamin 'ere."

"Please, Benny," she said, her voice crackling in her heavy phlegm like a sort of static, "could you give me your hand?"

Inside his mask, Mickey Mouse began to cry.

"Me *'and*? Give you me *'and*? Why, wot an idear! I don' fink *dat's* a bolt from da blue."

Because many of them were seeing straight now. And had

begun to drift toward the door. Lydia Conscience pushed Mudd-Gaddis's wheelchair. Pluto tugged at Mickey Mouse's arm and whispered something in his big ear the foolish but ultimately not unkindly Mouse couldn't quite make out, though he believed he caught the Dog's gist—which he hadn't at all—and, nodding, reluctantly joined him in the exodus, all the while looking back over his shoulder, rubbing his big white gloves against what he'd forgotten were only one-way black glass buttons and not eyes, and thinking, the not-so-standoffish softy Lydia Conscience had been told about in her dream, that perhaps it made better art not to be in on the very end of their performance, that perhaps there were some things best left unstated in theater, following, nodding, glancing back over his shoulders and rubbing his eyes, perhaps the only one to get out of there with his honor intact.

Because despite the fact that the children were dying themselves, they had gone and bought trouble anyway. Getting home free had been denied them, not having to apologize had. All they could hope for now was to cover their ass.

"Hey," Benny called, "where *you* off to then? Lydia? Charley? Hey, Noah," he called.

"Let them," Rena said. "Benny?"

"Yeah," he said, "sure," watching them leave.

The buddy system had broken down completely. Noah had thrown his arm about Tony Word's shoulder. Janet Order fell into step between Pluto and Mickey and dared them to speak once they'd left the confines of the room and were in the hall again. Pluto kept his own counsel, but Mickey Mouse, grown into his part, said he thought all of them had done a wonderful job.

"Do you think you could hold me?" Rena asked.

"Hold you?"

"I shouldn't ask. I know I'm a mess."

"Listen," he said, "are you going to be all right?"

"After that night," she said, breathing brokenly, "we explored the hotel, when we had all that fun . . ."

"What?" Benny said. He could hardly hear her. "What?"

"Oh," said the fastidious girl, "look at this bed. What I've done to the sheets." Some of her handkerchiefs, wadded, stained, had shaken loose from the sleeves of her dress, from her collar and waistband, from the hem of her skirt. They lay about her like ruined flowers, exploded ordnance. "Please," she said, "hold me. Just till they find us."

He held her, and it hurt where even her frail weight pressed against his chest, his belly, his heart. He held her, and she told him she'd never taken her eyes off him that day they'd all undressed on the island. He held her, and she told him she loved him.

"Oh, Benny, the good die young," Rena Morgan said, and died.

He was with her when Mary Cottle and the others found them.

"She said she loved me," Benny told them when they walked in.

"Oh," Mr. Moorhead said. "Oh, God. Oh," he said, as if suddenly it was all quite clear to him.

Which it was.

Because everything has a reasonable explanation. The physician had determined to bring no one along who he was not certain could survive the trip. It was her respiration, her terrible heavy breathing that had caused her spasms and loosed the poisons in her chest, the mucus and biles, the clots of congestion hanging together and preserving her life by the strings of the ordinary. The great prognostician had simply failed to factor her desire into the equation. He had missed his prognosis because he hadn't taken her sighs into account, the squalls, blasts, and aerodynamics of passion, all the high winds and gale-force bluster of love.

Bale wasn't the sort who necessarily saved the best for last, who felt, that is, he must earn his rewards. As a kid he hadn't dutifully done his vegetables in order to get to the meat, or eaten all his meat up in order to tuck away dessert. He wasn't anal enough for rigmarole and would occasionally, though he was never particularly fond of greens, use the spoon he'd just dipped into his trifle to take up his salad. "Eating around" was his term for the habit. Though this wasn't a habit either. He had no habits and noticed that Liam had inherited the tendency. (It delighted him, even when his boy was in hospital, to watch the child—the hospital trays with the meal's portions isolated and set in the tray's hollows and pockets like paints spread out on a palette made this easy to keep track of—and know that this piece of business came from him, from Eddy, or at least from his, the Bales', side of the family.) It wasn't exactly a blockbuster heritage and he made no great claims for it, but it was amusing nevertheless to be able to identify and claim—though he didn't do this either—the trait as strictly his own contribution. Because Ginny, he'd noticed, ate in accordance with secret and, within terms of the discipline, totally arbitrary principles of her own, or at least of her side of the family. He'd made no study, of course—he *wasn't* compulsive—but had observed that, though it was unknown to him and perhaps even to her, she had a sort of game plan, changed as often as good code. Sometimes it was as elementary as eating everything on her plate from left to right. Sometimes he didn't realize until days afterward—he *wasn't* compulsive, he wasn't compulsive and he wasn't anal; he had a good head for menus is all—that she had eaten her food alphabetically, or along the points of the compass.

So why had he waited almost a year to open that letter she'd left for him the day she'd gone off in the taxi, the letter he had assumed, assumed now, assumed at the time, would explain everything? Because he already knew why she'd left. Indeed, if Ginny hadn't left him it could only have been a matter of time till he'd left Ginny. Liam had been a remarkable child. In health remarkable: bright, good, cheerful, pleasant, thoughtful, generous, obliging, and kind. And in sickness remarkable too: all he'd been in health plus a saint of suffering. In sickness and in health. A self-contained marriage of true mind. (He might have taken vows, though he was better than that, better than vows.) To have remained together after Liam died would have been a constant reminder that they were not as good as Liam, that they'd been brought low. If time was to do its job and heal all things, then first the wound had to be taken off, covered over, removed. Liam must die and the Bales must separate.

So he knew why Ginny had left and why, it could even be, she'd taken up with Tony the Tobacconist. At the time he hadn't known that she had. Otherwise he'd probably have ripped open the letter at once, skipping over all the stuff that was sure to be there (". . . and the short of it, Eddy, is that Liam was simply too good. We should never have been able to recover from his loss. Even if we never mentioned his name again, darling, we should be reminded every time we called·each other's. We're both young and don't deserve to live in the shadow of his loss another thirty . . .") to get to the juicy parts.

So why? Who'd deliberately left his son's scrapbook at home, photos from the papers of the ill head-bandaged boy, and which, according to the very letter of his own topsy-turvy laws of reasoning, eschewing the good memories, preserving the bad, he could easily have afforded to bring along with him, but who'd left it instead unlooked-for in Putney, or for Ginny to take with her, her dead dowry, to her tobacconist, and who carried on his person only the black, dissolving shards of the memorial brassard, little more now than a kind of officially sanctioned death dust? So why? Why the letter? Who by inclination, and all the sugarotropism of those familial, historic, biologic, Balean, sweet-seeking genes, took dessert with his soup, appetizer with his coffee?

Because while he wasn't the sort who necessarily saved the best for last, wasn't dutiful about his veggies or anal enough for rigmarole, he had, in fact, a sense of the last, a knowledge and feel, that is, real as his pride in his own continuity in good Liam's eating patterns, for the conclusionary ripeness—an instinct, that is, for when worse came to worst.

So maybe he *was* anal, or at least retentive, squirreling away the best if not for last then for when it was most needed.

Though he thought he pretty much knew what would be in it. (They weren't *enemies*, after all, they loved each other, had been married almost fourteen years.) There'd be solace in it. Solace most needed.

And what else was there to do while Rena Morgan was being prepped in the Orlando funeral parlor?

They'd taken their terrified charges to the chapel off I-4 which Nedra Carp had discovered on their first morning in Florida. The nanny had organized a hasty, last-minute service for the little group of mourners, and it struck Bale that what

Nedra had told him—could it have only been a week ago?—about the chapel was probably true. It had the altar and pews, the stained glass and track lighting, and even a dried-out font sort of thing, vaguely baptismal, vaguely birdbath, but there was a real question in his mind about whether the place had ever been consecrated. Notices were everywhere in the pew racks that "a priest came on Sunday." What that left to be made of the young man in charge on the day of Rena's memorial service was also a question. Clearly, however, the child's death was probably the most important religious event in the history of the chapel. The pastor, if that's what he was—he wore a sort of gray modified cassock—seemed more affected than any of them. He could hardly get through a psalm without crying, and his brief eulogy stressed over and over again the pity of the little girl's having come all the way from England to Florida to die. He couldn't seem to get past the sheer mileage of the thing.

There were official representatives from the Magic Kingdom in attendance. Also, Matthew Gale and Lamar Kenny had shown up. They sat quietly in one of the rear pews. Benny recognized Kenny from their encounter at the elevator and pointed him out to Eddy. Mary Cottle recognized Gale as the young man who'd winked at Colin Bible at the Haunted Mansion and said nothing. Though by now, of course, the adults had pretty much pieced together a general idea of what had gone on that night. The Disney people were on to the false Pluto and had fired him. They'd fired Kenny, too, on suspicion of being the false Mickey Mouse, but Lamar, fearing he'd never work again and still believing he'd been duped into his phony audition, would admit nothing. Nor would Matthew Gale tell them otherwise.

"I got you into this," Gale told him.

"You bet," Lamar said.

"I won't let you down."

"He won't let me down," Lamar said. "Big deal. Top Disney dicks crawling all over the place watching us, and he won't let me down. Loyalty! Follows me everywhere as if he really *was* Pluto!"

Back at the hotel, Nedra had taken the children to the game room.

Colin, off to see what could be done about changing their tickets, called to say that they didn't have to be changed, that Rena would be ready in time for their flight the following day.

"What are they doing to her, do you think?" Eddy asked Moorhead.

They were sitting in the Coconino Cove, a bar just outside the Pueblo Room.

"They're embalming her. It's not generally done in Europe, but it seems to be mandatory in this country."

"Embalming her," Bale said. "What is that actually?"

"Well," Mr. Moorhead said, "it's pretty much what you'd think. They treat the corpse to prevent decay and putrefaction."

"Putrefaction," Bale said. "She was barely thirteen years old, for God's sake."

"She was old enough to fall in love," Moorhead said. He finished his gin and ordered another. "It's what killed her."

"Yeah, you said."

"It was the unforeseen complication."

"How do they do that?"

"Do what?"

"Prevent decay, prevent putrefaction."

"With preservatives."

"What, like in the rashers and bangers, you mean?"

"The Egyptians soaked their dead in brine and filled the body cavities with spices and aromatic substances."

"That's nice," Bale said. "A little attar of roses, a splash of Nuits de Paris."

"Then they drain the blood from her veins with a hollow needle called a trocar, which they use in conjunction with a tube called a cannula."

"Secrets of the ancients revealed," Bale said.

"To prevent the body from shriveling and turning brown—"

"Like an apple," Bale said.

"—they pump formaldehyde into the cavities in combination with alcohol."

Eddy set his drink down.

"They apply cosmetics. They apply masking pastes."

"Hey," Bale said, "I just remembered, there's something I have to do back in the room," and left the bar, returned to the room, and took Ginny's letter out of his suitcase.

I was his mother, Eddy [Bale read], I was his mum. I'm the one carried him those nine months, who lost her figure and still wear stretch marks like chevrons—my corporal, as it were, punishment, as it were.

Have the decency. Spare me your shock and outrage. Keep to yourself your reservations about my taste and sensibilities. Four years like these down one's craw and anyone's taste would have soured, SHOULD have soured, if, that is, any sensibility is still there to function at all. I don't need any crap just now.

It ain't all been dainties and plum puddings, has it, Eddy, our crusade? Passing the hat, doing our buskers' shuffle up and down the kingdom's avenues? For press and for public passing the hat, passing the hankie, touching it to the collective eye, the collective nose. God, Eddy, how we Hyde Park–cornered them with our despair, with our need and our noise. Our cause! Cause and affect! Anyway, our hats in our hands, our hearts on our sleeves, and our knees on the ground. Beggars! *Beggars, Ed!* Always for Liam, of course, never ourselves, of *if* for ourselves, then for the abstract motherhood and fatherhood in us, or if for Liam, then for some soiled and abstract childhood in him, some sentimental fiction of good order, natural birthright, the ought-to-be.

"Well of course," you'll be saying, "Well of course, you silly git, of *course* we'd a right to expect better than we got, of *course* Liam did. Of *course* it's good order, birthright, and proper dispensation for kids to grow up! Nothing sentimental there. No fiction about it. Childhood diseases are one thing—mumps and measles, chicken pox, croup. Maybe a broken bone or a tooth to be pulled. Rashes in summer from lessons botched in leaf identification. The coughs and sniffles and low-grade fevers. All the rocking-chair temps. The mustard plaster and the asafetida. Oils of clove and the hanging garlics. All the cuddle comforts—Epsom salts, vaporizers, and the Vicks reliefs. Your only *scaled* suffering, what the traffic can bear.

"But car crash and brain damage," you'll be saying, "paralysis? Your tumors and cancers and drowning accidents in surf?"

Don't get me wrong, Eddy. I think so too. I was his mother, I was his mum. And lived nine months longer than ever you did with superstition and fear, the 4 a.m. credulities, all the toxic heterodoxies of lying-in, all pregnancy's benighted, illiterate dread. Guilty for fried foods I'd eaten years before, the shadow of sugar incriminating me, of butter and egg yolk and marble in meat, all that candy, all those fish 'n' chips.

Even signs of life startling. "My God," I thought when he kicked, "he's got only one leg!" And "Christ!"—when I puked—"I'm upchucking bits and pieces of my kid!"

Doing bargains with God, you see: "If he's missing a finger, take it from his left hand, Lord," "Make him deaf rather than blind, blind rather than simple." "If he has to be ugly, don't give him bad teeth."

Jesus, the stuff I thought! "I'd rather he be homosexual than nearsighted." "If he's fat I hope he's tall." "I prefer he be bad at games than not have a sense of humor; I'd rather he didn't get the point of jokes than be stingy." "It would be better if he were a poor Tory than a wealthy Red."

That's not the half of it, of course. The half of it was another bargain, the half of it was this: "Let him have one leg, Lord. Take the fingers from his right hand and make him this deaf, blind, simple, rich, fat, Red. Rot his teeth, God, and let him be short, this clumsy, mean and ugly, humorless, nearsighted fag. Just let him be born alive!"

Not just let him live, Eddy. Let him be born alive. Because if he was born alive I took it for granted he'd live. It never occurred to me it could be otherwise. What did I know about vicissitude who could strike such bargains? Who assumed you paid the price of admission up front and were never bothered again; who suspected, perhaps even expected that at the outside there might even be trouble, hard times, say, but to whom it just never occurred that she'd still be alive herself and have to witness out-and-out tragedy?

But he was perfect, our Liam. From the beginning one of those rare, good-looking babies, alert and cheerful, sturdy, well. So even-tempered that if you didn't know better you might believe him actually thoughtful, actually circumspect. And wasn't his *gaze* clear? And wasn't his *grip* strong? As if he was trying to chin on the world with those perfect, tiny hands? Pull himself up, have a look round?

I was his mother, Eddy. I was his mum. And counted his limbs and totaled his toes, his fingers and features, doing the sums of my baby son like some holy arithmetic, as if I were a religious telling her beads, say, or as if I were counting my blessings.

But nervous . . . no, stunned, in the presence of such glory. The postpartum depression you hear about—I was his mother, I was his mum—is only a sort of stress, only a kind of strain, just the ordinary and decent apprehension of responsibility. His soft spot, for example, his fontanel, that dangerously malleable skullcap of infant membrane which I couldn't help but think of as a kind of quicksand, some treacherous maelstrom of the vulnerable it half scared me to death to clean, to go near with water, a washcloth and soap.

Or any crankiness that couldn't be accounted for within the limited infant parameters of shit or hunger or sleep, the explosive, inexplicable tantrum cholerics of incommunicado grief like a sort of willful madness, which was . . . well, maddening, mysterious to me because it seemed so arbitrary and implacable, like . . . oh, a cow howling, or the panic neighing of a horse, or any other inarticulate anguish of the beasts. "What? What is it, Liam?" I'd lean over his crib and ask. "What, child, *what?*" Or pick him up, rock him, spoil him, try to bribe his anger with my comfort, my still swollen maternals, the boneless, angleless fillets of my soft shoulders, my tender breasts, my featherbed lap, my mother-meat. Crooning, cooing, ah-ah-ahhing a promised protection I had no more faith in than he did, the distraught, crazed, wailing Liam.

Because that's what I thought, Eddy, that he'd actually gone mad, as out of control as a demon. Dry, rested, fed (spitting my tit out like an orthodox offered interdicted fruit) and outraged. No longer even bothering to reason with him through reason (my new mum's version of it anyway—love, a hug, a kiss, a squeeze), but cutting through all that and going directly to the recognized, time-honored lingua franca of all infants everywhere: that universal, gold-standard, pound-sterling, cosmic greenback, the comprehensive baby currency of distracting bauble. Shaking keys at him, offering my change purse, setting a ticking watch at his ear (which he wouldn't have heard anyway above that racket he made), giving him a shiny spoon to look at, a rattle to bang, textures to feel: crumpled paper, a penny, a string of beads, an orange peel, grapes, bread, the flesh of an apple. Concerned, Eddy—well, I was his mother, I was his mum—that there might be something intractable and unyielding and malicious at the core.

Which there was, wasn't there, Ed, only not what we expected, or anyway expected back in those days when we were both new to the game and didn't know the score.

Because you learn. Sooner or later you do. I did. Because standing over their cribs to see if they're still breathing doesn't keep them alive. Hard work does.

Though I'll spare you this part lest you take it into your head I'm complaining, which I'm not. Because things even out, they really do, and there's a certain clean democracy about everything. I'm thinking of those nine months of ungovernable dread, the seven I knew I was pregnant plus the two retroactive ones when I feared I might have done Baby some thoughtless injury just because I didn't know he existed yet. Because if those nine months were unbearable to me, and if it's true that you can never really share them, never really catch up, I ought to tell you that you can't share or catch up either with the times of greatest joy, those seven or eight or nine months when I knew he was out of the woods, or I was, that I was past my postpartum funk, that his soft spot wasn't going to sink in on itself and the crankiness was no cry of madness or doom but only some inexplicable inner teething, say, maybe just ordinary run-of-the-mill boredom, and we lay, infant Liam and I, gurgle to gurgle and coo to coo and skin to skin.

I was his mother, Eddy, I was his mum. I saw him raise his head, turn over, crawl, pull himself up, stand without holding on, take a step, walk. I heard him say "biscuit," I heard him say "mum." I pushed him in his pram. I was with him on the pleasure-ground, on the commons, on the heath. I took him to the Bingo, I took him to the high street. I took him to the kiosk, I took him to the caff. Oh, Eddy, we went everywhere, everywhere, Liam and his mum. We went to the tinsmith, to the coster and chandler. We rode in estate cars that the salesman would drive. I showed him the fishmonger, the chapman and publican, the chemist and cutler, the cooper and smith. We browsed at the stationer's. Estate agents opened houses for us. We had the builders in. And took the air at the poulterer's. Haberdashers and milliners set out their wares for our inspection. Everyone did, showing their goods, pitching their hope at us in the lively open market that's the world.

All for Liam's baby benefit, Ed, to train his urge and craving to their cheer. So that we went everywhere and did it all not just with whomsoever but with whatsoever the greengrocer and tradesmen equivalencies are for arcade and for bourse. Ever so much better than playing House it was, our sprightly little game of playing Planet, playing Life.

He wasn't a baby now. He was a little boy. And had seen enough, I think, of what was only merchandise.

For perhaps a month we'd been going to the parks, Liam rough and tumble with the kids, for when they showed him a toy, at least at first, I think he thought they meant to sell it to him, for him to buy it from them, and so he'd act standoffish, reluctant, disinclined, and ask with almost inattention, nonchalance, just what they thought they wanted for that thing, shaking his head whatever they told him, whatever they said, as I hadn't even known I'd been teaching him to. "Too dear, too dear," he'd say, driving his hard bargains like nails in the very air.

"No, darling, no sweetheart," I had to explain, "they only want to play with you."

I was his mother, Ed, ever so much longer than you were his dad. No, wait, I was. Because everything has a reasonable explanation, Eddy. No, wait, it does. It has to. Those dreadful nine months he was in my belly like rotten cheese, say, or something you eat that gives you bad dreams. And the four or five months it took his soft spot to heal, the two or three I couldn't get used to his crankiness, couldn't get used to him—because motherhood's not natural, Eddy, it's *not*, whatever they say; how could anything that dangerous, difficult, and strange be natural? How can spending all that time with something, all right, some*one*, but someone who doesn't speak your language yet and who doesn't have enough of his own to tell you his name or say his address, be natural? And how can it be natural to be at the constant beck and call of anything, all right, any*one*, anyone who lives within those barbarous parameters of shit and hunger and sleep and all the rest of the time, *all* the rest of the time, on bliss and on grief like a dancer up on point? *Natural?* How can it even be *good* for you? And then our years on the town; then—well, everything, the time I put in on call even when he napped.

You were at business. I had possession, enjoyment,

holding in fee simple and fee tail, in freehold and seisin, in dubious privilege and precedence, my mum's natural seniority, my tenure: all motherhood's time-serviced squatter's rights.

Jesus, Eddy, he'd have had to live another dozen years for you to catch up with me.

Which he couldn't, didn't. It being hard enough for him to make it through that first dozen. Which he barely could, barely did.

Though you certainly *tried* to catch up, I'll give you that. Seizing, it turned out, on his illness. Making his disease your cause. Like an entertainer on the telethon, almost, so frenzied you were. La! La, luv, it couldn't have been easy for you—my frame of reference isn't even his sickness, you know; it's that pregnancy, those seven lean months when I got so fat, my wary wait-and-see ways afterward—I know. It couldn't have been easy. Or shouldn't, shouldn't have been. Taking poor Liam's case, your case, over all their heads.

Over the heads of the doctors, of the interns and specialists, over the heads of the experts and scientists and the National Health, over the heads of the odds-makers, over the heads of the nobs and the honorables, of the chairmen of boards, of the media, of the movers and shakers, over the heads of the very public that pitched in with its pounds and its pennies to stretch out his life, at last taking it over the head of God and—what I can't forget and will never forgive—over the head finally of Liam himself. Who wanted to die.

Then, before he could, you had your idea about all those other poor kids and had already begun your inquiries, and I knew I'd have to leave you once Liam was gone. I can't live like this, darling. I can't live like this, Ed.

So. Well. That's about it.

Anyway, I shall have to stop now. I've called the taxi and expect it will be here quite soon. Although it's funny. To tell you the truth, I haven't the foggiest what I'm going to tell the driver. I've known for years, since Liam was first diagnosed, that we couldn't live together once he was dead. But I don't know where to go. I'm out of cigarettes. I shall have to get some. I'll ask him to stop at the tobacconist on the Upper Richmond Road.

Oh, and don't you know yet, Eddy, that grown-ups are more interesting than kids?

9

On the strength of all this, Bale left 627 and drifted down to the Fiesta Fun Center, the hotel's big game room, where Nedra Carp had been joined now by Colin Bible and Mr. Moorhead. The physician had left the Coconino Cove and was, or so it seemed to Bale, a bit unsteady on his feet. Colin, his duties as liaison completed between the Dream Holiday People, as they'd come to be known in the local press, the Orlando undertakers, and the travel agency making the arrangements with the two airlines that would be taking them first to Miami and then back to England, was recounting some of his difficulties. He'd had to pick out the coffin, a rather more ornate and expensive box than necessary, but one which could be paid for out of their contingency fund.

The travel agent, he said, couldn't have been more helpful. She'd handled nearly everything and been most sympathetic. "Really," Colin said. "I quite felt sorry for her."

Bale looked about the game room at their half-dozen surviving charges.

It was late in the afternoon. The children still wore the dressy clothes they'd worn to the service in the chapel. Except for Noah's tie, which the child had undone, and the collar he'd unbuttoned and the shirttails that had come out of his pants, and the pants themselves, partially unzipped and hanging from his waist at an askew angle, and the unhealthy, excited flush on his face, the children seemed calm, almost staid.

"Is that one going to be all right?" Eddy asked. "His eyes, his eyes seem too bright to me." Except for himself and the hotel's caricaturist, no one seemed interested.

Colin was still recounting the exploits of the afternoon.

It seems the woman had broken down in tears when she'd had to explain the carriers' policies regarding the shipment of Rena's body. The domestic carrier had agreed to accept Rena's passenger ticket as payment in full for her shipment as freight to Miami. They didn't have to, they said, but it was an unwritten rule and they would. On the other hand, the overseas airline required an additional $2.63 a pound overage. The casket was 220 pounds. Rena was 95 pounds. It would come to $828.45. "But the unwritten rule," Colin objected. Overseas airlines were bound by international agreements, the travel agent had said. There were no unwritten rules.

"He seems awfully excited," Bale said.

"She was still on the phone when I took it from her," Colin told them. " 'What about her baggage allowance?' I demanded of the agent on the other end of the line."

The man told him that the first 62 pounds were free but that they must pay an additional $2.63 for each pound above that.

" 'It never does,' I said. The fellow didn't know what I

was talking about. 'Her luggage,' I said. 'It can't weigh more than thirty or thirty-five pounds at the outside. We'll be wanting a credit on the difference, mate, or we're going to fucking sue you all over the goddamn sky!' He still hadn't a clue what I was on about. 'I told you,' I said. 'The kid's bags weigh maybe thirty-five pounds, the kid ninety-five pounds. You're charging her for a seat, so according to the international agreements she's entitled to her full baggage allowance. She's got twenty-seven pounds coming to her. At two sixty-three a pound that's seventy-one dollars and a penny. From eight twenty-eight forty-five. That's seven fifty-seven forty-four. The name's Bible,' I told him. 'Colin B-I-B-L-E. I'll see you tomorrow at the weigh-in! Oh, and mister,' I says. 'What's that?' he asks me. 'They'll *always* be an England!' I tell him and hang up."

"Now you know how *I* feel," Moorhead said, when Colin had told them all this under his breath.

"What?" Colin Bible asked the physician.

"I said now you know how I feel."

"How's that?"

"The son of a bitch," Moorhead said. " 'Well, at least she'll get a Florida death certificate out of it.' Imagine the son of a bitch saying a thing like that to me. 'At least she'll get a Florida death certificate out of it.' The son of a bitch." He was talking about the doctor who'd signed Rena's death certificate. Moorhead, who wasn't licensed to practice in Florida, hadn't been permitted to sign the document.

Bale was watching Noah, who'd been rarely to shops and who didn't know where he would get money for the big-ticket items, who couldn't read well or do his maths. He was watching Noah, who would not live to make money.

When Rena died, the little boy demanded that Moorhead turn over the rest of the hundred dollars he'd been holding for him. The doctor had heard about the incident in the shops but had given him his eighty dollars without a fuss.

Now all of them were watching Noah, who'd been changing five dollars at a time and taking his quarters to play each game, to play skee ball and air hockey, to play Asteroids and Space Invaders, Pac-Man and Donkey Kong. He did not seem even to be conscious of his scores but cared only about how many games he could play. But it was taking too long. Now he was depositing his money in as many machines as he could, pressing whichever button activated the first ball or the first sorties of invading terror craft, the initial extraterrestrial overflights, but without waiting long enough to use his joy stick before going on to whatever machine happened to be unoccupied. Soon children who were not even part of their group were watching him. Nedra Carp watched with her arm lightly about Janet Order's shoulders. The caricaturist made rapid charcoal sketches on sheet after sheet of paper. Noah turned to the spectators and indicated with a gesture that they come forward and play on his quarters. He put money in the soda machines but didn't bother to retrieve his drinks, in the gum and candy machines but, seeing he'd run out of change, went to get more before returning to the vending machines, and only then after making another deliberate sweep of the room. He pumped quarters into machines that were still activated and invited kids to come up and take the soda and candy and gum, as he'd invited them to play out his time on the arcade games.

"Noah," Nedra Carp called. "Noah? Noah, dear."

"Don't you think we ought to stop him?" Eddy asked Mr. Moorhead.

"No," the doctor said, "I shouldn't think so."

Bale looked at Colin.

"He's on a roll, mate," Colin said softly.

"Now *that* was a shopping spree!" Benny Maxine told the little boy when he was all out of money.

"Wasn't it just?" Noah said, beaming.

"You're de bloke wot broke de bank at Monte Carlo."

"Aren't I just?"

Bale left the arcade and stepped into an elevator. A guest turned to him.

"Floor?"

"Eight, please," Bale said.

He thought he could smell her strange, strong cigarettes in the hallway. "May I come in?" he asked.

Mary Cottle shrugged and stepped aside to let him pass.

He sat down on a chair by the table.

"They cleaned *this* place up."

"They offered me a different room," she said. "I didn't want it."

"No."

"Too many swell memories."

"Yeah."

She sat on the edge of the bed, facing him.

"So?" she said.

He repeated what Colin had told them about the casket, about the $2.63 a pound overage the airline was charging.

"He made them apply twenty-seven pounds of her own body weight toward the cost of the overage? Jesus!"

He told her about Noah and the machines, about the sketches the caricaturist had made.

"The kid hired someone to draw him spending money?"

"No," Eddy said, "Colin commissioned them," and explained Bible's scheme for getting effigies of the children into Madame Tussaud's.

"What I don't know doesn't hurt me," Mary said.

"Sure it does."

She shrugged. "Maybe," she said. "I guess."

"Could I have one of those?"

"You said you thought they were too harsh."

"Not by half."

"No," she said.

"I can't have one?"

"Sure," she said. "I mean, you're right. They're not too harsh. Not by half. Not by two thirds. Five eighths, nine tenths."

He leaned forward to take a light off Mary Cottle's cigarette. "Cheers," he said.

"Cheers," she said. They touched the tips of their cigarettes.

"This time tomorrow," he said.

"We'll be on our way home."

"We'll be standing in a queue. We'll be showing our passports and explaining about Rena and mopping our brows. We'll be extricating our underwear from the cheeks of our ass."

"Look," she said, "is that snow? Is it snowing?" She pointed her cigarette past his head but Bale didn't turn around.

"You're not so tough."

"It's that same freak weather."

"Funny," he said. "I don't feel the least bit purified."

"Me neither," she said. "Not the least bit. Purified."

"Why are you crying?"

"I'm not so tough."

"What's the matter?" he said.

"Oh, Bale," she said, "we lost one."

"It's not as if she had a life expectancy," he comforted.

"My God," she said, "we were gone a week. We lost one."

"I'm making my move," he said, and left his chair and got up to sit beside her on the bed. He stroked her face.

"Do you have anything with you?"

"What, a condom, you mean?"

"Yes."

"No," he said. "What about you? Aren't you on the pill?"

"No," she said.

"An IUD?"

"No," she said.

"A diaphragm? Foam?"

"Nothing," she said.

"Oh," he said, and started to move away.

She pulled him toward her. She undid his shirt, his belt, the button on his trousers. She raised her dress, she lowered her underpants.

"Will it be all right? Neither of us is protected."

"We lost one," she repeated, and Eddy helped her the rest of the way out of her dress. He undid her bra and held her breasts. He sucked her nipples. She placed a hand in his shorts and withdrew his penis. She held it between her palms and rubbed. "This is how you start a fire without matches," she whispered. Bale growled softly. "Easy," she said, "take it easy." She wanted him huge, immense, colossal. She wet her little finger and slipped it into his anus.

"Oh," he gasped.

"Easy," she said.

"Oh."

"Has it been long?"

"Yes," he said, "yes."

"Yes," she said, "take it easy."

She wanted him prodigious, vast, whopping, stupendous. She wanted his cock engorged, his balls filled with come. She wanted her tubes to dilate, her pudendum to run with grease. "Take it easy," she murmured, "ease off, take it easy, take it easy."

Then, at what instinctively she felt was exactly the propitious biological moment, she reached out and seized him, she reached out and brought him to her. She raised him on top of her and guided him into her body. She wrapped her legs about his buttocks and alternately squeezed, released, and squeezed, pressing his body deeper inside her own with each contraction, rocking him, inching him along her clitoris, easing him through the zones of her flesh and up the boneless scaffold of her sex, thinking, who'd not lain with men in years, who'd held them off with their activating poisons, the white agency of her soiled, provoked chemistry, all the radical synergistics of their deadly, complice, conspired force, who'd used mechanics, gadgets, gravity, vibrators, even her moistened fingers like so many machines, who'd explored her own almost articulated nerve endings till she knew them like the strings that raised and lowered the joints of puppets, thinking Now! Now! *Now!* Thinking of monstrosities, freaks, ogres, and demons, conjuring werewolves, vampires, harpies, and hellhounds, conjecturing maneaters, eyesores, humpbacks, and clubfoots. Thinking *Now now now now now* and inviting all cock-eyed, crook-backed, tortuous bandy deformity out of the bottle, calling forth fiends, calling forth bogies, rabid, raw-head bloody-bones. *Now,* she thinks, *now!* And positions herself to take Bale's semen, to mix it with her own ruined and injured eggs and juices to make a troll, a goblin, broken imps and lurching oafs, felons of a nightmare blood, fallen pediatric angels, lemures, gorgons, cyclopes, Calibans, God's ugly, punished customers, his obscene and frail and lubberly, his gargoyle, flyblown hideosities and blemished, poky mutants, all his throwbacks, all his scurf, his doomed, disfigured invalids, his human slums and eldritch seconds, the poor relation and the second-best, watered, bungled being, flied ointment, weak link, chipped rift, crack and fault and snag and flaw, his maimed, his handicapped, his disabled, his crippled, his afflicted, delicate cachexies with their provisional, fragile, makeshift tolerances. Invoking the sapped, the unsound, the impaired, the unfit. Invoking the milksop, the doormat, the played-out and burnt-out, the used-up, the null and the void. Adjuring their spirits in the names of Mudd-Gaddis, of Tony Word and Lydia Conscience, of Janet Order and Benny Maxine, of Noah Cloth, spending his money like a drunken sailor, and Rena Morgan, spent. On behalf of dead Liam and her own unnamed stillborn kids. Thinking, Not gone a week and we've lost one. Thinking, Now, now, goddamn it, *now!* And accepting infection from him, contagion, the septic climate of their noxious genes. Dreaming of complications down the road, of bad bouts and thick medical histories, of wasting neurological diseases, of blood and pulmonary scourges, of blows to the glands and organs, of pathogens climbing the digestive tract, invading the heart and bone marrow, erupting the skin and clouding the cough.

Now, now, now, now, now, now, now, she thinks, and calls upon the famous misfits, upon centaurs and satyrs and chimeras, upon dragons and griffins and hydras and wyverns. Upon the basilisk, the salamander, and the infrequent unicorn.

And upon, at last, a lame and tainted Mickey Mouse.

Obelisk